The ~

Cynthia Harrod-Eagles

Futura
Macdonald & Co
London & Sydney

For my sister Lesley
who helps me by being unfailingly interested
in What Happened Next.

A Futura Book

Copyright © Cynthia Harrod-Eagles 1984

First published in Great Britain in 1984
by Macdonald & Co (Publishers) Ltd
London & Sydney

First Futura edition published in 1984

ISBN 0 7088 2499 4

Reproduced, printed and bound in Great Britain by
Hazell Watson & Viney Limited,
Member of the BPCC Group,
Aylesbury, Bucks

Futura Publications
A Division of
Macdonald & Co (Publishers) Ltd
Maxwell House
74 Worship Street
London EC2A 2EN
A BPCC plc Company

FOREWORD

The break in the legitimate succession which occurred when James II fled to France in 1688, gave rise to extraordinary anomalies which tend to be ignored by the sort of history we learn in schools. This is no doubt because the traditional kind of historian likes his history divided up neatly into reigns or, even better, into dynasties.

The period from 1688 to 1714 is distressingly untidy from that point of view, and history books tend therefore to tidy the dynastic problem away. But for the people who lived at that time it was by no means a certainty that Anne would follow William, and George Anne, and if I have been able in this book to convey something of their confusion, I am content.

Amongst the books I found helpful were:

Maurice Ashley	*England in the Seventeenth Century*
John Baynes	*The Jacobite Rising of 1715*
Eileen Cassavetti	*The Lion and the Lilies*
*Daniel Defoe	*A Tour through the Whole Island of Great Britain*
*Celia Fiennes	*Through England on a Sidesaddle in the Reign of William III*
G. E. and K. R. Fussell	*The English Countrywoman 1500–1900*
M. D. George	*London Life in the Eighteenth Century*
M. G. Jones	*The Charity School Movement*
Alan Kendall	*Vivaldi, His Music Life and Times*
E. Lipson	*The History of Woollen and Worsted Industries*
R. W. Malcolmson	*Life and Labour in England 1700–1780*
Dorothy Marshall	*English People in the Eighteenth Century*
Charles Petrie	*The Jacobite Movement 1688–1716*
Charles Petrie	*The Marechal Duke of Berwick*
Christopher Sinclair Stevenson	*Inglorious Rebellion*
*Duc de St Simon	*Memoirs of the Court of Louis XIV*
E. S. Turner	*The Court of St James's*
T. H. White	*The Age of Scandal*
*Lady Mary Wortley Montague	*Letters and Works*

Contemporary Material

5

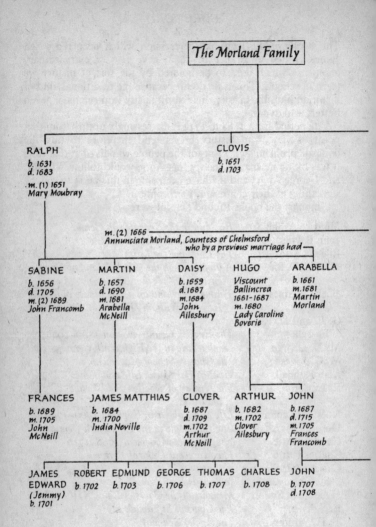

The Morland Family

RALPH
b. 1631
d. 1683
m. (1) 1651
Mary Moubray

CLOVIS
b. 1651
d. 1703

m. (2) 1666
Annunciata Morland, Countess of Chelmsford
who by a previous marriage had —

SABINE
b. 1656
d. 1705
m. (2) 1689
John Francomb

MARTIN
b. 1657
d. 1690
m. 1681
Arabella
McNeill

DAISY
b. 1659
d. 1687
m. 1684
John
Ailesbury

HUGO
Viscount
Ballincrea
1661-1687
m. 1680
Lady Caroline
Boverie

ARABELLA
b. 1661
m. 1681
Martin
Morland

FRANCES
b. 1689
m. 1705
John
McNeill

JAMES MATTHIAS
b. 1684
m. 1700
India Neville

CLOVER
b. 1687
d. 1709
m. 1702
Arthur
McNeill

ARTHUR
b. 1682
m. 1702
Clover
Ailesbury

JOHN
b. 1687
d. 1715
m. 1705
Frances
Francomb

JAMES
EDWARD
(Jemmy)
b. 1701

ROBERT
b. 1702

EDMUND
b. 1703

GEORGE
b. 1706

THOMAS
b. 1707

CHARLES
b. 1708

JOHN
b. 1707
d. 1708

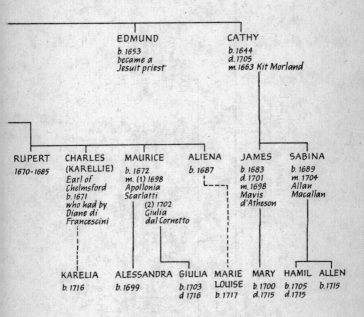

EDMUND
b.1653
became a
Jesuit priest

CATHY
b.1644
d.1705
m.1663 Kit Morland

RUPERT
1670-1685

CHARLES
(KARELLIE)
Earl of
Chelmsford
b.1671
who had by
Diane di
Francescini

MAURICE
b.1672
m. (1) 1698
Apollonia
Scarlatti
(2) 1702
Giulia
dal Cornetto

ALIENA
b.1687

JAMES
b.1683
d.1701
m.1698
Mavis
d'Atheson

SABINA
b.1689
m.1704
Allan
Macallan

KARELIA
b.1716

ALESSANDRA
b.1699

GIULIA
b.1703
d 1716

MARIE
LOUISE
b.1717

MARY
b.1700
d.1715

HAMIL
b.1705
d.1715

ALLEN
b.1715

JOHN
b.1708
d.1711

ARTHUR
b.1709
d.1712

JOHN
b.1713

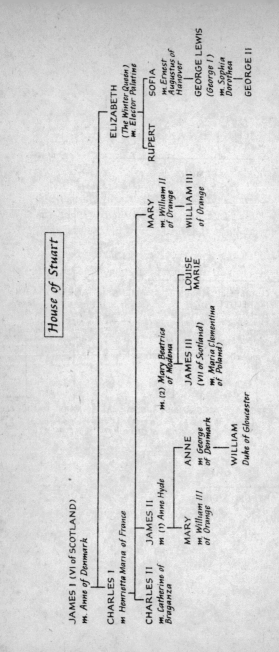

House of Stuart

JAMES I (VI of SCOTLAND)
m. Anne of Denmark

CHARLES I
m. Henrietta Maria of France

CHARLES II
m. Catherine of Braganza

JAMES II
m (1) Anne Hyde
m. (2) Mary Beatrice of Modena

ELIZABETH
(The Winter Queen)
m. Elector Palatine

RUPERT

SOFIA
m. Ernest Augustus of Hanover

GEORGE LEWIS
(George I)
m. Sophia Dorothea

GEORGE II

MARY
m William III of Orange

ANNE
m George of Denmark

WILLIAM
Duke of Gloucester

MARY
m. William II of Orange

WILLIAM III
of Orange

JAMES III
(VII of Scotland)
m. Maria Clementina of Poland

LOUISE MARIE

BOOK ONE

THE LEOPARDS AND THE LILIES

My light thou art – without thy glorious sight
My eyes are darken'd with eternal night.
My love, thou art my way, my life, my light.

Thou art my way; I wander if thou fly.
Thou art my light; if hid, how blind am I!
Thou art my life; if thou withdraw'st, I die.

John Wilmot, Earl of Rochester:
To his Mistress

CHAPTER ONE

That February day of 1689 had been frozen from its sluggish beginnings. The earth was bound in a pitiless frost like an iron glove that had never looked like easing; two hours after noon the light was already dying from a sky like stone. Dinner had been early, and of winter meagreness, but the maids had just gone round the house replenishing all the fires with stacked logs and pressed blocks of peat, so there was comfort to be had within each golden flickering radius.

The steward's room was small enough to be lit by its fire without candles, and here the family and the senior servants had gathered. James Matthias, the heir to Morland Place, who was only five years old, thought that they were like cattle gathered under one tree for warmth. He had seen the overwintering cattle bunched together like that, with the apprehension of hunger in their eyes. Later he could recall the meeting with great clarity, although he did not remember much of what it was about.

James Matthias, generally known as Little Matt, had wriggled in ahead of the others to get a good place on the floor before the fire, and here he was joined by his cousin, Arthur, Viscount Ballincrea, who was nearly seven and bullied Matt; as well as the dogs, Fand, the blue wolfhound belonging to the Countess, and his father's young bitch Kithra. The dogs shoved their hard, lean bodies against the boys until they had worked their way as close to the flames as they could, and then they collapsed on to their sides with sighs of content. Both had been rolling in cowdung, but it wasn't a smell Matt minded. The other children were too young to be included in the meeting, being all under two years old, and they were up in the nursery with Flora, the wet-nurse. It made Matt feel grown-up and important that he was not with them.

Having settled himself with the dogs between him and Arthur, who sometimes pinched him slyly just for the pleasure of hurting him, Matt looked about the room. In the black, carved fireside chair sat Matt's grandmother, Annunciata, Countess of Chelmsford, a person of such eminence to Matt that even when he was in the same room with her he could hardly believe she was real. She was dressed all in black, and round her throat she wore a glittering diamond collar, which had been given to her by King Charles II, while on her breast she wore the gold and diamond cross which was one of the Percy jewels, a Morland heirloom. The diamonds flashed brilliant rainbow colours in the moving firelight; Matt thought she was like the Queen of Winter in the legend.

Matt's father, Martin, who was Master of Morland Place, stood behind her chair with his hands resting on the chairback so that they just touched the Countess's shoulders. Matt loved his father dearly, but indeed, so did everyone. He was a small man, thin and wiry and brown-skinned like a hazel-nut, with soft, curly dark hair and small, dark-blue, twinkling eyes, and a mouth that seemed to smile even in repose; even now, when his face was grave and sad. He was the Countess's stepson for the Countess had once been married to Martin's father, Ralph Morland.

Sitting on the floor beside her chair were the Countess's two surviving sons by Ralph Morland, Charles, Earl of Chelmsford, always called Karellie, who was eighteen, and Maurice, a year younger. Behind this group were the representatives of the servants: Clement, the steward, whose forefathers had been stewards at Morland Place time out of mind, and his son Valentine who was butler; the chaplain, old Father St Maur, who had cropped grey hair and very bright dark eyes in his brown, wrinkled face; Jane Birch, the governess, sour-faced, sharp-tongued and heavy-handed; and the Countess's waiting woman, Chloris, very beautiful with red-gold curls and violet eyes.

Now Matt's eyes turned in the other direction, towards the man whose unexpected arrival that morning had caused this meeting to be called. He was Uncle Clovis, who was half-brother to Ralph Morland but much younger than he. Matt had hardly ever seen him before, though he knew quite a lot about him, for Clovis lived mostly in London where he acted as factor to the family's wool and cloth business, and also had some position at Court.

When everyone was settled, the Countess said, 'Let us hear your news. You may speak freely – we are quite safe here. There is no one in the house I do not trust.'

Clovis nodded and drew out from his breast a much-folded and much-stained letter. 'This,' he said, 'is from my brother Edmund in St Omer. No need, I think, to go into details of how it reached me–'

'It is better not to speak of those things,' Martin interposed quickly. 'What is not said cannot be repeated. Will you read it to us?'

Clovis held the letter in his hand, but did not look at it. He addressed the company as a whole, but his eyes never left the Countess's face.

'It is written mostly in a code Edmund and I have used from time to time, but I can tell you the gist of it. It says that King James reached France safely and joined the Queen and the Prince of Wales. King Louis of France has given them the Palace of St Germain, just outside Paris, for their home. He has been most generous to them, giving them money, furnishing the palace, redecorating the nurseries for the Prince of Wales. He treats King James with all royal state, and they are often together. They were together when the news came that Parliament has given the crown jointly to Princess Mary and Prince William of Orange. That was on the 16th.'

'Fast travelling, even for bad news,' Martin said gravely. 'They got the news almost as soon as we did.'

Little Matt remembered the day that the news had come, the shock first, and then the anger. Parliament had decided that the King, by leaving the country, had abdicated.

Prince William, the Dutch husband of the King's elder daughter Mary, was occupying London with his soldiers. Parliament had offered the throne to Princess Mary, but William had angrily refused to be his wife's 'gentleman usher' and had forced them to hand the crown to them jointly. Parliament had done so on condition that a Protestant succession was guaranteed, so that no Catholic might ever again sit upon the throne of England. That meant that after William's death, Princess Mary's sister Princess Anne must have the crown.

Matt remembered the Countess's fury. 'So Parliament takes it upon itself to pass the Crown of England from hand to hand like a parcel of tea!' she had raged. 'The Dutchman made King! The Prince of Wales removed from the succession! As if they have the right – as if they have the competence!'

'But at least there are to be no reprisals,' Martin had said, trying to comfort her. 'No action to be taken against those of us who resisted him.'

'He wants it to appear that he took the throne by public demand and not by the force of arms,' Annunciata had said bitterly. 'He will leave us alone until enough people believe the lie that the King abdicated – and then–'

Morland Place had been badly damaged during the siege following William of Orange's invasion. Matt tried not to remember those terrible days. The damage to the house had only been sketchily repaired as yet, and Annunciata and Martin expressed their fears readily enough to Matt, though they had not voiced them.

Clovis glanced at Edmund's letter again, and continued. 'The King was gravely shocked, of course, especially by the heartless behaviour of his daughters, but he and King Louis began to make plans at once.' Matt could feel from Clovis's voice that he was coming to the important part of the letter. 'King Louis is to give the King money and men enough to equip an entire expedition.'

The Countess almost rose to her feet. 'To England,' she said eagerly.

Clovis shook his head. 'Not England at first. To Ireland – the Catholics there will rise in support, and when he has Ireland, it will make a safe base from which to cross to England.'

'Who is to command?' Annunciata asked. There were questions in every face, but it seemed natural that she should voice them.

'The Comte de Lauzun will be commander in chief, but the King will go himself, of course, with the Duke of Berwick.'

'Berwick is a good soldier,' Annunciata said approvingly. 'My son Hugo fought with him against the Turks, and knew him in the Monmouth campaign. He spoke highly of him. It seems that the King is luckier in his bastard son than in his legitimate daughters,' she added harshly.

Now Karellie spoke for the first time. 'Mother,' he said, 'is not my lord of Berwick the King's son by Arabella Churchill? And did not her brother John Churchill desert the King for the Prince of Orange? I wonder that the King can trust him.'

'Berwick is sound,' Annunciata said abruptly. 'John Churchill cares for nothing but his own career. He is ruled by his wife, and his wife has Princess Anne safe in her pocket, and so they think the Protestant succession will offer them the best chance of advancement and riches. If Princess Anne is ever Queen, they hope to hold the highest places in the land. Remember that,' she added bitterly to her children, 'that is what Protestantism does – it replaces faith, duty, loyalty and obedience with self-interest. You saw how Princess Anne betrayed her own father . . .'

Martin's hands came down in a restraining sort of way on her shoulders, and Karellie, turning his face up to her, said gently, 'It's all right, Mother. Maurice and I have better examples to follow.'

'When is the expedition to be?' Martin asked Clovis, who was waiting patiently to return to the matter in hand.

'Very soon. They hope to land in Ireland in two weeks' time.'

15

There was a silence. Maurice was looking at Clovis, but not as if he saw him. Karellie turned his face from Clovis to his mother, gazing up at her with an eager, questioning expression. The Countess shook her head minutely at him, and then looked up at Martin, and Martin, searching her face, spoke at last.

'We must decide what to do.'

And now the Countess put her hand up to cover Martin's, which rested on her shoulder. Matt, watching, saw how white and long the Countess's hand was, how square and brown his father's; more than that, he saw how there was a strange quietness about them, as if they were alone together in a place away from everyone else. Their eyes, and the lightly touching hands, were exchanging messages in some way, as if they were reading each other's thoughts.

Finally the Countess said, as if the words continued a long conversation they had had that no one else had heard, 'No, you must decide what to do. You are the Master of Morland Place. It is for you to say.'

After that the talk went on for a long time, and Matt, growing weary, half-dozed amongst the dogs, letting the flow of words go over him like water, feeling the shape of them without listening for the meaning. Finally he slept in truth, and woke to Birch's hands pulling him up to his feet. Everyone was leaving the room, Clovis ushering them out quietly. Matt, looking round, half-dazed, saw the Countess and his father standing near the window, evidently waiting for privacy. Birch was tugging at his hand, and he stumbled after her, hearing the door of the steward's room click closed behind him, leaving those two quiet figures alone with the dogs and the firelight.

The cold outside in the great staircase hall woke Matt to shivering, and he picked his feet up and hurried with Birch and Arthur to get upstairs and to another fire. Birch dropped Arthur's hand to lift her skirts clear of the stairs, and Arthur said, 'I'm hungry. I'm hungry, Birch.'

'You're always hungry,' Birch replied in automatic rebuke.

'But I am. I had hardly anything at dinner.'

They reached the turn of the stair, and Matt, glancing down despite himself, saw the chequered tiles of the hall floor and remembered them strewn with blood and dead men. That was when the rebels smashed their way in at the end of the siege. He never wanted to remember, but the visions always broke through, triggered by certain things, always the same things, somehow unavoidable. He crossed himself, and seeing the gesture out of the corner of her eye, Birch softened.

'Well, well, perhaps I can find you something,' she said. 'Poor children. God knows what will come of all this. Poor things. Hurry on, now. We'll go to the nursery, and I'll see what I may have.'

'Will the babies be awake?' Matt asked, brightening. He was fond of the babies, as one might be fond of a litter of puppies. There was Arthur's brother John; little Mary Celia Ailesbury, the orphan daughter of Martin's sister, and always called Clover, because she was round and sweet – she was Matt's favourite; and Aliena, the Countess's new baby. There was something odd about Aliena, Matt knew – not about her person, but about her existence, for the servants whispered and broke off when Matt came near, and Birch always shook her head over Aliena sadly, though she was a lusty child, small and dark but strong. Matt knew better than to ask questions, just as he realized the servants knew better than to ask the Countess questions, or even to speak above the lowest of whispers. 'If the babies are awake, can I play with them?' Matt pursued. Birch shook his hand in mild reproof.

'Play with them, indeed. They're not toys, you know.' And then, glancing at Matt's face, she said, unexpectedly kindly, 'You can give Clover her pap, if you like. If you're careful.'

Matt was pleased; but all the same, apprehensive, for kindness from Birch surely portended some disaster.

The door shut with a soft click, leaving them alone in the tumbling shadows of the fire.

'Shall I send for candles?' Martin said, glancing out of the window. 'It's quite dark outside.'

'I can see well enough,' Annunciata said, turning to him. When Martin had told her that terrible day that the King had fled the country, she had known that it was the end for her, and she had wanted to die, had prayed for it. But miraculously, a little space had been granted them. Prince William had not sent soldiers to tear down Morland Place and throw her and Martin into the Tower; social pressures had not forced her and Martin apart; the children had not discovered the truth about Aliena. Annunciata's spirits had revived, and hope had sprung up in her, and with the hope, a fierce desire to live.

And now that she had had those few brief weeks of life, she did not want to relinquish it again. She had thought, when Martin came home and rescued her from the hands of the mob, the priest-killers, that the complication of their relationship would make it impossible for them to stay together. But now, looking at his dear face, she felt that those same complications, thicket after thicket of difficulties, made it impossible for them to part. Her love for him welled up in her, strong and joyous, bubbling upwards like the source of a mighty river. She clasped her hands together and pressed them against her breast-bone as if she feared that her ribs would spring open from the pressure of that flood.

Martin looked at her, and saw her face alight and her eyes brilliant with some strange and vivid joy, and he thought, dear God, there is no one like her! Two months ago he had seen her in despair, bowed, defeated, and he had thought that she would die. Worse than that, he had thought that she would go away from him. But now, look! From whence came that vitality, that spirit, he wondered? He smiled at her, and she held her hands out to him, and when he took them she laughed.

'Karellie will go,' she said. 'How he longs for a battle!'

'And Maurice?' he asked.

'I hope not Maurice,' she said. 'Karellie has it in his blood and in his heart, and he will make a fine soldier. Perhaps that is all he will make. But Maurice – Maurice has something else in him, more important than the change of dynasties.'

'My lady,' Martin said in mock reproach, 'what could be more important than the change of dynasties?' Everything that was alive of her was in his hands, as if the force of her energy flowed through them and into him like the strong current of a river. 'You will have to go abroad,' he said.

'What, now?' she said. She thought he was jesting. 'How should I desert my country now? I shall be needed here, to greet the King when he arrives.'

'Listen, my heart,' he said steadily, 'the campaign will not take days or weeks. It will take months. It will not be so very easy to dislodge the Dutchman – he is an old campaigner, and he has good troops. And he will want to secure his rear when he goes out to Ireland to face the attack.'

'He has left us alone so far,' Annunciata said.

'But he will not, once the King lands in Ireland. You are too well-known. You will draw attention to Morland Place. My dearest, it is not for your own safety alone I say this – God forbid that I should stop you flinging your slender life in the path of your enemies –'

It was only half a joke. She would never forget the horror of those endless moments when she held the staircase against the mob, while they murdered and mutilated her priest.

'Without you, I think he will leave Morland Place alone. You must consider the family.'

'You want me to go into exile?' she said. The very word was a horror.

'For a short time. Until the campaign is won, and the King restored.'

'And you, you will stay here, I suppose?' Her voice was

19

hard. She could endure anything, but to be parted from him.

'You forget,' he said lightly, 'I am already an exile.' She would not take that. She turned her eyes from him in pain.

'The King exiled you – the Usurper will pardon you. That is the way it works.'

'Not if I fight against him.'

Her eyes came back to him, alight with laughter. 'You? Ah, Martin, Martin!' And she pressed herself against him. She was laughing, but her cheek against his cheek was wet. He wound his arms round her, tightly, tightly, smelling the sweet smell of her skin, feeling the harshness of her black hair against his neck, and her hands strong against his back, pulling him closer. This was life, the touch of her; to be apart from her was death.

'Everything must be done, to ensure a swift victory,' he said, his lips to her hair. 'I have endured one exile. A swift assured blow, and the end to all this – that is our only hope.'

For a while they rested against each other, drawing strength, and then she freed herself gently and straightened, looking at him levelly, like a soldier. 'We have so little time,' she said. 'We must make plans.'

Clovis was to stay at Morland Place, as its guardian, and guardian of the fortunes of the children who were the future's hope. It was a grave burden to lay upon him, but there was no one else. The only other adults of the Morland family left now were Martin's sister Sabine who, recently widowed and childless, was running the three Northumberland estates, one belonging to the family, and two of her own; and Clovis's half-sister Cathy, married to cousin Kit Morland, who lived in Scotland where they had an estate and one sickly son.

'You will manage, I know,' Annunciata said. 'I am sorry to lay so heavy a task on you, but you are strong for it, and I hope you will forgive me.'

'I owe everything to you,' Clovis said gravely. 'And it will not be for long.'

'You will write and let Cathy and Sabine know?' Annunciata said. 'It will come better from you.'

'I dare say they will have their own troubles. There will surely be a rising in Scotland.'

'We must all help each other.' She bit her lip. 'I feel I should not be running away.'

He took her hand and pressed it. 'We have gone through all that. You know it is best.' His hand was warm and steady, and reassured her. He was strong with some strength that she had never traced to its source, not associating it with herself. Even Clovis did not know what it was precisely that he felt for Annunciata: he only knew that all his life his heart had slept in her shadow, and that though he had had many opportunities to marry, and marry well, there could be no place for any woman in his life while he served her.

It was hard to say goodbye to Father St Maur, whose spirit was willing to go with his mistress, but whose flesh was weak.

'The children need you,' Annunciata said to hide her emotion. 'To whom else could I trust their education and their souls?'

Hard to say goodbye to the servants, who had been so faithful, who had fought beside her, cared for her and been cared for by her for so many years. Hard to say goodbye to Jane Birch, who had been with her since she had first gone to London, almost thirty years ago, who had witnessed all the triumphs and griefs of her life. But the ague that had swept through Morland Place in the winter had left Birch feeble, and a sea-journey in early March would have been too much for her. She accepted that she must stay behind without comment, but when the moment came to part, her eyes, shallow with encroaching blindness, filled with tears.

'You are needed here,' Annunciata said. 'It won't be for long.'

'Yes, my lady,' Birch said, holding herself rigid.

Annunciata wanted to kiss her, but she knew it would break Birch's control, and that Birch would feel ashamed to cry in front of the other servants. So Annunciata said, 'Help Clovis. Look to the children. I shall come back very soon.'

'Yes, my lady,' Birch said, but her eyes spoke a different truth.

Hard to say goodbye to Karellie, who would be leaving the next day with Martin and some of the men for Ireland. Her tall boy, with his easy lounging grace, Ralph's height and colouring and features, nothing of Annunciata about him except the dark Stuart eyes. She had taken him aside the previous night and, with great pain to herself, had told him the secret of his ancestry: that Prince Rupert, whom Annunciata had loved, and whose mistress she had almost become, was in fact her father. Only intervention at the last moment had prevented that terrible thing, for Annunciata's mother had never disclosed her father's identity. The intervention had come in time to prevent the deed, but too late to change the love she had in her heart, which for ever afterwards must be shut away, hidden and denied. But it was important for Karellie, on the eve of such an important campaign, to know what blood flowed in his veins.

'You are a Stuart, Karellie,' she said, 'great-great-grandson of King Charles the Martyr, grandson of the greatest soldier the world has ever known. Your grandfather fought to preserve King Charles upon his throne. Now you will fight to restore the throne to King James, your cousin. Be worthy of the Stuart name.'

In the grey half-light before dawn they left Morland Place for Aldbrough, where a ship awaited them. Though planned hastily, this was no fugitive flight, and Annunciata was taking with her horses and servants and money and jewels, for she did not want to come a beggar to St

Germain. She took the baby Aliena, and Maurice; Dorcas to look after the baby; Chloris, a servant-girl Nan, her footman Gifford, a groom Daniel, and John Wood to attend Maurice.

The ground was still frost-hard, and they made good time, avoiding the deep, frozen ruts of the roads and riding over the open fields, where the stubble had long since been eaten by the overwintering cattle. They reached the little harbour in the early afternoon, finding the ship rocking gently at anchor between the grey sea and the grey sky, and were able to get everything aboard by dark. Then came the last goodbye of all. Gifford retreated, without being asked, to the edge of the foam, and Martin sent his armed escort to wait further up the beach, and that was all the privacy they could gain.

'My lady,' Martin said, taking her hands. Those two words alone were enough to undo her. Tomorrow he would ride off for Ireland, there to do battle for his king.

'Oh Martin, take care, take care,' she said. The salty wind whipped stray fronds of her hair about her brows where they escaped from her hood.

'As much care as may be,' he said. He drew her to him, and kissed her cheeks and eyes. They were damp and salty, but whether from the sea-wind or from tears he did not know. Her skin was cold under his mouth. He sought her lips, and they were cold too, but warmed under the touch of his. He closed his eyes.

'Oh God, I love you,' he whispered. 'Only you, for ever.'

The sound of the sea, coldly chattering on stones, and the whimpering of seagulls, blown like damp rags about the sky; the smell of salt, and broken seaweed. The tide would not wait for them. They clung together, even as they pushed themselves apart, and their eyes still touched when they stood separate.

'God go with you, Martin,' she said. 'Clovis will send me word, but write to me, if you can.'

'I will. God bless you, my lady. Oh, God keep you.'

Gifford came to help her on board, and as soon as she

was over the side, the sailors broke into frenzied action from their watchful stillness. Martin stood on the shore, huddled into his cloak against the freshening wind, and watched as the graceful little ship shook out her sails, gathered steerage way, and then span about and leapt eagerly towards the incoming waves. The darkness was deepening, and soon she was only a glimmer of sails and a thicker core of darkness in the murk. Martin was not aware of the moment when she disappeared, for he continued to stare after her into the darkness as if his mind saw with a clearer eye, following her progress over the cold, grey-green waves. At length one of his men came down to him, had actually to tap his arm to gain his attention.

'Best we get going, Master,' the man said gently. 'It's mortal cold, and the tide's coming in.'

Martin looked down with a start and saw the foam lipping almost to his feet.

'Yes,' he said. 'I'm coming now.'

The Château of St Germain was an ugly red-brick building on a medieval foundation, but its setting was beautiful, with gardens that ran down to the River Seine, and roof terraces that looked over the great game-forest that earlier French Kings had planted west of Paris. The forest teemed with game; splendid trees grouped around ornamental lakes, linked by broad, mossy rides; and beyond its curly dark poll could be seen, misty and beautiful, the roofs and spires of Paris.

Annunciata wrote to Clovis to tell of her kind reception there. The Queen in exile was warmer and more accessible than she had been at Whitehall, and was evidently also glad that Annunciata had not arrived penniless, as did most of the exiles. She granted Annunciata an apartment on the first staircase, which was the best, and made her a Lady of the Bedchamber, as well as making Maurice Gentleman of the Chapel Royal. Annunciata reported that the Queen was evidently deeply shocked and miserable at finding herself in exile, but that the King wrote cheerfully from Ireland, and the King of France and all the French royal family were generous and attentive. The Prince of Wales was thriving, and Maurice had written an anthem to celebrate his first birthday on 10 June, which the King of France had said was very good.

Clovis responded with frequent letters that arrived via his secret route. He could give little news of the campaign in Ireland, other than that Martin and Karellie had arrived safely, but he gave her news of the family. Martin's sister Sabine, unable, so it seemed, to endure her widowhood, had married her steward, a man called Jack Francomb. Clovis added that Sabine was expecting a child in December, so it looked as though the steward's comforting preceded his marriage with his mistress.

Cathy was also expecting a child, due in July. Kit had gone north to join up with Viscount Dundee, known as Bonnie Dundee, who was raising the Highlands for King James. The Usurper's army under Mackay was hoping for help from the Covenanters, but Dundee was the better general and the more popular man. A victory in Scotland would be of enormous help to the King in Ireland.

But on the last day of July the news came that though the Highlanders had won a tremendous victory over Mackay's army at Killiecrankie, Bonnie Dundee had fallen in the battle, and without his leadership the Highlanders were already drifting away, back to their mountains and valleys. And, in the same battle, Kit Morland had met his end.

Cathy's baby was born a week before the battle, a girl, and healthy. Cathy's pregnancies had been unfortunate, leaving her with only one child, and he frail, and Sabine, despite her condition, had gone with her husband to stay with Cathy at Aberlady and see her through her confinement. In gratitude, Cathy had named her new baby Sabina. Sabine had begged Cathy to go back with her to Northumberland and make her home there, but Cathy had refused, saying that her duty lay with Scotland and her son.

August brought another letter from Clovis, with no better news. The Highlanders had been thoroughly defeated at Dunkeld, and there was no hope of another Scottish campaign that year, and even if a leader could be found to replace Dundee, it was doubtful how much chance he would have of raising the Highlands again for some years. And Princess Anne's son, born at Hampton Court in July, whose life had been despaired of because he suffered from fits, had not only survived his first month, but was now actually flourishing with a wet-nurse and looked likely to survive. Princess Anne had named the boy William after her brother-in-law, a piece of essential tact, and the child had been given the title of Duke of Gloucester.

The news sank the exiled Court into gloom. William Duke of Gloucester provided the Protestant party with the thing they had signally lacked, an heir, a rival to the infant Prince of Wales. It became more than ever essential that the King should dislodge his son-in-law without delay; but Scotland seemed already lost, and the news from Ireland was, at best, uncertain.

CHAPTER TWO

July of 1690 had been hot, weeks of white glare. The streams had shrunk, the earth baked, and there was a film of dust over the dark green grass and the leaves of the trees. The harvests had been early and abundant, and the children, who would normally have been carrying and gleaning at this time, had nothing to do but run and play all day, and get themselves into trouble.

Two dusty boys came down to the Foss from High Moor Farm one afternoon when the shadows lay deep like sharp-edged cuts under every grass blade. They looked much alike at first glance, of a height and build, dressed in shirts, stout breeches to the knee, and nothing below but a caking of white dust. One had straight, bushy hair of fieldmouse brown, and a great many freckles: he was Davey, the youngest grandson of Conn the shepherd. The other had very dark, curly hair, though with the summer dust it looked almost as mousy as his companion's; and eyes of dark Morland blue that were bright in a face as brown as a hazel-nut: he was James Matthias, heir to Morland Place, the 'young master'.

Reaching the beck they tore off their clothes with a frantic eagerness, dropping them amongst the alder-roots, and jumped into the cool, brown, swirling water, shrieking with delight at the shock of coldness on their baked skin.

'Oh! It's so cold! I could drink it, I'm so thirsty.'

'Horses do. Look, Matt, can you do this? Matt!'

'I'm an old water otter. Look, Davey, look at me! I'm an otter.'

After a while they climbed out and stretched on the bank, the water rivering off them to soak the parched grass, the sun drying their hair. Matt lay back, propping his head on his folded arms, and squinted down at his

27

butter-brown skin. The water had already receded into single drops, each lying like a transparent pearl, perfectly hemispherical, and magnifying the texture of his skin like a telescope-glass. He squinted up at the cornflower-blue sky, and there were drops on his eyelashes too, so that for a moment he tried to make-believe he had been crying. But he couldn't remember how to be sad today, not today. He concentrated hard, remembering that he had no mother, that his father had gone to Ireland to fight the Usurper's army (once he had accidentally referred to the Usurper as 'king', and Birch had boxed his ear) but today the contentedness sat inside him like a good dinner, and he could not, could not make himself stop smiling.

'What are you doing? Grinning like an old dog,' Davey said. Davey was older than him, and went to school at St Edward's because he was clever and his mother hoped he would be a steward or a bailey when he grew. Davey's father was in Ireland too, with the Master and Davey's oldest brother.

'I was looking at the sky through the water on my eyelashes. It's funny. You try it.'

But Davey was dragging his shirt towards him. 'I want a plum,' he said. He had been carrying them in the front of his shirt, and it was now streaked a beautiful crimson colour. 'Most of them are all right. There's three burst ones.'

'That was when you fell down,' Matt said. 'Clumsy.' But Davey was not to be taunted. He did not want to wrestle, he wanted to lounge and eat.

'Here –' and he threw across some fat, purple plums that they had rifled from the farm on their way. Matt caught them and put them down in the grass, all but one, which he held to his lips and rubbed it back and forth, to feel the warm, silky, full feeling of its skin. It smelled wonderful; all the children were gorged on windfall plums this year, but Matt felt he could not get enough of them.

'I love plums,' he said, postponing the moment of biting it.

Davey rolled on to his front to inspect his before biting, and said, 'Remember the wasp?' He began to giggle, and Matt tried not to join in, because it was disloyal; but it had been funny, the time his cousin, Arthur, Lord Ballincrea, had snatched the plum that Matt was about to eat, and had bitten into it; only to be soundly bitten back, for there had been a wasp in it, unknown to any of them. Arthur's face had swollen up horribly.

'He looked like a pumpkin by evening,' Matt said with guilty pleasure. Arthur was eight, two years older than Matt, and had always lorded it over him. He was a big, heavily built boy, and bullied Matt, demanding by force of fist a homage from Matt, because Arthur had a title and he didn't.

'You must call me "my lord",' he would say, sitting on Matt and pummelling him; but pummelled or not, Matt wouldn't.

'Cousin Arthur,' he would say. 'Ouch! Leave me alone! Cousin Arthur, cousin Arthur, cousin Arthur!'

Snatching the plum from Matt had been typical of Arthur, but that time God had paid him back, for Matt didn't know the wasp was there, and if Arthur hadn't taken it *he* would have been stung instead. Matt believed firmly in God. Birch had told him when he was very little that God saw everything he did, even in the dark, and for a long time he had had bad dreams about huge eyes just outside the ring of firelight or candlelight. He was older now, and more sensible, and not afraid of the dark at all – well, not much, anyway. Once he had been out by moonlight, and he had looked up at the great silver circle floating free above the black tree-line, and thought that God's eye must look like that, brilliant and beautiful.

It was very peaceful, with the chuckling of the beck the only sound in the stillness of a hot afternoon. A dragonfly came along, hovering above Matt's face to smell him in case he was worth investigating. Through half-closed eyes Matt watched the brilliant, jewel-bright thing, and imagined that it was as big as it seemed through his eyelashes, as big as a horse; he imagined himself climbing on to that green-blue, sapphire back and riding away, soaring above the trees into the blue sky, flying to Ireland where his father was –

'Come on, don't fall asleep,' Davey said, startling Matt from his half-doze. 'I'm hungry. Let's go and see my grandfather. He's with the sheep on Popple Height. I expect he'll have something to eat about him.' Instantly, Matt was hungry too. They jumped up, pulled on their clothes, and ran out across the fields; soon they were scrambling up Popple Height to where Old Conn sat watching his flock.

'He looks like a lump of granite himself,' Davey giggled. 'I wonder if there's moss growing on him?'

Matt thought Conn looked not like a rock, though he was so still, but like a growing thing, brown and weathered, a tree perhaps, his no-coloured clothes not like man-made things at all, but like the foliage of some strange but belonging plant.

When they got close, they saw that he was not immobile after all. His bright eyes, half hidden in the wrinkled brown folds about them, were watching them, and his hands were busy with something in his lap. His crook lay nearby; and his two dogs panted and waved their tails in greeting, the young one running to the boys to sniff their hands, the old one merely grinning at them from the scrap of shade he had found beside the rock, his teeth very white and his frilled tongue very pink against his black muzzle.

'God's day to you, young master,' old Conn said when they got near enough.

'God's day, Conn,' Matt said, with the formal politeness he had been taught to use towards the people who would one day be *his* people. 'I hope you are well.'

'The heat suits me, young master, and so I thank you. Now then, Davey, what hasta been about? No good, I'll be bound.'

Davey, who had been trying to tease the old dog into playing, came and flopped down on the short, sheep-bitten

30

grass near his grandfather's feet and said, 'We were hungry, and we thought you might have something to eat.'

'You're always hungry. I've clap-bread, and ewemilk cheese, if that's dainty enough fare for you.' He reached down beside him for his pouch.

Matt felt Davey had been too abrupt, that it seemed like rudeness to come to a man to steal his dinner, so he said, 'But we do not want to leave you hungry, sir. Please don't trouble –'

'Na, master, what I have is yours. Old folk don't get so hungry as young ones.' He pulled out a flat, golden cake of oaten bread and broke it in half, giving half each to the boys; and a piece of white, crumbling ewe-cheese, wrapped in a cabbage leaf. 'Help yourself, young master. You'll find it all the sweeter, for the ewes have been grazing on wild thyme and clover and bergamot and all the herbs the bees love.'

'Does it really make a difference?' Matt asked, putting a crumb of the cheese into his mouth.

'Why, of course. What you eat is what you are; what the ewes eat goes straight to their milk.'

The boys were silent awhile as they fed their hunger, and then they had time to slow down and look about them. Matt watched the shepherd's brown hands, stiff and gnarled like tree-roots though they appeared, moving nimbly about the piece of carving in his lap.

'What is it you make, Conn?'

'A yolk for a sheep-bell, master. See? When I've smoothed it off, I'll make a notch here, and here, for to tie the thong of leather. Wooden yokes are better, though the folk down south use bones. A hip-bone from a sheep they use.' He made a sound of disgust in his throat. 'How would you like to have a man's hip-bone around your neck?'

Matt had no answer for that. He said, 'Have you been down south, Conn?'

'When I was young, about the same age as you. I fought for good King Charles, against Old Noll, God rot him.

Marched all the way south, past Nottingham. When I was a lad of fourteen.'

Matt didn't think fourteen was at all the same as six. Fourteen was grown up. But it seemed rude to contradict, so he said, 'What's the south like?'

'Down south is the same as here mostly. It's the folk that are different. Here, young master, come here and look about you. Look round, all around.' Matt scrambled up and obeyed, gazing out over the peacefully grazing sheep, over the open fields, some already ploughed up into strips, the folds curving with the folds of the land; others under stubble, fenced off with hurdles, being grazed by the fattening cattle; the silvery silent glint of the river Ouse and the twinkle of the becks; the white walls of York, fencing in its spires and chimneys; and everywhere around the walls the windmills, their great sails barely turning in the faintest of breezes. The sheep-bells made a sweet, deep clonking sound as they moved, and bees were busy amongst the short-growing herbs, and here and there a skylark shot up, climbing vertically to hover and shrill. And far off, farthest of all, were the lilac-blue smudges of the hills, the Hambleton Hills to the north-east, and the Pennines to the west. All familiar, safe, and beautiful. He looked at Conn enquiringly.

'I remember the time when it was all open fields, young master, no enclosed fields at all, no growing hedges, only hurdles. Well, times change. Up here they change slowly, down south they change fast. Down south they close off fields, each man for himself. They care nothing for each other, nor for their King, nor for God. 'Tis all profit with them, and if a man fall sick or get himself into trouble, they turn their backs, for fear it may cost them profit to give aid. They don't work together, share their fields and their harvests and their joys and their troubles. That's why the south is different.'

He turned his eyes, disconcertingly bright, to Matt's face. 'Remember what I say, one day when you are Master of all this. A man is nothing alone.'

Matt struggled for understanding. There were things he had thought only half in words, things he had been told and only half understood. He said, gropingly, 'Birch says that the Protestants think they can choose their King instead of letting God choose him . . . ?'

But old Conn had seen something amiss with the flock, and spoke sharply and in his incomprehensible dialect to his young dog, and she jumped up and raced off to fetch back a ewe that was wandering into trouble. When the crisis was over and the dog was back, jabbing her muzzle for praise into Conn's brown hand, the old shepherd said cheerfully,

'When men choose for themselves, they always choose wrong. Remember that too, Master Matt. Wives or Kings, they always choose amiss.'

The shadows were long and violet across grass yellow as fools' gold when Matt, having parted from Davey at Ten Thorn Gap, came trotting home at an easy, ground-consuming huntsman's lope. Morland Place was golden too in the late sun, the grey stones honey-gold, the lichen on the roof gorse-yellow, the west-facing panes of windows like square gold coins. The men released from the harvest early had been repairing the remaining damage from the cannon two years ago, and the house was almost as good as new. Young Matt was savagely hungry, Conn's bread and cheese a distant memory, and he wondered what there might be for supper. Pigeon pie, he hoped, for Uncle Clovis had been intending to go shooting that day. Pigeon pie with leeks, or rabbit stuffed with little brown onions! His mouth ran water in anticipation as he trotted over the bridge and into the yard.

He knew at once that something had happened; he could smell trouble in the air, even before one of the old women came hurrying out of the house scolding shrilly.

'Where have you been all day, young master? They've

been looking for you. You'd better come in at once. Tut! What a state you're in, all dusty and dirty.'

Old women always scolded, that was nothing; but there was something in her eyes, something in the set of her mouth that frightened him.

'What is it, Meg? What's happened?'

But she didn't answer him. 'Go you in, young master, right away. You're wanted,' she said, brushing at his hair ineffectually with the flat of her hand. He ran in through the great door into the hall, and stopped. Clovis was there, standing with Clement and Father St Maur, discussing something. He held a letter in his hand, and he was waving it as if giving instructions to Clement. Aunt Caroline, Arthur's mother, was sitting on one of the little hard hall chairs and crying. Now they had seen him: their eyes all rested on him, solemn and grave and warning.

'James Matthias,' Clovis said, and his formality was a further warning. 'There you are. Come here, child. I have some news for you.'

News, of course, could be good news, but Matt walked forward reluctantly, knowing it was not. The great hall was cool after the heat of the day, and his bare feet flinched at the coldness of the marble floor. Outside the sunlight poured down golden and perfect, and Matt longed to run out again, away, back to Conn and the sheep. The blue and gold day he had spent lingered in his mind like lovely music as his feet carried him inexorably towards the news they had for him, and he knew, without knowing why he knew, that there would never be another day like the one he had just had; that he would remember it all his life as the last day of his childhood.

The news came to St Germain. A terrible defeat, a battle by a river called the Boyne, tragic loss amongst the Irish-French forces of the King. A decisive defeat, coming as it did after a long and disastrous campaign; the King in flight, already on his way back to France with Berwick;

Lauzun, the Queen's special friend, staying behind to gather what was left of the army. The women waited, sick with fear. For days Annunciata walked the rooftop terraces, waiting for the first glimpse of the returning warriors, for news of life or death. From time to time Chloris would come to her and beg her to rest, or take food, or sit with the baby, or listen to Maurice play, but she only shook her head without speaking. A superstitious dread was on her that she must see the horsemen at the first possible moment.

At last the outriders came into view, galloping ahead, and straining her eyes she saw the distant, moving dot of the main party, like a many-legged insect, multicoloured. Now and then she saw a flash as the sunlight glanced off a helmet or breastplate or horse-ornament. For a long time it seemed to come no nearer, and then all of a sudden it was close enough to distinguish men and horses. It moved along the great avenue, disappearing from time to time under the trees. It was easy to distinguish the King. Soon she could pick out Berwick by his great height and his fair hair; then, her heart turning over with relief, she saw close behind him the silvery hair of Karellie. But so many of the others were small and dark-haired, that though she scanned them eagerly, she could not tell one from another. Then they were under the trees close to the walls and out of her sight.

Annunciata left her post at the parapet's edge and almost knocked Chloris over in her haste as she ran towards the stair.

'My lady!' Chloris called warningly, but Annunciata did not heed her.

Dorcas was hurrying up the stair as Annunciata reached it, and said breathlessly, 'My lady, my lady, they're here.'

'Yes, yes, I know. I saw them. Out of my way!'

'They are to be received in the Queen's gallery, my lady. I came to tell you,' Dorcas said.

Chloris caught up with them, and said firmly, 'You

cannot go down to the courtyard, my lady. This is not Morland Place.'

Annunciata paused, looking from one to the other, and then nodded painfully. 'Of course, etiquette must be observed.'

'Yes, my lady,' Chloris said, not without sympathy. 'It will be only a few moments longer.'

It seemed like days, weeks. She stood with the other ladies of the bedchamber behind the Queen on the dais in the gallery, watching the door for the moment when it would be flung open. And there was the King, looking bowed and grey and suddenly much older. In silence he crossed the floor, took his wife's hand to raise her from her curtsey, and stood looking down at her for a moment before taking her into his arms in a hard embrace. Annunciata was close enough to see that the King was crying, and it touched her unbearably. Over the King's shoulder she caught the eye of grim-faced Berwick, and he made a strange grimace at her whose meaning she could not interpret. But the King's informal gesture towards the Queen had released the flood-tide, and the courtiers were rushing forward to greet the returning soldiers who crowded through the doors behind the King and Berwick.

There to the fore was another tall, blond soldier, his dark eyes ringed with lack of sleep, his nose raw with a bad sunburn. Nothing more could restrain Annunciata; in a second she was across the floor and had her tall son in her arms, and he was holding her, and saying, 'Mother, oh Mother,' and she could feel his tears wet on her cheeks.

'Oh my darling,' Annunciata said, between tears and joy, 'you are safe. Thank God. You are not wounded? Oh God, you smell abominable. Are you all right, Karellie?'

Karellie could not speak, only held her tight and gulped like a child at his tears, and over her shoulder tried to return Maurice's smile of greeting. At last his grip loosened, and Annunciata put him back from her a little to look at him.

'I know I should not be so glad to have you back, since

36

it means you have been defeated, but my heart can only hold one thing at a time – the rest is beyond me. But where is Martin? Was he one of those who stayed behind?' Her eyes left his face to scan the rest of the party, but only briefly. If he had been there she would have known it. Then they came back to Karellie's face. 'Where is he?'

Karellie's dark eyes held her still. 'No,' she whispered. He shook his head, keeping his hands on her arms. The noise of the room receded, and she was held in a silence in which she could hear her own heart beating, each beat like a blow of pain. 'No, Karellie, no.'

'It was at the Boyne, Mother. In the thick of the fighting. I did not see, but one of my men told me.'

'No,' she said again. She was shaking her head, and the blood seemed to be rushing through it with a sound like the sea, like the sea at Aldbrough where they had said goodbye – but not for ever, not for ever!

'He was very brave, fighting on foot after his horse was killed under him,' Karellie was saying. She shook her head again, not wanting to hear any more. She had not believed that she could feel such pain. Voices boomed and faded about her; the pain in her throat was so terrible that she could not speak, and she seemed locked in a strange silence where she could see only Martin's face, his lips curving, his eyes smiling into hers. Darkness came welling from the corners of the room; they were speaking to her, trying to gain her attention, but she did not want to heed them, she wanted to go into that darkness and silence where Martin was, away from this pain that was all there was for her now. She wanted to die, there and then, so that the pain would stop.

A windy day in March 1691; a day of cold, gritty wind, though the sky, the pale blue of a robin's egg, spoke of spring being not far away. In Annunciata's memory winter was a mixture of twilight and fireglow. Like an invalid she had not strayed far from her fire, and her servants had

37

treated her like an invalid, wrapping her warmly against the icy draughts from the windows, moving softly about her, coaxing her to eat. She spoke little to them, hardly seemed to notice their presence; she moved like a ghost through her world, closed in with her pain, her eyes blank with uncomprehending misery. After the shock of Martin's death had come the gradual realization and then the terrible, bewildering loneliness. It rolled like a boulder on to her chest every morning when she woke, and she carried it with her all day until sleep finally released her.

She came to crave sleep as her one relief from unremitting pain, for sometimes in her sleep she would dream of him, and wake with tears on her face. In her waking hours she could only go over and over every separate memory of him, peopling her darkness with images of him which could not comfort, for they only brought it home to her again that he was gone from her for ever. She had no hope left; even in death she would be parted from him, for their love had been forbidden, and she was an exile not only from her country but also from her church. With him she could have faced exile, gone anywhere in the world and made a life. Without him, her exile was absolute and terrible.

Fand had spent most of his winter sleeping by the fire at her feet, roused only when Karellie dragged him out for exercise. For Karellie and Maurice exile was not so terrible. They had both lived abroad before, and both had their occupations. Maurice was kept happy and busy reorganizing the Chapel Royal choir and building up an orchestra to play the pieces he was composing for the King and Queen. Karellie had the company of his new friends, especially Berwick. Now there was no need any longer to conceal the fact that Annunciata was daughter of Prince Rupert of the Rhine, and in fact every reason to reveal it, her family could reap the benefits of their royal blood. Berwick was a duke and the illegitimate son of a king; Chelmsford was an earl and the great-great-grandson of a king. They had fought together in Ireland and come to like each other, and in the enforced idleness of St Germain their friendship had blossomed.

Through the winter, Berwick had been a frequent visitor to the apartments of the Countess of Chelmsford, and gradually he had been joined at her fireside by others, veterans of the Irish campaign, and veterans of Killiecrankie, known as The Jacobites, because in Latin their King's name was Jacobus. In the flickering light the voices would rise and fall, telling of old campaigns, of glorious charges, desperate stands, of courage and bitter humour, of dear friends fallen. Bored and lonely, the soldiers crept, like Fand, to her hearth, scenting sympathy and companionship, and though the Countess rarely spoke and seemed largely unaware of what went on around her, it was to her that they spoke.

They told of the wars against the Turks, of sieges under the merciless desert suns, when the wounded would weep like children because their wounds were black with feasting flies. They told her of the campaign against Monmouth in the west of England, when they marched through mud into which they sank knee-deep at every weary step. They talked of the civil war, of the glorious cavalry charges led by her father, noble and tall on his white horse. They spoke of Bonnie Dundee in Scotland, Lauzun in Ireland.

They spoke at length of the deaths of her own kin, her son Rupert at Sedgemoor, her cousin Kit at Killiecrankie, her brother Dudley Bard at Buda – Martin at the Boyne. She was a noble and beautiful lady, come of a great military family, and they brought her their stories because, poor men and exiles, it was all they had to give her. Their voices, through the winter, were an unreal background to the unreality in which she was living, but whether they knew it or not, whether she knew it or not, she heard them, and their open-hearted kindness laid a balm on her wounds. For death in battle was the common coin of them all, it was the holiness in them, and their quiet courage called to hers.

But now, on this windy spring day, they were leaving.

They had formed the King's private bodyguard, these hundred and fifty Scots Jacobites, most of them officers; but the King, struggling to support ever larger numbers of penniless exiles, could not pay them, and so they had asked the King's permission to leave him and enlist as private soldiers in the army of the King of France. The King, though loath to see them go, though ashamed that they should have to become common soldiers, could do nothing but agree. So they paraded for the last time, their helmets polished, their tunics immaculate, their beards neatly trimmed. Annunciata and her family stood behind the King on the steps with others of the Court, and the windows of the courtyard were crowded with white faces.

Slowly the King walked along the line, stopping to speak to each man. He took down the name of each of them in his pocket-book so that he should not forget any of them; the hard little gritty wind whisked their words away, but their expressions were eloquent. Then the King returned to the steps and mounted them and took off his hat, and bareheaded in the cold sunshine, his face wet with tears, he bowed to them. The veterans knelt, and for the last time gave him the royal salute. Then they rose and marched away, officers no more, to seek their deaths as strangers in a strange land, fighting for another king but theirs.

A week later, Karellie sought out his mother with a request. He found her in her apartment, and for the first time she was not sitting by the fireside, but at the window. True, her mind seemed far away, and he doubted whether she saw the gardens or the river, yet he sensed that since that day when the soldiers had left, she had begun to come back to them. He stood looking at her for some time before she noticed him. Her face was too pale and too thin, and there were traces of tears on her cheeks. She was wearing the black dress she had worn that day when Clovis had read Edmund's letter to them at Morland Place. It was growing a little shabby now. He remembered with pity how once there had been a time when she could not endure to wear the same dress thrice over, much less keep it for two years. Then Fand whined softly, and she made a small, fretful movement of her head, and turned to look at him.

'My lady mother,' he said softly, coming to kneel beside her, so that their faces were on a level.

'Karellie,' she said.

'Mother, I have something I must ask you.' She shewed no reaction, but her eyes were still on his, waiting. 'I want your permission to ask the King of France for a commission.'

'You want to leave me?' she said at last. 'Karellie – you will go away from me?'

'Mother, I can't help it,' he said gently. 'I can't stay here for ever, doing nothing. We have been here six months already, and I have no money but what you give me. It is no life for me, you must see that.'

She sighed, and he took it for assent and went on, 'So we thought –'

'We?' she interrupted.

'My lord of Berwick and I.'

'Ah, Berwick,' she said, as though that explained everything.

'We thought that we should try the French army. The King of France is mounting a new campaign in Flanders, and with our experience and birth, he would likely give us good commissions. He is going to ask his father this morning, and so I –' He could not endure her expression, and grew angry and defensive. 'I'm sorry, Mother, but you must see – our first loyalty is to the King, but . . .'

'Yes,' she said, cutting him off. 'I do see.' She stood up and walked away from him and back, restlessly, as an invalid grows restless with pain. He rose to his feet and watched her, and she suddenly seemed to him not like his mother at all, not connected to him in any way, a stranger whose house he happened to share. At last she stopped, facing him, and he saw that she had braced herself as if for some effort.

'Very well,' she said. 'Go to your good fight in Flanders,

my lord Earl. But remember that your first duty is to your own King, if he should need you.'

It was his permission, but he was dissatisfied, thinking she was angry. He hesitated, and made a vague gesture, as if to touch her. She shook her head, and then smiled, a strange, inconsequential little smile.

'No,' she said, 'it's all right. God bless you, child. God bless you, Karellie.'

The convent at Chaillot was a convenient distance from St Germain to ride or drive, and the Queen was a frequent visitor there. The order was a sister to the one she had hoped to join before she was persuaded to marry instead the English prince, James. She liked to go and talk to the nuns, walk in the beautiful gardens, take the sacrament and meditate in the peaceful surroundings, away from the pressures of the Court. The head of the convent, Soeur Angelique, was a middle-aged woman with a sensible eye and a brisk manner, like a kindly, efficient squire's wife of the middling sort. She was the Queen's closest friend and confidante, and it was to her that Annunciata turned for help in the autumn of 1691.

The woods through which she had ridden to Chaillot were beginning to be streaked with colours of Turkish splendour, rich crimsons and golds; the windows of the nuns' little parlour into which she was shewn were open, and below the window was a bed of marigolds, yellow and orange and dark-red, and scarlet windflowers.

Soeur Angelique sat quietly, her hands folded, waiting for Annunciata to tell her what troubled her, but when the silence extended itself she said at last, 'You may speak quite freely here, milady Chelmsford. Nothing you say will ever be heard outside these walls.' Still Annunciata could not find the words. 'How may I be of service to you?'

'I wish to come back into the Church,' Annunciata said at last. 'But – I fear I cannot.'

The nun waited for elucidation, and then said gently,

'Madame, God's love is greater than anything you can imagine, and for the truly penitent –'

'Ah, but that is the trouble,' Annunciata cried. 'I cannot repent, because I cannot say I am sorry for what I did. If time could be turned back, I would do the same again, gladly, gladly.' And she told Soeur Angelique about her love for Martin. It did not come easily, it did not flow from her – it was hard and painful, and yet there was a relief in speaking of what she had never been able to discuss with anyone, other than Martin himself. When she had finished, she stopped, and sat as though exhausted, looking down at her hands.

Soeur Angelique looked at her with pity, at the bent head with its loose, soft curls, which seemed so childlike to one accustomed to French ladies, who wore headdresses and elaborate fronts of false hair; at the long, beautiful hands which seemed somehow eloquent of grief.

'It would be a poor world, Madame,' she said at last, 'if God were not more loving and more generous than man, would it not? There are many who would not find it in their hearts to condemn you, and should not God have greater understanding than His creatures? Of course, we must have discipline, for without laws we should have chaos. But God has given to us, alone of all His creations, the ability to question, and to decide, and to worship Him in the subtlety of our minds.'

Annunciata looked at her with dawning hope.

'Confession, Madame, is unburdening ourselves of our guilt, and of our sorrow and confusion. We tell God that we are sorry that we have offended Him, we beg His forgiveness, we promise to try to do better in the future. Now, milady, can you say those things and mean them with your heart? Are you sorry to have offended God? Will you try never to offend Him again?'

Annunciata nodded, wordlessly, and Soeur Angelique stood up and held out her hand. 'Then come, Madame, come with me to the confessional. Father Dubois is here, who hears the sisters' confessions. Come and unburden yourself, and be forgiven, and then stay for Mass, and take the sacrament here with us.' Annunciata rose like an obedient child, and the nun led her towards the door, saying, 'The past is over and gone, and it is wrong to cling to it. Grief can come to be a vanity and a sin too, you know. God gives us life for a purpose. We must not waste His gifts.'

Later, Annunciata remained alone in the visitors' section of the chapel, divided by a screen from the part where the sisters sat. On the high altar the banks of candles had been snuffed, and only the sanctuary lamp glowed its eternal light; but to Annunciata's left on the small lady-altar the candles were lily-flames of pale gold, lighting the white cloth, the gold-and-crystal candlesticks, and the statue of Our Lady. It was a wooden statue, the robes painted blue and white, the face and hands painted gold, and it reminded Annunciata of the statue in the chapel of Morland Place. But this one was not so old, and the hands instead of being extended, palm upwards, were folded at the breast over a painted wooden lily.

She sat and gazed, alone, and at peace at last, once more returned to the bosom of the Church, to the safe and loving arms that had enfolded her all her life. She looked at the statue of the Lady, but what she saw was the face of the Lady at home, the worn, gentle, gilded face that she had adored so often; in the weariness of pain finally vanished, she could only think that it was the same thing, that all loves, in the end, are one – for otherwise, how could she feel closer to Martin now than at any time since they parted on the beach at Aldbrough?

In the spring of 1692 Karellie came back to St Germain, riding ahead of the main party. His mother's apartments were empty, but after a search he found Maurice in the chapel, alone, staring into space and playing odd unconnected notes on the organ. He betrayed no surprise when he looked up and saw Karellie, hands on hips, grinning down at him.

'Just where I suppose I ought to have expected to find you,' Karellie said.

'I was only thinking,' Maurice said. 'It's quieter here.'

Karellie clapped his shoulder. 'Are you not pleased to see me, little brother?'

'Of course,' Maurice said vaguely, and then frowned. 'But what *are* you doing here?'

'King Louis is back from Flanders, and Berwick and I have come to seek out our respective parents to give them the news. Great things are afoot, Maurice. And where is our mother?'

'She is at Chaillot, at the convent. She goes there a great deal now.'

'You sound disapproving,' Karellie said, mildly surprised.

'Well, I wonder sometimes if they aren't trying to make a Papist of her.'

'Why should that trouble you?' Karellie asked.

Maurice looked at him for a moment as if wondering how much he would understand, and then said, 'You know the Queen is with child again?'

Warned off, Karellie allowed the subject to be changed. 'Yes, I heard. The King must be delighted. If it is a son, it will be a blow to the Usurper. And perhaps it will dispel the warming-pan stories once and for all. It's a good omen for our new venture.'

'What new venture?' Maurice asked absently.

'Oh how hard it is to arouse your curiosity, little brother,' Karellie laughed. 'The King of France has decided to launch another attack on the Usurper on our King's behalf!'

'Has he? How kind he is,' Maurice said. 'But I suppose it is in his interest too, to remove Dutch William from the throne of England.'

'Kind or not, he's lending us the whole French fleet, with which to take the fifteen Irish battalions at present in

France across to England. If the help that has been promised in England meets them, it will be over in no time, and we shall be back in England by St John's Eve. Oh, think of it, Maurice, to have the midsummer celebrations at Morland Place again! The feasts, the dancing, the bonfires –' He caught sight of Maurice's expression and stopped. 'You don't feel the same way, do you? You have never felt homesick, like the rest of us.'

'One place seems much the same as another to me,' Maurice said. 'A bonfire burns as brightly in France as in England. And hunger gnaws an Englishman's belly as much as a Frenchman's.'

'But don't you long to go home?'

'Home? The world is home enough for me. God's eye can see me wherever I go, so how can I ever think myself far away? I can't help it, Karel,' he added anxiously, 'I don't think about things in the same way as you do.'

'I don't blame you for it. It's strange, that's all.' He hesitated. 'Why do you disapprove of Papism?'

Maurice gave him the same considering look. 'I don't know if you'd understand. I don't know if I can explain it. It's too *exclusive*.' Karellie watched him, waiting, and Maurice went on, feeling for words, 'God made all of us, you see, and we invented different ways to praise him – the Papists one way, the heathens another.' Karellie was trying not to look shocked, and he said, 'Look, when your hound-bitch whelps, you make the litter a bed of straw in the warmest place in the stable, where they'll be safe and contented. If one of the pups thanks you by licking your hand, you may grow fonder of that one than the others. But you don't throw the rest of the litter out to die in the cold because they didn't.'

Karellie turned his head away awkwardly. 'I don't think you ought to talk like that. It sounds – well, blasphemous to me.'

'I knew you wouldn't understand,' Maurice said. There was a silence, and Maurice broke it by pushing his stool

46

back and getting up. 'Would you like to ride over to Chaillot and give mother your news?'

'Will you come with me?' Karellie said doubtfully.

He was afraid he had offended his brother, but Maurice said cheerfully, 'Yes, of course, I need the exercise.'

They walked towards the door, and Karellie reached out a hesitant arm towards his brother, and Maurice, with a small private smile, moved closer so that the arm could be draped companionably about his shoulders.

CHAPTER THREE

The early part of June was always like a quiet haven between the storms of lambing and the storms of shearing. Little Matt had gone out early rabbiting on the edge of Wilstrop wood, and with two bucks in his carrying-bag he started home, taking the long way across Marston Moor, because he was in no hurry, and because the place fascinated him. And there he found his own sheep grazing on the good, sweet grass, and Old Conn sitting at his ease on the ridge known as Cromwell's Plump, because it was said to be there that General Cromwell had placed himself to dispose his troops at the battle of Marston Moor.

Old Conn acknowledged Matt's arrival with a nod, and a comprehensive glance that took in the rabbits in the bag, but he wasted no words on meaningless greeting. Matt sat down beside him to get his breath back, and together old man and young boy stared out across the moor towards the woods, while Matt tried to imagine the battle, the men and horses and cannon.

At length, as if he had heard Matt's thoughts, old Conn said, 'That were the year my son Conn, Davey's father, were born.'

'Were you at the battle, Conn?' Matt asked. He knew he was, of course, having heard the story before, but he never tired of hearing it again. 'Did you charge with Prince Rupert?'

' 'Course I were there. Me and Jack and Dick, we were the last three left, of those that went away with Master Kit. Jack had a terrible wound in his arm, and died of it, two weeks later. It wouldn't heal. That's the way it was on campaign. The longer it went on, the harder it was to heal your wounds. I was never wounded, praise God. Jack and Dick and Master Kit and me – and Hamil Hamilton, that

48

was brother to Master Kit's wife, he was our captain. By God, that were a battle. We were taken by surprise, but Prince Rupert rallied us, and we charged and charged again. Master Kit was killed, and Dick. I lost sight of Jack, and then I got knocked off my horse. In the end we had to flee, to the woods up there, where you been catching rabbits.'

He stopped and let that thought sink in. Where I've been catching rabbits, Matt thought, men, weary, bleeding, thirsty from battle, hid from the pursuing enemy.

'Some of us got away – not many. Lord Newcastle's men were killed, every one, over there where the sheepfolds are. Prince Rupert gathered us all together the next day to march us north to Richmond, but I'd had enough. Jack went on, with Captain Hamilton, and we never saw either of them again. I dropped out as we crossed the bridge by Watermill, and made my way back to the city.'

'And where was your wife all that time, Conn?' Matt asked.

'Why, she'd been travelling in the baggage vans with the other wives, and – and the other sorts of women. She was so near her time when we got to York that I'd left her at an outlying cottage that belonged to Garth the shepherd. He was killed on Marston Moor too, and when I got back to his house, my bairn was born, and so I stayed and took his job and looked after his wife until she died, not a twelvemonth later. And there I still am, young master, a good many years later.'

Matt sighed with content; every time Conn told the story, there were different little bits he put in.

'There you still are, and your son, and your grandchildren,' Matt agreed. 'Where's Davey today?'

'He's helping out at High Moor Farm,' Conn said. 'No place for idle hands at my house, not now there's a new mistress, like to breed like a summer yow, and a born wastrel, if I know owt about women.' Davey's mother had died the year before, and his father had married again. Evidently, Old Conn didn't approve.

'Is Ursula with child, then?' he asked.

'Seemingly,' Conn said with a grunt.

'Conn must be pleased,' Matt said cautiously. Old Conn fixed him with a bright eye.

'He's a fool, and he always was, and he always will be. He'd no cause to marry at all, not with a daughter of twenty-three who could have left her job and come home to tend the house and garden and the spinning. But he must needs marry, and marry a flighty bit with no more sense in her head than a mayfly. A parlour-maid, she was, and spoiled as a house-fed kitten. She knows nowt about tending crops and beasts, and cares for nowt but her white hands. Catch her scrubbing and scouring and digging and hoeing! When she spins she breaks her thread every minute.' This, Matt knew, was a great crime. Almost every household improved its income by spinning Morland wool into yarn, which was then collected by the agent and taken to the weavers. 'Remember what I told thee, Master Matt, that when a man chooses his own wife, he always chooses amiss.'

'But, Conn, didn't you choose your own wife when you married the fo –' He almost called her the foreigner, which was what local people had always dubbed Conn's wife. She had come from Bristol, and Conn had married her on campaign there with Prince Rupert. Bristol, to the Yorkshire folk who had never been farther afield than Leeds, was incalculably foreign, and Conn's wife had spoken with such an incomprehensible accent that for years she had been thought to be a Dutchwoman. 'When you married Conn's mother.'

Old Conn stared hard at him, as if wondering how innocent the question was, and then he said with massive dignity, 'That were different, young master. That were providence, which is to say the working of the Lord, for she and I met in a providential way when I was soldiering in foreign parts. And she was a good wife to me, God rest her soul, though she never bore me but the one son. But that was God's working too, and you can't argue with it.'

Now Matt asked in a small voice, 'Is it God's working too that the King should have been defeated by the Usurper's fleet?' Old Conn looked at him more kindly.

'Is it the talk up at the House, then?'

'It seems to be all they talk of,' little Matt said. 'Uncle Clovis – he doesn't exactly say so, but he thinks it is the end of everything. The defeat, he says, was so complete that the King of France will never lend our King any more ships or money.'

'I'll tell thee, young master, the King was hoping our navy would go over to his side, on account of him knowing them all, when he was Lord of the Admiralty. But when our ships see a Frenchy ship coming towards them, why they can't help firing at it. It would be against their nature to let a Frenchy ship past, now wouldn't it?'

'Even if it was for our King?'

'Even then. You see, master, the King made a terrible mistake when he left England, for now he's out of it, he can't get back without some foreign king's help. That's where the weakness is. And the Usurper, why he's got more sense than Lord Cromwell. He leaves folk alone, and most folk, they don't much care who's king at Whitehall, so long as they're left alone to get on with their own lives.'

'But our cousins at the Hare and Heather, they say that every night people lift their tankards to the King over the Water,' Matt said. Conn nodded, wagging his short beard like a sparrow wagging its tail.

'Ah, talk costs nothing, does it? They'll drink a toast to our King, and if the King comes back they'll welcome him. But they won't lift a finger to *get* him back, not while the Usurper leaves them alone.'

They were silent for a while, old man and young boy, pondering. Then Conn said, 'I'm sorry for your grandmother, the Countess – her most of all.'

'You don't think she'll come back to England?' Matt asked. He remembered her, glittering with jewels and sweetly scented, like a queen.

'Not while the Usurper is on the throne. When he dies

– who knows? There won't be no more expeditions for our King, take you my word, master. We must pin our hopes on the Prince of Wales. But it's sad for her to be in exile. I remember her from a little girl. Rode better than any boy, and could shoot flying, and rare pretty!' He was silent for a while, remembering the beautiful young girl, who was the image of that dashing young cavalry general who had led them to so many victories up and down the country. It was never spoken of, of course, but Prince Rupert rested the night after Marston Moor at Shawes, where the Countess's mother lived unwed, and nine months later a dark-haired dark-eyed baby had been born. Well, if Miss Ruth had not wanted to speak of it, then no one else could, in all courtesy, but Conn and some of the older men had guessed the truth of it rightly enough.

'So you think the Usurper will never be defeated?' Matt asked at length.

'Tha must make the best of it, young master, as must we all,' Conn said. 'There'll be no more expeditions for our King.'

'But what when the Usurper dies? Who will be king then?'

Conn's eye was bright and full of a strange sympathy. 'That will be thy 'heritance, to worry over that. I shall be with the Holy Virgin by then, and past worrying. Men sow their fields with wrong, but it's their sons and grandsons who have to harvest the crop.'

King James was so shocked and grief-stricken at the failure of the expedition which had looked so promising that he would not at once return to St Germain, but remained in Brittany, grieving, and wondering what he had done so to offend God that He set His face against the royal family. He was still absent from St Germain when, on 28 June, the Queen went into labour, and was delivered of a healthy daughter. Annunciata, waiting at the foot of the bed with the rest of the ladies of the bedchamber, could not help remembering that other occasion in Whitehall, when the Prince of Wales had been born. It seemed that poor Mary Beatrice was doomed to travail in misery, for then she had been surrounded by her enemies, and vile and wicked rumours had been seething in the corridors of the palace and the streets of the capital.

This time, though her labour was comparatively short and easy, the Queen was in great distress because of the continued absence of her husband and the failure of their attempt to regain their throne. Word was sent to the King at once, however, and he hurried, conscience-stricken, to his wife's bedside, where he embraced her tenderly and received his infant daughter into his arms, and said with tears in his eyes, 'God has sent her to us for a consolation.'

Annunciata looked at the infant princess, and thought how she came too late, like her brother. Had Queen Mary presented the country with an heir at the beginning of her marriage to the Duke of York, things might have gone very differently, for a fifteen-year-old Prince of Wales would have been a very strong inducement to the country to tolerate his father a little longer. Still, if there were any hope for them now, it lay with the prince. He was four years old, healthy, strong, beautiful, and sweet-tempered. If God gave him the chance, he would one day make a good king.

The new baby was so healthy that it was decided to delay her christening until King Louis came back from Flanders, which was in the middle of July. The ceremony took place in the chapel royal at St Germain, and was a lavish occasion. Maurice composed and directed the performance of a new anthem and processional, and at the feast afterwards he played the cornetto, and was loudly acclaimed. King Louis was godfather to the princess, who was named Louis Marie in his honour. The other godparent was his sister-in-law the Duchess of Orleans, known affectionately as Liselotte.

Liselotte was the daughter of Prince Rupert's brother Charles Louis, and therefore Annunciata's cousin; a cheerful, friendly, and unassuming woman, she took a great interest in Annunciata and her family. When Maurice had finished playing, Liselotte called Annunciata over and congratulated her on having such a talented son.

'And he looks so like his grandfather, don't you think? A real Palatine!' she cried sentimentally. Annunciata consented to this piece of romance – Liselotte had never seen Prince Rupert, other than in portraits, but her lively imagination sometimes ran away with her. 'You know, our aunt Sofie would so love to see him. I have mentioned him quite often in my letters.'

'That is very good of you, Madame,' Annunciata said. Aunt Sofie, the Duchess of Hanover, was Prince Rupert's younger sister, and had always been the great correspondent of the family.

'Not at all, my dear Countess. But you know that Aunt Sofie is greatly interested in the arts, and especially music, and she would so like to hear something of your son's. Now, it occurs to me, Madame, that if you were to take him to see her, she might well give him a position. Don't you think that would be wonderful for him?'

Annunciata assented again, but thought deeply about it afterwards. There would obviously be no more attempts at replacing King James upon his throne, and he was looking so old and ill that it did not seem likely he would live many years more. It was to the Prince of Wales they must look for their future. Nevertheless, for the present, her sons must have something to do. Karellie was happy enough soldiering for the King of France, and Aliena was still too small to worry about, but it was surely time she did something for Maurice. Hanover, to be sure, was a small and unimportant Court, but if he were to be given a position there, it would be a stepping-stone to greater things. And he had been happy enough when he lived in Liepzig, seeming to get on well with the German character. She decided to write to Aunt Sofie at once.

In the January of 1693, news came to Morland Place that John Ailesbury had died, leaving his entire estate to Mary

Celia. Clover, who had seen little of her father in her life, was not at all upset, and was far more concerned with the miniature portrait Clovis was having done of her, for his own delight. At six Clover was strikingly pretty, with her mother's fair features, grey-gold eyes and golden hair, and Clovis adored her quite extravagantly.

Being the only girl in the nursery, Clover was in a fair way to being spoiled, being as arbitrary and capricious as any small tyrant who had ever felt her power. She insisted on taking lessons from Father St Maur along with John and Arthur, and would have shone at them, for she had a very good brain, except that she would not apply herself. Also, she spoiled her cousins' concentration and Father St Maur's discipline by leaving the lessons when she had had enough, and by not coming in at all when she had something she preferred to do.

She learnt early that Clovis was the source of power in the house, and that the way to impress Clovis was to evince a love of learning, and so she would come to him in the evenings and beg him to teach her things. She did have a quick grasp of figures, and it was one of the sights that the Morland Place servants never quite got used to, to see Father St Maur and Clovis going over the accounts in the steward's room, with the small fair head of Clover between them, bent over the books with a scowl of ferocious concentration.

She also liked to accompany Clovis when he rode into the city or around the estates on business, sitting up in front of him on his horse, with his strong arm around her body and her little hands clasped over his. The cottagers and tenants thought it charming, and made a great fuss of her, bringing her out sweetmeats and flattering her more than was good for her. Birch and Caroline separately remonstrated with Clovis over the way she was being brought up, but to no avail.

'If she was a boy,' Birch would say, 'it would be well enough to have her cast accounts and draw triangles and read the stars. But what use is it to a young lady?'

And Clovis would say, 'Come, Birch, your own mistress, the Countess, is a very learned lady.'

'That's as may be, sir. The Countess was properly educated, and though it would not be my choosing for a young lady, she was at least taught all the accomplishments too.'

'You mean, embroidering and sewing and dancing?' Clovis said, smiling. 'Well, Birch, you cannot say that Miss Clover is not a young lady in that respect. Don't worry – I'll make sure she learns to dance daintily, and not show off her learning.'

'You'll never get her wed, sir, if you bring her up so different,' was Birch's warning, and Clovis would say lightly, 'She doesn't want to marry – she wants to stay with me. And I want her to stay, so we are all happy.'

When John Ailesbury died, the disagreement flared up more seriously, for Clovis refused to put Clover into mourning clothes.

'It's not right that a child should not mourn for her father,' Birch said in outrage.

Clovis retorted, 'I'm not going to have that pretty little thing dragging herself about in horrible black garments like a wounded crow. She's too pretty to be dressed in black. She's only a child.'

Birch was shocked. 'It's not proper. It's not right. What will people think? You should not fill her head with such consequence of herself, sir – you are doing her no service in making her vain.'

'She's pretty and she knows it. It would be a crime against nature to hide that prettiness in ugly clothes.'

And Birch grew so passionate that she overstepped the bounds of her servitude. 'Folks here about all talk of the way you have that child with you all the time. It's unnatural and wrong to want a little girl's company like that. You should leave her in the nursery where she belongs.'

Clovis, in fury and outrage, gave Birch her notice on the spot and sent her from his sight. Birch swept out in equal fury, and only when she reached the nursery did she give way to her tears. The house was in turmoil for hours, news of the quarrel spreading like ripples from a dropped stone. The under-servants crept about like dogs afraid of being kicked, but the older servants argued the matter furiously in undertones at every corner, freezing into unnatural silence when a member of the family came by. Caroline, hearing of the matter, took Birch's side and quarrelled with Clovis herself, then retreated in high dudgeon to the long saloon where she sat sewing so savagely that she broke her needle.

The children heard of the quarrel, too, and Clover at once rushed to comfort Uncle Clovis, sitting on his lap and winding her hands in his fingers winningly, and chattering to him in the way he liked, though he hardly seemed to be hearing her. John, on the other hand, ran straight to his mother and stood by her chair, giving her his silent support while she complained bitterly at the way she was treated in this house.

And Arthur and Matt quarrelled, and the quarrel ended, as usual, in Arthur using his superior weight and strength to subdue Matt, getting him on the ground where he could kneel astride him and pummel his body at his ease. The noise brought the servants running, Arthur was hauled off, and Matt was sent, dishevelled and bleeding at the nose, to speak to Clovis.

'What were you fighting about?' he asked, looking coldly at Matt. 'It is unseemly behaviour in the heir to Morland Place.'

Matt licked his lip and grimaced at the taste of blood. 'Sir, I don't really remember how it started. It was about Mrs Birch, sir.'

'What about Mrs Birch?' Clovis scowled.

Matt stared at him anxiously. 'About her going away. Oh please don't send her away, uncle. Arthur said she could go, and good riddance. He said she could go to France –'

'Well, so she could, I suppose,' Clovis said. He had not thought of where Jane Birch would go if she left Morland

Place, and had long since repented of his loss of temper. But perhaps she would be happier rejoining her old mistress.

'But, sir,' Matt went on, 'she's so old, and she might easily die on a long sea-journey like that, and when I said that to Arthur he only said that would be even better riddance, and that no doubt that was what you intended. But I know you wouldn't mean that, you couldn't. Oh please don't send her away to die, uncle.'

'It's all right, Matt, she need not go if she doesn't want to,' Clovis said. 'I don't mean her any harm. I was angry and hasty. I should be used to her sharp tongue by now. Go and tell her that I want her to stay, and send her here to me.'

It made a convenient excuse that did not involve loss of face, to forgive Birch on Matt's plea. Clover did not wear mourning; Clovis took over the management of her estate, making another burden to add to his already considerable responsibilities, not the least of which was governing Annunciata's affairs, and ensuring an income from her estates was paid to her abroad. He wished that she would come back to England and take over some part of the burden, but there seemed little chance of this happening. In the spring a letter came from her, addressed from the Court of Hanover, where she had gone with Maurice to try to get him a position.

'I intended to make only a short stay,' she wrote, 'but I am received with such kindness by my aunt that I find it hard to leave, and I have been here four months already. She wants me to make my permanent home here, but my duty lies with the King and Queen – I cannot desert them. But the duchess – or Electress as we must now call her, her husband having been made Elector at last, after a lifetime of effort in that direction – was delighted with Maurice, and has made him her Kapelmeister, which is a wonderful beginning for him. He is to teach the children in the royal nursery, arrange the state music, and write pieces for special occasions, and his wages are most generous.

'But though I am sure Maurice will be happy here, it is not a place where I could feel at home, for though my aunt is a lively, intelligent, generous woman, the rest of the Court is not like her. Her husband, and her eldest son George Lewis, are dull and sullen, having no interests beyond hunting and eating and drinking. I met George Lewis at Windsor when he was a young man, and was not impressed with him then, and he has not improved with age. He is married to a pretty, silly young woman, his cousin Sophia Dorothea, and they have two children. He loathes her so much he will hardly stay in the same room with her, and disports himself openly with mistresses, the chief of whom are two women of startling plainness, one very thin, one very stout, and both as dull as slugs. Sophia Dorothea retaliates by flirting with a handsome Swedish mercenary officer called Konigsmark, despite anything Aunt Sofie can do to make her behave more discreetly.

'The rest of Aunt Sofie's children are no more like her than her eldest son. Two of the older boys, Frederick and Charles, were killed a couple of years ago fighting against the Turks, and the youngest, a girl, was married at sixteen to the King of Prussia. The three left at home, Maximillian, Christian, and Ernest Augustus, are like their father in looks and temperament. The eldest has not even the wit to get himself married, though he is twenty-six.

'So you see I shall not be sorry to go back to St Germain, where there is at least witty conversation, and where the younger generation fills one with hope and not despair.'

Clovis read this letter with resignation. No, there was no chance that the Countess would come back to England, even though he thought that the Usurper now felt so secure on his throne he would have ignored the return of the exile, provided she made no trouble for him. He must continue to carry the burden alone; and so he did not see that anyone could blame him for taking innocent comfort from the company and adoration of pretty little Clover.

★

In the late summer of each year, Cathy Morland had a party of guests to stay at Birnie Castle in Stirlingshire for the hunting and shooting. It was one of the things that was expected of her, but she did it largely for her son's sake, for she would do nothing that would jeopardize his future. She still hoped that one day he would be Lord Hamilton, the title his father had fought to have restored to his branch of the family, and which would surely be his when the true King was restored to his throne. And if James was to be Lord Hamilton, he must have the right background and the right friends.

In the summer of 1695 her chief guests were her neighbours, the Macallans of Braco, who brought with them their son Allan and their ward, an orphaned heiress from the far north, named Mavis D'Atheson. Mindful that family connections were important too, she sent an invitation to Sabine to send her daughter Frances, and to Morland Place for Matt and Clover. She did not include the McNeill children, Arthur and John, in the invitation. Titles they may have, but they had no land and no fortune, unless Annunciata left them her estates, and Cathy knew Annunciata too well to suppose that she would ever let anything of hers fall into the hands of her first husband's descendants.

Matt was pleased with the invitation. He had not been away from Morland Place before, and the thought of travelling so far was exciting. He had met his aunt Cathy and his cousin James – they had visited Morland Place two years ago. Aunt Cathy was so sharp she made Birch seem like sugar-syrup by comparison; but she was intelligent, and treated Matt like an adult, which made it very different. Matt had heard the servants talking about her, how when she was a girl she had been very plain and had grown up in grandmother Annunciata's shadow, and so had come to hate her; that she had made a bad marriage at first, but when her first husband died she married her cousin Kit who was the love of her life and had gone to live in Scotland to be as far from Annunciata as possible.

Matt knew enough of servants' stories to dismiss much of this, but he had heard Uncle Clovis say that as Cathy had come to look forty when she was but twenty, she had the benefit of it now, for at fifty she still only looked forty. To Matt she seemed like weathered rock, worn away until only a solid core remained, and that core untouchable and unchangeable, and like rock, her beauty was her own and not to be compared with the beauty of flowers or birds.

Clovis was at first inclined to refuse the invitation, but Matt begged so hard to go that in the end he agreed, though he would not let Clover leave him for so long. Clover was indifferent, and in fact rather hoped that with Matt gone she might have even more of Clovis's attention, and so it was decided in the end that servants should be sent from Northumberland to collect Matt, and take him to Edinburgh, collecting Frances on the way. Aunt Cathy's servants from Aberlady House would then accompany the children the rest of the way to Birnie. Old Conn, when Matt told him, said that when *he* was a lad, the far north was so wild that you could not travel in it without an army, and Matt was impressed and rather excited until he discovered that Conn, despite his wanderings in the south, had never gone farther north than Yorkshire.

They reached Birnie Castle by 1 August. Three of the four wings of the castle were ruined, and wild wallflowers gilded the heaps of stones, and ferns grew from empty windows. Jackdaws nested in the north-west tower, and chacked and chattered amongst the crenellations, where once guards had stood surveying the horizon for marauders; pigeons nested in the gatehouse tower, and flew up with a rattle of wings when the children entered it at the bottom on their tour of inspection.

'These were the guard rooms,' James explained importantly, doing his duty as host, 'and there was a portcullis here – you can see the grooves, and up there are the remains of the chains.'

The visitors craned their necks obediently, but six-year-old Sabina had heard it all before, and looked bored.

'Wouldn't it have been fun, to stand guard up there, and throw stones and pour boiling oil on your enemies,' said Allan Macallan. He was ten, and well-grown for his age, a stocky, wiry boy with red hair.

Sabina didn't like his sandy eyelashes or his freckles, both of which made her shudder, and reminded her of a ginger cat that had lived in the cellar at Aberlady House and had the most horrible sore on its back. She was deeply in love with James Matthias, whom she thought the most beautiful boy she had ever seen, so she said contemptuously, 'I don't believe anyone ever poured boiling oil on anyone. It's just a stupid story.'

'But I've read it in a book,' Allan said – politely, because when one is a guest one must be polite, even to rude little girls.

'But it's miles from the kitchens,' Sabina said stoutly. 'It would be cold by the time they got it all the way to the top of the tower.'

'Oh Sabina, what does it matter?' James said impatiently.

'Perhaps they carried the oil cold, and had a fire up there to heat it,' said Mavis D'Atheson, in an effort to propitiate, and Matt hastened to agree with her. She was a few months older than him, nearly twelve, and already a lady. She had soft, mouse-fair hair which she wore ringleted, creamy skin, large violet eyes, and she wore fine dresses without pinafores or caps, which impressed Matt so much that he had already decided he wanted to marry her as soon as they were both old enough. He had never met a young lady of his own age before – only servants and commoners – and was therefore very vulnerable to her charm.

'Of course that's what they did – how clever of you to think of it. They could have had a brazier up on the roof,' he said. Sabina was annoyed that he had sided with Mavis.

'Well even if they had a brazier, it still wouldn't have been boiling by the time they poured it over the wall,' she said stubbornly. Her brother stepped in firmly.

'Now hush, Sabina. Let's go up here. The steps go nearly all the way to the top.'

They climbed the stone spiral. 'It does smell horrid,' Mavis said, drawing her skirts up fastidiously. Matt kept close behind her.

'Be careful. The steps are slippery,' he said. He hoped she might slip a little and he would be able to save her from a nasty fall. At the top they came out into the open, for the roof was missing entirely.

'This was the chapel,' James said. Above them arched a blue and windy sky, and through the windows in the half-ruined walls they could see the great spread of the moors, brown and purple and pierced with little glinting burns, stretching to the glowering hills, Ben Clach and Creag Beinn Nan Eun. Away to the north was the little town of Braco, where once the Roman legionaries had built a fort at the place where the Roman road ran away north-eastwards to Perth. From the windows on the other side they could see the soft greenness of Strathallan, and the Allan Water writhing this way and that like a silver worm, and beyond the low moor of Sherrifmuir, and more hills, plum-purple and riven with deep blue shadows in the strong sunshine.

Matt stood beside Mavis, where she stationed herself at a low place in the wall and gazed eagerly towards the north-west. The bright air made her cheeks pink, and blew soft fronds of her hair loose, and her eyes were brilliant with more than just the wind's teasing.

'Can you see your home?' he asked.

'I can see where we live,' she said, as if it were not the same thing. 'Over there, look. The windows catch the sun just.' Her accent was strange and lovely to him, making her voice sound slow and careful, as if each word were important and worth the choosing.

'You don't call it home?' he asked. She looked at him, and away again.

'I have no home. My home was far away, beyond those hills.'

'Tell me it,' Matt said eagerly. 'Tell me about your family.'

'My parents both are dead,' she said slowly. 'My mother was a Macallan, and so the Macallans are my cousins. That is why I live with them.'

'But your surname is not Scottish, is it?' he asked. She looked around for somewhere to sit, and he hastened to brush a convenient block of stone with his hands to make sure it was clean enough for her before she sat down. She had a slow way of moving, and a high way of carrying her head, which made her seem queenly.

'My grandmother was a Breadalbane from the far north, and she married a Frenchman named D'Ath, who died in exile with King Charles II. But she brought her son, my father, back to Scotland, and gave him the name D'Atheson so that her people would understand who he was. I am my father's heir, and all his fortune will be mine one day, when I am grown.'

'Well, then, you will be able to go home,' Matt said. She shook her head.

'My fortune is all in gold. They sold my father's land when my mother died, because there was no one to keep it.'

'What is it like, in the far north?' Matt asked, enchanted. She was so romantic and sad, an exiled princess, that she stirred his imagination as well as his senses.

'Dark, and silver,' she said. 'The tall hills cut out the sky, until you come to the sea, and then the sea and sky are like a silver shield.' They were silent for a moment, and then she said, 'Tell me about your home. It must be so different.'

But at that moment Sabina came running up and grabbed Matt's hand. 'Matt, come and see – you can go up these stairs where the tower was, and then it just stops, and there's a tiny room, with a bench and a sink, where the priests used to retreat, so small you can't imagine how they lived in there for a day, leave alone a month. Do come!' She flicked a glance at Mavis and said, 'Mavis had better stay here. It's too steep and dangerous for her, and she might get her dress dirty.'

To which Mavis merely assented with a serene smile,

and Matt, for politeness, was obliged to scramble up the tower with his cousin, though he would much rather have remained and talked. He consoled himself with the thought that there would be plenty of time to talk in the weeks to come.

Time there was, but not so many opportunities. The children had a degree of latitude in the safeness of Birnie that they all enjoyed as a contrast to their normal lives, and provided they remained on Birnie land, they were not required to be accompanied by nurses. The ruins of the castle were theirs to run and play in, and the old nursery wing was huge, and they could make as much noise as they liked without being reprimanded, and the moors were open for them to ride and walk. But Matt found it difficult to be with Mavis, for often James wanted to bathe, which meant the boys going off without the girls, or Allan wanted to hunt, which meant leaving Mavis and Frances behind, since Mavis did not care to hunt and Frances was too young. And whenever they were all together in the castle or the gardens, Sabina would be sure to seize Matt's hand and drag him away to see something or explore something or play at something with her. She simply did not seem to understand Matt's grimaces and hints that he would sooner stay where he was and talk to Mavis. Only in the evenings when they would sit around the great nursery fire – the castle was so chill and damp that even in the summer fires were necessary after dark – and tell stories, was he able to seat himself beside the object of his choice, and even then he could not talk privately to her, for Sabina was always at his other side, interrupting. He sometimes spoke a few sentences to Mavis in French, which Sabina did not understand, and that constituted the only privacy that Birnie afforded him. It made him all the more determined to marry Mavis when he was old enough, so that he could spend the rest of his life talking to her without anyone listening on his other side . . .

CHAPTER FOUR

Lessons at St Edward's school finished at six o'clock in the summer, and James Matt was one of the first to emerge into the sunny, dusty street. He was alone: his fellow pupil Davey, with whom he had kept up a constant friendship over the years, had not been at school that day, or for several days before it. Arthur, who was now fifteen, had been sent to Christ Church College in Oxford, though he was a little young for it, because it had become beyond either the school's ushers, or Father St Maur at home, to control him. Matt was not entirely sorry that Arthur was thus removed from the scene. Arthur had grown bigger and heavier since his voice broke, while Matt at thirteen was still small and slight, as his father had been, and until Arthur had gone away, no day had passed that Matt did not find another new bruise somewhere on his body.

But it made it lonely at home, for John and Clover were both away too. They had had the chicken-pox, which had somehow, miraculously, missed Matt, and Clovis had sent them to Sabine at Emblehope where the air was said to be very good for invalids. Flora missed them very much, and often sighed to Matt that she longed for the time when he would be old enough to marry and give her some more babies in her nursery; and Matt, glad to have someone to talk to about it, had told her about Mavis D'Atheson, and his plan to marry her as soon as ever he was old enough, which would be in two more years.

Flora had listened kindly, and at the end had said, 'Well, Master Matt, she sounds a very nice kind of young lady altogether.'

'Do you really think so? Do you think she's suitable?' Matt asked anxiously. He had never forgotten what Old Conn said, that men always choose amiss when they choose their own wives. Flora had said she sounded very suitable, but the answer had not entirely satisfied Matt. His quick ear had detected something lacking in her tone of voice, as if she were not taking the question seriously.

On school days, Matt left his pony, Goldfinch, in the stables of the Hare and Heather, which was just across the road from the school. The inn belonged to Matthew Morland, known to Matt as Cousin Matthew, though the family connection was so far back that it was impossible to gauge the exact degree of cousinship between them. Matthew had married the innkeeper's daughter of the Starre Inn in Stonegate in the city, a sweet-tempered, buxom girl named Mary Handy, and they now had two children, Ambrose, who was nearly seven, and Mary, or Polly, who was a year old. Ambrose, who was becoming very good at various jobs about the place, had Goldfinch all ready saddled and bridled when Matt came into the yard, and held his stirrup for him to mount like a proper little groom. Matt thanked him gravely, and asked after his parents, but Ambrose became tongue-tied and merely went silent and scarlet. He was all dressed in black, for his father's brother, Jacob, had recently died, falling from his horse in a race on Clifton Ings and breaking something inside. Matt thought it looked strange to see such a small child as Ambrose dressed in black, and remembered the quarrel with Mrs Birch over the question of black clothes for Clover. Uncle Clovis had been right in that, Matt thought.

Matt rode home over Micklegate Stray, across Hob Moor and through the gap in the sedges that people called Hobgate, crossing the Akburn at the shallow place where the three willows grew, where Goldfinch always liked to stop and drink. Matt sat idly, watching the clear running water dimple around Goldfinch's round hooves, and then a slight veering of the wind brought to his nostrils a terrible smell. Even Goldfinch lifted his head for a moment and wrinkled his nose, making the silvery drops dance and spring from his long whiskers. Soap-boiling! Of course, it had quite escaped Matt's memory that today was the beginning of washing-week.

Aunt Caroline had been in a passion that morning, for the washerwomen had finished at Beningborough Hall and had come straight over to Morland Place to ask if Lady Caroline wanted to start her washing a few days early, since the weather was so good. Otherwise, they had said, they were going off towards Leeds, and would not be back for nearly a month.

Matt remembered that Lady Caroline had called it blackmail, for the summer wash was the biggest, and needed the help of the professional washerwomen, but it was such an upheaval for the family that it needed planning for, and she had planned it for a week hence. Flora had reported to Matt that Lady Caroline had been on the point of sending the women away, and saying they would manage on their own when the time came, until Birch had pointed out that as the weather was so fine and Master Clovis was away in London, it would be foolish for Lady Caroline to cut off her nose to spite her face.

'Though it would have been our noses and our faces,' Flora had said to Matt, 'when all's said and done.'

And then, when it was decided to go ahead, Lady Caroline had inspected the stores and discovered that they were almost without soap, and there had been a terrific row with Mrs Clough, the housekeeper, for letting the soap get so low. Mrs Clough had retorted that she had intended to boil soap in time for the washing-day as originally planned, and Mrs Birch, who resented Mrs Clough's authority, had said that washing-day had to depend on the weather, and Mrs Clough had no business letting them run out of soap so close to washing-time. Mrs Clough had asked, acidly, what business it was of Birch's, and at that fascinating point Matt had had to leave for school. But evidently it had been decided to boil right away, and in Matt's experience, with the twin disorders of washing and boiling, the house would be a comfortless place.

When he rode up to the house, he saw that the green

areas all around the moat looked like tenterfields, with the freshly washed linen stretched out on poles and lines to dry, the thorn hedges that lined the path white with small linen like a mysterious snow-fall. He crossed the moat and rode into the yard, and saw two boys scurrying one way with arms full of wood, and two maids scurrying the other way with arms full of soiled cloth, and no cats or dogs or peacocks anywhere to be seen, sure sign that the human inhabitants were all moving about too fast for animal comfort. He hitched Goldfinch to the stable wall and went inside, and up to the nursery to look for Flora. He found her inspecting the nursery naps, and she turned to him with a hot and anxious smile as he came in.

'Oh, Master Matt, is it that time already? What a to-do there's been.'

'I can see that. There'll be no supper tonight, I guess.'

'There's not been no dinner, either,' she said resentfully. 'We've to work on empty stomachs, to get all done the quicker, but you can get some bread and cheese from the kitchen if you're hungry.'

Matt was starving, having had nothing since his dinner at school at twelve.

'How is it going?' he asked. Flora rolled her eyes.

'Her ladyship's in a terrible taking, for the housekeeper at Beningborough sent to Mrs Clough to say she's missed some pillowslips, and she doesn't think the washerwomen are honest, and so Lady Caroline says we've to take everything to her to be counted dirty, and then back again to her to be counted clean, and it all has to be written down, and Father St Maur said he wouldn't write down washing, it wasn't fitting, and Lady Caroline can't write numbers, only words, and Birch said she couldn't see to write, and then one of the washerwomen said *she* could write, and Father St Maur said what was the point of that, if it was her honesty that was in question, and then the washerwomen said what was that? There was such a to-do they nearly up and left. And Father St Maur said he had spent the best years of his life teaching maids in this house to read and write and when one was wanted none could be found.'

Flora paused for breath, and Matt said, 'So what happened in the end?'

She grimaced. 'In the end Valentine was called in to do it, and a fine sulk he made about it too, but there was no help for it. And now you're home I dare say they'll want to put you on it so that Valentine can get on with his own work.'

'It sounds as though I'll be better off out of here,' Matt said with a grin.

Flora patted his shoulder. 'You skip off, Master Matt, if you want. I shan't say I've seen you, unless they ask.'

'I'll go over to Davey's, and find out why he hasn't been at school. I hope he hasn't been ill. I'll get some supper there.'

'It'll be better than bread and cheese, anyway,' Flora said. 'But if he's got the chicken-pox, don't you go in. You come straight back, and don't touch anyone. We don't want that brought back here.'

Conn the shepherd's house stood sheltered by a coppice of elms, and the homecoming rooks were making a fine din high up in the branches when Matt arrived. The chained yard-dog barked in a bored fashion, and in a moment Davey's stepmother appeared at the open door, looking distracted. She had a baby in a sling of cloth across her front, suckling as best it could when her movements did not jerk the nipple from its mouth; her hands were thus left free for spinning. Like many of the local women she preferred to spin by hand, rather than with a spinning-wheel, for at a spinning-wheel a woman was tied, and could not move about to keep an eye on crawling children, straying hens, or boiling pots. Almost every good wife span Morland wool, for it made extra income for the household. The agent would bring the raw wool one week, the wife would spin it, and the agent would collect the yarn the next week and pay her in hard coin for her work. Many a woman was chosen for wife on the basis of how well she could spin – it was more important than how well she could cook or sew.

Ursula had been eighteen when Davey's father married her, and Matt remembered how pretty she had been – 'flighty', Old Conn had called her. She was not so pretty now, he thought sadly. She had had four babies since then, and had lost several of her teeth, and her hair was rough and uncared-for; her clothes were shabby and disordered, and she had either grown very fat or was pregnant again. She had a thick cord tied about her middle, into which the end of the distaff was thrust, and even though she was evidently flustered about something, her hands continued to drop and catch the spindle and wind the thread with an unshakable rhythm, as if they were nothing to do with her, as if they were separate animals. The movement of her arm as she caught the spindle jerked her nipple from the bairn's mouth every time, but it was evidently well used to this, and did not whimper in protest, merely nuzzled for it again and continued to suck.

'Oh, it's you, young master,' she said, and her tone was not precisely welcoming. 'I thought it were my master come home, and the supper not ready yet.' There was a smell of cooking from within the house which made Matt's mouth water. Had he thought about it, he would have known that her husband, Young Conn, was not at home, for the upstairs of the house was entirely filled with his loom, and the rattle of the shuttle and the regular double thud of the pedals could be heard from some distance when he was weaving. 'He's gone to help his father. What did you want?'

It was not hospitable. In the days when Davey's mother was alive, she would have asked him in and offered him food and drink before asking such a question.

'I came to see if Davey is all right. He's missed school, and I wondered if he was ill.'

'No, he's not ill. But his brother Bob hurt his foot and

71

can't walk and someone has to tend to the beasts. I'm sure I can't do it, with four bairns and spinning and getting meals and hoeing the beans and I don't know what else. The Lord He knows He only gave me two hands, and work enough for six.'

She frowned crossly, and Matt wondered whether she regretted having married Conn. Once she had been the prettiest girl in the village, and parlourmaid to a gentleman. But she'd been turned off when the gentleman married, for the new wife didn't like such a pretty maid in the house, and sooner than become a dairy maid she had accepted the proposal of the newly-widowed cottager-weaver. Conn had been good to her, and never beat her, not even when she burnt the dinner, but there'd been four babies, all close together, and then her stepchildren Betty and Bob, older than she, and Davey to feed and clothe, and the old man who to her mind was the worst of the lot and criticized her openly for her muddles . . .

And now she smelt the stew burning, and fled inside with an inarticulate cry. Matt tied up Goldfinch and followed her in cautiously. He rememered how the house had looked when Davey's mother was alive. Now it was unkempt and neglected, and it had a stale smell about it. There were dirty plates and pots on the big table, and in the corner the bed was unmade and covered with bits of wool, and on the shelf over the fire the treasured pewter did not shine. Ursula had no time for scouring and polishing pewter, as well as everything else. It was a small and rather bare house, but Matt had always found it comfortable, like a second home to him. The big room here was where they lived and ate and sat after work, and in the corner stood the bed where Conn and Ursula slept, and the cradle for the littlest bairns.

Through the doorway on the other side was the second room where Bob and Davey shared a bed, Betty and Old Conn had cots of their own, and a mattress was put down for the two older bairns at night and rolled up during the day. There was a concealed staircase in the stone wall that led up to the loom-attic above, and across the main room in front of the bed an open wooden stair that led to the root-store, where carrots and turnips and potatoes and onions and apples were kept, and sometimes a sack of oats or beans. In the great chimney there were always hams and bacons and sometimes fish hung up to smoke, and bunches of herbs and garlic hung on nails on the beams above the table. There was a little, cold, stone room leading off at the back of the house where the milk and cheese were kept, and where butter was made, and there was generally a cask of good October ale in there, and a hare or rabbit or pheasant or two hanging up to draw.

The house itself was not without its comforts. Besides the pewter, there was a handsome red rug on the floor before the best seat, a stout oak chair with a deal of carving about it, which Old Conn was said to have made himself in his youth. There were enough stools so that even the bairns did not have to sit on the floor, and a very handsome oak chest for storing the clothes; and a patchwork counterpane to cover the big bed in the daytime that was fine enough for a lady's chamber.

But there was a frowsty unwelcomeness about it now, and Matt's heart went out to Ursula, who was stirring the stew with one hand, holding her spindle clear with the other, and arching her shoulders against the hanging weight of the baby, who had fallen asleep, its drooping head in danger of being clipped behind the ear by the rim of the cook-pot.

'I'm sorry to intrude upon you, mistress,' Matt said in his politest voice, 'but since I am here, let me at least help you. The bairn's asleep – let me take him from you and put him to bed.'

She looked at him doubtfully. 'Nay, master, that isn't fitting work for you.' He came towards her, moving quietly as if she were an animal that might be startled. 'What does tha knaw about bairns?'

'I'm very good with bairns,' he said. 'My nurse Flora would tell you.' And though she looked apprehensive, she did not stir while he untied the ends of the cloth sling and carefully gathered the baby into his arms. Her back straightened instantly with relief, but she still eyed him a little nervously as he cradled the baby and looked into its sleeping, grubby face. 'Which one is this?' he asked. Its features were pretty, though it smelled rather unpleasant.

'That's Marigold, of course. Peter's asleep in his cot, thank God, and t'other two are out the back with Bob. What I s'l do when the littlest two are fit to run about I don't know.' Her voice took on the tone of returning grievance, and Matt went quietly away and tucked Marigold into the cot in the dark corner with her brother, and stayed soothing the bairns until they settled. When he turned again, Ursula had calmed herself, put aside her spinning, and was making oatcakes on the baking stone. She gave Matt a gap-toothed smile of conciliation.

'Now then, young master, that's right kind of you. Will ta stay for supper? Davey will be home soon enough. He's had the cows and geese out on the common all day, but his stomach will bring him home. Go you out the back and sit wi' Bob till then.'

'Can I help you? I could stir the stew for you?' he offered, but she looked distracted again.

'No, no, you're in my road here. I can manage.'

Out at the back, where the air smelled wonderfully fresh after the staleness within, there was a bench along the whitewashed wall of the cottage where it would catch the last of the sun, and here Matt found Bob, sitting with his legs stretched out. On the other side, where the cool-house was, the roof stuck out beyond the walls to make a shelter to keep the cool-house cool, and here under the eaves blocks of turf and small logs for the fire were stacked. Some swallows had nested above the fuel-stack, and darted in and out, feeding their young, and their *swee-swee* of a call was counterpart to the raucous clamour of the rooks.

Bob's foot was swaddled in bandages almost to the knee, and he glanced up anxiously whenever one of the children came near, while his hands were busy whittling oaken nails. It was a good job for a man tied by the foot, for wooden nails were always in demand and earned the whittler a few coins per dozen. Tom, the younger child, who was two, was playing with stones in the dust, pushing them with his forefinger and crawling after them. He was too young to be useful to the household yet; but Lucy, who was three and a half, was already employed on tasks suitable for her age, like collecting eggs or kindling or keeping the birds off the peas. At that moment she was fetching the hens in for the night, helped by a lame shepherd dog, and she strutted self-importantly when the visitor increased her audience.

Bob looked up and grinned self-consciously, and said, 'Now then, Master Matt. Tha finds me stuck here useless, I'm afraid.'

'How is it, Bob?' Matt asked.

'Well enough, master, well enough,' Bob said, though his face was flushed and anxious, and there was a white line of pain etched around his lips. 'But I can't walk on it, you see, and that makes things awkward.'

Bob's contribution to the household was to tend the beasts – the pigs, the geese, and three heifers that were the household's wealth – and to do the heavy work on their two acres of land, the ploughing and harrowing. The rest was Ursula's job. When not thus employed, he hired himself out as a day-labourer to farms round about. He was twenty-six, a red-faced, stocky man with hands like planks of wood, and the startling dark eyes that were the legacy of 'the foreigner', Old Conn's wife.

'How did you come to do it?' Matt asked.

'I was cutting grass over to High Moor farm, and the billhook slipped. It wasn't such a terrible cut, but it's gone bad on me, and so I can't walk.'

'Can I do anything for you?'

'Why, thank you, Master Matt. I were just thinking it's time to light up my pipe. The midges are a pest this time of night.'

So Matt fetched Bob's pipe and tobacco for him, and he

put aside his whittling and filled and lit it, and a little peace stole over his anxious face as he got it drawing nicely.

'Hasta heard the news about our Betty?' he asked at last. Matt shook his head. 'Well, she's to be wed, this day fortnight. Will Turner is his name, a nice young man from over Aksham Bogs, a horseman, he is, and well thought of.'

Matt was expressing his congratulations when Davey came back from folding the beasts, looking tired and dusty and not a little discontented.

'Come with me while I wash,' Davey said. 'Supper will be ready soon – are you staying?'

Davey washed the dust off himself at the cattle-trough with a great deal of blowing and splashing, and Matt thought how strong and brown his arms and shoulders were, compared with Matt's own. And his neck, arched and strong, was no longer a child's. Davey was growing up fast, and leaving him behind, he thought, and it saddened him.

As he dried himself roughly, Davey talked about Bob's accident. 'Grandfather won't let him alone about it, says that it's all Bob's own fault, because he's no more grace than an eel on a frozen pond. He says every job has its rhythm, and Bob rushes at things like a bull. Poor Bob's foot turned on a stone and that's the truth of it, but grandfather won't listen. Old people are a law to themselves.'

'You should be proud of your grandfather,' Matt said. 'He's the oldest man in these parts. In fact, you're the only person I know that *has* a grandfather.'

'It's a distinction I'd be happy without,' Davey grinned suddenly. 'Anyway, poor Bob's foot is really bad. Ursula won't dress it – she says it makes her sick – so grandfather does it, and nags away at Bob all the time. So I have to take the beasts out. There's nothing for them here. I've had them up and down the lanes all day.'

'How long will you be missing school?' Matt asked. Davey jerked his head irritably.

'I don't know. Until Bob's better I suppose. Someone has to tend the beasts. If the bairns were older it'd be different, but Lucy can't control three cows and ten geese on her own. I don't *like* it, you know.'

'I wish there was something I could do,' Matt said guiltily. 'How would it be if I came over after school each day and told you what we'd done, so you didn't miss out.'

Davey looked embarrassed. 'What, here? I couldn't, Matt, not in front of the family. Bob and Betty had no schooling to speak of, and Ursula thinks it very silly to keep me at school, when I could be earning money. It would be awful to do lessons in front of them all.'

'But you must have schooling, if you're to be a steward,' Matt said anxiously.

'*I* know that,' Davey said. 'But Ursula – oh well, there are four babies, and another on the way. One can't blame her.' This was not entirely clear to Matt, and he remained silent, as Davey added, 'Never mind, come on in to supper. It's rabbit stew. I caught the rabbits myself with a new snare I've invented. I'll shew it to you afterwards. It's a great improvement.'

Betty was the last to arrive home, for she had a long walk from the farm on the edge of Aksham Bogs where she was dairy maid. Matt would have known her for a dairy maid without being told, by her swollen red arms, and cracked and swollen red hands, the result of milking cows in the open in all weathers through the year. She was the oldest of the family, being twenty-eight years old, and had the dark hair and eyes of her grandmother, and a hard red face like a rosehip. She was kind in her quiet way, but she worked so hard that in the evenings she had no energy for anything but to eat, sit in silence for half an hour, and fall into her bed. She rarely spoke, and when she did, her voice was so quiet you had to listen for it. All the other children in the family had died young, except for the brother between her and Bob, who had died at the Boyne with Martin.

Conn said Grace, and they all sat down, and there was

silence while everyone stifled the first desperate pangs of hunger. Then as they slowed down, there was conversation, largely about Betty's forthcoming wedding.

'Will Turner is as good a soul as you would want to meet, and steady,' Bob told Matt. 'Betty met him at the midsummer fair last year, didn't you, Bet?' His sister nodded, eating steadily. 'They've been walking out ever since. He's twenty-nine, and he's got near on thirty-five pounds saved.' Bob looked to Matt for his amazed approval.

Conn said quickly, 'That's all right, our Betty's got thirty pound saved up. She's a good match for him. She knows all about tending beasts, and she can spin and sew and bake and make cheese, and everything a man would want in a wife, and she's as strong as an ox.'

Matt was calculating in his head while Conn spoke, and worked out that Betty must have saved two-thirds of her annual wage as dairy maid for the last twelve years to have thirty pounds saved up. Will Turner would have earned more as a horseman, but his saving was also impressive. He must indeed be a steady man, not given to drinking or tobacco, or the countryman's vice of gambling.

Conn went on, 'They've found a cottage out at Dringhouses. It's only got an acre, but it's got good common rights. They'll have grazing on the moor, and on the champion once the crops are in, and they've right of cutting turf and furze and brushwood on the moor, and collecting acorns and lichens in the woods. With sixty-five pounds they can furnish the cottage, and buy some pigs and chickens and an in-calf heifer and maybe a couple of sheep. Betty can take in spinning, and Will can take in harness to mend – he's right handy with the needle and palm – and that will pay their rent. Oh, they'll be all right.'

He smiled, vastly pleased with the prospect. He only hoped his little ones, if they survived, would do as well as his daughter.

'Lucky for them they don't live down south,' Old Conn said, tearing bread with his sharp old fingers. 'There's precious few cottages down south. The great lords pull them down, so as to have common rights to themselves.'

'Oh, you and your down south,' Ursula said in exasperation. 'Anyone would think you'd been to China and back the way you talk. We've all heard enough about your down south.' She glared at the old man, and he glared back, his little eyes bright with malice.

'Woman, hold your tongue,' he said. 'I didn't live to my age to be snapped at by a viper of a woman who ought to know better than to speak at all. When I remember –'

'Oh hush, Father, hush, Ursie,' Conn said anxiously, for Old Conn frequently compared Ursula unfavourably with her predecessor, and it made for unpleasantness in the house. 'Remember we've got a visitor.'

'Aye, and he'll be our master one day,' Old Conn said, 'and a good master at that, because he listens to the words of folk wiser than himself. There's some,' he added venomously, 'that never heed anyone, and clack like spoons in empty bowls instead of listening to good advice.'

Ursula drew breath to retort, and Conn broke in quickly to prevent her. 'I know Betty would take it very kindly if you was to come to the wedding, Master Matt. There'll be good food and good ale and plenty of music.'

'Why, thank you,' Matt said, delighted. 'I shall have to ask Uncle Clovis, but if he says I may, I shall certainly come.'

Clovis made no objection, and Matt, armed with a suitable bride-gift, went along on the day and enjoyed it more than anything he remembered. Betty looked almost handsome in her wedding finery, and was moved to tears by Matt's present, and thus rendered even more inarticulate than ever. Will Turner was a nice little brown nut of a man, smaller than Betty, and with legs already bowed from a lifetime of horses. He hadn't a tooth in his head, but his eyes were bright blue and merry, and his leathery hand shook Matt's warmly in a way that made Matt want to trust him.

The feast was plentiful, and everyone ate until they ached, and drank so much that had they not danced it off, they would all have been incapable long before the end. Matt took along his father's bassoon, and won everyone's approval by playing some merry measures for the dancing, and all the favourite songs for singing while they rested between dances. It was very late when he was fetched home by a faintly disapproving servant, and he was so tired by then that he had to concentrate on not falling off his pony. He thought all the way home about Betty and Will in their new home, wondering how things would go for them, and hoping they would have good health and good fortune, and that not too many of their children would die. He wondered again about his own marriage, and longed to be bringing Mavis D'Atheson home, as Will was now bringing his Betty. When I marry, he thought, I want the wedding to be just like that one.

It was only a few days later that Matt learnt through a servant that Bob had died. He had been cheerful at the wedding, though obviously very sick, and he had not been able to dance, but had sat in a corner with his foot propped up on a stool and protected by a basket, for anyone brushing against it made him almost faint with pain. Matt had thought his flushed face and glazed eyes had been due to good ale, for he had spoken cheerfully to Matt when he passed by; but it must have been the wound fever after all.

Matt was greatly saddened, for he had known Bob since he was very small, and had been fond of the man, as of an older brother. Davey had been absent from school all this while, and when Matt was finally able to go over to the cottage to pay his respects, Davey told him that he would not be coming back to school again.

'But why?' Matt asked, aghast. Davey gave him a

significant glance, and led him outside to the privacy of the cattle-trough to talk.

'My stepmother's doing,' he said abruptly. 'She says it's nonsense to keep me at school, and that we can't afford it. If my father takes over Bob's beast-tending, there'll be less time for him to weave, and in any case, there's Bob's wages from his day-work to replace. She's another bairn on the way, and who knows when *that* will stop. She's young, she could have twenty years of child-bearing ahead of her.'

'But Davey, what will you do?' Matt said.

'I'm to stay here and tend the beasts, and take odd jobs when I can, until Lucy and Tom are old enough to mind the cows. That'll be two years, I suppose. Then I'm to go as a live-in servant on a farm, wherever a place can be found for me, and send my wages home for the family.'

Matt stared, aghast. 'But Davey, you can't!' he cried. He knew what that kind of servitude meant. A live-in man on a farm that kept maybe only one man, a dairy maid, and a couple of small boys, would be old before he was twenty-five, for the long hours of gruelling work without respite and with no opportunities for rest or recreation were killing. And if he was sending home his wages, he would not even be able to save up, like Will Turner, for a place of his own. He would be chained to his servitude for life. 'You can't!' he cried again. Davey looked at him resentfully.

'It's all very well for you to say I can't. I can't do otherwise. I have no choice in the matter. I'm not a lordly young master like you, with wealth and servants and a beautiful house.'

'But you have such a good mind,' Matt said, ignoring the hostility in Davey's voice. 'You mustn't waste it.'

'I don't have any choice. Besides, what use is a brain to me? You don't need to be able to read and write to herd cows or plough or dig turnips or stook hay. Education is wasted on the likes of me.'

'But Davey –' Matt began, and now his friend turned on him angrily.

'Oh stop but-Daveying me! What's it to you, anyway, *Master*? Why should you care whether I waste my brains or not?'

'I'm your friend, Davey,' Matt said, hurt. Davey looked at him with cold and calculating eyes.

'There's no friendship between the likes of me and the likes of you. That's for children. Well, you may be a child still, but I've had to grow up. I'm not your friend, I'm the son of your tenant, and I'll have to bow and knuckle my forehead to you for as long as we both live. And in a couple of years you'll order me whipped for insolence if I speak to you like this. It's time you grew up, Master Matt, and found friends from those of your own sort.'

Matt stared at him in uncomprehending misery. It was the first time Davey had ever called him 'master'. They had gone to school together, sat at the same desk, done the same lessons, played together, snared rabbits and swum and run and got dirty together, bound each other's cut knees and shared each other's dinners, since Matt was five years old; and never in that time had Davey ever hinted that there was any difference between them. He did not know what to say, and in the end he could only turn away and walk blindly in the direction of home, breaking after a moment into a stumbling run.

Davey watched him go, swallowing at the intolerable lump in his throat. A few tears broke past the rigid barriers he had put up, and he knuckled them away angrily. There was no time for such softness now. But he watched, all the same, until the slight, dark-haired figure of his friend – his *true* friend – had disappeared from sight beyond the line of thorns before turning with a sigh to go in.

CHAPTER FIVE

The Bluebird House was a very discreet place in a quiet street of Hanover, and Maurice and Karellie, having got good and drunk, had gone there without being able to remember who first suggested it, and had stayed there all night – or for as much of the night as was left. Now in the sober light of morning they had all got into one bed for company, and the two men were sitting up and talking while they waited for coffee to be brought them.

Maurice had been chatting to his whore, who seemed to be passably interesting to him, and had a light of intelligence in her eye. Karellie's girl, who was lying on his chest with her arms wound round him, seemed less alert.

'Why do you always get on so well with your girls?' Karellie asked crossly, as Maurice and his girl laughed heartily at something. 'All *you* seem to do is talk to them.'

'Perhaps it's *because* I talk to them,' Maurice said genially. 'After all, this is business to them, so why should they enjoy it? A conversation must make a pleasant change.'

Karellie heard this heresy with an open mouth. His companion yawned widely and smiled at him and said something which he didn't understand. 'Well,' he said, 'even if I wanted to follow your example, I'd never make any sense of their terrible language. They sound like ducks quacking.'

'I think she was swearing eternal love to you,' Maurice laughed, lifting an arm to accommodate his girl as she leaned across to talk to her partner in sin. In a moment the two girls were having a cosy conversation *sotto voce*, and Maurice sat up the straighter and said, 'Well, my dear, now you have been expelled from France, what are you going to do with yourself – apart from getting drunk and picking up doxies?'

'I wasn't expelled from France, only from the army of France,' Karellie pointed out.

'Same thing in your case, and Berwick's. It must have been hard for King Louis –'

'Hard for him? How can you be so forgiving, when he has acknowledged the Usurper as King of England?'

'My dear, he had to,' Maurice said. 'He was forced to make peace in Flanders, and the Usurper wouldn't miss an opportunity like that to make King Louis toe the line. You know the first draught of the Treaty of Ryswick insisted that he expell the whole royal family from France, but King Louis wouldn't have that.'

'You seem to know all about it,' Karellie grumbled.

'We aren't entirely cut off from the rest of the world at the Herrenhausen,' Maurice said sweetly. 'And in reason, Karel, if Louis recognized William as King, then it would be inappropriate to have the King's son and the King's cousin serving in his army, wouldn't it?'

'If you say so,' Karellie said, unconvinced. Maurice smiled.

'How disagreeable you are on waking, my brother. It must be the wine. You used to be so sunny-tempered when we drank only ale.' Karellie gave an unwilling smile. 'That's better. So tell me of your friend Berwick. He married, didn't he? Does he love his wife? Are they happy?'

'Oh yes, it seems so. He married Patrick Lichfield's widow, you know, and took on her son as well, but the boy adores him. They have one of their own now, as well. But Berwick is furious about having to leave the army. Neither of us could stomach sitting around at St Germain – it's so gloomy now – and in any case, there was no honour in being the mere pensioner of a pensioner of the King of France. The Prince of Conti offered Berwick his house down in Languedoc, and he took his family and went.'

'But what will he do there?' Maurice asked.

'Be a country gentleman, he says. But I can't see it. He'll get so bored.'

There was a knock on the door, and it opened to admit two servants carrying wooden trays containing platters of fresh white bread, wooden cups, and a tall pot whose fragrance filled the room.

'Ah, coffee!' Maurice cried, pushing his girl off his shoulder to free his hands. 'You know, when we were boys and Father St Maur used to tell us stories of ancient Greece and Rome, I used to think I had been born in the wrong age, and wish and wish I could have been a noble Roman. But that was before I discovered that they had no hot coffee in Rome.'

When they were served, and the footmen had gone away, Maurice asked again, 'So what are you going to do now?'

'Find some other army to serve in. Soldiering seems to be all I'm fit for. And I like it. It's something to be done, that I can do well, and it's straightforward – no intrigues or doubts or puzzles. Just orders – a town to besiege, a wall to be sapped, a hill to be held, an enemy to be charged. Nothing one can't understand.'

'Poor Karel,' Maurice said gently, 'you do find life a puzzle, don't you?'

'Well, don't you?' Karellie said, turning his dark Palatine eyes to his brother.

Maurice looked at him for a moment, and said, 'You know, even if our mother hadn't told us about her being Prince Rupert's daughter, I think I would have known sooner or later. Your eyes, for instance – and all of our mother's features – so like Aunt Sofie.'

'You like Aunt Sofie, don't you?' Karellie said.

Maurice smiled. 'I love her dearly. She is a sensitive, thinking woman and she surely does not belong here in this nest of boors – no, it's all right, neither of them speaks English. You know, Francesca Bard came here to visit a while ago – Dudley Bard's mother, Prince Rupert's mistress long ago – and Aunt Sofie took her in, and persuaded her to make her home here for good. Now there are many

85

women in Aunt Sofie's position who would refuse to have someone like Francesca under their roof.'

'So you are happy here?' Karellie asked.

'Not entirely,' Maurice said. 'There are many things I don't like. I love Aunt Sofie, but there is no one else here in whom I have the least interest. The rest of the royal family are dull, and the heir apparent, George Lewis, positively unpleasant.' Maurice glanced at the girls to see they were busy with their bread and coffee and chatter, and said, 'You heard about the Konigsmark affair?'

'Not in detail. There was some mystery –'

'Mystery indeed. Konigsmark disappeared, and it seems certain that he was murdered, either by, or on the order of, the Elector or the Elector's son. George Lewis divorced his wife, as he had a perfect right to, although I don't believe for a moment that she actually did anything with the man. It was all just a game to her, poor silly child, but her behaviour was immoderate and people had been talking. But he not only divorced her, he also sent her away to be imprisoned in a big lonely house miles from anywhere, and he not only forbade her to see her children, he also forbade her to have any visitors at all. Now that was just plain spite. That poor creature, who lived for company and chatter.' Maurice shook his head. 'No, there are enough things here that I don't like to make it easy for me to leave.'

'Are you leaving?' Karellie asked, surprised.

'Soon. I don't know where I shall go, but I must go somewhere. Perhaps to Italy. Do you remember at St Germain, the Venetian ambassador, who said to me, "Young man, the soul of music is Italy, and the soul of Italy is Venice"?'

'I remember,' Karellie said. 'And I said –'

'You said that judging by his clothes and jewels and servants, Venice was certainly the purse of Italy at the very least.'

They both laughed, remembering.

'We had *some* good times at St Germain,' Karellie said wistfully.

Maurice said, 'Of course we did. Now tell me the latest news from there. How is our mother? And our little sister – what of her?' Karellie's expression was peculiar, and Maurice pursued, 'She must be growing beautiful now. At ten she is almost a woman.'

'The King has certainly been impressed with her, though I think more by her learning and manners,' Karellie said evasively. 'He has asked our mother if she can be brought up in the royal nurseries as a companion to Prince James and the princess, and he has promised to make Aliena a maid of honour to the princess as soon as her household is formed.'

'Well, that is good news. Our mother must be delighted.'

'She is,' Karellie said shortly.

'Though it will be lonely for her, not having Aliena with her. She has no one now. But tell me, you did not answer before, is Aliena beautiful?'

Karellie turned troubled eyes on his brother. 'She's quite the most beautiful child I've ever seen. She's learned, and graceful, and accomplished. She sings like a bird, plays the virginals, rides like an Amazon, dances like a swan gliding about a lake, converses in Latin, speaks French and Italian so well you would think they were her own tongue – oh, there's no end to the list of her graces. And with all that, she's as modest and sweet as – oh, I don't know.'

'And beautiful,' Maurice pressed him gently, feeling his way towards the heart of Karellie's trouble.

'Like a little porcelain statue, delicate white skin, deep blue eyes, soft curling dark hair.' Karellie stopped and swallowed down some constriction in his throat. 'Maurice, I think I shall have to tell you. It's burning inside me like an arrowhead. I shall have to tell you.'

'Tell me, then, dear brother. What is it about our sister that troubles you?'

'I did not notice at first, but as she grew older, the

87

resemblance became unmistakable. And then I began to piece together things I had noticed when we were in England, and things people had said, and gossip I had overheard from the servants. Maurice – she is the spitten image of Martin. Martin – is – her – father.'

There was a silence, as Karellie looked at his brother, waiting for the significance to sink in. Maurice only smiled, and Karellie felt constrained to be more specific.

'Don't you see, it means that – our mother – was Martin's lover.'

And Maurice laughed, gently, and pressed his brother's hand. 'Oh Karel, is that all? I have known that for – oh, for as long as I can remember. Of course they were lovers. Of course Aliena is his child. How could she be otherwise? Our father had been dead a long time when she was born. Did you think she was a gift from God?'

'But don't you care? Doesn't it shock you?'

'Why should it?' Maurice said, and then, seeing Karellie's expression added, 'Look, Karellie, they were no relation to each other. Not by blood. She was only his stepmother, and that's nothing but a legal tie. You know we grew up regarding him almost as a father – he was more like a father to us than our own father was – so why should she not come to regard him as a husband? Who is hurt by it?'

'But Aliena – is she our sister? Or our brother's daughter? I can't encompass it.'

'What does it matter? It's only words. There is not enough love in the world for us to condemn it or turn it away, wherever we find it. Martin was a fine and a brave man, to whom we owe a great deal –'

'Oh, I don't blame him,' Karellie said with some bitterness. Maurice looked anxious.

'Karellie, don't grow a spite against our mother. To hate her would be to hate yourself. You must understand what she did, and forgive it, if you feel it needs forgiving. But you must not hate her.'

'But how can I ever trust – ever trust – a *woman*? After this?'

'Oh Karellie!'

'I adored her so. She was like the sun and moon to me –'

'Perhaps that is the trouble. Why don't you regard women as human beings, like yourself?'

'Like me? But I am a man.'

Maurice gave it up. 'When I go to Italy, will you come and visit me? Perhaps you can find an army to serve in, in Italy,' he said, changing the subject firmly. 'And we'll find you some pretty girls to adore. Speaking of which, I think I have some unfinished business on hand here, with this dimpled little thing –' And he put his arm round his girl and made her giggle, though she looked up at him with speculative eyes. His trouble was that all women seemed to him flawed and imperfect. How could he ever fall in love? He could not believe that he would ever find a woman perfect enough to rival music in his mind as a subject for adoration. It seemed likely that neither of them would marry – already at twenty-six and twenty-five they must be a worry to their mother – and then what would happen to the title? Poor mother. Poor Karellie. He concentrated on kissing the willing little whore, but his mind strayed to the beautiful Aliena, and he wished that he could see her, just once, before she grew imperfect like the rest of the world.

Henry Aldrich, Dean of Christ Church, was a handsome man, with the sort of plump, sweet face that might almost have been thought womanly, had it not been for the firmness of the delicate features and the level, intelligent eyes. Clovis had met him several times in London, at meetings of the Royal Society, and at the Office of Works in company with Christopher Wren, his friend and mentor: Aldrich, Wren and Richard Busby, the headmaster of Westminster School, were a trio frequently seen about London and Oxford, united by their common love of architecture.

That love had induced Aldrich to take Clovis on a tour of the buildings before the dinner to which Clovis had been invited one day in the summer of 1698, and they strolled around the great quadrangle, admiring the new statue of Mercury which had replaced the old ball-and-serpent fountain in the central basin, and the elegant bulk of Wren's gigantic domed tower which had been built over the gatehouse to house the bell, Great Tom, which had formerly hung in Christ Church Cathedral steeple. Every night the bell tolled out one-hundred-and-one strokes as a signal that the gates were being shut, the number being the number of pupils in the original foundation of the college.

Clovis looked and admired; they talked a little of this and that, as will educated and cultured men; and then Aldrich brought up the subject which Clovis had been anticipating.

'I thought it better to speak to you quietly and informally about this,' he said, 'because, indeed, I am in rather a delicate position.'

'It is about Lord Ballincrea, I take it,' Clovis said.

He had half expected Arthur to have been sent home in disgrace before now, and the reason for the omission was revealed when Aldrich turned to him with a sweet smile and said, 'I am no saint, as you may have heard, Morland. Wine, tobacco, extravagant entertainments, I am no stranger to them. In fact, the gentlemen commoners say that they only ape me when they indulge in their fashionable debaucheries. So I am in rather a delicate position when I come to speak of your stepson.'

'Of his debaucheries?' Clovis asked non-committally.

'I can't send him down for misbehaving, which he does, or for being a bad influence on the other young gentlemen, which he is. But I can ask you whether you would consider taking him away voluntarily, and placing him somewhere else, somewhere –'

'Where he will do less damage?'

'Shall we say, somewhere where he will be happier and

more useful. He is not helping himself, and I am afraid, his debaucheries being so heedless, that he will come to serious harm if something is not done. He is younger than most of the other young gentlemen, and perhaps therefore less amenable to reason. For his own sake, Morland, will you not take him away?'

Clovis frowned in thought. 'The difficulty is that he has already been removed once "for his own sake". I sent him here earlier than is customary because he was uncontrollable at home. And what could I tell his mother, who dotes upon him?'

'As to the latter, I may tell you frankly that if he does not kill himself with debauchery, I shall have to think seriously about sending him down for his political extravagances.'

Clovis looked surprised. 'I did not know he had any political interests.'

'How sincere his expressions are I don't know. But the feeling here is very Whig in temper, and he is known to have strong Jacobite sympathies, and some of the meetings in his rooms are suspect. If I have to, I shall use that to remove him.'

'I see. Then obviously I shall have to forestall you, to avoid the scandal. But it leaves me with the problem of what to do with him.'

They mounted one of the flights of steps from the recessed green to the gravelled walk, and moved towards the entrance of the Great Hall. Clovis guessed from this that the Dean assumed the conversation was almost over.

'I think I can help you there,' he said. 'Your stepson, for all his faults, is not stupid, and he has what seems to be a very sincere interest in architecture. Why don't you set him in the way of learning it? It will keep him occupied, give him a respectable and satisfying way of earning a living, and may even be the making of him. Vanbrugh has been commissioned to build a new house for the Earl of Carlisle on the ruins of Henderskelfe Castle, which you know is not far from York. I can give you a letter of introduction to Vanbrugh, recommending him to take on Lord Ballincrea as a pupil.'

'I didn't know Vanbrugh was an architect,' Clovis said. 'I thought Talman was to build the house.'

The Dean paused in the doorway and turned to look out over the quadrangle. 'Howard has quarrelled with Talman – relations are very bad between them, bad enough I believe for a lawsuit to be talked of. And Van has not designed anything before. But he is the most dedicated of amateurs, and I have seen his preliminary designs for the new castle, and I tell you Morland, they will cause some heads to turn. Hawkesmoor is helping him, and Wren has had his head bent over the plans, in between scurrying from the site of St Paul's to the site of Greenwich Hospital. They were all here a month ago, looking over Tom Tower, and I shall be very surprised if the new Castle Howard does not finish with a dome-and-lantern.' He glanced up at the great tower, and then smiled at Clovis. 'I am very glad we managed to get our dome up first – but then, I believe you have an even earlier example of Wren's obsession at home? He tells me he built a dove-cote in the style at Morland Place.'

Clovis smiled too. 'Yes, for Lady Chelmsford. It was a whim of hers. You have discussed it with him?'

Aldrich spread his hands. 'I must confess that I did discuss my little problem – in the most discreet terms, of course. I can promise you, therefore, that a letter of introduction from me would not be entirely ignored.'

'You are most kind, sir – and I appreciate your discretion in this matter,' Clovis said. 'But I must discuss the matter with the boy's mother before I make any decision.'

Aldrich nodded. 'As you please. And now, shall we go in? I have a consignment of real French claret which I am eager to have your opinion of – let us not inquire how I came by it. And perhaps after dinner you might be interested in looking over some plans of my own, for replacing Peckwater Inn?' His smile grew impish. 'Since I shall have to ask for substantial subscriptions for the work, you may as well see what you will be paying for.'

From Oxford, Clovis had to ride to London on business, where he went first to Chelmsford House in St James's, and then, leaving his horse at a tavern with instructions to have it fed and rested and taken to Milk Street, he went down to the Whitehall Steps to get a boat. This part of London was sadly deserted now, thanks to an invalid and widowed King, and an increasingly invalid heiress apparent. Dutch William preferred Hampton Court, for the smoke of London exacerbated his asthma. Princess Anne, who had recently had yet another miscarriage, was beginning to suffer from gout, and she preferred to live out at Kensington, where her son Gloucester had his household, London not being considered healthy for the young princeling.

When in London, the Usurper now had to use St James's Palace for his Court, for Whitehall, scene of so many triumphs and splendours, was no more. In the January of 1698 a Dutch serving-woman of Colonel Stanley's was drying some clothes too close to the fire, and they caught. They set light to the furnishings, and before anything could be done the whole house was ablaze. Had the Court been in residence perhaps the palace could have been saved, but there were not enough people on hand to do much about it. The old timber buildings caught and blazed like oakum. A hundred and fifty houses, all belonging to noblemen, and including Ballincrea House, were burnt to ashes, and another twenty were blown up with gunpowder in a vain attempt to halt the blaze.

Of the palace itself, only the great banqueting hall had escaped – the rest was gutted, and now, though greenery was beginning to grow over the horrible fire-scar, the river-bank was marred by the hollow, blackened shell and the heaps of rubble, and the wounded trees of the privy gardens. The Usurper had come once to pick his way fastidiously through the ruins, and had muttered something about rebuilding it one day, but no one believed that he would, and already the better bits of the rubble were beginning to disappear, as people took them away for buildings elsewhere. Clovis mourned a great opportunity lost – here there could have been raised a great, new, beautiful palace in the Palladian style that would be the envy of Europe. Instead, little by little, people would build in a jumble of styles, as the fancy took them, on their old sites, just as they had in London after the Great Fire.

At the Steps, Clovis turned his back on the blackened ruins and took a pair of oars as far as the Custom House landing – a pair was cheaper downstream, and he enjoyed the luxury – there to see about releasing some goods from bond. Then he walked up to Lombard Street to see his banker, and went to the Bell Inn, off Gracechurch Street, to take his dinner. He was hungry, and found himself in luck, for the dining rooms had a good board spread that day. He regaled himself with venison pasty, roast chicken, pease pudding, lobster, asparagus, and strawberries with clotted cream; but though they offered him wine he took only small beer, for he had more business to conduct and wine in the middle of the day made him sleepy.

From there he walked up to Edward Lloyd's coffee house and spent an hour reading the newspapers and listening to the gossip while he took a dish of coffee, and then he went down to the Morland warehouses at Bell Wharf. Finally, footsore and weary, but with the knowledge of a good day's work done, he walked back to Milk Street. Here he kept the small, narrow house that had belonged to his mother and father, long ago, when he was only a child. He kept it up mostly out of sentiment, for it would have been just as easy to go to an inn when he was in London; but the house held dear memories for him, and was still furnished with the things his mother had chosen and cherished. He had hired an old couple, Goody Teale and her blind husband, to look after it. They lived on the ground floor, and were taking the sun on a pair of stools at the door when Clovis walked up.

The old woman nodded to him and said, 'There you are, then, master. The boy brought your horse and put him up, and put the saddle in my kitchen. And your visitor's upstairs, waiting for you.'

'Visitor?' Clovis said. 'I wasn't expecting anyone.'

'He give his name, but I disremember it now,' she said vaguely. 'A gentleman from up north.'

Up in the parlour, Clovis found Jack Francomb, smiling genially, stouter and browner by a year since Clovis had seen him last, and wearing the same coat of green velvet that was finding its job more and more of a strain as time went by.

'I couldn't come to London without seeing you,' he said, clasping Clovis's hand and wringing it cheerfully. Clovis eased his fingers out of the grip with caution. 'They told me at the Custom House you were in London, but I'd just missed you. Have you any ale in the house? I've a day-long thirst on me.'

'I could send out for some,' Clovis said, 'but why don't we go out and have some supper somewhere?'

'By all means. I'll pay. I want to talk to you anyway.'

They took supper at the White Horse where there was a good ordinary and reliable ale, and talked business and exchanged news.

'How is Sabine?' Clovis asked. Francomb shook his head.

'Not too well. She eats and drinks too much,' he said.

'Can't you restrain her?'

Francomb opened his blue eyes wide. 'Me? She's twice my size! But the bairn is flourishing. Little Frances – as pretty a little wench, and clever! I have a dancing master twice a week, you know, to teach her to dance and play the spinet, and you should just see her. Tinkling away on the keys and singing 'Barbary Allen' like a little Court lady! When I came away I asked her what I should bring her from London, and she said, "Papa, bring me a basinet".

95

So I say, "Why, hinny, what should you want with one of those?" and she said, she would learn to play it, for she heard that the ladies in Court all play it and she would be like them. She meant basset, of course. She thought it was a musical instrument.'

He chuckled delightedly at the story, and drained his tankard. 'Well now,' he went on, fixing Clovis with a bright blue gaze, 'so I hear from that sister of yours there's to be a wedding, and right soon.'

'Is there? I haven't heard from Cathy for a while.'

'Aye, that sickly son of hers, to that rich heiress she's been stalking, Mavis D'Atheson – a good match, plenty of money there. And she's wise to wed the boy quickly, for he's a grey shadow with that asthma of his. Cathy treats him with blackberry smoke, but it does no good. So she'll get him wed, and let's hope he gets the maid with child before he turns blue for good. He won't make old bones, that one. Seems a shame to wed that pretty little thing to a cripple boy, but there!'

Clovis said that it was a good match, and that he did not know James was so ill. Francomb went on, 'There's something else I think perhaps you don't know. That boy of yours, that young James Matthias, he's been writing letters to the D'Atheson girl.'

Clovis stared. 'I certainly didn't know. Letters?'

'I'm glad you don't know, for I wouldn't like to see a falling out between you and Cathy, for the fact is the boy has it in his head he wants to marry this lassie, and writes her letters full of love and poetry and such matter. Cathy won't give it up now, for anything, and the contract's signed too, and the settlement's all agreed, so you'd better have a word with young James Matthias, before there's trouble.'

'I didn't know, and I'll certainly speak to him. But why does he think he will marry her?'

'Oh, it's a thing they worked out for themselves on his summer visits there, you know the way children do. My little Frances swears she'll marry me when she grows up,' he chuckled. 'But the boy has taken his own fairy story seriously, and writes his letters starting "My dear sweetheart and mistress" just like a book.'

Clovis thought, poor little Matt, if he is seriously in love with the girl it will be a sad shock for him, especially after losing his friend Davey. 'I'll attend to it as soon as I get home,' Clovis said. 'I'm obliged to you for mentioning it.'

'Now look here, Clovis,' Francomb said, leaning forward conspiratorially, 'the best thing to take his mind off it is to get him betrothed at once. He's old enough – what is he, fourteen? Why not make a match between him and my little Frances.' He sat back to watch the effect of his words, and then added, 'The estates ought to come together, it's right and fitting. You won't find me ungenerous. And she's as good and pretty a lass as ever you saw.'

'But she's only eight,' Clovis said.

'Going on nine,' Francomb said.

'Very well, but it would still mean a long betrothal before they could wed, and I'm not in favour of long betrothals. Young Matt will need a wife and children before Frances is ready.'

'Five years, that's all. We'll do it when she's fourteen, no fuss.'

'Five years is too long. I'm sorry. I'd like a match, and I agree with you that the estates ought to go together, but we can't wait until Matt is twenty to wed him. Besides, Frances is his first cousin, and there's a great deal of inbreeding already among the Morlands. I worry about it quite a lot. But what do you say to a betrothal between your Frances and young Lord Rathkeale? They are much more of an age.'

'What, Ballincrea's brother? But he's nothing, no money, no land, naught but a title,' Francomb objected.

'I shall probably settle half my estate on him – I have no children of my own,' Clovis said. Francomb grinned.

'Promises are pie-crust. When tha does it, let me know. Until then – we'll wait and see.' He shook his head to indicate the subject was closed, and said, 'Now what's this I hear about your young kinsman Maurice?'

Maurice had gone to Naples in the spring of that year, with a letter of introduction from the Electress Sofie couched in such glowing terms that he was invited to stay as a guest at the royal palace for as long as he liked. There was a great deal of music-making there, particularly opera, a form in which Maurice was not versed. He attended a performance of the opera *Psiche*, and afterwards was introduced to the composer, Alessandro Scarlatti, who was Maestro di Capella of the royal chapel – the equivalent to Maurice's position at Hanover.

Scarlatti was twelve years older than Maurice, but a man of such energy and charm that Maurice felt instantly that they had been lifelong friends. They had a great deal to talk about, both being interested in exploring the new techniques of harmonic music which were replacing the polyphonic forms in which they had been trained. Scarlatti was interested primarily in opera, Maurice in developing the orchestra, and they had many ideas to exchange.

Very soon such intimacy had grown between them that Alessandro invited Maurice to come and live with him at his home, and Maurice gladly accepted. It was a teeming, noisy, happy house, filled with Alessandro's voluble wife, and his ten lively children – Pietro, Alessandro, Apollonia, Flaminia, Cristina, Domenica, Giuseppe, Caterina, Carlo, and the baby Gian Francesco, their ages ranging from nineteen down to three. Maurice had great fun learning their names and how to distinguish one from another, for they all moved about so fast that it was some time before he was certain how many there actually were of them.

He was treated with a flattering degree of consequence – the little children all wanted to sit on his lap, and begged him for stories; the older boys wanted to know what it was like to live at other Courts, and what Karellie's experiences of battle had been like, and the middling girls waited on him hand and foot, their eyes modestly downturned, but flashing him occasional glances of admiration. He found it very hard to concentrate on his work, and wondered how Alessandro had ever managed to produce anything at all with such delightful distractions around him.

But at least Alessandro was not likely to be distracted in the particular way Maurice was. It was only a matter of days before his eyes began, unbidden, to seek out Apollonia from the crowd of children, and to miss her when she was not in the room. She was sixteen, the oldest of the girls, and therefore perhaps more serious and quiet, having had the responsibility of younger siblings all her life. Maurice noticed her first because of her beauty, and soon came to the conclusion that here, at last, was perfection. Her honey-coloured skin was smooth and unblemished, her jet-black hair fine as silk, her large eyes as dark as Karellie's, her figure small and dainty. She it was who brought him his cup of wine and saw to it that it was filled, and when she bent over him, her eyes on the flask, her lips pressed lightly together with concentration, he found his heart beating so hard that he could hardly find his tongue to thank her. And when she had finished, sometimes she would look up at him, a fleeting glance into his eyes, so innocent and shy that it made the bones melt in his body.

It took only a few weeks of such delicious torture for Maurice to become convinced that he would never write another note unless he soothed the gentle fever, and so he asked his host and friend for the hand of his daughter. Scarlatti was delighted that his daughter would be marrying the brother of an English earl, who might one day be earl himself, and who, besides, was a musician and composer of no little talent. He gave his permission readily, and the wedding was planned for the first possible date. A feast there should be, as lavish as money could make it, and music – the bride's father should compose music himself! – and as for the bride, she should be dressed all in white lace, for nothing else was fine enough for such pure beauty. Maurice's gift to her was pearls, which she wore for the ceremony about her smooth golden throat. He was dressed in sapphire blue silk and black velvet and a great deal of lace, and the young couple looked so handsome together that Alessandro insisted they commission the Court painter to take their portrait. While they were still enduring the sittings, a gift arrived from the bridegroom's mother, a very handsome necklace of emeralds for the bride, and a letter full of love and congratulations not unmingled with tears. If Maurice felt guilty about anything, it was of cheating his mother of his wedding.

But apart from that, he could not feel in the least sad. He was in love, foolishly, passionately, with this dainty Latin goddess. He wanted to bring her white flowers, and doves, and diamonds, and the seven stars of Orion, and heap them in her lap for offerings: instead he brought her what he could, the product of his mind and soul – he brought her music, and on the third day after their marriage, he began his first opera.

CHAPTER SIX

James Matthias was in the Lady Chapel at Morland Place, where he had taken refuge, as a dog, played-with and played-with by the much-loved children of the house, will finally creep under the table with his ears down. He leaned against the marble memorial of his ancestors, Robert and Eleanor, and idly ran his fingers over the lion that supported Robert's head. Eleanor's rested on a unicorn. The lion and the unicorn, England's symbols. Around the frieze ran the words, 'The brave heart and the pure spirit, faithful unto death. In God is death at end' – lion and unicorn again. Were they like that, he wondered, the Morland Master and Mistress of a hundred and fifty years ago? Did Robert feel like him, badgered, burdened, and above all, lonely? Or did his Eleanor hold the warm place in his heart, so that every day seemed full of good things?

Matt was sixteen – his sixteenth birthday had just passed – and a man, though his legal minority would last two years more. He was, everyone said, very like his father, and like his father, would never be tall. Flora said there was nothing of his mother in him, and it saddened him a little, for it seemed to him that his mother was rejected and forgotten by everyone. Even he had no memories of her – his earliest memories were of Lady Caroline, of the rustle of her silk dress and the perfume of her skin. Of his tall red-haired mother who, Flora said, could ride any horse in the stable better than a man, he remembered nothing, and no one would ever talk of her. She had died when he was three. When pressed, they would tell him she had been killed by robbers while on a journey, and then hastily change the subject. And Matt's own treacherous features celebrated his dear father in every respect, without reference to the other parent.

He was an orphan, and that was a lonely thing, though all his life he had had a good home and kind guardians and servants. He was well aware that Uncle Clovis was good and conscientious, Lady Caroline gentle and lady-like; that Birch in her rough-tongued, hard handed way was devoted to him, and Father St Maur had a father's care of his mind. Flora, who had nursed him at her breast, loved him in the rough, careless way that mother cats love their kittens, though she loved Clover and John more, having nursed them more recently than him. But he had no one of his own, no one to love him exclusively, no one to whom he could confide his thoughts and from whom to seek comfort.

He had hoped Mavis D'Atheson would become that all-in-all to him, until the rude awakening came, when he was told that his letters to her had been intercepted and read, when he was forbidden to write to her again, when they told him that she was to wed his cousin James. They had been married going on two years now, and in April there had been a child, a daughter, Mary. Mavis was far, far beyond his reach now. That had come close on the heels of losing his friend Davey. Davey had left school to tend his father's beasts and land, and now he had gone away altogether to work on a farm somewhere, in order to be able to send home his wages for the maintenance of his little half-brothers and sisters. Matt did not even know where he was: since Davey had rejected him, he had not paid any more visits to Conn's house.

He was sixteen, and he knew burdens rested on him'—not just the management of all the Morland estate, which after all was merely a task to which a man could apply himself, in which he could hire subordinates to help him. In his slight body, in his slender loins, rested the last hope of the Morland line, the legitimate succession. If his parents had been alive and there had been brothers beside him in the nursery, he might have been sent to University like Arthur, or on a Grand Tour with a tutor. There would have been years of learning and maturing and pleasure before the matter of his marriage became urgent. But there were no brothers, no parents, only him. After him, the line passed to his half-brothers, Charles Earl of Chelmsford, and Maurice, and they were both in exile – Karellie, at the last bulletin, serving in the army of the King of Poland in company with a great many other English, Scottish and Irish exiles; and Maurice in Florence, where he was Maestro di Capella at the Palace of Ferdinando di Medici, the greatest patron of music in Europe.

So he must wed and get a son, lest the line die with him. He must breed. His loneliness was like a crystal cave; he was walled in, seeing and hearing the world around him, but unable to touch it. And today his bride was to arrive at Morland Place, he was to see her for the first time. Uncle Clovis had chosen her for him. They were to be wed here, in the chapel, in two weeks' time, and then – the breeding, he supposed, would begin. He knew about it in theory – the Morlands were horsebreeders, after all, and then there were the dogs and sheep and peacocks and all the other beasts everywhere around – but of the practical aspects of it, he knew nothing. He was aware that he was in some ways immature for his age – from what the servants said, Arthur could well have become a father many times over since he was fourteen. But Matt had always been more quiet and thoughtful than Arthur, and had led a life sheltered by the sheer volume of things he had to do and to learn. In the last eighteen months, since Christmas '98, he had not even been at school – he was taught at home by Father St Maur – and so had not had other growing boys to talk to. Most village boys, he knew, considered themselves men at fourteen. They could have told him. But it would be impossible to ask any of the stable boys or young male servants.

All today they had been pursuing him around the house with their clacking tongues and silly demands – dear Flora trying to brush him down and tidy his hair as if he was five years old, Birch snapping at him to comport himself like a man and not shame her when the time came, the other older females of the house giving him sly looks and silly grins and telling him stupid sentimental things about love and weddings. He wished today was over. He wished it wasn't happening at all. He had no wish to meet face to face this strange girl whom he would have to – breed with. So he had taken refuge in the quiet coolness of the chapel.

But here in the chapel, more than anywhere, his responsibilities were brought home to him – here where generation after generation of Morlands had worshipped, where the walls were decorated with marble memorials to the industrious breeding of past Morland Masters. There was no respite here. The burden was his, and he could not lay it down, for there was no one else to carry it. He pushed himself off the marble sarcophagus and went to kneel on the prie-dieu before the wooden statue of the Blessed Virgin and, looking up into her face, made a short prayer to Her for help. Her soft golden face, worn by time – she was older by far than the house – and the slender, offering hands calmed him, and he rose to his feet in a resigned frame of mind, as the door of the chapel opened and the old dog Kithra came across to him with a clicking of nails on stone, heralding the arrival of Clovis, looking for him.

'She's here,' Clovis said without ceremony. 'Come on.'

India Neville was fifteen, but looked older than Matt, a fine, big, well-grown girl, only too evidently physically mature. She was handsome, straight-backed and free-moving, with a high colour in her cheeks and glossy black hair. On first seeing her, Matt thought she looked like a well-fed, well-groomed black filly led out for the race.

Had he lived a less sheltered life, he would have seen her before, for she was well-known in the city – but Matt never went into the city, except to the Minster for special observances, and occasionally on business with Clovis. India lived with her mother in vexing poverty in two rooms in a house in Lady Peckett's Yard. Her father had been a merchant adventurer – India was named, in gratitude, after the source of his wealth, though he never vouchsafed which of the Indies was referred to – and had amassed a considerable fortune, but he had died inconsiderately and suddenly at sea, leaving all his money in trust for India, to be released when she should marry. She had been only nine at the time, and since then her mother's primary task had been to keep alive, and to keep India healthy and attractive, until the first possible moment she could be married off. Mistress Neville had had a desperate struggle, and only by letting the house on Fossgate and moving into the two rooms in the Yard could she afford to live at all. Six years of scrimping and pinching had left their mark on the mother, who was worn and shrill and nervous, but she had remained true to her faith in that never had she allowed India to suffer privation during those years, even when it meant taking in sewing to afford the kind of food which alone could produce that well-nurtured look in a girl.

Of course, there had not been leisure or energy during those years to attend much to India's education – and, in any case, since marriage was the goal, education was only necessary insofar as it would make India more attractive as a bride. India had been taught to walk and dance gracefully by an exiled Huguenot who gave lessons in a room in Tanner Row; Mrs Neville had taught her to sew, to speak a few words of French (which she practised on the dancing-master, to his distress, for her accent was impeccably Whitehall) and to play the virginals. Otherwise, India's mind had all the unblemished bloom of ignorance of a butterfly's wing.

Mrs Neville kept in contact with her husband's merchant friends, and by the beginning of 1700 there could have been none amongst them who did not know of the existence of India and of Mrs Neville's intentions for her. Clovis was one of the last to hear about the girl, for he spent so much time in London and elsewhere that his business in York was usually carried out by an agent, but when he heard he went straight round to investigate. The poverty of their surroundings, in comparison with the fortune locked up so inaccessibly, moved him. He saw that the girl was healthy and handsome; he verified the amount of the fortune, and that it would be released unconditionally on the girl's marriage; and he made his offer. The girl came of good family – the Nevilles were one of the most ancient and respectable families in the north – and the complete lack of living relatives other than the mother was an advantage. He must get Matt wed as soon as possible – here was a girl whose sole object in life was to wed. Clovis and Mrs Neville came to an early and amicable agreement.

On being introduced to Matt for the first time, India's thought was 'But he's only a child' and then, 'He won't give me any trouble'. At the end of the day, when she and her mother retired to the guest chamber, and her mother asked her how she liked her future home, she said, 'It's a horrible old house, mother, so old-fashioned and small. But some of the furniture is good, and we can change everything once we're settled. And the horses are wonderful! I do so long for a horse of my own. But can he really be sixteen?'

'Master Morland assures me – my dear, he could not possibly be lying, he is very respectable,' Mrs Neville said, coming across to unlace her daughter. She had grown accustomed to the function of lady's maid, and the action triggered a thought. 'We must be sure to get a large advance from him to get you a really good lady's maid before the wedding. One who knows about hair and garniture. It makes such a difference. He will arrange for the wedding clothes, of course, but I shall need some new things. And, my dear, don't forget to mention my allowances when the subject arises.'

'Yes mother, I'll see to it,' India said briskly, her mind on other things.

When she was undressed and clad in her nightgown, her mother took the brush to brush out the long black hair and said, 'India, my dear, I think perhaps it is time we had a little talk. Such beautiful hair you have, though quite where it came from I cannot tell, for your poor dear father was bald as an egg, and before he was bald his hair was quite nondescript, a sort of mouse-brown. What was I saying? Oh yes, I must have a little talk to you about marriage – about the private side of it.' India smirked at her reflection in the mirror – a circle of polished silver, not a proper glass mirror as she would have expected. She'd order plenty of those once she was mistress of this dusty old tomb of a house. Her eyes, which were hazel and changed colour according to her mood, shone greenish like a cat's in the candlelight.

'Yes, mother?'

'Well, dear, you know that when a man and woman marry, they sleep together in the same bed, and, well, dear, they *cohabit*.' Mrs Neville met India's bright cat's gaze and looked away again hastily. 'Now, dear, your husband will want to do things to you which you may find, well, frankly, unpleasant. But it is his right to do those things, and you must allow him to, however distasteful it is to you, without complaint. My advice is, take hold of your lower lip with your teeth and bear it. It is necessary, so that you will become with child. And India dear –'

'Yes, I know, I must have children. That's why I'm here – to safeguard the Morland line,' she said impatiently. 'I only hope that boy is old enough.'

Mrs Neville was shocked. In silence she brushed the long tresses smooth, and then said, 'To continue, dear.' She was a conscientious woman, and intended to say the things that must be said, however distasteful. 'There is no need to continue with those things after you are pregnant, and once you have a reasonable number of children, it will be up to you to regulate your husband's animal nature according to your own conscience and the needs of the nursery. If your early children live, you may not need to do it any more after the first few years.'

'Yes, mother,' India said. She smiled at her reflection, watching the way the deep dimples came in her cheeks. She had practised that smile night after night in the shabby little room she slept in, and tried it out, with devastating success, on Monsieur Fragarde, the dancing-master. Poor, silly, dusty, Fragarde. How ridiculous he had looked upon his knees, begging for her favour. How contemptuously she had bid him be silent, chided him for his presumption. It had been exciting, the way he had looked at her, the sensation of growing intensity over the weeks, and that day when, finally, he had broken bounds and kissed her, and let his hand stray to her shoulder, and then to her bosom . . . She had let him, just for long enough, and then jumped up, outraged. Oh, it had been such fun!

Briefly her mind flickered towards the quiet little dark-haired boy she was to marry, and a mute enquiry formed itself in her mind. But she dismissed it. No, there would be no excitement there. She would do what she had to, and otherwise please herself. He would give her no trouble. He would be easier to handle even than dusty old Fragarde.

India stood meekly in her white satin under-gown and bent her head forward so that the maid – the new one, from London, who called herself Millicent – could lift the over-gown over her head. There were a few moments of discreet threshing and flailing before she emerged at the top, and Millicent and Birch pulled the gown down and settled and smoothed the rich silk.

'It's such a beautiful colour,' said Lady Caroline happily. Birch teased out the great fullness of the under-gown's sleeves so that they billowed from India's elbows, and then fastened the clasps. The sleeves of the over-gown were much shorter, and split down the sides, held in two places by the jewelled clips, so that the white satin could be puffed out through the gaps. The over-gown was of a rich and delicate shade between primrose and gold, and the sleeve and bodice clips were set with yellow agates.

'Master Clovis knows cloth, my lady,' Birch said, stepping back to see if she had puffed out both sides evenly. 'He's known it all his life.'

'The colour suits you perfectly, my dear,' said Lady Caroline. In the great bedchamber all the women of the house were assembled to watch the dressing of the bride – all except Cathy, who preferred to talk business with Clovis downstairs. Caroline's gown, of pale lilac silk, was her own favourite colour, although she had grown so pale and thin of late it no longer suited her, though no one would tell her that. She smoothed its skirt lovingly as she sat on the end of the bed, with Mrs Neville on one side and Sabine on the other. Clover, Frances and Sabina made a row along one of the window seats; Clover, now thirteen, looked enviously at India, Frances, ten and a half, was making up stories in her head about it, and Sabina, who was a month off eleven, glared with hatred at India, for she had always planned to marry James Matt herself, and comforted herself by imagining that India was dead and they were dressing her for her funeral.

India now sat down so that the new maid could do her hair. Here Birch could not compete, for she could not see well enough, though she had dressed the Countess's hair and was certain she knew better than this flighty new girl, who in any case wore too much face-paint for a maid, even a fashionable lady's maid. But Millicent's fingers were nimble and skillful enough.

'The colour's well enough,' Sabine said, 'but it's not to my taste. Too wishy-washy. I like bright colours that you can really see.' She was holding a bowl of candied fruits, and as she spoke she rummaged through them for a sugared apricot, her favourite. She had grown enormously fat of late, and her once pretty features were blurred and distorted by flesh. When she was not eating, she was hunting, and though she now had to have a heavyweight of a horse, she hunted with no less vigour or enthusiasm. Francomb said to Clovis that they didn't need hounds, for it was enough to frighten a stag to death to see Sabine thundering down on it like Jehu, yelling fit to start landslides. Even her riding habits, in defiance of tradition, were in bright yellows and greens. 'Now this,' she continued, wiping her sugary fingers on the mustard-yellow skirt of her gown, 'is what *I* call yellow.'

'I remember my own wedding,' Lady Caroline said dreamily, 'twenty years ago in this house. It was very beautiful. And even though I was not marrying a Morland, we were allowed to use the great bedchamber. This very bed –' She realized suddenly what she was saying, and stopped abruptly.

Birch took pity and covered for her by saying, 'This bed is very ancient, made over two hundred years ago for the Master of Morland Place for his marriage. All the Morland heirs have been born in this bed, and many of them have died here too.'

India gave the great ornate bed a single glance of distaste, and Lady Caroline, intercepting and misunderstanding it, said gently, 'It is a noble duty to provide your husband with an heir. A thing any woman can be proud to do.'

Sabine, who had notably failed to provide either of her husbands with an heir, said sourly, 'Duty, aye, and let's hope she has better luck than some of us. For the Countess's sons don't look like helping much – one of 'em unmarried, and the other with nothing but a daughter to show. And now his wife's dead, I hear, Caroline? Not that it'd do much good, with him in exile, if she had given him a son.'

'If all did fail,' Caroline asked hesitantly, 'where would the estate go?'

'Cathy's son James, if he should live so long,' Sabine said shortly, and looked at India. 'Better get to it, mistress.'

Father St Maur performed the ceremony, and though he was old and frail now, his voice still rang clear and steady over the familiar words. All the family other than the exiles, and all the servants, and as many of the tenants as could be crowded in amongst the distinguished guests, attended, for the marriage of the heir to Morland Place was an important event. Matt, in his shyness, looked younger than ever in his beautiful wedding clothes of white-and-gold damask and sapphire-blue satin, and stood awaiting his bride with such an expression of apprehension that

Cathy leaned over and whispered to Clovis that he looked as if he had far rather get on his pony and ride back to school for refuge. Arthur, back from Court for the occasion – he had been serving in the household of the Duke of Gloucester, his mother having refused to consider his apprenticeship as an architect – was his attendant, and the big, heavy, red-faced youth looked far more of a bride-groom than Matt.

Then the bride came in, attended by Clover and, incidentally, by Kithra, who was not accustomed to being forbidden the chapel and had made three attempts to get in. Clement, at the door, fielded the old hound and made him sit at his feet, and smiled at the bride as she went past. She looked very lovely, walking tall and proud in her golden gown, her hair dressed in soft flowing curls, the front part taken back and knotted with white flowers and a diamond clip at the back. Around her throat she wore a necklace of pearls that formed part of the Morland jewels which would be hers to wear for her lifetime; it had originally been a gift from Edmund Morland to Mary Esther Chapham on their wedding-day. The priceless Black Pearls, always traditionally worn by the mistress of Morland Place on important occasions, had disappeared during the Revolution and the attack on Morland Place, either stolen in the sack of the house, or hidden by someone now dead and unable to tell of the hiding place.

After the Mass came the feast, such a feast as had not been seen at Morland Place since Ralph Morland married the Countess. A small army of cooks had been hired from York and from London, and all the family's plate, the store depleted since the days before the civil war, but still impressive, was taken out and polished. The house was decorated with flowers – June was a good month for that – and orange trees in pots flanked the doorways, and over each door was tied a garland of bay and rosemary for good luck, interspersed with heather, representing the Morland family, the whole wound together with ribbons of blue and white silk. In the hall were hung the wooden shields displaying the Morland achievement of arms that had been used at Caroline's wedding, together with a new one shewing the arms of India's father, which she would bring into the family – a white saltire on a red background, differenced with a cross moline.

Because of the large number of guests, Clovis had decided to serve the feast in the buffet style that the Countess had favoured for her parties, and the tables were set out in the great hall, covered with damask cloths and decorated with flowers and ivy leaves. There were whole geese, salmon, and chickens, a peacock dressed with his tail erect and his breast gilded, scarlet lobsters with their claws erect, and pies – venison, rabbit, chicken, asparagus, Florentine, and crayfish – whose crusts had been built up into representations of various houses, Morland Place, Chelmsford House, Shawes as it used to be before it fell into ruins, Windsor Castle, St James's Palace, Edinburgh Castle, Birnie Castle and, as a centre-piece, Versailles, with all its turrets gilded. There were cold meats and sallets and fruits and sweetmeats, bowls of sugared apricots and comfits, scarlet mounds of strawberries, junkets and blanc-manges, and delicious little tarts of stewed fruits – goose-berry, raspberry, blackcurrant, and cherry – covered with custard and mounded over with cream.

Outside, for the tenants and servants, an ox and pigs and chickens were roasted in the cook-pits, trestles were set up, and ale flowed a-plenty. After the feasting there were entertainments and dancing, during the course of which the couple were ceremonially bedded by the senior members of the family, firmly excluding Arthur in the cause of seemliness. The cup was handed, Father St Maur spoke the blessing, the curtains were drawn, and the elders went away, leaving the bride and groom alone in the dark. The bride's first action on hearing the door close was to leap out of bed, and Matt thought for a moment that she was running away. Not that he would have blamed her – he would have liked to run away himself. He knew nothing of this girl, and though she had appeared very beautiful to him in the chapel when they were married, he could not find any attachment in him for her, which made it seem strange that he was to do such intimate things to her.

But she only went to the windows and drew back the curtains. It was almost midsummer, and the sky was still filled with a soft afterlight. She stared out of the window for a moment at the revellers beyond the moat, and then came back to the bed, leaving the bedcurtains open too.

'I hate to be in the dark,' she said. Matt watched her, dim but visible, climbing in beside him. She did not seem at all embarrassed or nervous, and this daunted him still further. 'It's hateful to be shut up here. I'd far sooner be out there dancing, would not you?'

Matt did not answer. His bride, still sitting up, leaned over to look at his face, her long hair swinging loose and tickling him. He put a hand up to fend off the hanging silken ropes.

'Or would you not?' she added thoughtfully. 'Have I misjudged you? Have you, after all, an appetite for this, when I thought you had not even the stomach?' He did not quite know what she was talking about, and lay still, like a small animal menaced by a bigger. She ran her hand over his face and then slipped it under the covers, and down his body. He drew in an involuntary breath, and she smiled, but did not remove her hand. 'Come, that's better. It seems you are a man, at least. Well, since it must be done, let's do it.' She removed her hand – to Matt's brief and piercing disappointment – and with swift movements drew off her nightgown, flinging it from her and leaving her strong, white, and womanly body naked. She took Matt's hand and guided it to her breast, holding his fingers to her nipple until it stiffened under his touch. Then she lay down with him, and began manoeuvres of her own. There was silence, except for the sound of their breathing, and the occasional rustle of sheet. Matt, feeling his body stretch itself into unknown spaces of delight, was half joyed and half terrified, for it seemed something was happening without his will or consent. In the dark, she did not seem so much a stranger. From time to time he caught the glint of her teeth when her lips parted in smile or grimace, a light on her hair or eye; her shape seemed already known to him, and the smell of her, sweeter than he had expected, but also stronger, became something he could not remember not knowing.

'There – now – gently, gently – like that,' she said.

'Is this it?' he asked, forgetting that she could not know, any more than he.

'Yes,' she said. 'Slowly, don't rush,' she admonished. 'Ah!'

Time was suspended, and he did not notice the dark growing until it was absolute, for he saw with his mind's eye when his physical eye could see nothing. A long dream of unimaginable pleasure spun itself softly around him, and the revellers outside had finished and gone home before Matt drifted off to sleep with his face pressed to his bride's shoulder. The last thing he heard was her voice saying softly, with the glint of a laugh, 'Like a duck to water!' but he was too sleepy to wonder what she meant.

In the June of 1700 Karellie visited Maurice in Florence, and found him working furiously on the last pages of his opera *The Martyrdom of St Apollonia*. The opera had begun as a romantic comedy, and was translated halfway through to a tragedy by the death of his wife in the course of miscarrying her second child. The first, a daughter whom Maurice had named Alessandra, after her grandfather, was a little over a year old, and flourishing; in the court of Florence, the handsome young widower had no difficulty in finding women willing and eager to care for the child while he plunged himself into his work.

Karellie came to sympathize, and found his sympathy impossible to give, for Maurice determinedly would not talk about his wife, and turned every conversation firmly from the personal to the musical, and after a while Karellie gave up. He found it difficult to discover what Maurice had felt about his beautiful young wife. On the wall of the apartment hung the portrait taken of Maurice and Apollonia just after their wedding; all the works he had written in the two years of their marriage were dedicated to her; yet he never spoke of her, and his emotional state seemed closer to anger or ecstacy than grief.

Karellie, between campaigns, had come in the company of a friend, a Venetian nobleman who was, like himself, a mercenary, though not an exile. Francesco was the son of the Duke di Francescini, who had left home to become a soldier of fortune when his father had married a second wife with whom Francesco could not get along. The second wife now being dead, the young man had come to make peace with his father, and had invited Karellie along as a buffer state. The diversion to Florence had not been unwelcome to him: he was willing to postpone the difficult interview as long as possible, and help Karellie to debauch his brother for a few days or weeks in the interests of healing his sorrows.

'In fact,' Francesco said idly one day, 'why don't you come with us to Venice when we move on? It is an essential part of your education – no musician can call himself complete until he has been to Venice, for that is where the soul of music resides.'

Maurice had heard this from denizens of all the cities of Italy, and was not impressed, but Francesco was insistent.

'We live for music in Venice. Every action of our lives, from waking in the morning to lying down at night, must be accompanied by music. Our eating, drinking, our devotions, our celebrations, weddings, funerals, everything we do – there is no one in Venice who does not make music in some way. Why, if three men meet on the corner of a square in the course of an evening stroll, they will at once form a band and give a concert, and the passers-by will join in. You must go to Venice, my friend, and the sooner the better. You are wasted here at Florence. In Florence music is merely an art. In Venice it is a passion. It is life itself.'

115

Maurice listened with mild amusement, but Karellie joined in eagerly.

'Oh do come with us, my brother! I am sure the change will do you good – it will inspire you. You must be growing stale here.'

'Come and stay at the house of my father,' Francesco added. 'He will be delighted and honoured. It will enhance his reputation greatly to have such a talented musician and composer in his house. He is a great patron, you know, and will invite all the most important people in Venice to come and hear you.'

In such a vein they worked upon him, and though Maurice merely shrugged indifferently, when his opera had been performed with no more than moderate success at the Pratolino he found himself gripped by a terrible feeling of anti-climax. He had been both happy and productive in Florence, but everything now reminded him of Apollonia, and without her presence the palace seemed less bright and beautiful, somehow tarnished. He had adored Apollonia, and made her his inspiration, his Muse. In many ways he had hardly known her – he could not well have said what she really felt or thought about anything, for she was to him a symbol, an image of perfection. He had placed her upon a pedestal and adored her, and had not required or wanted to know that she was flesh and blood. Yet without her, Florence was no different from any other place. He became bored and restless, and soon agreed to go with his brother and friend to Venice.

He had little to pack, besides his clothes, his instruments, and his manuscripts, for in two years he had never bothered to acquire anything. Apollonia's clothes and trinkets he sold or gave away. Karellie thought that he wanted nothing to remind him of her, that he would even have given away the child if he could. He was certainly prepared to abandon the portrait, but Karellie insisted on removing it from its frame and packing it, and it was Karellie, too, who found a woman, a very young widow named Caterina Birnisi, to take care of the baby. They set off towards the end of July, and travelled slowly, stopping in Bologna and Padua, and arrived in Venice in mid-August.

The duke received them kindly at the elegant Palazzo Francescini, an ancient building of pink marble whose cool and airy rooms contained treasures, collected over centuries, of furniture, paintings, silver, porcelain, statuary, and glass that made even Maurice stare. The initial interview between Francescini and his son was painful but brief, and Francesco broke through it to embrace his father, and kneel for his blessing, upon which he was entirely forgiven and restored in the most satisfactory way. As Francesco had predicted, the duke was enormously pleased and proud to have Maurice as his guest, and Maurice was flattered to find that the duke had not only heard of him, but had also heard some of his music, and begged to be allowed to consider himself Maurice's patron.

'You must stay here, for as long as you like – I positively cannot permit you to be anyone's guest but my own while you stay in Venice. Perhaps when you have discovered how much Venice has to offer, you may be persuaded to make your home here permanently.'

As to Alessandra, there was no difficulty. She could be accommodated in the nursery along with the duke's five-year-old daughter by his second wife, with Caterina to take care of her. The duke was enormously proud of his daughter, Diane, and on the first evening, after the men had dined, she was brought down to be displayed and praised like the foremost of his treasures. She was a charming child, tall and well-grown for her age, with red-gold curls, blue eyes and porcelain-white skin, and a proud and haughty carriage which suggested that even at five she had already learnt how to get her own way in all things. She was introduced to the English lord and his brother, and nodded graciously to them with all the dignity of a matron. Maurice concealed a smile at such grown-up gravity in so small a child, and noted, with amused interest, that she paid far more attention to Karellie – The Marechal

Comte de Chelmsford as he was introduced – than to simple Signore Morland. Karellie was plainly enchanted by her, and willingly gave the homage she appeared to expect. As a great treat she was asked, and consented, to sing to them.

'Already she has a beautiful voice,' her father said. 'I have a tutor for her, who is training her for the opera. In a few years –' He waved a hand to indicate the heights to which she would climb. Maurice offered to accompany her on the harpsichord, and the child arranged herself with professional care by the instrument and sang three songs. Maurice, prepared to discover that the father's praise was more partial than exact, was surprised and impressed by the clarity and sweetness, but above all by the power of the child's singing. When she had retired, he asked the duke whether she would really sing opera.

'But of course,' the duke said, and explained that in Venice it was quite usual for well-born ladies to give concert performances, and indeed was thought greatly to their credit. 'Music is our aristocracy,' he said. 'To excell in musical performance is the aim of everyone, and those who do go everywhere and are much feted, whatever their original rank in life. We have in Venice four Ospedali, where female children are placed – orphans, illegitimate children, some the product of noble families, some the offspring of our wealthiest prostitutes – and the best of them are trained for musical performance. The finest performers in Venice come from the Ospedali, particularly the Pieta, in which I have an interest. They have the best teachers, and frequently marry into the best families when they are old enough. When anyone in Venice has a great celebration, he hires the orchestra from one of the Ospedali – I do not decide on the date until I have discovered that the orchestra of the Pieta is free.'

Maurice was much interested in that, and the duke promised him that he would take him to the Pieta at the first opportunity. 'But tomorrow we go to St Mark's,' he said firmly. 'That is where the best music is. You must hear our famous red-haired violinist, Vivaldi – no visit to Venice is complete without that. On the day after I will take you to the Pieta. And now, my dear sir, if you are not too fatigued, would you honour us with some music? I have heard that you are unrivalled on the cornetto. Would you favour us with a piece of your own?'

It took Maurice no more than a few days to discover that Venice was his spiritual home. Though he was seeing it at the worst time of the year, when the heat was almost insufferable and the canals stank abominably, yet it spoke to him, and he felt he could never leave here. The duke was all kindness, and would not hear of Maurice living anywhere but at the palace, and his patronage was extremely useful to Maurice, for he introduced him to all the most important people. Maurice was amazed, not only at the beauty of the women, but at their freedom, for they seemed to be able to go about as easily as men, and were so accessible that at first he had difficulty in telling the patrician ladies from the wealthy courtesans. They pursued him mightily, and his following was in no way inferior to Karellie's, for as the duke said, music was the aristocracy in Venice. But there was nothing to tempt Maurice in the elegant, richly clothed, painted ladies; they were all too human and imperfect. With their lively minds, beauty, and frank, intelligent converse, they reminded him of his mother, as he wrote to her in his, now more regular, letters.

'You would be at home here, mother. Can I not tempt you at least to visit?' he wrote.

Karellie left Venice in October to visit Berwick, recently remarried to a young Jacobite beauty, his wife having languished and died in the marshes of Languedoc. Maurice, unable to accept idleness even in Venice, sought some kind of employment, and the duke, though repeating his offers of unconditional hospitality, helped him. In November 1700 Maurice became Maestro di Cornetto at the

Ospedali della Pietà, and in December added to that the post of Maestro di Trompetto. His task was to teach cornetto and trumpet to the young girls, who lived in the cloistered manner of nuns, and even wore white uniform dresses very like habits. Despite this, they were lively, gay creatures, full of high-spirits and frequently, Maurice found, difficult to control, but very gratifying to teach, for they were all talented and eager to learn. Music was their life; because of their origins, they were known only by their Christian names, and when any further identification was required, they were distinguished by the name of the instrument they played, so *Silvia dal Violino*, or *Adriana dalla Tiorba*.

And it was thus that Maurice was introduced to a fragile-looking, dark-haired, dark-eyed girl of fourteen known to him only as Giulia dal Cornetto. When he first saw her, she was wearing the white habit of the Pietà; her luxuriant dark ringlets were tied out of the way with white ribbon, and into the knot of curls she had tucked a white flower. She stood before him shyly, her eyes turned up to him from under dark lashes, her long-fingered, white hands clutching her cornetto, which seemed too big and heavy for her, though she was the star amongst the cornetto girls. A man with a weakness for wine would do well not to lock himself in a wine-cellar – from the first glance of her dark eyes, he was hopelessly in love.

CHAPTER SEVEN

The death of Lady Caroline a mere three weeks after the wedding did nothing to disturb Matt's dreamlike honeymoon. He was sad, of course, and attended the obsequies with a grave face, but his mind could hardly be said to be on it, though he managed to keep his eyes from his wife during the ceremony. Lady Caroline's death was so sudden that Arthur was unable to come back from Court in time to witness her last moments, though his brother John was at the death-bed. When he received news of her death, Arthur wrote back that since he was too late to say goodbye to her, there was no point in his leaving, especially since the Duke of Gloucester's birthday was close on hand, which he, as a Gentleman of the Bedchamber and a captain in the Prince's private army, ought to attend.

By the beginning of August, however, Arthur was back from Court, and this time for good. The Duke of Gloucester's birthday party at Windsor had been a splendid occasion, complete with banquet and firework display, but the Prince had woken the next morning with a fever and a sore throat. The doctors called in to attend him had bled him and prescribed rest and quiet, but by the evening he was obviously seriously ill. For four days he lay in a delirium, holding the hands of his mother and father, who never left his bedside, and on 29 July he died, taking with him the hopes of the Protestant party. Since his birth the Princess Anne had borne four sons who had died within hours of birth, and suffered four miscarriages, and now her childbearing days were over. Her grief, and that of her husband, affected even Arthur, and he arrived home in a subdued mood. Clovis, while sympathizing deeply with Princess Anne, knew that the Prince's death must have been a good thing for the Jacobite party, for Princess Mary was dead, and the Usurper old and ailing, and who was there to succeed but the legitimate heir, the Prince of Wales? He wrote with discreet hope to Annunciata.

These things passed Matt by almost unnoticed. He was obsessed with India. He spent every moment of every day with her, lay wrapped blissfully in her arms all night. She expressed a wish to learn to ride, and he took her out to Twelvetrees and taught her on the old schoolmaster gelding, Hastings, and she shewed an immediate and such a skilful grasp of the art that within a fortnight he was choosing for her a horse of her own, and ordering a special saddle and bridle to be made for her. The animal he selected was half-brother to his own new horse, Star; a handsome coal-black gelding named Midnight, great grandson of Ralph Morland's famous black stallion, Barbary. Midnight was a beautiful horse with a great conceit of himself, and very showy paces, but for all that reliable enough for Matt to trust him with his beloved bride. The tack he had made was of black leather tooled in silver and decorated with silver beads; India at once ordered in a dressmaker to make her a riding habit of black velvet trimmed with white ostrich feathers, which Birch said sourly was most impractical. Dressed in it, and mounted on Midnight, she was quite spectacular, and the villagers and servants loved it, and rushed out of their houses to wave when she went by.

Once she had learned to ride, she and Matt were out every day, and he took her over all the estate and introduced her to his tenants. She liked sitting upon an eminence and being told that 'all this belonged to her, as far as the eye could see', but had less patience with the tenants, whom she said were ugly and smelled bad, and though she was polite to them for Matt's sake he thought it best to limit her visits, lest they be offended. When they were not riding, or walking about the gardens, Matt dedicated himself to amusing her within the house, playing cards with her, or playing to her, or listening while she sang. Even when she sat and sewed, he was on hand to find her scissors, thread her needles, pick up her handkerchief, or fetch her rose-flower water.

'She leads you about like a bear by the nose,' Birch said to him once, and he was so angry that he would not speak to her for days. Had she been anyone else, he would have dismissed her; so the servants, though they shook their heads over his infatuation, kept their comments to themselves. Matt neglected his work to attend his bride, but Clovis took over that burden too, saying that everyone should have their honeymoon, and Matt was still young. So there were visits and parties and banquets and balls, and the dressmakers came every day loaded with silks and laces, and India grew daily more fine and Matt daily more proud of her. The only thing which gave him any qualms at all was the amount of time she spent giggling and gossipping with her maid Millicent, of whom Matt had from the beginning no great opinion.

He tried to wean her mind to higher things and, shocked that she was unable to read or write, offered to teach her.

But she only laughed gaily and said, 'What should I do with books? Even if I could read, I would never have time to. Why, I'm busy from morning to night.'

Sometimes when she sewed he tried reading aloud to her, hoping that it would awaken an interest in her, but it proved hopeless. She would listen for a few minutes, an expression of eagerness on her face, and then would interrupt him in the middle of a sentence to ask her mother's opinion of her work or comment on the good fit of her new manteau, and Matt would know she had not been listening, and that the eager expression had been designed to please him.

It was the same if he tried to talk seriously to her; after a few words she would break in to say, 'I must tell you of the woman I saw today riding into the city, with her hair dressed in such a curious way, I could hardly stop staring at it. What a mercy it is one has hair that curls naturally! I could not endure to look so forced as she did, not for twice my fortune!'

These things saddened Matt, for he had hoped that marriage would provide him with a complete companion, someone in whom he could confide utterly. But they were small matters beside India's beauty, charm and vivacity. She was prodigally extravagant, and her extravagances amused him, for it delighted him to give her things and watch her pleasure as she unwrapped a new present from him. He bought her a pair of clips for her hair in the shape of two sprays of blossom, all in diamonds, and was deeply moved that she altered the style of her hair to accommodate them.

One day he took her down to the strong room and took out all the boxes of jewels to shew her, and she cried in excitement, 'Oh Matt, they are lovely. I must put them on at once.'

'What, all of them?' he said, amused. She clapped her hands.

'Yes, all of them, at once. Come, you shall help me.' And she stood like a statue while he lifted out piece after piece and put them on her, until the boxes were empty and she glittered like a Spaniard's haul, and then obliged him to run and fetch a glass so that she could see herself. Her eyes glittered as brightly as the diamonds, and her cheeks were flushed, as she gazed at herself, and Matt felt his stomach churning.

'You look – fabulous,' he said in a strange, husky voice. She turned to him, an odd smile on her lips.

'Lock the door,' she said, and when he hesitated, 'Do it! Quickly!' He obeyed her, his hands trembling, and she made him pull out a bundle of furs to make a couch for her. 'Now you shall lie with me, just as I am, all covered with jewels. Yes, yes, now! Hurry!'

His excitement was so great that he could barely fumble with his fastenings. He had never in his wildest dreams imagined anyone like her. Afterwards she sighed with content and rubbed her face against him. 'When I was a child, and we were so poor,' she said, 'I dreamed of jewels like these, and the man who would give them to me.'

The next day Matt bought her a greyhound bitch with a diamond collar, and she thanked him with a smile that melted his bones, so full was it of shared secrets and promises. He was utterly bewitched, and very happy, and thought he could not be happier, until November, when she told him she was with child.

'It means we must not continue to do those things that delight us so,' she told him, stroking his cheek with one soft hand, and her eyes looking deep into his made him blush all over, 'but it is only for a short time. And there are other things we can do, just as pleasant for you.'

The advent of her first pregnancy changed India's attitude to Morland Place and its inhabitants. Until then she had been happy just to enjoy herself, spending money and enslaving her husband, but once motherhood entered her calculations, she began to realize that as mistress of Morland Place she had great power.

'It was lucky Lady Caroline died when she did,' she told her mother one day while she was dressing. Her mother, an early riser from long habit, often came to her room and broke her fast with chocolate and bread while India was dressed. Matt was attending Mass in the chapel, as he did at that time every day, and so they were alone with Millicent and the dog, Oyster. Matt had given up trying to persuade her to attend the morning Mass. She said once a day was enough for her, and he told Clement that the mistress was not strong, and needed to sleep longer in the mornings. Clement, recollecting the energetic, firm limbs and healthy colour of the mistress, agreed gravely.

'If she had not,' India went on, 'I should have had to persuade her to go away and live with her brother, and that might have been difficult to do. There are too many people living here on my money. I cannot see why I should pension half the world.'

Mrs Neville, who was herself a pensioner, said nothing. Millicent, wielding the brush and comb over India's glossy black head, said, 'Big houses always have a lot of dependents hanging on their coat tails, madam. When I worked for the Earl of Bennendon –'

'Yes, yes,' India said, not caring for any more stories of Millicent's past service, 'but I have not gone to all the trouble of getting married in order to have my fortune released, only to see it spent by a parcel of good-for-nothing beggars. Arthur and John, for instance – quite penniless –'

'Lord Ballincrea is very good looking, madam,' Millicent put in. 'And mightily smitten with *you*, if I may say so.'

'You may *not*,' India retorted, and then, her curiosity whetted, 'has he said anything to you?'

'Oh not to me, madam – not to a servant. But one only has to see the way he looks at you. Such a fine gentleman! And a title, too.'

'A title and nothing else,' India said with spirit, but with a shade of thoughtfulness behind it.

'I think Master Clovis Morland is intending to do something for Lord Ballincrea and his brother,' Mrs Neville said helpfully. 'He has money of his own, and no children to leave it to.'

'There's Clover,' India said with venom. 'It's indecent the way that child hangs about his neck. I wouldn't wonder if he leaves everything to her, though goodness knows she has enough of her own. I don't know why *she* has to live here on my charity.'

'Well, dear, she is only a child still,' Mrs Neville said. 'She's only thirteen.'

'She's old enough to make me blush for shame with her dallying and smirking at Clovis. But let her just get to fifteen, and I'll have her out of the way, married in two minutes, the very moment she's old enough. And John Rathkeale. Now my own child is on the way, I shall have enough expenses without them. And there are a lot of servants who will have to go – that horrible old priest, and that evil old woman Birch for instance. We can't have the house filled with cripples, eating their heads off and doing nothing.'

'Your husband is very fond of them,' Mrs Neville said with a hint of warning. 'He wouldn't like them to be turned out to go hungry.'

'He's sentimental and foolish,' India retorted, but less briskly, for that foolishness was to her own advantage. She resolved to be rid of Father St Maur and Birch, however. 'I am going to reorganize this house, and things will be done the way I want from now on. And we must have some new furniture, and lots and lots of mirrors. In fact, I think it would be a good thing to pull this house down and build a new one.'

'One thing at a time, madam,' Millicent said, and added, 'of course, Lord Ballincrea is mightily interested in architecture. Had you thought of asking him what he thinks of Morland Place?'

Clovis had been too busy since Caroline's death and Matt's marriage to worry about Arthur's future, and since his return to Morland Place, Arthur had been occupying himself with his own pleasures in such a way that Clovis had almost forgotten his presence. His spell at Court had matured Arthur, confirmed him in his vices, and taught him that reckless behaviour was not ultimately to his advantage. He hunted a lot, spent a great deal of time in York, in his favourite coffee-house, in the upstairs rooms of one or two inns where young men of like mind gathered, and in the discreet whorehouse in Skeldergate, and since he managed these things without getting himself into trouble, Clovis, bowed with work and worry, did not notice him.

Arthur noticed India, but only to observe that she was handsome, that Matt was a fool, and that she would give Matt trouble enough before she was done. But that was before she turned her charm on him. A spell of bad weather in February 1701 confined them all to the house, and Matt to his bed with a bad cold. India was all concern, and ran up to visit him every hour and soothe his brow and tell him he must sleep and have absolute quiet, and in between she sat in the drawing room with Arthur. Clover and Clovis, as usual, were busy in the steward's room with accounts, John preferred to read in solitude, and so India had Arthur to herself. She occupied herself with sewing, a dainty and ladylike pursuit; her pregnancy was hidden by the graceful folds of her pale blue dress with its loose overskirt of lace; her hair was dressed high on her head with pearls, and falling behind in a mass of dark curls; she knew exactly how she looked, and exactly what effect it would have on Arthur, when with shining eyes she looked up and fixed her gaze on him.

'It is dull to sew without conversation. Pray talk to me a little, cousin Arthur. I do so want your opinion on what to do about this house, for there is no one else here who understands architecture as you do.'

Arthur knew it to be the most blatant flattery, but the day outside was grey and bleak and wet, and she made a charming picture, sitting in the glow of the great log fire with her greyhound at her feet in its glittering collar. He stretched his legs out before him, gave her a smile of insolent ease, and answered.

The wet spell lasted a week, and at the end of it, India told Matt that, while it was essential for her to have some fresh air, he was not yet strong enough to get out of bed. 'You will bring your cold on worse than ever if you get up too soon. I shall only go out for a little carriage ride, very slowly, with the window half down, and Arthur can come with me to make sure I'm all right. You must not disturb yourself, my darling.'

Two days later, Birch went to Clovis.

'It's time you did something about Arthur, master,' she said abruptly. 'Did you not have some plans for him, before her ladyship wanted him sent to Court?'

'Why – yes,' Clovis said. 'But what troubles you, Birch? Is he getting into trouble that I don't know about? I thought he was behaving himself very well these days.'

'It's him and the new mistress, sir,' Birch said. Clovis stared.

'Why, you surely don't mean that –'

'I don't say there's any harm to it – yet,' Birch said implacably. 'But I know Arthur, and I can see the new one has nothing much to her.' Clovis frowned at that, but she went on notwithstanding. 'Idleness breeds trouble, master, and the two of them have nothing to do all day but get ideas into their heads. If you take the advice of an old woman that has seen it all before, you'll get Arthur out from this house and into some occupation.'

Clovis hesitated, unable to believe that there was anything in it; but Arthur had always been a favourite of Birch's, and if *she* spoke against him – oddly enough, what convinced him was that she called him 'Arthur' and not 'Lord Ballincrea' as she usually did. He nodded.

'Very well. Say nothing of this to anyone. I will see what can be done.'

Clovis worked quickly. The following day he took Arthur with him when he went into York, and for the next week kept him always about him on one pretext or another; and at the beginning of March Arthur was taken to meet Sir John Vanbrugh in York. Arthur went sullenly, feeling in the first place that his illegitimate pleasures were being interfered with and secondly that it was ignoble for a man of his birth to be expected to 'learn a trade'. But from the beginning of the interview his ideas changed. Vanbrugh brought Hawkesmoor with him – they were both on their way back to the site of the new Castle Howard after a trip to London – and Arthur took an instant liking to both of them. He knew both by reputation, of course, and Vanbrugh's bawdy plays were a recommendation in themselves to Arthur's mind. Moreover, the only thing in the world that Arthur was interested in, besides Arthur, was architecture, and as soon as the two men began to talk about their plans for the Henderskelfe site, his pose of weary superiority dissolved and within minutes he was leaning across the table and talking with an eagerness that made him look sixteen again.

So matters were happily agreed, and Clovis guaranteed to pay Arthur a generous allowance for as long as he stayed with Vanbrugh and Hawkesmoor and behaved himself. India was no more than faintly annoyed at the removal of her admirer, but Millicent soon discovered from the servants what was at the back of it, and when she reported it to her mistress, India was furious, and determined at once that Birch should go. She confronted the old woman in the nursery, where Birch was going over the linen in preparation for the new occupant, expected in May.

'Did you want something?' Birch asked coldly. India's eyes narrowed at the insolence.

'I just came to tell you that you have interfered for the last time in this household. You would do well to remember that *I* am the mistress now.'

'When you are worthy of that title, I will give it to you,' Birch said calmly, and went on with her sewing. India reached forward and snatched it from Birch's hands and threw it on the floor.

'I warn you, old woman, you had better not cross me,' she said. Birch looked at her without fear.

'You cannot harm me. I have been in this household more than thirty years. I spoke to Master Clovis for your good as well as everyone else's, as he knows well.'

'Master Matt is my husband, and he has the final word in this house.'

'Master Matt would not take your side against me. I was his governess before you were ever known to him.'

India smiled with triumph. 'We'll see which of us he believes,' she said, and left in a flurry. A little while later, Birch was summoned by a servant child to speak to Master Matt. Matt looked embarrassed, and spoke to Birch without quite meeting her eyes. In the background, India sat, her hands folded over the bulge of her pregnancy, her expression gentle and meek.

'Birch, the mistress tells me that you have spoken

harshly to her, and refused to address her as "mistress".
Now I know that you have been a long time in this house,
and I know you sometimes speak more shortly than you
mean to, but I must ask you to shew a proper respect to
my wife.' India sighed, just audibly, and Matt added, 'And
do exactly as she says, without arguing. It is very bad for
her in her condition to be crossed in any way.'

Birch stood rigidly, looking neither to left nor right.
'Yes, master,' she said. Matt felt rather ashamed.

'That will be all,' he said, and Birch went away without
a word. A little later India contrived to meet her on the
stairs, and gave her a smile of sweet triumph.

'You see?' she said. 'Don't cross me in future, or it will
be the worse for you.'

She passed on, and Birch continued her slow way to the
nursery. She sat down in her chair by the window where
she could get the best light, and picked up the lace-
trimmed baby's shirt in which she had been making a tiny
darn. Her eyes were tired and she could barely see what
she was doing, but she would not let any of the other maids
attempt the repair, for this was the silk and lace shirt that
King Charles II had given to the Countess for the first of
her babies, back in 1661, almost forty years ago. Birch
remembered the hard time the Countess had had giving
birth to the twins; it was during that labour that her own
tender love for her mistress had been born. How long the
Countess had been away! Birch was sixty-five years old, a
good age for a woman. How much longer could she last?
And would the Countess ever come home again? Birch
missed her more than she had ever believed she could; and
now she was obliged to call this shallow little flirt 'mistress'
in the Countess's place.

Tears began to prick her eyes, and she put the baby's
shirt carefully from her so that they should not fall on the
delicate silk and mark it.

On the day after Matt's seventeenth birthday India gave

birth to a healthy son. There was great rejoicing at this advent of a new heir for Morland Place, for there had been times, since the revolution, when the people had thought that the Morland fortunes were doomed. The baby was christened James Edward, which Clover, standing proudly as godmother, immediately contracted to Jemmy, and the nickname stuck, just as had her own.

Clovis now felt able to spend more time in London, where other Morland matters had long since been demanding his attention. Matt, though still besotted with India – more so, indeed, since she had presented him with an heir – was gradually taking over the running of the estate, and with Clement and Father St Maur to watch over him, Clovis felt he would not go far wrong. India, in spite of what Birch thought of her, was proving an energetic mistress of the house, and though she left the day-to-day details to Mrs Clough, she had already dismissed some servants whom she said were inefficient, organized thorough cleanings and polishings, got in new curtains, counterpanes and bedhangings, and was gradually changing the look of the interior of the house.

Thus it was that Clovis was in London when Parliament passed the Act of Settlement in June, by which the throne was to pass to Princess Anne on the death of the Usurper, and on her death to Annunciata's Aunt Sofie of Hanover. It was an extraordinary piece of work. Without half thinking, Clovis could name two score people with better claims to the throne than the Electress but, of course, they were all Catholics, and the Usurper, backed by the Whig party, wanted to make sure of a Protestant succession.

Sofie of Hanover, Clovis thought, would make a good Queen, from what Annunciata had told him about her; and she was granddaughter to King Charles I, sister to Prince Rupert, and one of the best of the Palatines, intelligent, generous, able. But after her would come her son, George Lewis, as dull and unpleasant a creature as could be found, and after him his son George, both of them foreigners to the hilt. It occurred to Clovis to wonder whether the very unsuitableness of the Hanoverians might turn the tide in the Jacobites' favour. Perhaps the Whigs had at last overreached themselves? It seemed likely that Princess Anne would succeed peacefully to the Usurper, for she was well-loved, and daughter to the King; but she was not a strong woman, and might not live long. When she died, surely there could be no doubt that the country would prefer the Prince of Wales to the boorish Guelph family?

And then another idea occurred to him: had Prince Rupert married Annunciata's mother, Annunciata herself could well have been named Queen by that same Act of Settlement and, being Anglo-Catholic, might have been the means of uniting the two opposing parties of Catholic and Protestant sympathies. Strange thought! Except for the trifling, though insurmountable, matter of her illegitimacy, she and George Lewis had exactly the same relationship to the throne of England, both being great-grandchildren of King Charles I through his daughter Elizabeth, the Winter Queen. Clovis contemplated Queen Annunciata all evening, and it made him chuckle. It was the only piece of amusement the Act of Settlement ever afforded a Morland.

Clovis was still in London in September when the news came from St Germain that King James was dead. A letter from Annunciata followed very shortly with more details: the King had been ailing since March when he suffered a stroke, and during the summer he had travelled to Bourbon to take the waters, and had come back saying he felt better, but everyone had known it was only a matter of time. He had died quietly with his family around him at three o'clock in the afternoon of 16 September. King Louis of France had at once acknowledged the Prince of Wales as King James III of England, and the young King, now thirteen, had issued a manifesto setting out his right to the English throne.

There were immediate diplomatic protests – the English ambassador at Versailles left without taking leave of King

Louis, and the Usurper dismissed the French ambassador from the Court of St James – and King Louis wrote an apologetic letter to say that he had only acknowledged the Prince of Wales formally as his father's heir, but had no intention of attempting to restore him to the throne. The Usurper was not impressed, and put a Bill of Attainder through Parliament to say that James Stuart would be executed without trial if he ever set foot in England, and made it a treasonable offence for any English person to write to him or send him money.

Meanwhile the Queen had written to Princess Anne asking her help in making reparation to her half-brother. Spain, Savoy, Modena, and the Pope followed France's lead in declaring James king, while Holland and Austria sided with the Usurper and formed a triple alliance against the France-Spain allies. It was obvious to Clovis that there was going to be another war in Europe, for France had now recaptured all the disputed areas of the Spanish Low Countries, and since King Louis's grandson had been proclaimed King of Spain, France controlled all the ports on the Channel coast. The rights of King James III would be a side-issue in what was truly a struggle to maintain the balance of power, but whether the war would favour King James or harm his cause it was impossible to tell. Wearily, and with a sense of futility, Clovis went home to Morland Place for Christmas.

Sabine and her husband and little Frances had come down for the season but the Scottish Morlands were in mourning and stayed at home. Poor Cathy's son James had given up the unequal struggle for his life and had died on the third of December, just four weeks before his eighteenth birthday, leaving behind him no son, only a twenty-month-old daughter Mary. When the news came Matt mourned his cousin genuinely, but gave no more than a thought of passing pity for Mavis, widowed at eighteen: so strong was India's hold on his heart. They had not yet resumed sexual relations, although India's 'other things' continued to enslave and at least partly satisfy him. She had spoken to him frankly and openly about it.

'Of course I want us to have lots and lots of children, darling,' she had said. They were preparing for bed, and she had come and sat beside him on the edge of the bed and captured his hand in both of hers, and was gazing into his face with a frank and innocent appeal that he found irresistible. 'But I don't want to be worn out with child-bearing before I'm twenty. I've seen what happens to women, and you wouldn't want your wife to become a wrinkled old hag, would you? If I did, you'd run off after younger, prettier women and break my heart.'

'Oh India, how could you think it?' Matt said. 'I'd never, never –'

'I know, darling,' India interrupted him, pressing her soft fingers over his lips, 'but I wouldn't want to put you to the test. Besides, if I am forever with child, I shan't have any time to devote to you, shall I? So let us have our babies a good bit apart, shall we?'

'Of course, my dearest,' Matt said. 'Anything you say. You have only to say the word. We'll have as many babies as you want, and when you want.'

'That's my good, sensible husband,' India murmured, leaning towards him, pressing her lips over his and allowing her hand to stray from his waist downwards. Matt felt the familiar hot, feverish weakness stealing over him. In her hands he was helpless, as if all his bones were melting. He lay back upon the bed and, gazing up at her through half-closed eyes, he surrendered himself to her magical power and his overmastering love.

Arthur came to Morland Place for Christmas, and Clovis thought him greatly improved by his months working on Castle Howard. He had an air of maturity now. He drank less, gave up smoking his foul pipes, since India said she could not abide the smell, talked to Clovis in a sensible and interesting way, and generally made himself pleasant. Matt made John Lord of Misrule for the season, and Arthur helped his brother arrange games and teases, and kept the fun fast but not furious. He also arranged the Boxing Day hunt, and at the ball in the evening danced with all the plainest girls who seemed to lack partners. Remembering Birch's fears, Clovis observed Arthur carefully in relation to his dealings with India, but he seemed to treat her with a perfectly grave courtesy as mistress of the house, and nothing else, barely sparing her a glance when she entered a room. There was obviously nothing between them, Clovis thought with relief.

On the day after Boxing Day, India decided to go into York and visit her mother's cousin, her only living relative apart from her mother. Matt offered at once to go with her, but she would not hear of it.

'She is old and tedious, my darling, and I would not by any means trouble you to be bored by her. But I ought to pay her my respects.'

'Why do you not bring her here? I can send some servants to fetch her, and she can spend the season with us,' Matt said.

'Oh no, that wouldn't do,' India said with a frown. 'She is old and frail and would not care to leave her home. No, it is best if I visit her.'

'But I do not like you to travel alone at this time of year,' Matt said. India laughed gaily, making her long curls bob and sway.

'I shall not be alone – Millicent will come with me. And besides, it is not really travelling, to go two miles into the city. There is no snow, the weather is perfectly fine, and I shall be back before dark. Now what is there to worry about?'

'Still, you should have someone with you, in case of accidents. Let me send a groom with you.' India frowned again, and opened her mouth to argue, and Matt added, 'No, better still, let me ask Arthur to accompany you as far as your cousin's house. I know he is going in to York on business today, and I'm sure he would not mind taking you there, and collecting you on his way back.'

'I do not like to trouble him,' India said, and then sighed

and smiled. 'Well, if it will make you easy in your mind, dear husband, I shall let you ask him. But pray tell him it was not my idea.'

Matt smiled and took her hands. 'Always so thoughtful,' he said. 'Don't be afraid, I shall make sure he knows it is my foolishness that binds burdens on him.'

India stepped close to him and kissed him, lightly like the touch of snowflakes upon his lips, and cheeks, and eyes. 'My dear, thoughtful husband,' she murmured. 'I do believe that no woman was ever so fortunate in her husband as I.' Trembling he closed his arms round her, and when she eventually pulled away, it was to look into his eyes with an expression that made his blood rush about his body in hot tides.

'Tonight, dear husband,' she whispered. 'Tonight. I think we have waited long enough, don't you?'

India reported her elderly cousin to be in such poor state that she was obliged to visit her on most days through the rest of December and January. Arthur's business in York made it possible for him to accompany her during the Christmas season, but when Christmas was over he left Morland Place to go back to Henderskelfe. By that time, however, Matt had become inured to the idea of the daily visits, and as long as India went accompanied by Millicent, he raised no objection. She was never away long and, in any case, since they had resumed sexual relations he was in a dream of bliss where anything she asked for could be hers. He went about his work during the day with a remote smile upon his lips, living for the night-time.

Clovis went back to London as soon as Christmas was over, for matters were boiling up in Europe, and in February war was finally declared between the Triple Alliance and France and Spain. The Usurper appointed Marlborough as his commander-in-chief, and King Louis responded by appointing Berwick a general under the commander-in-chief Villars, and on his recommendation recalling the Marechal Comte de Chelmsford. Annunciata wrote to Clovis of this; their correspondence had had to be carried on in increasing secrecy since the Act of Attainder, but with Clovis's connections there were always ways.

'Karellie seems much changed to me,' she wrote, 'quieter and so much older; not at all like the child who shocked and amused us all so many years ago at Morland Place. He remains very attached to Maurice, and spends a great deal of time in Venice, and talks with warmth of Maurice's host and his daughter. The latter is, however, a child not yet ten, and so I have still no hopes of his marrying and getting an heir. He seems not much interested in women, though they are very much interested in him.

'The King received him very kindly. He seems disposed to be generous to my family, for like his father he is very faithful where he loves. He has appointed Aliena as maid-of-honour to the Princess Louise-Marie, as his father promised to do, but indeed he is fonder of Aliena than the Princess is. The three of them are much together, but as Aliena has shared the King's lessons for so long now, the conversation is mostly theirs, and they are like two brothers with a younger sister.

'My dog Fand died in his sleep three days ago, and with Banner gone, I seem to have lost all contact with Morland Place. I cannot replace either of them here. How I long for home, how far away it seems!'

On the day that this letter arrived, the Usurper suffered an accident while out riding, for his horse tripped on a mole-hill, and tumbled him off. He broke his collar-bone, but it seemed that he must have done other damage to himself as well, for a week later he was dead. There was no one to mourn him; indeed, in the taverns people drank a toast to 'the little gentleman in black' whose excavations had hastened the Usurper on his way to a better place. He had been a foreigner, and that was an unforgivable sin as far as Londoners were concerned, and there was great rejoicing at the accession of Princess Anne, who was English through-and-through. This was not the time,

Clovis could see, for renewing the Jacobite cause. But Princess Anne was thirty-seven, and though that was not a great age, she had had seventeen pregnancies, and was stout and gouty, and could not be expected to make old bones. When she died, that would be the time to recall the King to his throne.

Clovis had never failed in his attentions to Princess Anne all through the Usurper's time, and now that she was Queen, she was disposed to be grateful to those who had stood by her in less propitious days. Clovis began a delicate negotiation with her, the more delicate because its purpose could not be spoken of directly. The situation was complicated by the fact that Karellie was now a marechal in the French army; but Annunciata had been lady-in-waiting to Princess Anne's mother, and had known Princess Anne since she was a small child, and in her own person was no more guilty than many another Jacobite not in exile. Moreover, Annunciata was a blood-relative, even if it was on the wrong side of the blanket; and Princess Anne had continual, if brief and quickly dismissed, stirrings of guilt over her abandoning of her father and brother. Clovis worked gently and delicately upon her, in between talking of horses and promising the Princess first refusal of the best of the new batch of Morland colts.

The Coronation took place on St George's day, 23 April 1702, and on the following day Clovis wrote to Annunciata with a description of the occasion, and a carefully phrased invitation: if Annunciata cared to come home, she might. Anne could not receive her at Court, but would allow her to live quietly in whichever of her houses she chose, without molestation or persecution.

While King James II was alive and the Usurper on his throne, it was not an invitation Annunciata could have considered, for it would have been an act of gross treachery in her eyes. But things were different now. James III was a minor still, and it was possible to regard Anne's possession of the throne as a regency, and to expect the King to take his proper place when Anne's death came to her. Annunciata had been in France for thirteen long, weary years; she was fifty-seven-years old, and she longed inexpressibly for home.

Chelmsford House was vacant, and as it had been carefully tended it was the work of days to prepare it for the Countess, to hire suitable staff and to air and clean the rooms. Birch came up from Morland Place to supervise the preparations, more glad than she could ever tell anyone to be leaving India's domaine and to be returning to the service of her true mistress. Clover, who was approaching fifteen, came too, needing no prompting to be where Clovis was, and eager for the excitement of London and the return of such an illustrious person as the Countess, of whom she had heard stories all her life. She became Birch's right hand, and under her direction smoothed covers and arranged flowers and directed the hanging of newly-cleaned pictures and tapestries.

Finally the news arrived that the Countess and her household – Chloris, Dorcas, Gifford, and Daniel, Nan having stayed behind to serve Aliena at St Germain – had landed at Greenwich and were coming up the river in a sailing barge. They landed at London Bridge, where Clovis met them with a fast oared boat, to bring them on the Whitehall Steps, leaving directions for the luggage to be brought on after them. It was June, and nearing the longest day, and the sky was full of light. The river smelled sweet with mallow and fern and reed, and the banks were heavy with the intoxicating froth of elderflower, and high above the swallows skimmed back and forth and shrilled their high sweet cries. From Whitehall Steps it was but a short walk to Chelmsford House, and at nine in the evening the Countess of Chelmsford stepped over her own threshold once more and into the great black-and-white-tiled hall. Jane Birch was there to meet her, made her deep curtsey, and then just stood and stared with trembling lip. She and the Countess were old women, and they had not expected ever to meet again.

'Oh, my lady –' Birch said. Annunciata shook her head.

'Don't cry. Please don't cry,' she said desperately; but it was an impossible request. Annunciata wanted to put her arms round her old servant and friend, but Birch's rigid propriety made that impossible, and the two women stood stiff as soldiers, four feet apart, and wept.

BOOK TWO

THE THISTLE AND THE ROSE

Coquette and coy at once her air,
Both Studied, tho' both seem neglected;
Careless she is, with artful care,
Affecting not to seem affected.

With skill her eyes dart every glance,
Yet change so soon you'd ne'er suspect them,
For she'd persuade they wound by chance,
Tho' certain aim and art direct them.

William Congrave:
Hue and Cry after Fair Amoret

CHAPTER EIGHT

Annunciata celebrated her return to England by taking to her bed with a severe rheum-and-ague, and once there, displayed no strong desire to get up again. As if exile had itself been a sickness, she came home like a convalescent, weak, uncertain, weary. Her own bed with the grey taffeta drapes and the scarlet brocade counterpane was a haven, both comfortable and elegant – comfort and elegance having been in short supply in France. On the wall opposite her bed was Wissing's portrait of her, shewing her son Rupert offering her his sword; to the right, on the black lacquered dresser, stood the silver ewers and basins engraved with the Ballincrea arms that had once belonged to her son Hugo; to the left, in the corner, stood the almost life-size black marble statue of a negro boy which her first husband had brought back from Naples. All around her were her own treasured possessions. It was enough to lie there in peace, watching Birch and Chloris moving about the room as they unpacked and inspected her clothes, remembering happier times.

Many visitors came to the doors of Chelmsford House, for although the Countess' presence in London was unofficial, there were old friends wanting to greet her, place-seekers hoping for advancement, and others who simply wanted to gawp at this notorious woman. But few were admitted, and her illness made a convenient excuse for Gifford who, splendid in a new livery, had been rewarded for his faithfulness by being made major-domo. Even after Annunciata had risen from her bed, and was venturing so far as to walk about her garden, or drive in the little chariot in St James's Park, she maintained her seclusion, receiving her contact with the outside world by means of the daily visits from Clovis. Apart from one short visit to Morland Place, he had stayed in London since June.

'How will they manage without you?' Annunciata asked him one day as they breakfasted, late and leisurely in the garden, upon cold beef, Wensleydale cheese, white bread and black cherries. 'Won't everything come to a halt without your direction?'

'I hope I have trained my subordinates better than that,' Clovis said. 'Besides, Matt has been taking over more of the responsibility over this last year. I think the time will soon come when I can leave everything to him.'

'Not before time, I should think,' Annunciata commented shortly. 'He is no longer a minor.'

'He is only just eighteen,' Clovis protested, 'and running the whole Morland estate is a huge task for a boy who has only recently become a man.'

'His father did it from the age of fifteen,' Annunciata said.

'But his father was an exceptional person,' Clovis said gently.

'Yes –' Annunciata said. Here in this garden, on this very seat, she and Martin had sat eating cherries on the day Hugo came home to destroy their peace.

Clovis watched her face for a moment, and then said, 'He does so long to see you. Will you come home? Even if only for a visit.'

Annunciata came back from a long distance, frowning slightly as she tried to grasp his meaning. Then she said, 'Oh, you mean little Matt.'

'Not so little now. He has started growing again in the past year. He will be taller than his father. Will you come home? We could choose you a horse,' he added temptingly. Annunciata smiled at the blatant bribery.

'Oh, not yet, not yet, Clovis. Let me be for a while. I want just to savour being home for a while, enjoying the peace. Next year – after Christmas. And,' she added firmly, 'I shall not only choose a horse for myself, I shall want a dog, too. Tell little Matt I shall certainly come and be his guest next year.'

They had much business to catch up on, and Clovis had to render in detail an account of how he had taken care of her property in the years she had been away.

'The wars have been a drain on us all,' he told her on one of his visits. 'On you more than on the main Morland estate, for as you know it is land tax that pays for the wars, and for Matt the land tax is partly balanced out by the higher price of exported wool and cloth. But your revenues are all from property. However, I think you will be happy with the way things have gone overall. Besides paying a pension to you, I have been able to make some good investments on your behalf in the East India Company, and there is a considerable surplus in hand.'

'Enough to rebuild Shawes?' she asked. He looked sideways at her, not knowing if she was serious or not. She had been talking about rebuilding Shawes for thirty years.

'That would depend on how ambitious your plans were. Do you really mean to do it, after all this time?'

'Well I have to live somewhere, and Shawes is, after all, my home.'

'You could stay at Morland Place.'

'No. I don't think so. It would be too – painful, after all that has happened. Besides, little Matt will have his own family to house and care for. There won't be room for me.' She looked over the pages of neatly written accounts, and said, pointing, 'Whose hand is this? It is not yours, I know.'

'Oh, that's Clover's writing. She casts accounts very neatly, doesn't she? She often helps me that way.'

Annunciata looked amused. 'What else do you teach her, I wonder? I'll wager it isn't to dance and flirt.'

Clovis was defensive. 'She is a happy child, and does all the things children do. If she likes to be with me and help me with the running of the estate, what harm is there in that?'

'No harm, except that mathematics will not help her to get a husband.'

'She's too young to be wed. In time –'

'Clovis, she is fifteen by my reckoning,' Annunciata said seriously. 'You must not make the same mistake as Ralph and Martin made with her mother. She is a pretty girl with nice manners, and she has a good fortune. You must bring her here this winter for the Season, and we'll soon find someone for her.'

Clovis searched about for an excuse. 'But you will not care to go into society, even in a good cause. You said you wanted to be peaceful.'

Annunciata patted his hand. 'Please don't worry about me. I can entertain suitable candidates quietly at home. I have influence enough, even if I am here unofficially.' She looked at his downcast face with sympathy, and added gently, 'Your special friendship with her will not be destroyed, only altered. You must not be selfish with her.'

He placed his own hand over hers. 'You left Aliena at St Germain. How did you find the strength?'

She looked away, her eyes distant again. 'I thought of my mother, who sent me to Court, and never troubled me again. She did not even come to my wedding – my first wedding, I mean. But I have come to understand it. It is enough that she exists. I love her, she is all I have left of him; but she is her own person, and must make her own life, as I have made mine. Being alone will make her strong. I would not have her weakened by my shadow.'

In the silence that followed, Clovis sighed. 'You are right, of course. I will bring her back to London. I think she will want to stay until India has had her confinement, but after that –'

India was brought to bed on 1 October of a second son, whom they named Robert. At Chelmsford House, Annunciata and Clovis drank a toast to the new child before Clovis departed to pay his congratulatory visit to Morland Place and fetch Clover to London for the Season.

'What is she like, this wife of Matt's?' Annunciata asked

curiously. 'You have hardly mentioned her. Where does she come from?'

'Her father was Neville the merchant, with the big red house on Fossgate,' Clovis said.

'I remember,' Annunciata said. 'He married that pale, wispy little creature whose father had an estate at Holtby.' Clovis told India's story, and Annunciata went on, 'Well that seems satisfactory – and the Nevilles are perfectly respectable – but what is the girl like?'

'Strong and energetic,' Clovis said vaguely. 'Pretty, too. Matt adores her, that's plain to see. I thought at first he would never settle down to his work, for he was always hanging about her when he should have been attending to business, but once Jemmy was born things changed. I think *she* probably set him straight. She has a mind of her own.'

'Strong and energetic with a mind of her own,' Annunciata said musingly, and turned down her mouth. 'However, she is evidently fertile, and that's the main thing.'

Clovis burst out laughing. 'My dear Countess, imagine Ralph's relations saying that of you when you married him!'

'That was entirely a different matter,' Annunciata said, but she smiled all the same.

Christmas at Morland Place was a jolly one, and the house was full to overflowing. Annunciata remained at Chelmsford House, but insisted that Clovis should take Clover home for the month. Cathy was too ill to travel, and stayed at Aberlady, with Mavis and little Mary to bear her company, but Sabina, who had been staying at Emblehope for the hunting, was brought to Morland Place by the Francombs, and Arthur and John were both home.

India, quite recovered from the birth of little Robert, was brimming with energy, and invited a number of young bachelors of good family from York to stay, in addition to one or two families.

'With Clover just back from her first Season in London,' she said to Matt, 'and Frances and Sabina coming to stay, we must have lots of dancing, and that means lots of young men for dancing-partners.'

'You are so thoughtful,' Matt said admiringly. 'But if you are in the room, the girls will still lack for partners, for all the young men will want to dance with you.'

India laughed, and her eyes shone. 'Oh my dear, I account myself quite an old matron now. They won't even notice me – a mother of two!'

'You're more beautiful than ever,' Matt said, and meant it. She leaned towards him and rubbed her cheek against his, and his hand strayed helplessly and automatically to touch and stroke her. If she were not so insistent that he did his duty by the estate, he felt that he would be quite happy to spend his whole life at her side, kissing and caressing her.

Everything was done in the best of style, and the food was both lavish and elegant. Most of the servants liked and admired India, but the cook positively worshipped her, for under Clovis's direction, during Matt's minority, there had been little scope for his skills. Food at Morland Place had been plentiful, but plain and wholesome, no canvas for a great artist. This Christmas, inspired by India, he excelled himself. The centrepiece of the whole season's feasting was the collosal Twelfth-Night cake, which was three feet in diameter and decorated to be a perfect miniature of Morland Place in beautiful detail, right down to the marzipan peacocks who spread their paper tails on the sugar drawbridge.

As well as the feasting, there was of course music and entertainment of all kinds, all the favourite Christmas games and, every night, dancing. India danced with the best of them, and Matt, though he could hardly get a dance himself with his own wife, stood at the side of the room and watched her with pride and love as she flew tirelessly up and down the sets, conspicuous in her peacock-blue satin, with the Queen's Emeralds glittering at her throat.

India's mother, who no longer lived at Morland Place – India had rented her a house in York as soon as the second child was born, saying she would be happier there with her old friends – had come to stay for Christmas, and sat by the big fire at the north end of the long saloon to keep Sabine company. Sabine had grown grotesquely stout and could no longer dance, though she watched India with a gleam of approval in her eye.

'By God, she reminds me of myself at that age,' Sabine said, reaching with an automatic hand for another sugared apricot from the dish at her side. 'I used to dance every dance once, though you wouldn't guess it to look at me, madam. Dance all night long, when I was that age.' She shrieked with sudden laughter, making Mrs Neville jump. 'Sweet Mary, look at her going up the set with my husband! How she makes him leap! Who would have thought he had it in him to dance so spry!' The couple turned at the end of the set with a flurry, and Sabine waved a sticky finger at them in encouragement. 'I vow and swear, she does him good, that wench of yours, madam. Look at the colour in their cheeks.'

Mrs Neville murmured something, though she thought the colour in Jack Francomb's cheek more suggestive of apoplexy than good health. Sabine sighed.

'And they'll be up at dawn to go out hunting again, I'll warrant. I used to be the same, you know, before I got so cursed fat. Now it's two men's work to get me up on a horse.'

The dance ended, and the dancers scattered like spilled beads from the centre of the room to the sides, for a brief rest before the next began. Frances and Sabina came to flop on the cushions beside Sabine, fanning themselves vigorously. They were both going on fourteen, almost women and not quite yet ladies, and they were having wonderful fun. Frances was plump and fair and snubbily pretty, while Sabina was thin and dark and thought herself plain beside her cousin, though her face had a vividness that was far more striking. Sabine reached out and tapped her panting daughter on the shoulder.

'Now, Fanny, you've had some pleasure – you had better go and rescue your poor father before he takes an apoplexy.' She looked across at Matt, standing nearby, and said, chuckling, 'For shame, Matt, to let that wife of yours wear out the old folk!'

'Papa's all right, mother,' Frances said. 'He likes dancing with Mistress Morland.'

'Oh, I know he likes it,' Sabine said, 'but I'm afraid his heart may give out. Now, Master Matt, dance with your pretty wife, for pity.'

Sabina jumped up at that and seized Matt's hand in both hers. 'Oh no, he promised to dance with me. Did you not, Matt? You promised!' And Matt, looking down into her passionate face, had not the heart to deny her.

'Well, yes, I did say –'

Sabine spotted Arthur, coming to look for a partner, and called him over with the imperiousness of one who has no more reason ever to be shy. 'Go and dance with India, Arthur, before she kills my poor Jack. And, Fan, go fetch me some more wine, quickly, before the music starts again.'

'I was just going to,' Arthur said through gritted teeth, while Frances pouted crossly at being made to fetch and carry; but the music began before she had gone a yard from her place, a young man bowed to her, and she was off in a flurry, with no backward glance for her mother.

'Why do you keep dancing with that clown, Francomb?' Arthur asked India disagreeably as they made their sedate way up the line of the next dance.

'Only charity, my dear, the merest kindness,' India said imperturbably. 'I had to rescue him from that fat old wife of his, horrid old creature! How she could marry him, I don't know. She ought to be ashamed.'

'You seem to have his welfare close at heart,' Arthur growled. India squeezed his hand.

'Don't look so grimly, people will think we are quarrelling. Lord, you can't think I would have any interest in a man whose breeches are five years old at the least, and who has no more idea of garniture than my horse! Why, indeed, Midnight is far better company, and handsomer.' Arthur smiled a little, unwillingly, and she followed up her advantage. 'Besides, dear, you have been dancing a great deal with Clover, haven't you? Now it would not be a bad idea if you were to marry her, don't you think? After all, you must wed soon, and an heiress, and a nice quiet girl who would give you no trouble –'

'India, for God's sake,' Arthur said, gripping her hand tighter. 'I don't want to talk about Clover, or marriage. I want you. You know how much I want you. Will you let me tonight? For God's sake, I'm fretting my bowels to fiddle-strings over you. What more do you want?'

'No, darling, not tonight. Arthur! Don't hold my hand so tight, you're hurting me! No, listen to me. I can't tonight. Not yet. You know how easily I get with child.'

'Well, when, then?'

'Not yet,' India said crossly. 'Lord, I do my best for you. You like what we do, don't you?'

'You know I do, but I want you properly. It's killing me, this business of half –'

'Hush, no more, or I shall get cross,' India said, frowning. 'I shall tell you when. Don't annoy me, or it will be never. Now smile a little – people are wondering.'

That night India sat on the edge of the big bed in the great bed-chamber, her eyes closed with suffering, a cold cloth held against her forehead. Matt looked down at her with concern, and she smiled faintly.

'I'll be all right, darling,' she said. 'It's too much wine and too much dancing. You know these headaches of mine.' Matt sat down beside her and stroked her hand gently.

'My poor darling. It was too much for you, so soon after little Robert.' He looked at her flushed face and closed eyes for a moment, and then said, 'Shall I sleep in the bachelor's wing tonight, so that you can get a really good, quiet night's sleep? It won't take me a minute to get a bed made up.'

India opened her eyes and smiled tremulously at him. 'Oh darling, you are so good to me. You know, I think I really would like just to be alone tonight. I think it would do me such good.' She lifted his hand to her lips, and her eyes shone with a trace of moisture. 'You're so kind to me. I don't deserve it.'

'Of course you do, darling,' Matt said. He drew her to him and kissed her forehead. 'You mean everything to me, and your health is my greatest concern. Sleep late tomorrow morning. I'll give instructions that you are not to be disturbed, and you can send Millicent for your breakfast when you wake.'

When the house was quiet at last, India slipped on a loose robe and went out through the dressing room, where Millicent was sleeping on the truckle bed, down the chapel stairs and into the steward's room. The fire was still glowing red, and its glow threw the dark shadow of the man upwards and made his face a clown's mask.

'All serene?' he asked.

'Perfect,' she said, and walked into his embrace. She felt the hard, barrel-shaped body under her hands, smelt the warm, male odour of him, tasted the sweet pungency of his tongue in her mouth. Red and dark the room closed round her like a womb, and she abandoned herself to the ecstasy of her growing desire. After a long time, however, she said, 'No.'

'What do you mean, no?' She could not see his face, but she heard the cynical smile in his voice.

'Not everything. Not yet. I get with child so easily. Besides, there is plenty of time.'

'Is there?' he asked with the same, lazy humour. She felt uncomfortably as though he had known everything she was going to say before she even came into the room.

'Well, isn't there?' she countered, a little tartly. 'After

154

all, if you want me so much, there are ways to arrange things. Here, in York, in London, in Northumberland. Unless you are too devoted to that fat old wife of yours.'

The hands on her breasts moved lazily up to her throat and gripped a little, and there was threat in the gesture, though the voice did not change. 'We are not here to discuss my wife,' he said.

'*I* know that,' she said. 'But do you? If you want me, you can have me – but in my own time.'

'And on your terms,' he said, and chuckled, as though it were not at all a settled thing who should decide the terms. He thrust his tongue into her mouth again, and then said, with the dark laughter still in his voice, 'Oh but you smell of bitch, my lovely, so I'll take my chances. I'll have you.'

India surrendered again to his attentions, though with a faint feeling of uneasiness in her mind, that things had not gone quite as she meant them to. He ought to be the suppliant, deeply grateful that someone as rich, as beautiful, as high in society, should condescend to him, yet it was almost as if *he* had had the last word. But there was a powerful fascination about him. Her mind was wary, but her body wanted him, and as long as she could control him, it would be all right.

The first year of the war ended when winter closed the campaigning season in the Low Countries, and Karellie went to spend Christmas in Venice, where Maurice had promised him 'the maddest celebration of his life'. Maurice had taken his pupil Giulia from the Pieta in October and married her, and they were both still living at the Palazzo Francescini, with the duke and his daughter, and Maurice's daughter Alessandra. Karellie was greeted with a warmth which made him realize, by the sheer contrast, how lonely his life was.

'So how is the soldiering going?' Maurice asked him cheerfully.

'Inconclusively,' Karellie said with a shrug. 'We neither win nor lose. Sieges, withdrawals, tactics. Nothing like the great cavalry charges of our grandfather. I tell you Maurice, soldiering is not what it was.'

'I dare say men have been saying that since time began,' Maurice smiled. 'At least one thing is the same, however – you have your winters to yourself. I hope you may be able to stay for the Carnival, to hear my new opera.'

'Is it good? Are you pleased with it?' Karellie asked.

'Yes, and yes, but I don't know how the public will like it. It is not like what they are used to. But we must develop, we must explore. I please my patrons with their little bits and pieces for their banquets and birthdays, but meanwhile –' His eyes grew distant. 'The problem, you see, is that the strings are so crude, it is difficult to do anything but make a noise with them, and the harpsichord continuo has too little scope. I am reshaping the orchestra, Karel – flutes, oboes, bassoons, even trumpets – they will all play their part.'

'Yes?' said Karellie helpfully, and Maurice laughed.

'You don't know what I'm talking about, do you? But look, here is a page of my new piece. Now, you see, instead of two threads making their own patterns, regardless of each other, as they would in polyphonic music, we have two threads – melody and harmony – running along together, supporting, blending, entwining.' He looked at his brother, his eyes bright. 'Like making love to a woman, Karel, think of it. One presses, the other yields!'

'Now you are talking a soldier's language,' Karellie laughed. 'It all looks very complicated.'

'It is,' Maurice said, 'but exhilarating! It's like driving a four-horse chariot – sometimes you wonder whether the whole thing won't run away with you, but when you have control, you feel such a sense of power!' He turned the page, reading it, hearing it in his mind. Then he glanced up at his brother, seeing him left out. 'Of course,' he said dismissively, 'my former father-in-law maintains that counterpoint is the only true music. He's as stubborn as a mule. But he sent me such a kind letter when I married Giulia.'

'How is she? Are you happy with her?' Karellie asked shyly. Maurice touched the music lightly with his fingertips, as if he was touching her face.

'She is lovely, and such a help to me. She can play any instrument, you know, and read what I write on sight. If I am not sure of a passage, I have her to come and play it for me.'

'And you love her?'

Maurice cocked his head a little, not sure what Karellie meant by the question. Then he said, 'You should get married yourself, brother. It's high time you got an heir. There are so many lovely women in Venice, we must see if we can't get you fixed up before you leave for the wars again. There will be no shortage of candidates, once the news is passed that the Marechal Comte de Chelmsford is here!'

But Karellie only looked awkward. 'No, Maurice – don't. I couldn't. I –'

'What is it, brother?' Maurice asked gently. 'Why, you love women – and they love you. That's obvious.'

Karellie shook his head. He had no words to explain how he felt about women, how they frightened him, with their soft, powerful bodies, their dark, closed, treacherous minds; how he made himself free from their dark, cobwebby, clinging magic by shutting his heart and mind tight away while he conquered their bodies. With camp-followers or prostitutes, with children or old women, he felt safe, but all the others –

Maurice, seeing he could not or would not explain, took pity on him and changed the subject again. 'Did you know mother is talking again of rebuilding Shawes? You know that she went home to England?'

'Yes,' Karellie said abruptly. 'I had heard.'

'Oh Karellie, why do you mind so much?' Maurice asked, unlucky again in his choice of subject.

'It's a betrayal – of everything,' Karellie said, his face averted. Maurice looked at him helplessly.

'You're so *absolute*,' he said. 'It doesn't do.' Karellie turned abruptly.

'*You* wouldn't do it,' he said.

'You're wrong – I might, I might easily. Perhaps one day I will.' But there was no use in talking about that. Maurice said cheerfully, 'Now you must come up and see the children, or I shall be in trouble with them both. Alessandra has been practising to say your name all day, and I must get you to her before she forgets it –'

On Twelfth Night they exchanged the traditional gifts, and Karellie waited until last of all to give his to little Diane. He had scoured the markets of every town in Flanders for the right thing, and now as he watched her unwrap the red silk parcel, he was as nervous as if he had been choosing a gift for a mistress. It was a necklace of flat silver links overlaid with deep blue enamel, leaving a clear pattern of flowers in the centre of each link. She looked at it for so long he thought he must have got it disastrously wrong, but then she looked up at him. She did not smile, but she gave him one flashing blue glance that went straight to his heart.

'Put it on me, my lord Earl,' she said, standing up and presenting him with her back. He had to kneel down to manage the job, and when he had fastened it, he kissed the downy nape of her neck. The child span round with a disconcerted look which she quickly changed to one of scornful fury.

'You take liberties, sir,' she cried. Karellie managed to keep a straight face though it amused and touched him to see this child of seven aping the fine ladies of the city.

'I beg your pardon, Principessa. You must forgive me, for it is your beauty which overpowers me.'

She smiled at once – a child's smile – and held out her hand. 'I forgive you.'

'Then I am emboldened to ask for a favour. Will you sing for me?'

The duke, watching from his fireside chair, laughed and clapped his hands. 'You have the way to her heart there, my lord! She has been making ready a song for you ever since we knew you were coming. Yes, yes, sing for us, *cara*.'

'Maurice, you must accompany me,' Diane said imperiously, taking up her stance at the side of the harpsichord, and Maurice slipped obligingly into the seat and waited for her nod. It was a delightful song, and Diane's voice was very pure and clear, but most of all it was the look of her that he knew he would never forget; the way she stood, so erect and proud, her hands clasped just above her waist, her head flung a little back, with the candlelight making her reddish hair pure gold.

When it was finished she turned to Karellie so eagerly, childlike once more, and said, 'Well, sir, what did you think of my performance?'

'It was more than wonderful. It was divine,' he said. 'I shall call you that if I may – the Divine Diane.'

She was pleased, and laughed, and put her hand up to touch the necklace. 'I liked your gift,' she said. 'You must come next Christmas too.'

Her father laughed at that and said, 'What, so mercenary, so young? Invite him for himself, little one, not for his gifts.'

Karellie, watching her face, saw she was hurt, and knew she had not meant it like that, and said quickly, 'If you command it, Principessa, I shall come. I shall come every year if I can.'

She nodded and smiled, looking at him with shining eyes. The duke said heartily, 'Perhaps you will marry him, little one, when you grow up.'

Now she was baited too far, and she swung round on her father, angry and hurt. 'I shall *never* marry!' she cried passionately. 'I shall be a great singer!'

It was Twelfth Night, the night of prophecy, Karellie

159

remembered, and he shivered with a brief and sudden foreboding.

'Sing again for us, Principessa,' he said. 'Sing us something that Maurice has written.'

Soothed, she took up her stance once more, tall for her age in her straight-skirted, white lace gown. If I had married when Berwick did, Karellie thought, I might have had a daughter like this by now. But already he felt less lonely.

New Year's day was so fine and soft, so perfect for scent, that everyone in the family turned out for it, even Sabine, who was heaved by main force on to the back of a stout, weight-carrying mare, and was immensely proud of it.

'I hear Queen Anne follows the hunt in a two-wheel chariot, now she is too fat to ride,' she shouted, her voice ringing round the yard. 'Well, I am near ten years older than she, but I can still get myself across the back of a horse, eh, husband? We'll shew these striplings a thing or two!'

India, resplendent in dark hunting green, with a hat two feet across and almost obscured by feathers, curled her lip at this speech from her vulgar aunt, but Francomb, not yet mounted, walked across to his wife, placed his hand over her foot, and smiled up at her.

'Why aye, hinny, we'll shew 'em. They have no hunting here to compare with Blindburn. This is chasing butterflies on a bowling green, next to our hunting at home.' And Sabine looked down at him with grateful affection, and sat up straighter on her hairy-legged horse, feeling the pressure of his big hand on her ankle long after he had gone to mount up.

India rode at the head of the procession beside Matt, and their two horses, almost identical except that Matt's had a white star, and India's one white coronet, matched their steps and arched their necks so that they danced along with their muzzles almost touching, their bridle ornaments ringing together and striking fire from the early sun. Matt's eyes were on his wife, admiring the grace of her carriage, the long arc of her neck, the bright colour of her cheeks, brushed now and then by a drooping feather from her preposterous hat. Last night – the memory of last night warmed him down to his toes – last night they had resumed married relations. He had been hesitant, though longing for her. He had said, 'My darling, are you not afraid you will get with child? It is so soon after little Robert. I can wait if I must –'

But she had put her fingers over his lips and drawn her to him, whispering, 'Oh my dear husband, I am in God's hand. If He wills it, so be it. But I cannot endure any longer without you.'

It had been a wonderful night, and this morning – just look at her! The love she had for him made her brilliant, he thought. Bright as a peacock, darting like a swallow, the centre of attention, her ready wit, her laughter, her beauty, drawing all eyes. And she was his! he crowed inwardly. Midnight and Star danced along, lifting their forelegs high, carrying their tails like banners.

India turned to meet his gaze, and said, 'Husband, I have been thinking. Now that Clover is fifteen, it is good time that she should be married, don't you think?'

Matt smiled inwardly, and said, 'What made you think of that so suddenly?'

'It is not sudden. I have been watching her all this Christmas. I was wed at fifteen, my love, and have not regretted it for one moment. And I have thought of the perfect scheme – she should marry your cousin Arthur!' She waited, pleased, for his reaction. He turned it over in his mind, and she prompted his consideration. 'She has a fortune, but comes from an obscure family –'

'The Ailesburys are a very respectable and old family in their own country,' Matt said. India went on as if he had not spoken.

'And Arthur has a title and a coat of arms, but no estate, and as far as I can see, no income at all, other than what he earns. It is not fitting that Lord Ballincrea should have to earn his living. If he married Clover, he would not have to, and she would be Viscountess Ballincrea.' She stopped with the air of one who has just uncovered a treasure to public gaze. Matt grinned.

'She'd like that,' he said. 'I suppose any woman would. Well, it is a good scheme, I give you, and it is kind of you to concern yourself with my family –'

'My family too, now. Your concerns are mine, dearest husband.'

'– but you know, I am not Clover's guardian. Clovis is. But I shall put it to him, never fear. I'll speak to him later today.'

India leaned closer. 'Do not say it was my idea, husband. Put it to him as your own thought. I would not have him think I am impertinent. I have the greatest horror of impertinence.'

'My modest darling,' Matt smiled. 'Very well, I shall put it to him as my idea, first and last.'

The hunt was fast and furious, for the scent was good and the ground firm, and the family was soon well spread out, the first flight out of sight of the tailenders. Matt somehow got separated from India, and he did not know how that could have happened, for he had had his eye on her almost every moment. It must have been when we crossed the stream and had to jump that thicket of furze, he decided. She must have struck her own line through the trees and got parted from us. They lost the stag in the trees somewhere, and when they came out on the other side they halted to breathe the horses.

Matt walked Star round in circles, for he was sweating and Matt did not want him to get cold, while keeping an eye out for the rest of the field. Sabina broke from the trees on the chestnut he had lent her for the day, and came cantering over to him. She was in stout black, with a small hat with a curly brim, her one flash of colour a crimson feather that turned over the brim and round her ear. She was growing up, he realized, and growing into an attractive young woman. He halted Star as she came up, and the two horses touched noses, and Star put his head down to graze.

'Having a good run?' he asked her cheerfully. She nodded, making the feather bob. 'I'm glad to see you have kept up with us. We seem to have lost my wife – I hope she is all right. I am thinking of sending one of the servants to look for her before we set off. She may forget where we are going to draw.'

Sabina looked at him rather oddly, he thought. Was it strange to be concerned for his wife's safety?

'She's quite all right, I'm sure,' Sabina said. 'I saw her a while ago. She had Master Francomb with her –'

'Oh, well, he'll take care of her,' Matt said. 'He's a fine huntsman.'

'Yes,' Sabina said, still with that strange look. She leaned forward to him across her saddle. 'Matt –' she began hesitantly. He raised an eyebrow. 'Matt, I –'

'Yes, Sabina, what is it?'

She bit her lip, and then shook her head. 'No, nothing. Never mind it.' Matt looked at her with concern for a moment, and then reached over and patted her hand. Whatever was worrying her, he supposed she would tell it in her own time.

'I think the horses have got their wind. Shall we go on and draw the high coppice? Ride beside me, little cousin, do. I do not feel right with an empty place there.'

'Will you send a servant back?' Sabina asked in a small voice.

'Oh no. If you say Francomb is with her, I shan't worry. He'll take care of her.'

CHAPTER NINE

In February 1703 Annunciata gave a dinner at Chelmsford
House. It reminded her a little of the early days at St
Germain, for all the guests were male, and all united by
one common interest; though this time the interest was
not soldiering but architecture, for the Countess of Chelmsford had at last made the firm decision to rebuilt her house
at Shawes. She had invited her old friend Christopher
Wren, now head of the Queen's Board of Works, to dinner
to discuss the matter, and from those small beginnings the
thing had developed. It happened that Wren's second-in-
command at the Office of Works, Sir John Vanbrugh, was
in London for the season, and Wren suggested that he
come along too. Annunciata then thought of inviting Henry
Wise, the royal gardener, to be in on the discussions;
Vanbrugh, on receiving his invitation, said he would bring
along Nicholas Hawksmoor, who was also in London.

At the same time Annunciata received a letter from
Clovis saying that he wanted to come up and discuss the
possibility of a marriage between Arthur and Clover, and
that he would bring Arthur to London, as Annunciata had
not yet met him since her return from exile. They made
another two guests at what was becoming a definite
Occasion; last to be invited was Henry Aldrich, Dean of
Christ Church, whom Annunciata met in the Park. She
knew him slightly, and on his enquiring kindly after
Arthur, she remembered that it was by his patronage that
Arthur had been made respectable, and that he was a
distinguished amateur of architecture. She began telling
him of her plans, and ended by inviting him to dinner.

First, however, there was the meeting with Clovis and
Arthur to be got over. They arrived in the early afternoon
of the day before the dinner, and Annunciata thought at

once that Clovis was looking drawn and fagged. He was unnaturally pale, even though it was still winter, and there was a line of fatigue etched about his lips. She made him sit down at once by the fire, and herself drew off his riding boots, in spite of his protests, and sent for hot wine for him.

He smiled wearily at her and said, 'I shall be well enough, Countess. Let me but rest a while.'

'They have worn you out over Christmas,' Annunciata said, leaving him and sitting in her own chair. 'You should have stayed here with me, and been quiet. You forget you are no longer a young man.' Clovis smiled more broadly.

'How can I think myself not young, when I am younger than you, and you are the most perennially young of women?'

'Oh, hush!' Annunciata said. 'Bring forward that young man lurking by the door and present him. I think he has had his fill of staring.'

Clovis beckoned to Arthur, who had been standing quietly at the door, and indeed had been staring, for the Countess, his grandmother, was a legendary figure to him, and he could hardly believe that she had substance in reality. She stood up as he came across the room: he saw a tall woman, whose face was of such beauty it was impossible to associate it with great age, though he knew she must be old. Her hair, dressed without lace or flowers, was curled on the top of her head and fell in a tail of curls behind, and was as black as a young woman's; her eyes, large and very dark, were bright and gave her face a look of youthfulness and vitality; her features were fine, proud and stern, her lips full and soft-looking in a way that would have told him, had he been a student of physionomy, that her nature was passionate. There were diamonds at her throat – part of his mind calculated their value with respect – that glittered with many-coloured fire against the white skin of her neck and breast. Her dress was of deep crimson velvet, simply and richly cut, the skirt divided and drawn back to reveal the petticoat beneath of quilted crimson silk embroidered with gold threads. From the heavy lace of her sleeve ends her forearms emerged, white and smooth and innocent of jewellery. He was used to rich women displaying their wealth in a multiplicity of bracelets and rings, and the nakedness of her arms and hands was strangely affecting – both innocent and sensuous. She disturbed him, and he did not understand enough about people to know why she disturbed him. All the same it subdued his normal arrogance, and he approached her with a quiet humility. He had intended to salute her with a hearty kiss and call her grandmama: but that was before he saw her. Faced with her, he gave her involuntarily the respect he had not thought he would bestow on her.

'My lady, may I present Arthur, Viscount Ballincrea; your grandson,' Clovis said genially. Arthur made his leg, with a deep flourish, and then, finding this was not enough, went down on to one knee and remained there until Annunciata bid him rise. She studied him as he came across the room, seeing a tall young man – not as tall as Karellie, but an inch or two higher than most men all the same – of considerable girth and weight, dressed in good, though not extreme, fashion, with a blond periwig that hung over his shoulders but not all the way down his back.

The face – she did not recognize the face. She studied it for something of her own, or something of her son Hugo's, but he was entirely a stranger. She supposed he must look like someone on Caroline's side of the family. He was plump and fair with pale eyes and light eyelashes: she guessed that his own hair would be blond with a pinkish tinge, for he had freckles around his eyes and that indefinable look of gingerishness to his pale skin. He was entirely a stranger, and she felt a surge of great relief pass through her.

Her first husband, Hugo, had inflicted a great hurt on her when she was very young, and she had never forgotten or forgiven it. She had come to hate him; she had hated the two children that she had borne him, Arabella and Hugo; she had thought that she must hate Hugo's son Arthur.

But there was nothing of either Hugo or herself in Arthur, and it was as if a troublesome ghost had been laid. She was prepared to like, even to favour, this heavy young man in the sheer relief of being released from that burden of hate.

'Sit down and be easy, sir, I am glad to see you,' she said. Arthur took a chair between her and Clovis, and Annunciata continued, 'Well, let us to business. Clovis proposes a marriage between you, Lord Ballincrea, and Mary Celia Ailesbury, who is his ward. What have you to say to that?'

Arthur was startled by the abrupt turn to business, and could only stammer, 'I – I – have no great objection, my lady – but –' Annunciata dismissed him with a glance and turned to Clovis.

'Have you spoken to either of them? Have you thought about settlements?'

Clovis smiled. 'You go so fast, Countess! I am hardly coming to terms with the thought of my little one being old enough to marry, and you have them parcelled up and dispatched in two minutes.' Annunciata laughed at that, and Arthur saw how beautiful she must once have been.

'Very well, I accept your reproof. But my dear Clovis, if it must be done, by all means let it be done quickly. I have not a man's love of lingering over business. If you will let the girl go, and they neither of them have any great objection, then I will give it my blessing. And since the girl has a great deal, and Arthur nothing but his name, I will make a settlement on him, so that he will not be ashamed. Arthur, I have a house and a small estate in Kendal, and it seems to me that it would be appropriate for you to have property in the same country as your wife. If you marry Clover, I shall give you that estate, and you may do as you please with it.'

'Your ladyship is generous,' Arthur said. He thought briefly of India, but it was hard to keep her in mind in the presence of the Countess. He did not care about Clover one way or the other, but a man must marry, and all his life he had longed for an estate. If he pleased the Countess, perhaps she would make him her heir. He smiled carefully at her. 'I am your ladyship's servant. Whatever you decide, I will abide by.'

The Countess gave him a thoughtful, penetrating look, and then turned to Clovis. 'Well, then, cousin, it is up to you. Shall we make a bargain? You must give her up some time, you know – best swallow the draft quickly and have it done.'

She extended her long white hand, and it was made rosy on one side by the firelight. Clovis seemed to look at it for a long time, and then he straightened in his chair and extended his own, and they clasped. The two hands seemed to hover, disembodied, in the afternoon gloom of the room, white against the dark Turkey carpet and the red-gold flames of the fire.

The dinner-party was a most successful occasion, and Arthur was forced to see how elegantly things could be managed by someone whose taste equalled their wealth. It could have been very difficult, one woman entertaining seven men: he imagined India doing it, and knew that it would have been very different. Annunciata talked to the men as an equal, without shyness, without flirtation, without reserve. Her mind was as good as theirs, her education better than some, and yet there was no challenge in her manner. She was frank and easy, and with all that, perfectly feminine. She was dressed all in white, white satin with a white lace over-dress, the skirts held back by large pink artificial roses, the bodice sewn with pearls and crystal spars, the same diamonds at her throat, her dark hair dressed high with pearls. She sat at the end of the table, like a snow-queen; Aldrich was on her left, Kit Wren on her right, and when she laughed or spoke to them, they bent forward like trees stirring in an unseen wind.

The food was simple and elegant, the table service restrained and magnificent. The table was lit by three great silver candelabra, each holding eight candles, and they sat in a pool of light surrounded by darkness that grew as the afternoon closed into night. When they had done eating, they all retired to the drawing-room while the table was cleared, and then went back to spread out plans upon its surface and talk and point and discuss. Arthur felt as though he was in a dream, at the centre of which sat the black and white and glittering figure of the snow-queen. Against the dark mahogany of the table her naked white forearms gleamed as she pointed to some detail of her plan. The men grew heated and argued, not angrily, but passionately. She called Wren 'Kit', and Vanbrugh 'Van'; they wrangled, Kit for his own brand of restrained elegance, Van for the sumptuous Palladian splendour, and the latter called on Hawksmoor and Arthur to support him.

'Castle Howard – it will be most of all a *feminine* palace,' he cried, 'now won't it, Ballincrea? Support me, man! Does not your ladyship desire to be cradled in a voluptuous white temple, suitable to your beauty?'

'Does my ladyship?' Annunciata said. 'I don't know that she does. Remember Van, I am Yorkshire born and bred. Grey stone and harsh lines are in my blood.'

Wren picked her up eagerly. 'But of course, that is what I have been trying to tell these amateurs,' he cried. 'A building must look as though it has grown out of the place where it stands. Yorkshire –'

'The Plain of York, remember,' Vanbrugh broke in. 'Hardly harsh country, Kit. Green and fertile.'

'A feminine palace will not do for Lady Chelmsford,' Aldrich entered the discussion. 'Beauty, great beauty, wants a frame, a setting – not a rival beauty. Her palace must stand guardian over her, strong, serene, not sprawl like a courtesan.'

Annunciata threw Aldrich a look of amusement and interest and sympathy to which he replied with a slight bow and a dark glance of enquiry. Vanbrugh picked up the argument again, and the talk went on, ebbing and flowing like the candle-shadows, while the watchful servants came and went with wine and biscuits, tended the fires, trimmed the candles. At length they all retired again to the drawing-room, with the decision made that they would draw up their rival designs for the Countess's approval, one from Aldrich and Wren, one from Vanbrugh, Hawksmoor and Ballincrea. In either case, Henry Wise would lay out the gardens for her. The conversation turned to other matters, the war, Court gossip, such as it was, politics, horse-racing. At last Wren called for his coach and left, offering transport to Vanbrugh and Hawksmoor, and Wise called for a link-boy and walked across the park. Clovis, claiming to be, and looking, dead-tired, retired to bed, and Arthur, feeling *de trop*, made his bow too. As he left, he looked back, and saw the Countess and Aldrich standing by the fireside, both leaning on the chimney wall with one foot on the fender like mirror-images of each other. He closed the door and went to bed, his head whirling with new ideas. He had the feeling that something enormously important had happened to him that night, but he could not yet tell what it was.

Matters proceeded smoothly. Clovis rose from his bed the following day determined to go through with the giving away of his ward, and the lawyers were called in to draw up the marriage settlements. Annunciata, as promised, gave her Kendal property to Arthur and to his heirs got lawfully upon the body of Mary Celia Ailesbury. The contract was drawn up: the whole of Clover's property passed to Arthur as her dowry; an annual income from Arthur's newly-acquired property was settled on her in return; the contract was signed by Arthur, and by Clovis on Clover's behalf, and the thing was done.

Clovis then proposed to go back to Morland Place to acquaint Clover with her fate and to prepare for the wedding, which he said might as well take place in March since there was nothing to wait for. Arthur left at the same time for the Lake country to inspect his new property and determine whether there was a house suitable for the receiving of his bride, and Annunciata continued to pore over the plans for the new house. She would make her first visit to Morland Place for the wedding, and remain in Yorkshire for the rest of the spring and summer to see the building started – if she could get her architects to agree on something by the beginning of March.

Clovis wrote from Morland Place a week or so later to say that there was a very small hitch, in that India was suffering from the strain and worry of running the great household and had accepted Matt's advice to go away for a month. She was to stay at Emblehope for a complete rest, and the wedding would have to be postponed until she returned in April. Annunciata wrote back that April was by far a better month for a wedding, and that Wren and Vanbrugh were slowly finding a compromise for her house, and that Henry Aldrich had invited her to go and stay in Oxford for a week or two, and that she would be glad for the change to accept his invitation and would travel on to Morland Place from there.

'I am sure he has an unspoken reason for asking me,' she added. 'He must have seen my name on the list of subscribers for Dean Fell's additions to the buildings, and since he will soon be collecting subscriptions for his own proposed improvements, he will no doubt want to make sure of my sympathy.'

But Chloris, as she packed Annunciata's trunks, shook her head doubtfully. Dean Aldrich was a charming and gentle man, she thought, but she had hoped that in the years since Martin's death, the Countess had learned better sense than to become involved with charming and gentle men. There was no doubt that the Countess was looking younger and happier since that dinner party, and that she had taken to singing in her bath, something she had not done for fifteen years.

India came back from Emblehope in radiant good health, and greeted Matt with such excitement and affection that he knew at once that his endurance of her absence was rewarded.

'You enjoyed yourself then, my dearest?' he asked her wistfully. India put his hand to her lips and looked at him with shining eyes.

'Enjoyed myself? Well, as much as I could enjoy myself, away from you. I missed you so terribly, dear husband, but I am feeling so much more rested and strong. I'm sure it was worth the loneliness. And I have had long talks with your aunt Sabine and all the ladies of her acquaintance about the wedding and the Countess's visit. You can't imagine how terrified I have been, husband, thinking of such an eminent visitor, and wondering what one was to do about it. But I have collected good advice, and some interesting receipts, and I think now I shall be able to do you credit.'

And to prove how well she was feeling, she plunged herself into a frenzy of preparation which flattened everyone in the house like the passing of a great wind. Her energy was boundless, for as well as preparing the house and the food, she had endless sessions with dressmakers, both on her own behalf and Clover's, harried the gardeners from corner to corner over the floral decorations and fresh fruit and vegetables, arranged for all manner of entertainers and singers to come up to the house to be interviewed by Matt with a view to providing the Countess with the kind of entertainment she would have come to expect in her stratum of society, and still had the time to go riding with Matt by day, and make passionate love to him by night. Matt became accustomed to the bemused expressions on everyone's faces, and knew that his own was just as bemused, if tempered by rapture. The only person who was not swept up by India's energy was Clover, who seemed miserable and withdrawn, and managed to disappear for the greater part of every day. When she was cornered and driven into the great bedchamber for a fitting of her wedding clothes, she went with no enthusiasm, and

India had to provide for her the excitement she felt a bride ought to feel.

'Lord Ballincrea – such a distinguished young man – such a fine old title – so handsome – such a wonderful dress – really you are the luckiest of girls!' she would cry, and construe Clover's silence as assent.

On the day before the Countess's arrival, the house was finally ready, and everyone sank into grateful immobility, like autumn leaves released by the wind to settle to earth again. After a few hours in the evening of sitting in silence, everyone drifted off to bed early. Clovis sat up alone in the steward's room, pretending to do some work and in fact merely staring into the fire, too weary even to think. He went through into the chapel for half an hour to make his devotions and to try to bring himself to a more peaceful state of mind, so that he would sleep, and when he returned he saw the steward's room door open, and went in to find Clover, with a wrapper over her night clothes, sitting in his chair, waiting for him.

The sight of her, looking just as she always had done, round childish face and golden head, bent over his desk as if she were going to write out his purchases for him – the familiar sight of her moved him almost to tears. She looked up as he appeared in the doorway, and for a moment they simply stared at each other; then he saw her lip begin to tremble, and he crossed the room in a swift stride to gather her in his arms, to sit in his own chair and draw her on to his lap as he had done so many times since she was a little, little girl. She put her arms round his neck and rested her face on his shoulder, and for a long time they sat in silence.

At last he pulled his handkerchief out of his sleeve and pushed it into her hand, and she straightened up and blew her nose and wiped her eyes carefully, and then rested her damp hot cheek against his and stared with him into the dying fire.

'It won't be so bad, you know,' Clovis said after a while. 'You will find you enjoy having a household to run. You'll have your own servants and horses and you will be able to have anything you like to eat, and go visiting your friends in a fine carriage.'

She didn't answer, and he knew that was not it. It was having to marry Arthur – but what could he say to that? He had known women terrified of being married who had enjoyed it afterwards. Others had thought of it with distaste and come to accept it, though liking it no better. What could he say? In any case, there was nothing to be done about it. Blunderingly, he continued reassuring her.

'You'll have children, of course, and that will be nice –'

'Nice?' she said in what sounded like astonishment.

'And once you have an heir, or perhaps two, you need not –' Impossible to go on. He held her tighter, and she turned her face to kiss his cheek. His little girl, his little, golden, grey-eyed girl.

Her lips pressed again and again to his cheek, as if she did not know how to leave off; she said, between kisses, with desperate passion, 'Oh, I wish I could marry *you*!'

He wished it too, but he said, 'That is how children talk, Clover; a child wants to marry her father –'

'I love *you*,' she said with a child's clear simplicity. 'All I want is to be able to stay with you. Why can't I?'

It was not a question to which she expected any answer: it was the more heart-breaking because he knew she accepted the unkind fate as a child accepts the edicts of adults, not liking them, but not questioning them. In the end he could only rise up and walk upstairs with her in silence, and kiss her goodnight at the door to her room. He saw her in, and then went away to his own narrow bed, his shoulders stooped with more weariness than one day's.

It was a true April day when Annunciata came back at last to Morland Place; a high blue sky, filled with billowy white clouds with half-hidden dark edges; a day of hypocritical sunshine and sudden, capricious rain. She came by coach, for she had not yet a riding horse on which she would care to go two hundred miles, and despite the rain showers she kept the window down all the way so that her view was unimpeded. She knew the moment when she came on to Morland land; she would have known it, she felt, if her eyes had been closed. The very grass seemed to smell different; the bird calls and the sound of the running brooks, spring-swollen, seemed interspersed with the whispering voices of ghosts, human and animal, the ghosts of her childhood and young womanhood. Chloris and Birch and Dorcas sat in sympathetic silence, their eyes turned tactfully away. Annunciata longed to speak, or to sing, or to shout, to release the pressure inside her head, but the swelling silence was too great. She was dumb with feeling too much, remembering too much.

It looked the same, but different. The trees had all grown, yet many things seemed smaller than she remembered. The track was narrower and rougher, but it seemed further from the road to the house than her memory had told her.

When they were still out of sight of the house the coach bumped to a halt, and Chloris, leaning out of the window, said quietly, 'Someone has come to meet you, my lady. I'd say it was Master Matt. I'd know him anywhere.'

Annunciata nodded, and Chloris reached up to tap on the coach roof, and in a moment Daniel had opened the door and put down the step, and Gifford was there to hand her out on to the grass. The sunlight seemed dazzling after the coach, the air smelled too bright, and there a little way off was a manservant holding a handsome black colt with one white star – unmistakably a Morland horse, she thought, and her Morland heart craved such a horse for herself – and coming towards her was her grandson James Matthias – Martin's son.

She had prepared herself for the meeting, but found herself quite unprepared in the face of his reality. He was taller than Martin had been – Clovis had said he had taken to growing again – and about two inches taller than herself. He had swept off his hat; he wore no wig, and she saw at once that the soft dark curls to his shoulders looked and would feel just like Martin's. He bowed low, and straightened up, and she had to force her fingers to uncurl from each other so that she could extend her hand to him. He came close and took it, and bowed over it, with the nicely adjusted manners Father St Maur would have taught him – courtly, but not flamboyant.

He was Martin's child; there was nothing, she saw with triumph, of Arabella in him, except perhaps for that extra height. Everything of his face was Martin's, except for the eyes, and they, though dark blue as Martin's had been, were like her own, like her own father's. Yes, there was Rupert's blood in this boy. He smiled a welcome at her and said something – she was too distracted to understand what – and continued to survey her with a frank and open satisfaction.

That was the puzzling thing – the expression of the eyes. There was in them a childlike innocence that did not go well with his manly size and bearing. Martin's eyes had been filled with humour, wisdom, and wit from the time he was fourteen. At fifteen he had taken over his father's business and run it with quiet power and discretion. But James Matthias was almost nineteen and twice-over a father, as well as Master of Morland Place, and yet his eyes were the eyes of a child.

The right things were said, Annunciata got back into her carriage, and they set off again, with James Matthias riding alongside on his handsome black gelding. Annunciata puzzled a little, and then dismissed it, with the thought that whatever it was, it did at least curb the power that Martin's son might have had to hurt her.

The servants were all lined up in the great hall to receive the Countess. Many of them were known to her, some old friends who had said goodbye to her fourteen years ago, others were new, strange faces with familiar names, the children of former servants and villagers. Clovis was there, and Arthur, and a pale, mouse-fair youth whom Annunciata had no difficulty in recognizing as Caroline's second son John Rathkeale. Father St Maur stood nearby, his eyes swimming with tears he did not bother to try to hide, and behind him nursery maids – could that really be little Flora? – holding the two lace-petticoated babies.

But those things could hardly be noticed, for the centre stage was taken by the three women, an older woman in a low widow's cap, evidently Mrs Neville – the 'pale, wispy thing' of Annunciata's memory – and Clover, looking suspiciously red-eyed, and the new mistress of Morland Place. Annunciata could not help staring. India was the epitome of fashion: her high-heeled shoes, whose rosetted toes peeped out from under her petticoat, made her taller than all the women and most of the men present; her petticoat was a mass of frills, as was the bodice of her over-gown, whose skirt was drawn back and tucked up with a cascade of ribbons; her sleeves drooped lace halfway to the floor; she had three patches on her handsome, high-coloured face; whose expression was fixed in a smile of welcome; and her hair was frizzed on top of her forehead in front of a lace fontage three stories high, with trailing lappets that fell to her waist, and a lace-and-ribbon decked cap behind with a huge butterfly bow. Such was India's self-confidence that for a moment as she bustled forward, Annunciata felt herself ridiculously under-dressed, and wanted to shrink under the shadow of the trembling lace tower that bore down on her.

'My *dear* Lady Chelmsford,' India cried, 'do let me welcome you to Morland Place – and indeed, to England, where you have been much missed all these years, let me assure you!'

The impertinence of this young woman in welcoming her, not only to the house which she herself had ruled for so many years, but to her own native land, quite took Annunciata's breath away, and she had taken the offered hand automatically under the influence of the fulsome smile before she knew what she was doing.

'You must look upon this house as your own, and stay here for just as long as you like. I promise you we shall be more than delighted to have you here. Indeed, we are quite hoping you will make it your home,' she added with a gay laugh and a glance at her husband. Annunciata, about to remark that it *was* her home, was arrested by the glance and the reception it received from Matt, who was watching his wife with an expression of almost lunatic adoration. So that was it! she thought. That was what kept this man a child. It was a situation that would bear watching, though she knew nothing against this young woman, by report or observation, except for self-conceit.

Her words were waited for in silence, and she said, 'Thank you, mistress Morland. I am glad to be home.' It was enough for the moment, set loose another flood of words from the young woman, allowed Annunciata time to look about her. In this hall she had received guests, Ralph at her side, with his great hounds, Bran and Fern. Dogs ought to have longer lives, she thought painfully. Her own Fand had been one of Fern's progeny. Once she had rebuked her daughter Arabella with the words, 'While I live, *I* will be mistress of Morland Place.' Oh, how are the mighty fallen, she thought wryly. But she was being introduced to various people who deserved her attention, while the new mistress chattered on.

'We have prepared the west bedroom for your ladyship, as some of the servants remembered that was the one you used to like when you were here – and now, here is Father St Maur, my sons' tutor, whom I am sure you remember.'

Now she simply had to say something. 'Father St Maur has been my chaplain, and tutor to my sons and grandsons, madam, since long before you were born.' No ceremony with her priest: his arms were round her like a father's loving embrace, and she rested her head against his shoulder for a moment, aware that his arms were trembling and that it was not just emotion that made them do so – it was age, too.

'I'm sure your ladyship would like to go to your room at once,' India was saying, no whit abashed by the snub, 'and then we shall have tea in the long saloon. Shall I have hot water sent up to your ladyship?'

In the west bedroom, alone with Chloris, Birch and Dorcas having remained below to give direction to the menservants about the luggage, Annunciata said, 'Is that creature really mistress of Morland Place? When I think of myself, of Mary Esther before me – even Mary Moubray – Chloris, can that deplorable young woman really have taken my place?'

'No, madam,' Chloris said easily. 'She may be the master's wife, but she cannot take your place as mistress.'

Annunciata looked gloomy. 'I'm afraid in the modern climate of things, it may come to the same. Oh dear, I shan't like staying here. The sooner Shawes is rebuilt the better – but then she'll be my neighbour, and will be forever calling on me.'

She flung her hands up in a gesture of comic dismay, and Chloris laughed and came across to help unlace her travelling dress.

'I can see why Birch didn't like her,' she said. 'Poor creature! She's very young, you know, and may well improve with age. After all, contact with your ladyship cannot but teach her something.'

'Ignorant and bold – and, sweet Mary, so remorselessly fashionable!' Annunciata said. 'I feel a hundred years old, Chloris. Oh long gone are the days when I led the fashion at Court! Do you remember when the outer circle used to copy my dresses and ornaments?'

'And painted their faces to try to look like you without paint,' Chloris said, glad to see that her mistress had retained her sense of humour at least.

'Do you think, if I asked her privately, Mistress India would give me advice on how to dress?'

'I should think she might even be capable of that,' Chloris said and the two women began to laugh, and the thought of Annunciata asking India's advice amused them so much that they laughed until they had to sit down weakly on the bed, and Annunciata's hair sprang loose from its pins. When Birch came in a little later with two maids bearing cans of hot water, they were still sitting there, red faced and bright eyed, and to Birch's dim vision the Countess looked younger and prettier than she did fourteen years ago when she had last sat on that bed.

The wedding went very well, and Annunciata could find nothing to fault, except that the bride's dress had obviously been chosen by the mistress of Morland Place. It was so decorated with ribbons, artificial flowers, frills and lace that Annunciata was reminded of a clothes-horse on which several people's best gowns had been hung; and the bride's fontange was so high that she overtopped her bridegroom and was in danger of catching light on the chandeliers. Arthur, however, was almost as frilled and ribboned himself, and his blond periwig hung over his shoulders and spread over his back down to his waist, and was decorated in the middle of the back with a large blue bow. He was evidently happy with the marriage, and cast India several looks of great triumph, which Annunciata intercepted with some puzzlement. He had inspected his new property and found it better than he had hoped; moreover his new neighbours in Westmorland were disposed to treat him with a flattering degree of respect, and he had already received two commissions to design new houses for people of quality in the Lake country, which he promised he would 'fit in with his commitments at Castle Howard'. His neighbours were left with the impression that he alone was designing and building the Earl of Carlisle's new palace, and were deeply grateful that the viscount was so affable as to spare them the time. Gentleman, landowner, viscount, architect, and possessor of a beautiful and docile wife: Arthur saw himself as very comfortably placed, and crowed over what he hoped was India's discomfort at finding herself no longer required by him.

After the ceremony came the feast and entertainments, and they ate to the accompaniment of music. India had acquired from somewhere a fine counter-tenor and a small orchestra, which she felt would strike the right, sophisticated note; after the feast there was dancing, and India positively banned any of the usual rumbustious country dances, and ordered the orchestra to play only Court dances, for she did not want the Countess to gain the impression that they did not know how things were done up here in Yorkshire. Annunciata found it all very tedious, for she had no one interesting to talk to, and was continually having to give polite praise, for which India's appetite was voracious.

The next day was better, however, for while the new couple were paying their formal visits, Annunciata begged to be taken to the stables and shewn the horses, and when India discovered that the Countess did not scorn riding and hunting, she gave orders for a hunt to be organized, and for a mount to be placed always at the Countess's disposal.

'I shall give myself the great pleasure of accompanying your ladyship,' India said, 'although I must take care not to ride over rough country.' She looked down with a becomingly modest blush. 'I think your ladyship may have guessed why. I am of great hopes that I may again be with child.'

Annunciata expressed her delight at the news – and indeed, it did argue a most convenient fertility – but begged India by no means to risk her health by riding with her. 'I have been riding over these fields since I was three years old madam, and am quite safe and happy riding alone, with a servant. You must take care of yourself, madam, I insist.' And India, delighted with the Countess's affability, allowed herself to be persuaded.

A visit to Shawes, in company with Clovis. The old house was partly in ruins, and much of the stone had been carted away by people to repair old buildings or begin new ones. 'You have left it too long,' Clovis said. 'A good job you have come back now, before it all disappears.' The bathing house was all right, except that some of the glass had been broken, and inside the rain had damaged some of the plaster-work. But otherwise 'the Countess's folly', as the villagers called it, had not suffered. She walked from one room to another, admiring anew, and remembering: with Martin she had planned it, watched its building, and he had teased her about it, and he seemed present there, more than at Morland Place.

'I'm glad this has survived,' she said. 'I will build the new house around it. And use the old stone for the new house. As Kit Wren says, a house must look as if it has grown from the ground it stands on. We will start at once, next week, if the men can be found.'

Clovis looked at her with amusement. 'You look like a child with a new toy,' he said. 'Can you really care after so long about a new house?'

She nodded slowly, looking about the ungrazed field where one day Henry Wise would lay her gardens. 'Life gives us nothing, Clovis, only takes away. But there are two things we can do to immortalize ourselves, two things that go on growing after we are dead. One is to have children, and the other is to build houses.'

'I have never done either,' Clovis said, and she saw with quick contrition that his face was bleak. He really had minded very much about losing Clover. She took his hand and pressed it.

'Morland Place owes more to you than to anyone,' she said. 'Without you, the family would have been lost. *That* is your immortality.' He smiled, but she could see he was not comforted. She drew his hand through her arm and walked with him, lifting her skirts clear of the long damp grass with the other hand. 'Tomorrow,' she said brightly, 'you shall take me to Twelvetrees and help me choose a horse. You promised me one of the good colts, Clovis, and I shan't let you fail me. *And* a dog. Has any of the good hounds whelped recently? I should fancy another blue like dear Fand, or what do you say to a brindle? You always had sound advice.'

That night as Chloris prepared her for bed, she said, 'We must devote more time to cheering Clovis. He has had so much work and worry and so little pleasure, and he of all people deserves to be happy now.'

'Yes, my lady.'

'And, Chloris, I have been wondering what happened to the Black Pearls. I don't see Miss India wearing them, as I

182

would have expected, though she does seem very fond of the Queen's Emeralds.'

'Ah, I heard about that from the servants, my lady,' Chloris said, coming closer and lowering her voice. 'It seems that everyone thinks the Black Pearls are lost, or have been stolen. There are rumours enough, and the favourite one is that someone conveyed them out of the house at the time of the Revolution and no one knows their hiding place. Thrown in the moat, one says, and down the well another, and a secret compartment in the outer wall yet another.'

Annunciata looked surprised. 'Have they not looked in the hiding place under the altar? I put them there myself during the siege.'

'I did not ask directly, my lady,' Chloris said, 'but by indirect questioning I gathered that no one knows about that place.'

'The priest – Father Cloud – saw me hide the things away, but he was killed, God rest his soul. Clement must have known about it, he was with the family so long, and his father was steward before him,' Annunciata said musingly.

'Well, my lady, if he knows, he has not said anything. But the altar furnishings are in place – someone must have got *them* out.'

'Martin would have done that as soon as it was safe. I suppose he didn't think about the Black Pearls.' She was thoughtful for a while. 'Well, I shan't say anything either. Let them stay where they are. They are safe enough – and I don't think I care for the idea of the present mistress wearing them. Do you think she would do them justice, Chloris?'

'No, my lady,' said Chloris. 'They are better where they are.'

CHAPTER TEN

They were happy days, happier than Annunciata had expected or hoped for when she came back from exile, and there was nothing she saw at Morland Place to distress her. Little Matt, despite that strange innocence which Annunciata had noticed, made a kind and industrious Master, erring if at all on the conscientious side, for there were things which he could well have left to underlings which he did or oversaw himself. India, who was pregnant again, was being a model wife and mistress, except for a predilection to fancy herself unwell. Twice during the summer she insisted that it was too hot at Morland Place and that her health demanded a trip away; once for a week in Harrogate to visit the baths and take the water, and once, during the hottest part of July, for three weeks in Northumberland. Annunciata, seeing her bloomingly healthy face drawn into an expression of patient suffering, decided that she was merely bored and wanting a change of scene, and on the whole could not blame her too heavily, for she herself had found childbearing at Morland Place tedious when she had been young.

The household settled down with its additional members very well, and Annunciata curbed her desire to interfere over things she would have preferred done otherwise. Mrs Clough was still housekeeper, Clement the steward, and Father St Maur the chaplain, and between them they secured a continuity from which matters deviated only in detail. Birch alone seemed unhappy, and withdrew into herself, grim and silent. She retreated to the nursery, where at least in the presence of Flora and the babies she could feel herself in a familiar province, and there she stayed almost all the time, quitting it only when India paid one of her rare visits. Annunciata noted with approval that

India was not disposed to interfere with the nurturing of her babies, and she herself went to the nursery only once, out of politeness to Flora, for the new generation was still at the uninteresting stage. Later, Annunciata thought, with a faint, pleasant anticipation, she might enjoy walking in the gardens with her great-grandchildren – when they had reached a more reasonable age.

For a moment, she had enough to occupy her without that. There were visits to be made in York, to the few acquaintances from the old days whom it was still possible to visit; and out of courtesy, to her tenants. She looked, desultorily, for a house to rent for the summers to come, for she did not think she would want always to stay at Morland Place. Once or twice she met Vanbrugh and Hawksmoor for dinner at the Starre, to discuss the progress of the building at Henderskelfe, and on one occasion they were joined by William Thornton, the local man who was building a new house for the Bourchiers at Beningborough. The Bourchiers were close neighbours and old friends of the Morlands, and Annunciata visited them in their old Elizabethan house and walked with them over the site of the new building, which was at a short distance, further from the river and on higher, firmer ground. Thornton was interested in the new ideas of Vanbrugh and his companion, and one day they all rode over to Henderskelfe together to see the site of Castle Howard. It was a journey of about sixteen miles from York, but the roads were such that it took them nearly four hours, even on horseback, and the visit and travelling occupied a whole day from dawn to nightfall.

A great deal of her time was taken up with her own building project, and on most days she rode, or walked over the fields, to Shawes to see how things were going on, and to talk to the foreman, a handsome and almost incomprehensible 'incomer' from Newcastle, and the carpenter, John Molesclough, who was the son of Chloris's brother and very like Chloris to look at. Building a new house, she discovered, was very like having a baby – it seemed a long time from conception to delivery, and in the early days there was no indication, beyond imagination, of what the finished product would look like. But it was as satisfying as having a baby, and far less personally inconvenient, and Annunciata revelled in it.

When her time was not occupied with these things, she rode. She found she could not have enough of simply taking out her horse and riding over the familiar and long-missed land of her childhood, where every field, hedge, tree and eminence had its memory. Matt, in a manner reminiscent of his grandfather Ralph, made quite an occasion of 'choosing a horse for the Countess', and took the whole family over to Twelvetrees, where he had had an awning set up under which they could sit while the best of the young animals were paraded, and a picnic dinner of considerable style was served to them *al fresco*. India almost twittered with excitement over the daring and elegance of the occasion, and had to be restrained from extending the invitation to the whole of fashionable York.

Annunciata went along with it all, though from first glance she had no doubt as to her choice, for she firmly believed that choosing a horse had to be a matter of love at first sighting, or the proper rapport would never exist. All the animals brought out for her were handsome and had good conformation, and some of the blacks were magnificent, but she had always favoured the chestnuts which were the Morland speciality before the coming of the stallion Barbary, and it was a chestnut which now called to her. It was a four-year-old gelding, with the barb conformation – the combination of strength and delicacy that was so affecting – of his black great-grandsire, and the autumn leaf colouring of his Morland granddam.

He had no white hair on him; his mane and tail were so long that the latter brushed the daisies as he walked, and the former hung to his shoulder, fading from russet to orichalcum to pure gold at the fringed ends. He stood square beside the boy who led him, his delicate leaf-shaped ears pricked forward, his dark gentle eyes looking, it seemed, straight at Annunciata as if he had known her in the warm dream of his mother's womb and had only been waiting for the moment when they would meet. She stood up and went towards him, her fingers extended, and he whickered softly and shifted his small forefeet in the bright emerald grass. When he was saddled, Annunciata mounted and rode him round the paddock. Perhaps, she thought, there is reincarnation for the animals whose souls are too lowly for heaven; perhaps Goldeneye and Banner and this colt were all one. He was for her, she knew. She went through the motions of examining and trying others, so that Matt's occasion should not be lessened, and then made her choice aloud.

'An excellent choice,' Matt cried. 'And what shall you call him?'

Annunciata had no hesitation. 'Phoenix,' she said.

Choosing a dog was a different matter, for a dog must be taken as a pup, and is chosen for its strength and size, its character being a matter for creation by its master. Matt gave her the best of the litter of the best brindled Morland bitch, a big strong whelp with a white breast-mark and an almost black face, which gave it the look of a diminutive highwayman. Annunciata called it Kithra, which, like Fand, was one of the family's traditional names for their hounds, and its training took up whatever time she had spare from everything else. It proved amenable to training and by the time she left Morland Place in October, Kithra was already in a fair way to becoming a good and useful companion.

The whole family turned out to say goodbye to her. Clovis, who had been up and down to London several times during her stay, had come to Morland Place for the harvest, and said, 'I shall be leaving for London soon. I shall see you there.'

'I am stopping in Oxford for a week or two first,' Annunciata warned him, and he smiled up at her, resting his hand on Phoenix's shoulder.

'Your new friend?'

'It is pleasant to have an *intellectual* friend,' Annunciata said gravely, but her eyes sparkled with amusement. Clovis's tired face lit for a moment.

'That is what I have always said about you, my lady. Well, I shall see you in London at the end of the month, then. We can sample the new season's plays together if you have the mind.'

'I look forward to it,' she said. A moment later she was riding away out of the yard, and looked back to wave one last time, seeing the bobbing, elegant headdress of India white above the grey head of Clovis and the shining bald pate of Father St Maur, and her mouth curved in a smile of sudden affection for them all.

It was the last time she saw Clovis. He set out for London in the second week of October, reaching Aylesbury on the nineteenth, where he broke his journey at the Rose and Crown. He had taken a little light supper and gone straight up to bed, saying he felt very tired, and asking to be called at first light. The servant who had gone to call him in the morning had found him dead in his bed: he had apparently died peacefully in his sleep – a death, Annunciata thought through her tears when the news was brought to her, that God reserves for those he specially favours.

By his own request, expressed in his will, Clovis was buried beside his parents at St James's Picadilly, and his funeral was so well attended that there were not seats enough for all, and many had to stand at the back and even in the porch, spilling over into the churchyard. It was a tribute to his selfless life, and his universal quiet kindness. The anthem was sung by the pupils of The Girls' Charity School in nearby Carnaby Street, a school for the daughters of poor people which had been founded by subscription in 1699 and in which Clovis had interested himself from the beginning both personally and financially. Merchants, courtiers, tradesmen, all classes were represented in the congregation, and the Queen sent her treasurer, Lord

Godolphin, to represent her, for Clovis had been a faithful servant of the Crown in the Navy Office and later in the Treasury. Old friends from both offices attended, as did almost all the members of the Royal Society, and the entire staff of the Office of Works from Sir Christopher Wren downwards.

When Clovis's will was read, it was discovered that his wealth had been far greater than anyone had supposed, but the disposal of it came as no surprise. Apart from various pensions to old servants, and a large legacy to The Girls' Charity School, and another to St Edward's School at York, the whole estate was left to Clover, now Lady Ballincrea, to be held in her own right and disposed of as she pleased. It gave Clover an extraordinary freedom, for normally a married woman's property all belonged to her husband, and thinking it over in the dark days of winter, Annunciata wondered whether Clovis was thus expressing a distrust of Arthur, and giving Clover the power to withstand any ill-treatment her husband might inflict on her.

Annunciata spent Christmas quietly at Chelmsford House, subdued by the loss of another old friend. Christmas at Morland Place was also subdued, for India had her third child on Christmas Eve, and the labour went harder with her than before, leaving her very weak for the whole Christmas season. It was another boy, and they called it Edmund. Father St Maur performed the christening, and at New Year Annunciata received a letter from him asking her if he might leave Morland Place and come to London to become her chaplain once more. For reason he gave only that he felt too old to be a proper tutor to the boys growing up at Morland Place, and that he wished to end his days peacefully in the service of the person whom he had always regarded as his mistress.

Annunciata had no objections – indeed, she was delighted, stipulating only that Matt must give his free consent – and at the end of January, despite the weather Father St Maur travelled to London. He arrived grey and pinched with cold, and Annunciata hurried him to the fire and plied him with hot wine.

'This haste argues some more urgent reason for leaving than your age, Father.'

The old priest shook his head. Later, when he was able to speak, he said only, 'I was eager to come home, my lady. Having been given my leave, I could not bear to wait any longer.'

He took no ill-effect from his journey, and Annunciata was happy to have her own confessor, and to be able once again to converse with a man who not only knew her, but had largely shaped her mind. But there remained in her mind some small doubt as to why he had left Morland Place so precipitately. She was sure that something had happened, but since he did not tell her, she could not ask him.

In the spring of 1704, John Francomb came to London and presented himself at Chelmsford House, requesting an interview with the Countess. Annunciata received him kindly, having always had a distant respect for the steward-turned-master, and he wasted no time, but came straight to the point.

'My wife has had a letter from her aunt Cathy, to say that she has made a match between her daughter Sabina and young Allan Macallan of Braco, and it brought me to think of my own daughter. She is fourteen, going on fifteen, and if it has your approval, I am minded to make a match between her and your grandson John McNeill. What say you to that?'

Annunciata raised her eyebrows at such bluntness, and said mildly, 'Fourteen is young to be wed, Master Francomb. And John is still at university, has not even had his Grand Tour yet. What reasons do you have for thinking I might approve of the match?'

Francomb leaned forward, rested one elbow on his broad thigh, and fixed her with his bright blue gaze.

'My lass is an heiress of a large estate. Life being so uncertain as it is, the sooner she gets wed and with child the better. She'll be fifteen in December, woman enough for the job. Now, my lady, there will be no shortage of suitors for her, rich as she is, and pretty into the bargain. But I thought of young John first, so I'm making you the first offer.'

Annunciata smiled to herself and said, 'Your reasons, sir?'

'Are simple enough, madam. First, the lad is a likely enough boy, and he has at title, and the reversion of his brother's. Second, I am not so unjust as to ignore what's proper between me and your family. The property was all my wife's, and ought not to go to a stranger. Now there's no Morland lad of good age, so the next closest is your son, you being a Morland by birth. And third, the young people know each other, have grown up together, and I think are very fond of each other. I have spoken to my own little Fanny about it, and she says she would like to marry John. And on my way here I stopped off in Oxford and sounded out the lad, and he was cheerful enough to it.'

'Do you think it important that the children should like the idea?' Annunciata said. Francomb nodded vigorously.

'In this case, I do, my lady. It might not signify so much when the couple lives in London or some part of the world like Morland Place where there's plenty of society. But up in Northumberland, at Blindburn or even at Emblehope, it's an empty, lonely kind of country, and it can be a bleak sort of life, with no seeing of a new face for months on end. Now two young people not caring for each other, but shut up together with no relief, not even to get out of the house when the snows are down – well, put it to yourself. It would be a bad sort of life, would it not?'

Annunciata acknowledged the justice of the argument. Francomb sat back as if his work were done.

'You say the young people like the idea?'

'Fanny's all for it, and the boy – well, he's a shy lad, but he looked right pleased with it.' He looked at her shrewdly for a moment, and said, 'You got that other grandson of your off your hands cheaply enough, but here's an even better bargain, for I'll make the match for nothing. Fanny will have everthing of her mother's, and they'll not need more than that.'

Annunciata laughed at that. 'You drive a very easy bargain, sir! I find it hard to resist you.'

'Don't then, madam,' he said, and there was a caress in his voice and eyes that she knew was part of his performance, part of the way he won people to his side. 'Shall we shake hands on it?'

She knew she ought to think about it, to argue over terms at the very least, send him away with a cool appointment for a week's time; but there was something in his bluntness that called to the masculine side of her nature. With a smile that shewed her white teeth, she reached across and struck his brown palm with her own, and he grinned triumphantly back at her.

'We'll seal the bargain with wine,' Annunciata said, calling for a servant, 'and you must stay and dine with me.'

'I shall be delighted to stay as long as you like,' he said, with a calculating look. Annunciata looked into his blue eyes and felt his attraction. It would have been pleasant, she thought, just for a little while to be a serving woman, so that she could take advantage of that mute offer; as herself, it could not be done. But there was no harm in indulging in an evening of his masculine company and discreet flirtation. The servant entered, and she sent for claret.

The next day, after first Mass, Father St Maur asked to speak to her privately. He seemed ill-at-ease, and when they were alone, he asked her, 'My lady, it may seem to you a strange question, but I would like to know what that man is doing here, why he has come.'

It did seem strange, but there was no reason why the

priest should not know, and frowning a little, Annunciata said, 'He has come to make a marriage settlement, between his daughter and my grandson John. What is your reason for asking?'

Father St Maur's face was red, and he seemed to have difficulty in phrasing an answer. 'I – I have a reason, but it is not one I can readily tell you. But I would recommend you – ask you – not to have anything to do with him. I do not think an alliance between your grandson and anyone of his family would be advisable. I have reason to think – to think any contact between our family and him a thing to be avoided.'

Annunciata stared at him in astonishment. 'You have reason to think ill of him?' St Maur did not answer. 'Father, I insist on an answer. You cannot, surely, think it consonant with Christian feeling to cast doubt on a man without naming your reasons? A priest, Father, ought to have more charity.'

St Maur turned desperate eyes on her. 'My lady, I cannot tell you. Child, I ask you to trust me. You have known me for most of your life, and I hope in that time I have given you good advice. Can you not accept my word without question?'

'No, I cannot. I have judgement of my own, which you amongst others have taught me to use. I cannot hear a man condemned without reason.'

'I cannot tell you what appurtains to the secrets of the confessional,' St Maur said, his cheeks trembling with emotion. Annunciata stared at him coldly.

'Then you should not have spoken. Leave me now, and never speak of this again.'

The old priest left her, his face red and his eyes moist. Afterwards she was sorry she had spoken so harshly to him, but she could not regret her action. It was monstrous to offer accusations against a man without stating the reasons. Besides, even if St Maur knew something to the man's detriment, it did not make the match any the worse a match. And besides again, she had struck hands on it, and not for anything would she go back on her word.

Work on the new house at Shawes was progressing steadily. That summer, when she went to Yorkshire, Annunciata stayed only a fortnight at Morland Place before moving to a rented house in the city, for she felt, as she had not felt last year, that her presence caused a certain amount of tension. Perhaps it was because Birch and Father St Maur had both deserted Morland Place for her household. It could not, she decided, be due to any antipathy on the part of the new mistress, for after she had moved to York, India visited her there very frequently, though she never stayed long. Annunciata gathered that she also visited her mother in the city quite regularly, which accounted for Annunciata's bumping into her so often in different streets all over town.

Annunciata stayed less than three months in Yorkshire that year, for in the middle of August the news arrived from London that General Marlborough had won a great victory over the French at a village in Bavaria called Blenheim. The French, it was said, had been completely routed, and had suffered heavy casualties, one report putting the numbers as high as forty thousand. There was great rejoicing over the news, for the French were the old enemy, and generations had grown up believing that the French army could never be defeated on land. Marlborough was the hero of the day, and toasted in every tavern; the Queen was 'good Queen Anne'; Agincourt was on every lip; England's fortunes were to rise to a pinnacle of glory.

Annunciata felt herself alone in not sharing the joy, though there must have been others as well as her who thought of the King, living by the mercy of the French. But the forty thousand French dead must include many friends, and she feared lest the number include Berwick or Karellie. She hastened back to London. She had inherited from Clovis the correspondence with his brother Edmund, her former protege, at St Omer, and if there were bad tidings, they would come from him, and she would receive them more easily and privately in London.

Edmund wrote at length. Karellie and Berwick were safe, though twenty-three thousand French had fallen and fifteen thousand been taken prisoner. Annunciata witnessed the great procession which carried the Queen in a splendid coach to St Paul's cathedral for a thanksgiving service in September. She rode, jewel-bedecked, quite alone in her coach save for Marlborough's wife Sarah, proof, if any were required, of the esteem in which the Churchills were held by their mistress.

Matt's interest in the victory at Blenheim was overlaid by a more domestic crisis. He had been aware of a certain restlessness on the part of his wife during that summer, and though her health had been good, and she had not been forced to go away during the hot months as in previous years, she spent a great deal of time away from him in one way or another, visiting in the town, at Beningborough, and simply riding around the estate. He was afraid that she might be unhappy, for she seemed to spend an unusual amount of time in the chapel for one who had never before been punctilious in her devotions. The new priest was a tall, thin, sandy individual, with pale eyes and a protruding Adam's apple, who had only recently been ordained and had never had a living. Matt had interviewed him on Father St Maur's recommendation, and had thought him sincere and well-educated, finding him willing to fall in with all the other tasks that a domestic chaplain usually inherited.

It was only towards the end of the summer that Matt began to realize that India did not altogether take to Father Byrne. Her manner towards him was cold, and on one occasion, when she and Matt were alone, she burst out with a passionate request that he should not be allowed to dine with them.

'But, my dearest wife, the chaplain always dines with

the family. What can he have done to incur your wrath?' Matt asked anxiously. India walked rapidly up and down the room.

'Nothing. Nothing at all. It is simply that I wonder if he is the proper person to have charge of our dear children. I do not think him at all a superior person, I assure you.'

'He is very well educated,' Matt said doubtfully. 'And Father St Maur recommended him –'

'Oh if the sainted Father St Maur says so, then undoubtedly he is perfection itself,' India cried shrilly. Matt went to her to try to soothe her.

'My love, tell me what he has done to upset you.'

'Nothing. Nothing at all,' she said, and gave a strange, sarcastic laugh. 'He is most *correct* in every way.'

She would say nothing more, and so Matt had to drop the subject, and after that he thought she must be trying to overcome her antipathy, for she seemed to spend more time than ever in the chapel, as well as going to the priest's room at odd times to 'confess herself' or 'seek spiritual guidance' as she put it. But in August, shortly after the Countess had left hurriedly for London, India came to Matt in the steward's room where he was writing letters, her face very flushed, her eyes strangely bright, and her hair a little awry.

'Husband I must speak to you at once,' she cried without preamble. He stood up, dropping his pen in his surprise.

'My dear, what is it? What's happened?'

India began walking rapidly up and down the room, holding her skirt back with one hand and turning with an angry swish at the end of each four steps. She was evidently much agitated, but she did not speak at once. Matt watched her with apprehension. 'My dear, tell me. I cannot help you unless you speak.'

'I hesitate to speak, husband,' India said, 'because it goes against my nature to say ill of anyone, particularly someone for whom you have a regard. I have the greatest horror of appearing malicious or petty, as you know –'

'My darling, if one of the servants has been insolent –'

She interrupted him with a harsh laugh, and he went on, 'You know that your happiness is the most important thing to me. You must not think that I would put a servant before you. That would be a very misguided loyalty.'

'It is not a servant,' she said, and then clapped her hand over her mouth as if she had not intended to give away so much. Matt's heart sank.

'It is Father Byrne,' he said. She did not deny it, turning her eyes away, her cheeks burning. 'What has he done? Come, dearest, it is your duty to tell me, even though you hate to speak ill of someone. Think of our children. We have a responsibility to them and to the servants not to house anyone unsuitable. Has he been insolent to you?'

India appeared to make up her mind. She stopped her pacing and turned to him with bright, intent eyes. 'Matt, I have tried to like him, truly I have.'

'I know – I have seen it. You are magnanimity itself.'

She laughed again, the same harsh, sarcastic laugh. It pained him to hear it. 'Yes, I have been generous, and this is how he repays generosity. I do not mind for myself – it is for you. That he should so abuse *your* kindness to him, quite overcomes my natural modesty. Otherwise I should have spoken sharply to him and said nothing more, trusting there would be no recurrence. But I love you so much, my dearest Matt, that I cannot endure that his – his *ingratitude* should go unpunished.'

'But what has he done?' Matt asked patiently. She lowered her eyes.

'I – I hardly like to tell you.' He waited in silence, and she went on, 'I went to him a little while ago, to ask his advice about a spiritual matter. While I sat there, talking to him, he – he – he flung himself to his knees and avowed himself in love with me.' There was a short and breathless silence, and she hurried on as if to prevent him breaking it. 'I bid him be silent – I chided him as gently as I could – my modesty was offended, and I wished only to hear no more of it. Then he seized my hand and kissed it, and cried that his love could not be concealed any longer, that

197

he *must* speak of it. I reminded him that he was a priest, and I a married woman. I told him that he must be silent and never utter a word of it again, and I got up to go, but he pursued me on his knees. A ridiculous sight!' Her voice rose and her face flushed as if the memory of it outraged her still. 'I flung him off and ran out of the room, and went, I know not whither, until my heart had stopped pounding. Then I knew I must come to you.'

The silence was longer this time, and during it the colour faded from India's cheeks and she became quite pale by comparison, and sat down abruptly in the chair by the fireside as if she would faint. It galvanized Matt to action. He crouched beside her and rubbed her hands.

'My love, my dearest, I am so sorry. It must have been the most terrible shock to you. Have no fear, you will never see him again. You did right to come to me. Go out into the garden now, and walk until your spirits are refreshed. Before you return to the house, he will be gone, I promise you.'

India looked up at him with tears in her eyes and an expression of such relief that he realized all at once how the priest had terrified her. He escorted her to the door, bid the servant waiting outside to send Millicent to her mistress in the rose garden, and to send Father Byrne to the steward's room at once.

The priest came in five minutes. He stood before Matt looking paler than ever, but shewing no apprehension or guilt in his face. His brazenness stung Matt to anger.

'Well, what have you to say for yourself?' he demanded. 'I may add that the mistress has told me everything, so there will be no use in your adding untruth to your other crimes. How dare you behave so, to one whose shoes you are not fit to untie? Do you know, that she would have concealed your wickedness out of the kindness of her heart, had not her loyalty to me forced her to speak. You are not worthy of such generosity. What can you say in your defence?'

The priest said gravely, 'May I know of what I am accused?'

'You know very well. Do not bandy words with me, sir!' Matt cried.

The priest did not react to the anger, only said again patiently, 'Yet every accused man is at least allowed to know of what he is accused.'

Coldly, Matt told him, using India's exact words as far as he remembered them. The effect on the priest was remarkable. He did not look embarrassed, ashamed, afraid, he did not cast down his eyes or beg forgiveness. He only looked at Matt with a look of extraordinary sadness, almost of pity. He seemed to consider for a long time whether to speak or not, and then at last said, 'I have nothing to say, sir.'

'Nothing at all?'

'Nothing.'

Matt turned away, in astonishment, anger, and unease. He picked up the pen from the table and proceeded to ruin its nib without noticing, and then flung it down and turned to face him again.

'I do not blame you for falling in love with my wife. We needs must love the best when we see it. I do not even blame you for being so overcome as to express it. But to shew no remorse, no regret – have I not shewn you kindness?'

'You have been a kind and just master,' the priest said, still with that terrible pity in his eye. Matt avoided the glance.

'I have promised my wife that you shall be out of the house before she returns to it. Had you asked for mercy, I should have sent you from here with my protection. As it is, I dismiss you summarily, without wages or character. Pack your bag at once, and be gone within the hour, and do not speak to anyone in that time. And I advise you most strongly to go as far away from here as possible, and never to speak of what has happened in this house, for I am not without influence, and I shall certainly use it if I have cause.'

'I would not grieve you more than you are already,' the priest said gently. 'I shall never speak of it, I promise you. God bless and keep you.'

And he turned and went, leaving Matt feeling strangely as if it was he that had committed the ungrateful act, and had yet been forgiven by the sandy priest.

India was in high spirits that evening, though Matt could see they were not natural, and that the laughter would take little pushing to tip over into tears. He tried to soothe her, and after a while insisted that she sit and sew while he played to her, and this at last broke through the artificial barriers, and made the tears come. He hastened to comfort her, and told Millicent to take her off to bed, bathe her forehead in witch-hazel, and brush her hair well to calm her. When he went to bed himself, an hour later, he found her awake and calm, her eyes puffy and her eyelashes wet. She looked like a child, and his heart was rocked with pity. He undressed and slipped into bed with her, and took her in his arms, and she snuggled against him like a child. For the first time in their marriage, he felt strong and protecting, older than her, wiser; for the first time he felt that *he* was in command of the situation, and not her. He comforted her without words for a while, and then kissed her, and began gently to take off her night-gown. She did not resist, but acquiesced, softly and almost sleepily, and he made love to her in great tenderness until she came shudderingly to a climax. Then he gathered her once more into his arms, cradled her head on his shoulder, and said, 'Now sleep, my darling. I will always take care of you.' And she gave a little sigh, and he felt her smile before she drifted off into sleep as he commanded.

The next day India's spirits were normal again, and at

breakfast she interrupted his reading of letters and newspapers to say, 'I suppose that I had better begin looking for a new chaplain tutor at once, for it might take a long time to find the right one.'

'*You* look?' Matt said in astonishment. India dimpled at him lovingly across the table.

'Dear husband, of course I shall let you interview them, for form's sake, but I must be the one to make the final decision. After all, you chose the last one, and look what happened. I am sure my judgement is sounder than yours, for you are so unworldly and good, anyone might impose upon you, as that dreadful man did. Now dearest, smile and look agreeable. You know I am right.' Matt smiled reluctantly, and she buttered another piece of bread with a jubilant smile. 'I shall go into York this very day and begin my enquiries. I am so busy, I hardly know how I shall find the time, but it shall be managed somehow. Millicent, tell Clement to order the horses immediately after breakfast. And go up now and put out my clothes. And prepare writing things – you shall take down a letter for my mother, since I shall not have time to visit her today.'

And Matt could only smile across the table at her. 'My dear, you are magnificent. Nothing daunts your spirits.'

'Oh, I never was one to weep and mourn. What's done is done,' she said.

It took India a very great time to find the right man, but in January she said she thought she knew where he was to be found, and by February he was installed at Morland Place. He was twenty-five, and had had several places before, of which he had been deprived by a number of strokes of singularly bad luck. He was a well-built, well-spoken man of average height, with fair curling hair, blue eyes, and a fair, Grecian face, and he dressed in an unexpected degree of fashion considering his limited means. His name was Anthony Cole.

'It is right that we should have a man who dresses properly,' India said, when Matt, after the first interview, expressed doubts about Cole's high-heeled boots. 'Remember he is to bring up our sons. You want them to be gentlemen, don't you?'

'There is more to being a gentleman than dressing properly,' Matt said mildly.

'Well, he can teach them to walk, and stand, and sit, how to enter a room, and bow, how to take off their hats – he knows all about such things, I warrant you. *And* how to address persons of quality, which is more than can be said of that other nasty creature,' she added, as if it were the killing stroke.

'Yes, but he will also have to train their minds, dearest, and you have said nothing about his education.'

'Lord, you can tell he is educated by the way he speaks,' India said impatiently.

'But his schooling? His qualifications?'

'I am sure he said he was at Oxford,' she said quickly. 'In fact, I am convinced of it. Yes, I remember distinctly he said he was Christ's College and knew your cousins. In fact, I believe they shared the same tutor.'

Matt almost laughed, but suppressed it, for she could be easily angered on the subject of education, and he thought she felt deeply her own lack of it.

'I will see him again, my love, and ask him. Now, be easy, I will not go against your choice, but I must find out that he is able to teach our boys. You would not like them to grow up like savages, would you?'

She flew to him and put her arms round his neck and rubbed her face against his. 'But when you have asked him, you will take him on, won't you?'

'Yes, my darling, if that's what you want. Provided –'

'Oh thank you, darling, thank you. You are the best of husbands,' she purred, pressing kisses all over his face and lips and eyes. He tried to laugh it away, but his body stirred to her as it always did, and he closed his arms about her and began to kiss her in return. She broke away after a while and said, 'Now, darling, you must not ruffle me – I have so much to do.'

'India –'

'No, no, not now, dear husband. What would the servants say?'

'Damn the servants –'

'No darling, no. Tonight. Wait for tonight.'

'Oh. Very well then,' Matt growled. She pressed one last kiss on his forehead and danced away, Oyster running close behind, trying, as always, to press his head against her skirt. 'Tonight – you promise?'

'Promise!' she called back as she whisked out of the door.

CHAPTER ELEVEN

Despite his promise, Karellie did not spend the Christmas of 1704 in Venice, for he had received news that his friend Berwick was at St Germain with his duchess, and Karellie could not resist the opportunity to see him again. They had not been posted together since the previous year, for Berwick had been sent as a special envoy to the Court of Spain. Berwick had been very unhappy there, disliking the atmosphere of intrigue and the over-elaborate etiquette, and had from the first been convinced that the French ambassador was plotting to discredit him. He longed for active service and, when he was finally recalled to France, he applied for French nationality, in order to further his military career, and to improve the position of his wife and children when he was away on campaign. Queen Mary, as head of the Council of Regency, gave permission on the King's behalf, making the condition that Berwick would always put himself at the King's disposal if required, to which Berwick readily agreed.

Karellie was kindly received on his return, for he had distinguished himself in the campaigns so far. He was glad to see Berwick again, and was pleased by the Queen's kindness. His only embarrassment was on meeting his sister Aliena, for he had never been able to accept what he knew of her begetting, and all through his journey he wondered how he would feel when he came face to face with her again. He did not have long to wait to find out. The King received him in the presence chamber – he was sixteen now, a tall, slender boy with the big bones that shewed he would be taller yet. His skin was fair, his features fine like his mother's, his eyes very dark and expressive like hers, his hair light brown, inclining to fair. He was very gentle of speech, grave but not solemn or dour, very kingly in his bearing. Karellie knelt to him, feeling that here was a true king, whom it was a grace to serve.

The King said, 'Rise up, cousin. We are very happy to have you here. Christmas is a time for families to be together, don't you think?'

It was an extremely gracious reception, and Karellie glowed inwardly with pleasure. To call him 'cousin' was a piece of great generosity on the King's part, considering their blood relationship was an illegitimate one. But then, he had had some practice in calling Berwick 'brother' without any hint of embarrassment.

'I am very glad to be here, Your Majesty,' Karellie said.

The King smiled and said, 'I know that you will want to greet your sister. She is walking in the gardens with the Princess, and you have our leave to go there at once. We are both very grateful to your mother for leaving her here – she has been a very dear companion to us both.'

'Your Majesty is most gracious,' Karellie said, and inwardly he thought, *that* is why I am so affectionately received – because of her. He rose and made his exit, with the thought that he must suppress his unease at all costs; if the King and Princess valued Aliena so highly, he must not do less.

'La Consolatrice', as the Princess was known, was twelve now, a pretty and vivacious young girl with her mother's large, dark eyes, and auburn lights in her brown hair that many a Court lady would have given a fortune to possess. Karellie saw her at a distance, playing some kind of game amongst the hedges of the yew walk – it looked like tag, for there was a great deal of darting here and there, and before Karellie could reach her, a flying figure ran out from the hedge beside him and bumped into him so hard he had to catch her to stop her falling.

'Well, Mrs Nan, this is a fine way to greet a friend,' he said setting her back on her feet.

Nan stared up at him for a moment in bewilderment,

and then cried, 'Oh, my lord, I did not recognize you for a moment. I beg your lordship's pardon –'

'That's all right. It looks like a good game.'

'I am supposed to catch her highness and my lady, but not too quickly,' Nan explained with a sly smile, 'but I dare say they will have better things to think about now. Wait here, my lord, I'll go and call them.'

But there was no need, for the Princess came out from her hiding place to see why there was no pursuit, and instantly gave up the game and put on her formal manners, and Karellie, a little touched, walked gravely towards her and made his lowest bow.

'Your highness.'

'My lord of Chelmsford. It is good to see you here. We have heard great things of you in the last campaign. Your sister will be glad – Aliena! Come out – there's a visitor.'

A slender figure in a dark russet cloak darted out from the hedge, and stopped dead beside the Princess. Karellie looked, and his heart seemed to stop for a moment, for around great beauty there seems a kind of stillness and silence, as if nature itself draws breath. Aliena was seventeen, and Karellie had not seen her since she had grown from childhood to womanhood. She was not tall, but her upright and graceful carriage made her seem so. Her cheeks were bright with the cold air, the breath clouded from her parted lips, her eyes seemed to reflect the curving arch of dark-blue sky, clear and sparkling sky as only midwinter or midsummer affords.

Oh, but she was beautiful. Karellie with a soldier's experience of beautiful women, with a courtier's recollection of beautiful women, with the beauties of all of Europe from Versailles to Venice for comparison, was rendered speechless by her beauty; and more even than her beauty, by the expression of her dark blue eyes, for as well as her father's looks, she had evidently inherited his gentle, tender, wise and witty character. He loved her on sight, and the visual proof of her parentage only added a sharp edge to that love, that it might cut deeper into his heart.

'Here is your brother, Aliena,' the Princess said, with the pleased air of one bestowing a gift she knows will be welcome. 'I hope you will make him stay for a good, long time. Did you know, my lord, that there is to be such a grand ball at Versailles, the Twelfth Night ball? We have both new gowns for it, have we not, Aliena?'

Aliena smiled, and Karellie guessed that new gowns did not often come the way of this exiled Princess. It touched him, and he wished he had had the sense to bring something pretty from Venice for her. To come empty-handed seemed monstrous now – but there was time, still, before Twelfth Night.

'The Princess's gown is of amber velvet. I promise you, my lord, that it will be worth staying to see her.'

The Princess stepped closer and tucked her hand through Aliena's arm, and said, 'I'm afraid I shall never be able to look as well as your sister, my lord. She is a true beauty.' From another princess, it would have been a blatant call for flattery, but he could see that Princess Louise-Marie was simply speaking the truth as she saw it. He opened his mouth to reply, but the Princess said, 'I am sure you will want a little time together, and so I will go in ahead of you, Aliena. Come, ladies. We shall meet again soon, my lord, at vespers.'

She gathered her women, received his bow, and left them. Aliena watched her go and said, 'That is like her, to leave us in private. Shall we walk, brother? It is too cold to stand still for long.'

Karellie offered her his arm, and they turned and strolled along the yew walk, with Nan a few paces to the rear, giving them privacy. Karellie looked down at the delicate hand resting on his sleeve, and wondered what there was to say. At last he said, 'When I went away, I left a child. Now you are a woman. I find it hard to adjust to the idea.'

'I am just the same inside,' she said, 'I have missed you all.'

'Tell me about your life here. Are you happy?'

'Oh yes. It is very quiet most of the time, except when

we go to Versailles or Fontainebleau. We sew a little, read, make our devotions. Sometimes we go to Chailly with the Queen. We do our lessons, of course. James – the King and I take lessons together, with some of the other young men, and afterwards I teach the Princess what I have learned. She has her own lessons, but she likes to try to keep up with us. She likes us to be together, the three of us.'

'The three of you,' Karellie mused, smiling. 'How well that sounds! You are very fond of them both, I gather.'

Aliena looked a little puzzled. 'Fond?' It seemed a strange idea to apply to her King and his sister. 'I – belong with them,' she said, struggling for words. Karellie pressed her hand.

'I understand,' he said, and he did, a little. 'What is the King like?'

Her face lit up. 'He is all goodness,' she said. 'He is never out of temper, or cross, or sharp-tongued, whatever happens. He is always cheerful – not quite merry, for he is rather grave by nature, but he likes others to be merry about him. We have such wonderful talks – I believe we talk all day long. He is interested in everything you know.'

She talked on, and Karellie had no difficulty in seeing how much she loved the King. He hoped that it would not cause her grief, for sooner or later the King would have to marry. Observation would tell him how the King felt about her. It was only afterwards that he realized how quickly he had passed from feeling awkward and embarrassed at the thought of meeting her at all, to being deeply concerned that she should not be made unhappy.

The great ball in the Galerie des Glaces at Versailles was a magnificent occasion, as one would expect, but what impressed Karellie most was the sense of family that existed, the genuine, affectionate kindness between the French royal family and the English. And into this family, by further kindness and graciousness, he was accepted, being made to feel that he was welcome both by virtue of his blood and by virtue of his services in the army of France. The King and his young sister were the centre of attention, and in her new gown of amber velvet the Princess attracted the warm compliments of the old King Louis, who said that she reminded him of her great aunt Marie Mancini. But always, wherever the royal couple were to be found, one pace behind them was Aliena, and though her gown was an old one made over, she was more striking even than her young mistress. The King danced with his sister, and Karellie danced with Aliena, and all heads turned to watch the four young people pass up the set.

Sometimes they changed partners, and the King danced with Aliena while Karellie led out the Princess, and Karellie had the opportunity to watch his sister and gauge how the King felt about her. They were perfectly matched as dancers, and whether they were silent or conversing, Karellie had a feeling of complete trust and comfort between them. Yet it was not like man and woman, nor yet quite like brother and sister, but something in between – perhaps the accord of two young soldiers fighting side by side, the love of two perfect equals.

The King danced with his sister and with Aliena, and with one or two of the ladies of the French royal family, but mostly with his sister, although the ball went on until four in the morning and he danced every dance. Karellie wondered at that, and asked Aliena whether the King ever danced with other young women. She shook her head.

'The King does not care to dance with any lady he has not known for a very long time, unless it is a relative. He is very – reserved.' She looked up at Karellie as if judging how much she might tell him, and then went on in a lower voice, 'You see, the King his father left a letter of very detailed advice for the governing of his kingdom and his life, and there was a very special instruction to be careful in his relationships with women. The late King spoke feelingly of his own dear-bought experience, and cautioned the King most pointedly. I think he has taken it very much to heart. He does not want to give his mother and sister any distress of that nature, and wishes to avoid what he thinks of as dangerous temptation. So he never has to do with strange ladies, and in our own Court hardly speaks to any female person except the Queen and Her Highness.'

'And you,' Karellie said. She looked up with her burning-blue eyes.

'And me. But then, I am one of the family to him.'

There was information and warning in her look. Was she telling him that he need not fear for her heart, that she knew how things stood with the King? He did not want her to have to practise patience and acceptance. Whoever she loved ought to love her; whoever she wanted she ought to have. He felt himself swell with indignation and the desire to protect, and even as it happened he wondered at himself. But she was, after all, his sister. In that moment he had almost forgotten the other half of it.

The early months of 1705 brought interest and amusement to Annunciata, for the Queen, in recognition of Marlborough's great victory at Blenheim, had decided to give him the royal manor at Woodstock, and to pay for a new house to be built there along a grand design. The choice of architect seemed simple, for Wren was head of the Board of Works and already building the new St Paul's cathedral and the palace at Greenwich, and was undoubtedly the most eminent architect of the day. But Vanbrugh, calling upon the Countess at Chelmsford House one morning, told her that the commission was to go to him.

'All purely by chance, Countess, I assure you,' he laughed. 'I met Marlborough at the play last night, and we talked about it for a bit, and then I said, very casually, "Why, your grace, I hear you are to have a new house built at Woodstock", and he said, just as casually, "Yes, Sir John – would you like to build it?"'

'You are an opportunist,' Annunciata laughed. Vanbrugh shrugged.

'I could not refuse so noble a duke and hero, madam. What would you have me say? Besides, Wren is so busy, with St Paul's and Greenwich, he would not have the time.'

'And you, Van, are busy with Howard's castle and my new house – how shall you have the time? At least Wren is in London most of the time, not two hundred miles away in Yorkshire.'

'Ah, but I couldn't resist it, Countess! He talked a little of it – no expense is to be spared. It is to be the Versailles of England, a proper monument to England's greatest general and finest victory. Oh, you know the sort of thing.'

'I read it daily in handbills,' Annunciata said drily. 'But tell me, what plans have you? After your design for Henderskelfe, how can you surpass yourself?'

'Frankly, madam, I don't know. I think Henderskelfe will always be my favourite – does not a mother love her firstborn best? The first fruit of my brain has everything in it that I want to do. But I shall manage somehow.'

'You must be sure to keep me informed of the progress. I should not want to miss a moment of Versailles' history,' Annunciata said. 'But you will not neglect my own small monument, will you?'

Vanbrugh kissed her hand. 'When I die, they will find *Shawes* carved upon my heart,' he promised.

Vanbrugh made his model, and Christopher Wren was sent to Woodstock on the Queen's behalf to estimate the cost of creating the reality. He came back with the news that it would cost £100,000. The news was staggering – why, Castle Howard in its most recent estimate was only expected to cost £50,000. The Duchess Sarah told the Queen that it was nonsense, and that she was by no means to permit such scandalous extravagance. But Marlborough and Vanbrugh together were so enthusiastic that the Queen agreed to pay the sum out of her own incomes, and consequently the foundation stone was laid in June – eight foot square, and inlaid with the words 'In memory of the Battle of Blenheim, June 18th 1705, Anna Regina'.

Annunciata's own modest scheme, whose estimated cost

was a mere £18,000, was progressing well. Vanbrugh, on one of his visits to the site with Annunciata, said, 'Much as I love Castle Howard, and the grand design, I'm not sure your house will not be the most exquisite of all. A palace in miniature. I can see why great painters like to turn their hands to miniatures now and then – it prevents a coarsening of the spirit.'

Arthur was once more working under Vanbrugh, and with Annunciata's permission had been given charge of the work at Shawes, where he had introduced one or two ideas of his own. Annunciata, who thought her grandson deplorable in looks and dull in character, was surprised at his grasp of architectural principles, and gave her opinion that he must be an architect by instinct, since he surely could not be one by intellect. He had settled down happily, it seemed, with Clover, though there was not yet any sign of a child. Clover did not come to Morland Place with him. Arthur said that she had become a regular businesswoman, and that all her years of helping Clovis run the Morland Place estate had given her a taste to govern her own concerns in person. Privately Annunciata thought it the best thing possible for her to have something to occupy her thus, especially as it kept matters out of Arthur's hands. Though her observation of Arthur had given her no evidence of debauchery, she could not, would not trust him.

That summer, which brought the wedding of John Rathkeale and Frances Francomb and their departure on a European Grand Tour by way of combining honeymoon for both and education for John, brought other changes in the family. Cathy Morland died quietly in her bed at Aberlady House, of no particular cause it seemed, other than old age. It shook Annunciata badly when the news came, for Cathy was only a few months older than she, not yet sixty-one. But then, she comforted herself, Cathy had never been strong from babyhood, and had suffered a great deal of ill-health as well as great unhappiness in her life, and had, moreover, been living for many years in Scotland which was next door to being completely outside civilization.

'The Palgraves live long,' she said to Chloris. 'Look at my aunt Sofie.'

Chloris, who had heard all this before, nodded. 'Besides, madam,' she said, 'your parents were strong healthy people, not like poor Miss Cathy's.'

'True,' Annunciata comforted herself. 'And I am as strong as ever I was. I still ride and walk and dance with as much energy as ever. I can outride most young people, if it comes to that.' And to prove it, she called for Phoenix to be brought and rode him out to Marston Moor and galloped him until he was tired, and Kithra whined and sulked all the way home.

Cathy missed seeing her first grandson by only a few weeks. Sabina was still in mourning black when she presented Allan Macallan with a son, whom they called Hamil. Cathy's will had left everything to Mavis's child Mary, for Allan would inherit his father's estate and his children were therefore provided for, but for the present the two families continued to live together, dividing their time between Aberlady House in the winter and Birnie Castle in the summer. It was a comfortable arrangement, for the three adults had grown up together, and they felt it would be pleasant for their children to do likewise.

Sabine's death in the autumn came as less of a surprise, for she had evidently been living by leasehold for some time, as she grew fatter and fatter and redder in the face. Her death took place probably as she would have liked it. She had hunted that day, having been heaved by main force on to the back of her heavy horse, and had thundered with the best of them after the staghounds, only stopping when, short of breath, she had complained of pains in her chest. She had left the hunt and ridden home in the company of two servants when they drew the second covert, and before she reached home she had dropped the reins with a grunt of surprise, clapped her hands to her breast, and tumbled like a stone from the saddle. The servants had run to her and tried to revive her, but she was quite dead. She was forty-nine years old, and considering her mode of life it was a good age for her to reach.

Jane Birch died at the New Year. She was seventy-three, and had been growing more feeble all that year, but Annunciata found it harder to accept her death than that of the others, for Birch had been with her since her first Season in London, when she was fifteen. It was a lifetime ago, and more even than Chloris, Birch had witnessed all the sorrows and triumphs of her life, often sharp-tongued, often critical, but never less than entirely loyal. Annunciata could not do less for her old friend than to take her back to Morland Place, despite the winter weather. Jane Birch had been born a Londoner, but of latter years she had always referred to Morland Place as home, and it had been home to her and her mistress more than any other place.

Matt gave his permission for Birch's coffin to be placed in the crypt, until Shawes was finished, for Annunciata wanted to have her friend buried near her, and planned to move the coffin when the new house was ready. Father St Maur came too, and it was he who conducted the funeral service in the chapel at Morland Place, with the new priest, Father Cole, assisting. St Maur's voice trembled as he spoke the oration – he and Birch, as governor and governess to the Countess's children, had been close friends – and at one point it gave way altogether, and Father Cole, smoothly and tactfully, filled in the words until the old priest had recovered himself. It was a moving ceremony. Even India, vastly pregnant, wept real tears, though she had hardly known Birch. Matt, watching her with concern, was surprised at the tears; Clement, who knew more of the truth, was indignant.

After the service there were funeral baked-meats to be taken, and Annunciata got into conversation with Father St Maur's successor, and found him interesting, with a lively mind and more experience of the world outside the priesthood than was often the case. Matt told her that he had made himself thoroughly at home in the short time he had been there, and that the servants all liked him very much. He was willing to be useful in many little ways about the house and grounds, helped with the accounts, was knowledgeable about gardens and horses, taught the under servants to read and write, was training a choir of small boys from the village, was diligent about visiting sick tenants, and was giving Jemmy and Rob their first lessons.

'A very paragon,' Annunciata said drily. Matt looked proudly at his wife, vast in much-frilled black, overseeing the burnt ale.

'India chose him. She is a wonderful judge of character. I was quite wrong in my previous choice, but she has got it right this time.'

Annunciata discounted all of this as fatuous nonsense, but said, 'He does seem a pleasant young man, indeed, and handsome for a priest.'

India went into labour the day after the funeral, no doubt brought on by the emotional strain of the day, and with very little trouble produced her fourth child, a boy, a long, dark baby with a great deal of hair and an unexpectedly large nose for a baby. India told Matt that he was to be called George, which annoyed Annunciata greatly, since the name George to her was anathema, calling to mind the George Lewis who was intended to usurp the throne from King James.

Matt, caught between wanting to humour his wife, whom he loved, and wanting to humour the Countess, whom he respected, said, 'It is a good name, Grandmother, and a compliment to Queen Anne – and you have always liked her husband Prince George, have you not?'

'I have not objected to him. He is a perfectly harmless man,' Annunciata said. 'But the fact remains it is a German name, and belongs to dull, German men. It does not belong to a Morland, or a Stuart.'

But Matt, though apologetic, had no mind to cross India, especially when she was still in childbed, and so the infant was christened George by Father Cole, and Annunciata, though polite, took her leave for London, despite being requested most cordially to stay until the good weather and the building season began.

In London there were more serious concerns, and Annunciata longed for Clovis, so that she could have immediate and detailed knowledge of what was going on at Westminster and St James's; though Vanbrugh, as honorary member of the exclusive Whig club, the Kit-Kat, did his best to keep her informed during his visits to London. The matter was the long-debated question of the union of England and Scotland, an idea that first saw the light of day when the thrones were united in the person of James I of England. It had been a dear wish of Usurper William, and had he lived he might well have engineered it himself; as time went on it was growing more urgent, for the Hanover succession was likely to depend largely upon it.

The Scottish Parliament had the right to offer the crown of Scotland to anyone it liked upon the death of Queen Anne, and in 1703 had passed an Act declaring as much, and not guaranteeing the succession in Scotland to George Lewis. If on Anne's death the throne of Scotland was given to King James, it would give the French a convenient back door into England, and would make it easy for James to conquer England from there. The Whigs were nervous at the prospect, and in December 1705 passed an Act to say that the Scots should be treated as aliens and trade with Scotland restricted until the Scottish Parliament settled the crown of Scotland on the English successor.

The Border trade was important for Scotland, and it was enough to induce the Scottish Parliament to agree to negotiate, and when Annunciata arrived back in London the plans had already been made for commissioners from both countries to meet in April at Whitehall for the preliminary discussions. A union between the countries would be a triumph for the Whigs and make the Hanover succession more likely, but Annunciata could not believe that the Scots would ever consent to the union. She also had her doubts about Anne's eventual choice falling on George Lewis: she had never forgotten his snubbing her when she was just a young girl, and had always loathed even the sound of his name; and she was also known to have grave feelings of guilt about her behaviour towards her father.

There were strong links with the Court at Hanover – the husband of Annunciata's half sister Ruperta had recently been sent to the Herrenhausen as a special emissary of the Queen, and there was a plan mooted to bring Electress Sofie and her son to England so that they should be on hand when Anne died; but equally there were strong, though hidden, links with St Germain, and Annunciata knew, through Vanbrugh's gossip, that few of the Whig lords, even the great Marlborough himself, had not made their devoirs to King James, to be on the safe side. That summer, in June 1706, James's eighteenth birthday brought his minority to an end, and the Council of Regency was dissolved. This fact, together with the looming possibility of union between England and Scotland, made it more and more likely that there would be an invasion soon on the young King's behalf. Annunciata knew that her position would be dangerous in such an event, and began, very circumspectly, to make plans for flight if necessary.

The Treaty of Union was passed by the Scottish Parliament in January 1707, and there were riots in Glasgow and Edinburgh, and the news-sheets all talked of the possibility of bloodshed, civil war, and invasion. In London there was a thanksgiving service at St Paul's, with a splendid procession and speeches about the most glorious day of Anne's reign. The union was deemed to begin on 1 May, and the elders of the Kirk of Scotland declared 1 May a day of fasting and mourning for the country's humiliation. Annunciata received word from Edmund at St Omer that Colonel Nathaniel Hoocke had been sent to Scotland as a special emissary, to sound out the great lords on the possibility of a rising. She knew Hoocke, whom she had met at St Germain when he had joined the Irish guards there – he had been one of the visitors to her fire that first long winter. She had known of him before that, indeed, for he had been chaplain to the Duke of Monmouth and had accompanied him during the rebellion, escaping into hiding after Sedgemoor. After two years he had thrown himself on the mercy of King James II, and when the latter had pardoned him, he had shewn his good faith by converting to Catholicism and later going into exile with him. He had fought at the Boyne with Karellie, and was about five or six years older than her son.

Even before Hoocke had reported back to the King at St Germain, eight Scottish lords had travelled secretly to France to beg the King and King Louis to come to Scotland and lead the Scots against the English who had taken away their independence. From Edmund, Annunciata heard that their eloquence had moved both kings, and later when Hoocke reported that the whole nation was ready to rise and that troops numbering nearly thirty thousand would be available, a definite plan for an invasion in January was put in hand. Annunciata burnt the letter very carefully, and sat for a long time deep in thought.

Her own position was difficult. She was in England unofficially, and by the favour of Queen Anne, but if there was an invasion, she would almost certainly be either arrested or expelled as dangerous. Yet if she went now to Scotland, or abroad, she would alert the Queen's agents. She ought, of her duty to her King, do everything she could to aid him, but the thought of Morland Place was unpromising. Little Matt, completely preoccupied with his estate and his wife; frivolous India, recently delivered of her fifth son, Thomas, and with a full nursery to occupy her; would they have time or will to spare for the King over the Water? She did not think either of them cared a jot who sat on the throne of England, provided they were left in peace.

And further north, what of the other Morland households? Frances and John in Northumberland, young people with no particular reason to love King James, would they rise? In Scotland, without Cathy's firm hand on the reins, would they rise? And should she warn them of the plans, so that they could be ready, when to warn them might give them the power to betray the rising, deliberately or accidentally?

In the end, she decided that the best and safest thing was to do nothing, except that she wrote to the King at St Germain promising him money to the limit of her estate should he need it; and she kept a small trunk packed with essentials and her jewels, ready to take flight instantly the rebellion began.

Matt was riding home one day at the beginning of winter, his cloak pulled up about his ears and his hat pulled down against the sharp and icy little wind – 'lazy wind' the people called it, for it was too lazy to go round a man but passed straight through him. Star, eager for his stable, was putting his feet down well, pulling lightly against the bit as he trotted smartly over the firm track down from Shipton Moor towards the village. Matt was aware of feeling pleasantly contented with his lot. He had just concluded a good deal over the sale of one of his horses, and was going home to his supper a richer man by five hundred guineas. At home India would be waiting for him, looking radiant as she always did at this stage of pregnancy. All his five boys were healthy and growing apace. Jemmy, who was devoted to his tutor, was shewing signs of being a scholar like his father; and tomorrow Matt had promised to hold the ceremony of breeching Robert, who was just five. Provided he could get home before it got too dark and cold, he would have nothing to complain of. He had five miles or so to go, and he put Star into a hand canter, letting the horse pick his own way across the rough ground.

In the village he was forced to come back to a walk, and then to halt entirely, for he came across the route of a funeral procession. Funerals were as common as blackberries, especially at this time of the year, and Matt doffed his hat automatically, taking note that though it was a poor man's funeral, nothing had been stinted that could be afforded. Matt's pity was roused when the bier came past, for on it was the coffin of an adult and two tiny ones as well, and as a man passed next in the position of chief mourner, Matt concluded sadly that it was a mother and two children that had died.

As he passed Matt, the man looked up briefly, and Matt saw a grief-ravaged face that seemed vaguely familiar. And then the man stopped altogether, and Matt cried out, 'Davey, man, is it you?'

The procession straggled to a halt, and Matt flung himself from his horse and went impetuously towards Davey, hands outstretched, forgetting in his pleasure that they had parted with harsh words so many years ago; forgetting, just for a moment, that Davey was mourner in a funeral procession. Davey's rigid immobility reminded him. He dropped his hands, but could not prevent his face from breaking again and again into a grin of delight, which he would instantly repress in view of the bitter occasion. Davey looked at him with a kind of weary pity, behind which, if there was any pleasure it was well concealed.

'Master Matt,' he said. 'Yes, it's me. You come across me at a poor time.'

'Davey – oh Davey! Is it – are you – ?'

'My wife, sir, and my two little boys. Smallpox, sir,' Davey said expressionlessly. Matt's face was a battleground of emotions, and Davey observed him wryly.

'Oh Davey, I'm so sorry. God give them rest, and grant you acceptance. Poor Davey! I am so glad to see you, but so sorry that it is at such a sad time. But what have you been doing all this while? I have thought about you, often and often.'

'Have you, master?' Davey said, looking at him oddly. 'I've thought about you, too.'

'We were friends – it's natural. But look, I am holding up your procession. Shall I walk with you? Would you let me?'

'You, master? Attend a pauper's funeral?' Davey said harshly.

Matt looked uncomfortable. 'Not that, Davey, by all the evidence. Not a pauper.'

'I shall be when this is done. I have lost everything, and I sold all I had left to give them a decent funeral, for I would not have them laid away like discarded rags. But when they are laid to rest, I shall have nothing but the clothes on my back. So now you know. I'm a pauper, for all that counts.'

'You are still my friend, Davey. Let me walk with you.'

Davey pulled himself up stiffly, and gave a queer little bow of his head.

'If you will,' he said. There was no more said. Matt sent off his servant with a message for Morland Place, and took his place beside Davey, leading the indignant Star. The torches seemed to burn brighter as the dusk deepened.

After the funeral Matt took Davey with him to the village inn, and took a room for the night for them both, for it was too dark to travel on.

'Where would you have slept?' Matt asked. Davey shrugged.

'Under a hedge, if I could have found one safe from the constable. If the constable found me, I would have been whipped out of the parish as a beggar. You are keeping bad company, Master Matt. What would Father St Maur say?'

But Matt sensed behind the bitterness that Davey was glad to see him, and did not blame him, so he held his tongue and sent for supper for them both, and by his silence encouraged Davey to talk. By the time they had finished, he had heard the whole sad tale. Davey had gone to work for a farmer, and by dint of working every hour God sent, and saving almost to the point of madness, he had got enough to wed a servant girl with savings of her own.

'A good girl, master, though not pretty. Hard working.

Older than me, of course. But a good girl. You would have liked her, I think.'

Their joint savings were just enough to buy a tiny cottage with common rights on the edge of the moor, and they had set up as long before he had seen his sister Betty set up – but with less money, and in harder country. At first things had gone well enough. Davey had taken day work, as had his wife, and they had kept a few pigs and chickens and a goat, and grown their beans in their scrap of garden, and cut turfs from the moor. But then Alice had become pregnant, and after a while grew too big to work. It had been more of a struggle, but they were surviving. Then the pigs got swine-fever, and that was the death-blow to their hopes.

The babies had been born, twin boys, and Alice, already beginning to feel the pinch of hunger, had not had enough milk to feed them. The goat's milk had not agreed with them, and they had had to buy cow's milk to keep the babies alive. They could not replace their pigs. They lived on beans and eggs and cabbage, but Alice was growing weaker, and needed better food. They killed one of the chickens, so there were fewer eggs; then another; then their master, who owned the cottage and the land around, had told them they must leave at the end of the year, for he wanted to improve the land. Davey had begun, desperately, to look for a place, but a man with a dependent wife and two babies was not wanted when a single man could be found.

'The smallpox came almost as a release,' Davey said, his face indistinguishable in the gloom, turned away from the candle. 'First one of the babies took it, then the other. Alice nursed them. She was so brave, she never let me see her weeping. Then she got it too. She was too weak – she was starving to death in any case. They all died within hours of each other. God knows why I was spared. God keeps such knowledge to Himself.

'So I sold what we had, the furniture, such as it was, and the blankets and pots, and paid for the funeral. She had so little in life, I wanted her at least to have a decent funeral, poor girl.'

There was a long silence. They had finished eating, and there was only the wine left.

Davey said diffidently, 'I'm not accustomed to wine, master. It makes my tongue loose.'

'Davey, come home with me,' Matt said abruptly. Davey looked up at him, and Matt knew he had been expecting it. 'Work for me,' he said, knowing Davey's pride must be comforted.

'What as?' Davey asked. Matt opened his hands.

'God, I don't know. Be my steward, my bailey, butler, manservant, clerk, I don't know. Be my right hand. Be my friend. I have *need* of you, Davey. I don't know what title to give the need.'

Davey said slowly, 'I have to be able to believe that you do, Matt. Is it laughable? I can't afford pride. But I have nothing in the world – it is all that I can afford.'

'I want to help you, because I love you,' Matt said simply, 'but I am only saying the truth. I do need you. I have always needed you. I never had a brother, you see. I have no one to help *me*.'

Davey looked at him now, and his expression softened. There was no denying such generosity. His eyes were bright with the tears he had avoided until now. He did not call him master, not then. He put his hand out across the table, and Matt placed his own over it, and Davey said, 'I will come home with you. I will serve you in whatever way I can. Thank you.' Matt shook his head, unable to speak, and Davey added, 'Now I owe you my life. I'll repay that debt, one day.'

CHAPTER TWELVE

Karellie stood in the meagre shelter of a three-foot stone wall on the harbour-front at St Omer and huddled deeper into his cloak against the piercing February wind. Everything around him was grey – the grey walls of the harbour, the grey water slapping with a cold, oily sound against the dockside, the iron-grey sky, tearing into great scuds of wet cloud as the wind rose, and beyond the harbour, the grey, tossing, foam-shaken waste of the sea. Beyond it all lay England, green England, their objective, and Karellie stared hungrily into the murk as if he might catch a glimpse of his homeland.

Soon it would be dark, and time again to do the round of his men before retiring to his cramped billet in the town. They seemed to have been here for ever, doing nothing. Karellie's men had had the misfortune to be amongst the earliest to march into St Omer, so it was their fate to wait on the others. All through February the French and Irish soldiers had assembled here and at Dunkirk, where the ships also had been brought in a few at a time. The idea was to avoid any sudden congregation of ships and men that might alert possible English spies to the forthcoming invasion, for General Cadogan was at Ostend and in constant contact with Whitehall. So the slow assembly went on, and the firstcomers waited.

Fortunately, Karellie's men were still in good spirits, despite the bickering that had been going on amongst the upper echelons. Forbin and de Gace had been at daggers drawn from the beginning, Admiral Forbin holding that the whole plan was folly, for he said there was no guarantee of any support in Scotland, no port secured to them where they could definitely land safely, and no line of escape open if they should fail, since their heavy transport ships were slow and unweatherly. The King and the Minister of Marine had taken his advice so far as to exchange as many of the transports as possible for fast, light privateers, but still Forbin, who had charge of the naval side of the enterprise, was having difficulty in equipping his ships, and quarrelled with General de Gace, in charge of the army, about the noise and activity of the soldiers which was bound, he said, to draw attention to them.

Karellie had taken the opportunity while he was in St Omer to visit his uncle Edmund, Clovis's brother, at the seminary; a grey, shaven-head priest of fifty-four, with a strong resemblance to Clovis. Edmund received Karellie warmly, and they talked for some time about family matters before inevitably passing on to a discussion of the invasion. Edmund, Karellie found, was well informed about current affairs, for his life-long position as foreign correspondent to the family had caused him to build up a network of informants. He was not entirely sanguine about the chances of success.

'The time is right, of course. The union has disaffected the Scots, and the King has reached his majority, and there is a great deal of hostility in both countries to the idea of the Hanoverian succession,' he said. 'But I'm afraid Forbin is right about some things. Six thousand men is not enough, without definite promise of help in Scotland, and despite Hoocke's efforts, not one single man has actually promised to come to arms when the King lands. Hoocke is a good man,' he added, 'but his enthusiasm for the cause leads him to exaggerate the amount of support in Scotland.'

'But this is the time, you say?' Karellie said. 'After all, if not now, when?'

Edmund looked at him sadly. 'I'm afraid whenever the King attempts to regain his throne, he is going to have to rely on the King of France for help. And that means attacking when King Louis is ready. Whether this attempt fails or succeeds is immaterial to the King of France. It will at all events be a diversion from Flanders, you see, and he hopes that England will be forced to recall ships and men and thus give Louis an advantage, a chance to win back the ground he has lost to Marlborough.'

Karellie was shocked. 'You are wrong, I'm sure. The King of France is devoted to our King, and wants nothing more than to help him regain his rightful place.'

'That too, of course,' Edmund said.

Karellie thought about that conversation as he watched the light fading from the grey sky. He did not like to have to consider complexities such as that. He wanted life to be simple. Perhaps Edmund was wrong, he thought. A gull came flying in from the seaward, hurtling with the wind and turning with a desperate lurch and flap at the wall to make a clumsy landing a few yards from Karellie. The gull jerked back and forth until it had adjusted its balance to the tug of the wind, and then turned its head sideways to stare warily at Karellie with its dark, distant eyes. Karellie felt the cold wind fingering its way down between his cloak-collar and his neck and he thought suddenly of Christmas in Venice, of the heat of the fires, of the brightly-lit rooms, almost as bright as a summer day, there were so many candles, and of the song-bird in a gilded cage which had been this year's present to Diane.

'It will not sing so sweetly as you,' he had said, 'but it may serve to amuse you when you are resting your own voice.'

Diane was twelve, and growing tall, and she had begun to turn up her hair and wear headdresses. She was more on her dignity now, and did not laugh so readily, and sometimes, when they were alone together, he would catch her looking at him in a way that disturbed him, though he did not know why. But at Christmas she had been pleasantly childlike, reverting to her old ways, playing games and singing, and playing snap-dragon with burning raisins for the sake of the children, Alessandra, now eight, and four-year-old Giulia. It had been a bright and lovely time, lights, warmth, splendid food, spiced wine, brilliant colours reflected from every side by the host of glass mirrors, elegant men and beautiful women dancing and laughing and exchanging gifts and sly kisses. It was a good, warm memory to take out and polish now on this cold bleak afternoon.

Diane had been angry with him for missing a Christmas, and he had had to work hard to make it up to her by telling her stories of other Courts and the rich and famous people he had known. Maurice had been quieter and more withdrawn than before, for he had lost his second wife in childbirth, and was feeling it dreadfully.

'I shan't marry again,' he told Karellie one evening when they were alone over their claret. 'I find perfection, and I despoil it. She would still have been alive if it had not been for me.'

Karellie tried to comfort him, but he would have none of it. He immersed himself more in his work, and what comfort he had he seemed to get from teaching his daughters music, and overseeing the career of Diane, whose voice was now strong enough for her to give occasional public performances, to her intense delight. Only Maurice's stern discipline prevented her from accepting every invitation to perform and thus ruining her voice altogether. Karellie had left reluctantly when the call came from Versailles, for the Carnival was almost upon them, and Maurice's former father-in-law, Alessandro Scarlatti, had arrived for the production of two of his operas in the Teatro San Giovanni Cristostomo. The reunion between him and Maurice had been lovely to see, as was his delight in his granddaughter, whom he pronounced the image of Apollonia. Then he had drawn his granddaughter upon his knee and begun to talk music with Maurice as if it were nine hours instead of nine years since they had last met. Karellie had listened for a while, bemused, and then had crept away to play with little Giulia, whom he felt was more his intellectual equal.

The gull gave a harsh cry and flapped away off the wall, bringing Karellie back to himself with a start. It was almost dark, and as he turned he saw his man, Sam, coming towards him. It was that which had startled the bird.

'News, my lord,' Sam said as soon as he was near enough. 'The King has left St Germain and is on his way here.'

'Thank God. Perhaps then we can start,' Karellie said. Sam turned down his mouth.

'Well, my lord, a man who knows about these things says the weather is brewing up for gales. They always have them at this time of year. If the King doesn't get here soon, we'll be stuck here for weeks.'

Karellie shook his head. He knew nothing of sea matters. 'I dare say they have taken that into account in their calculations. They must know of the gales. What news of my lord of Berwick?' Berwick had been stationed in Spain for the last year, but had left at once on hearing of the expedition. He would be serving as a private gentleman, because of the agreement he had made when he became a French citizen.

'No more news, sir. He should be here before the King, at any rate. Will you come into supper now, my lord? It's growing late.'

Up in the town the first lights were shewing at windows, and their yellow glow at once made the dusk darker. Karellie felt tired and cold and hungry, and the thought of supper suddenly became of extremely cheering importance. 'Yes, I'm coming now,' he said.

The King arrived at the beginning of March, but was evidently unwell, and the following day it was reported that he was seriously ill with measles. His sister, Louise-Marie, had been recovering from measles when he left St Germain, and evidently he had caught the disease from her. For three days he lay in bed running a high fever, and during this time it was reported that a squadron of thirty-eight English warships had moved up from Ostend to Gravelins, only two leagues away, evidently aroused by the activity at Dunkirk and St Omer, and there was talk of abandoning the whole enterprise. But on the fourth day the wind changed, lifting the fog and driving the English ships away, and the King, though too weak to walk, had himself carried on board the flagship *Mars*, and ordered the embarkation without any further delay.

Karellie was still on the harbour-side when a group of horsemen rode up, wearing the French royal livery. The leader stopped a soldier and asked a question, and after a few more exchanges the soldier indicated Karellie, who had been putting off going aboard until the last possible moment. He had no great love of sailing. The messenger rode towards Karellie and saluted, and then recognized him.

'Marechal le Comte,' he said with a bow, 'I beg your pardon for disturbing you, but I have here a message from the King to the King of England, and I cannot discover where he lies. I beg you will help me, my lord, for it is a matter of great urgency.'

'His Christian Majesty is now on board,' Karellie said, 'and as he is ill, I doubt whether he will want to be disturbed. But if you say it is urgent, I will take you there.'

Karellie led the way to the *Mars*, still tied up, but ready to be cast off. Her gangways were up, and since the messenger did not care to leave his horse in the confusion of embarking soldiers, Karellie agreed to carry the letter to the King and was taken up on a chair for the purpose. The King was in bed in his cabin, and when Karellie was admitted, he found the tiny room crowded with senior officers.

'I apologize for disturbing you, Your Majesty, but a letter has arrived from Versailles which the messenger insisted was most urgent.'

'Thank you, my lord Earl,' the King said, holding out his hand, 'but I must beg you to remember that I am to be known as the Chevalier St George. I do not wish to be called King until I set foot in Scotland.'

Karellie bowed assent, and the King unrolled the letter and read it. A strange expression came over his face, and when he came to the end of the letter he looked round the officers assembled before him with an expression of wry amusement. 'It is from the King of France, who now wishes to cancel the whole expedition, for various reasons. But, gentlemen, I think you will all agree that this letter arrived too late. So unfortunate, but it did not arrive until after we had sailed, and so I had no opportunity to comply with His Catholic Majesty's wishes.' A murmur of laughter went round the group, and Berwick caught Karellie's eye over the heads of the others and gave a small nod of approval. The King, always gracious, dismissed Karellie. 'Thank you for your trouble, my lord Earl. Perhaps you would like to return to your ship now? I am sorry that you had a wasted journey.'

Karellie bowed and departed, and shortly afterwards the fleet sailed.

A month later what remained of the fleet struggled back against the contrary winds into Dunkirk, battered, seasick, weary and despondent. They had never been able to land in Scotland at all. The English fleet had known only too well what they were doing; contrary winds had delayed them three days at Ostend, and by the time they arrived at the Firth of Forth, there was a squadron of English warships waiting for them. They anchored by the Bass Rock off North Berwick and made the signals they were supposed to bring out the Jacobite army on shore to secure their landing, but no one came, and at daybreak they had to sail away or be trapped by the warships.

They had lost three ships and eight hundred men, and had achieved nothing. Word was passed around that Louis had never meant the expedition to succeed and had given Forbin orders not to allow James to land in Scotland, whatever happened. Karellie formed part of the escort that accompanied the King back to St Germain, where he was greeted with tears by his mother and sister, who had given all their meagre resources, including all their jewellery, to help finance the expedition.

'I have never known the Princess to complain before,' Aliena told Karellie privately, 'but she cried last night and said that they would have to live in such poverty from now on that even if the King were ever to be restored to the throne, they would none of them know how to behave like people of rank.' She looked keenly at Karellie. 'Is it true what they are saying, that King Louis meant the matter to fail?'

'I don't know,' Karellie said. It seemed likely, but even if it were true, what use was there in saying it? 'I don't know. We have all lost a great deal, not just in terms of money.'

'Yes, Karellie, I know,' Aliena said gently. 'The Princess Anne has named everyone in the expedition guilty of treason. Now you can never go home.'

Karellie almost laughed at that. 'I am no worse off than I was before on that count,' he said.

'I wonder how it will affect our mother,' Aliena said. 'I hope she will be all right.'

Karellie did not want to think about that. He hesitated, and then said, 'Aliena, why don't you go to Venice, and stay with Maurice? I could take you there myself, before I return to duty. You would be happy there, I'm sure, and you would at least have your family around you.'

Aliena looked at him curiously. She had known for a long time that Karellie did not feel entirely at ease in her company, and was touched that he should concern himself for her welfare. 'I thank you, brother, but I could not go,' she said. 'My place is with the King and my Princess. I cannot leave them, especially not now.'

It was only a short while later that the King came upon them, where they had retreated into a corner of the old nursery in order to be private. He stopped short when he saw them, and said, 'I'm sorry – I did not mean to – I did not know you were here.'

'You cannot think that we mind being interrupted by *you*,' Aliena said, smiling.

'Privacy is hard to come by in a palace,' the King said. 'I am sorry if I have intruded upon yours. But now that I find you together, perhaps I might speak to you. I have been wondering –' He hesitated, looking from one to the other, and Karellie prompted him gently.

'Yes, sir?'

'My lord Earl, do you think there would be a place for me in the army of the King of France? I feel so despondent and restless here. I cannot bear to remain idle, especially after – it is much on my mind you see, and there is nothing to distract me.'

'I am sure His Majesty would be delighted, sir,' Karellie said. The King was looking at Aliena now.

'I know what you're thinking – that I should not desert my mother and sister at such a time. But what use can I be to them? I cannot cheer them, being so sad myself. And my presence is a burden on the pension which supports them. Is it not best that I do something to support myself and keep myself cheerful?'

He seemed really anxious to have her opinion, and when Aliena answered it was without formality, as equal to equal, and Karellie realized that there was more to the relationship between his sister and the King than he could readily understand.

'You have decided already, and so I will give you the answer you want,' she said. 'Yes, it would be better for you to be busy, provided that you do not neglect your work of state on that account. You know that your mother and sister will miss you sadly, but you know also that their lives can and will proceed without you without much alteration.'

The King looked relieved, and smiled at Aliena with thanks. 'Then I shall ask King Louis at once. I am sure it for the best that I gain some military experience before I try again to regain my throne. After all, when the Scots come out in arms, I shall have to lead them in battle against my opponents, and it would be a poor thing if I had no knowledge of soldiering, and had to rely on others for experience.'

'You are in the right, sir,' Karellie said. 'The campaign

in Flanders this year will give you all the experience you need, if the past is any guide.'

The King beamed at him. 'I do not forget, my lord Earl, who was your grandfather. I look to you to give me the benefit of your advice and guidance when we serve together in the cavalry.'

Karellie bowed. 'I shall be honoured to help you, sir, if I can.' Inwardly he smiled, for the Chevalier St George was no different from any other nobly-born young man thirsting for glory and longing to exchange the scented inactivity of the drawing-room for the excitement of battle, whatever excuses he gave tongue to.

The King left them, and only then did he notice the sadness in Aliena's eyes, and realized what a difference it would make to the women of the royal family if the King left them. He renewed his offer to escort her to Venice, saying, 'Now that the King will not be at St Germain, you will have no reason to stay.'

'More reason than ever,' she replied. 'I cannot leave my Princess now.'

In the summer of 1708, Father Cole asked for, and was granted, permission to absent himself for a period of two months in order to visit his sister, who was ill. This, at least, was the excuse given, and though Davey had sincere doubts as to its truth, he at least was glad of the priest's absence, since it gave him something direct to do, in taking over temporary charge of Jemmy. He had not been entirely happy since returning to Morland Place with Matt, for when Matt said he did not know what he wanted Davey to be, he was only speaking the truth. Davey had led a somewhat confusing existence ever since, hovering uneasily somewhere between the servants and the family, and no one seemed to know how to treat him or whether it was possible to give him orders or not. He did odd things, where he saw they were needed, rubbed down Star or brushed or mended Matt's clothes, or ran errands, or wrote letters, or gently removed troublesome petitioners from his master's path. He thought sometimes that he was like the squire of a medieval knight. If they had gone to battle together, he would have been Matt's armour-bearer, he would have been Bedivere to Matt's Arthur. Matt, unworldly as ever, did not notice that Davey felt at all awkward about his place, and treated him as a friend rather than a servant, thanking him whenever he did anything for him, and consulting his opinion over matters both of family and national politics.

When the Countess came back to Shawes in the spring, Davey found a friend in Chloris. Shawes was well on the way to being finished – enough, at any rate, was done for the Countess to take up residence there – and the Countess made a precipitous move in March and seemed to dive into Shawes like a fox into its hole, not venturing out for some weeks. The reason became apparent when the news broke of the abortive invasion, and when, in April, Queen Anne outlawed all who had helped in it, Shawes positively quivered in its attempts to avoid notice, and the shades were not even drawn back for some days. But further details of the outlawing revealed that Chelmsford's name was not on the list, and Shawes sighed with relief and opened its doors again.

And then it was that Davey met Chloris, and in the course of several conversations she revealed to him that she had once been in something of a similar situation to his.

'The old master, Ralph, used to say that I was her ladyship's clown,' Chloris said. 'When I first came to her, I was employed as wet-nurse to her babies, but that was never all I was, though no one but the old master ever had a name for me. Now I suppose I'd be called her waiting-woman, but that's less than the truth, as the other was.'

'At least you had an official place to begin with,' Davey said. 'I think it's harder for me.'

'In some ways, yes,' Chloris said, 'but you are more nearly on a footing with your master than I ever was with my mistress. If he wants to call you friend, why can't you be generous enough to accept it?'

'Because – you know it is impossible,' Davey said, outraged that she should criticize him so lightly. She looked at him shrewdly.

'Ah yes, I know it, and you know it, but *he* doesn't. Let him think that's what you are, and let your heart dictate what he wants done. And never mind any other titles.'

So Davey looked for what needed doing, and did it, and tried not to feel out of place. But when the priest went away, and the nursery maids complained that Jemmy was too much for them to handle, Davey stepped quietly in, with a sense of relief, to take care of the young heir to Morland Place. Jemmy was seven, dressed now in a much-frilled miniature version of the clothes of a gentleman of fashion, complete with muff and periwig, and even thus hampered managed to get into a great deal of mischief. Robert, who was not yet six, was fat and fair and placid, and though he was also out of petticoats, he was no trouble to the maids, and liked most of all to trot about hand in hand with Flora and be told stories of the fairies and spirits who lived thereabouts. Edmund and George were still in frocks and the province of nurses, while Thomas, who was a little over a year old, was still sharing the wet-nurse with his new brother Charles, born in February.

Matt was only too pleased to have his friend look after his firstborn, and when Jemmy was brought before him, he bid the boy sternly to respect and obey his new tutor in everything.

'He has an excellent mind, Jemmy, and you would do well to learn from him as much as possible,' Matt said. Jemmy looked up at him solemnly, and then looked towards Davey as if wondering if his father could possibly be right about such an undistinguished person. Despite his blond periwig and his ruffled sky-blue coat, Jemmy was the image of his father and grandfather, his natural hair soft and dark and curly, his high-cheekboned face handsome and sensitive, with the long mouth and vivid dark blue eyes that made them so striking.

When the child had gone, Davey said to Matt, 'There's just one thing – if I am to have him for the summer months, may I do something about his clothes?'

'His clothes?' Matt said vaguely. Davey was hesitant.

'You see, I'd like to get him out of doors, away from the servants and the nursery, for everyone's sake. Remember how you used to like to run wild with me, in just shirt and breeches? Remember how much we learned about life that way? I'd like to take the boy riding, and walking, and swimming, and give him his lessons sitting on the top of a hill in the fresh air. And we can't do those things when he's dressed up like a – like a –'

'Peacock?' Matt offered, smiling wryly. 'Yes, all right, I know you cannot say so without being rude. Frankly, it is his mother's humour to dress him so elaborately. She says he must look like a gentleman before he can learn to act like one. She may be right. But perhaps, just for this summer, you might have your way. I shall be from home a good deal, Davey, so you will have to manage without my support.'

'I'll keep out of the way,' Davey grinned, 'and have him properly dressed for dinner, so she'll hardly notice.'

Jemmy was not at first entirely convinced that the change was for the better, for he had liked the consequence of strutting about in adult clothes, even though they were hot and uncomfortable, and the wig a positive penance. The servants all admired him tremendously, and he was a godlike figure to Rob and Edmund. He treated Davey, who did not even *look* like a gentleman, with some disdain at first, but after a few days, when he had discovered the delights of running about the fields and immersing his hot dusty body in a cold stream, he began to listen to Davey more attentively.

Davey found Jemmy's mind active, and not yet entirely spoilt, though he had already learnt the trick of ignoring everything but what would produce a good effect with the least effort, in order to impress Mama and Papa. But Davey would not be impressed, and soon he found Jemmy's mind agape for sustenance like a fledgling bird.

In the course of their long rambles and conversations, most topics were touched upon, and when architecture had its turn, it was natural for Davey to promise to take Jemmy over to see Grandmama at Shawes. As Vanbrugh had promised the Countess, Shawes was a palace in miniature. Faced with the old stone from the original house, it seemed to grow peacefully from its foundations, an elegant rectangular building of two stories, with servants' quarters in the attics. It was built around the central great hall, a magnificent feature which rose through two stories, its groined cove ceiling supported on massive fluted pilasters, set against the walls, and the whole lit from above by the glazed lights in the great dome. The massive door in the front, north face, opposed the door to the terrace on the south face, and a transverse passage ran straight through the house from east to west on both levels, offering magnificent vistas through decorated arches from one end of the house to the other.

As at Morland Place, the great staircase was housed in a separate hall to the west of the great hall: a grand cantilevered staircase of three flights, made all of oak, strengthened within with iron. The treads were parquetried, and the balustrade was of delicate wrought iron, and on the two half-landings were panels of raised plaster mouldings, shewing the heraldic achievement of Ballincrea and Chelmsford.

A short, curved wing on either side of the main block on the south side led, to the west, to the bathing house, set in formal gardens, and to the east, to the service wing and the stables beyond. From the terrace on the south side the gardens would run down to the stream, which was to be widened and dammed and generally made worthy of the house, but at present all this was still in the minds of the Countess and Henry Wise, for nothing had yet been done about it. There remained much to be done indoors as well

237

– the plaster mouldings, the carving – Gibbons had agreed to oversee this – the *trompe l'oeil* paintings in the wall-panels – but these things were details. The grand plan was clear and evident.

Even Jemmy was suitably awed by the grandeur of the house, and by the stateliness of the hostess. Annunciata, just then brimming with relief that Karellie was safe, was in a mood to take notice of her eldest great-grandson. Jemmy's social manners were at least perfect, and he shewed to his best advantage when he was making the correct obeisances and speeches to the noble lady. She condescended to shew the child around the house, and then called for her horse and accompanied them on a sedate ride around the perimeters, describing, mostly for Davey's benefit, what it would look like one day. Here Jemmy spoilt his previously clean slate.

'But when your ladyship dies, who will it all belong to then?' he asked, and Davey fancied there was a gleam of his mother in his eye. The Countess looked at him coldly, and Davey attempted mediation.

'Master James, I think, wondered whether with so much to do, your ladyship would see the completed plan.' This was hardly better. He blundered on, 'My lord of Marlborough, I heard, asked Master Wise to plant none but full-grown trees at Blenheim, because he would not live to see saplings grow to maturity.'

Annunciata's cold stare, now directed at him, made Davey want to giggle in despairing amusement. She said, 'You may assure yourself, and Master James, that I have every intention of enjoying the completed Shawes for a great number of years. Shall we go back?'

She turned her horse, and headed towards the house; but as her profile passed him, Davey felt sure he saw the corner of the Countess's mouth twitching too.

It lacked an hour until dinner when he and Jemmy rode back into the yard at Morland Place, and Davey decided it was good time to shew the boy how to look after his own horse. He demonstrated the art of untacking, petting, and rubbing down, and as he watched the child fumbling with the unaccustomed tasks, he talked to him a little about horses, for horse-lore, he felt, could not be learned too early, and if a man was to be at ease about horses, he had to play amongst their legs as a child, as Matt had done, and eat his bread and cheese perched upon a manger.

When the horses were done, and pulling contentedly at their hayracks, Davey lifted Jemmy up on to a manger, and produced a couple of sweet, wrinkled store-apples and let the boy relax, and chatter to him as he would. It was while they were thus engaged that the doorway was darkened, and Davey looked up to see the mistress with one of the nursery maids behind her.

'A groom said you were in here,' she said without preamble. 'May I ask what you think you are achieving by teaching my son to behave like a stable boy?'

Davey jumped down from the manger, and lifted Jemmy down, and said quietly and politely, 'There is still plenty of time, madam, before dinner. I assure you the boy would have appeared before you in exactly the manner you like.'

'He is not doing so *now*,' she said. 'Nurse, take Master Jemmy away, and wash him, and dress him like a gentleman's son.'

The nurse scurried forward, with the ducked head of one who expects to be cuffed on passing: the mistress had a reputation for lashing out when crossed. The nurse grabbed the child's arm with the suggestion of a pinch, and hustled him out into the hot sunshine, and in the silence that followed Davey heard the beginning of a howl, quickly cut short. Then there was only the sound of the steady pull and crunch of the horses eating, the rustle of their feet in the straw. The mistress continued to stare at Davey, and since she was in a position of superiority, with the sun at her back, he was unable to stare back; but he felt an unusual tension about her. She was almost as tall as he, with an upright figure; she looked good on horseback, which was how he thought of her, when he thought of her at all. She was handsome, he admitted, but there was something cold about her, something predatory that tempered the respect he felt he ought to have for Matt's wife. She had completely recovered from her last delivery, and with her high colour and shiny hair he thought she looked like a well-fed horse. But now there was this strange tension. She was dressed for riding, and she switched her crop against her leg in the irritated manner of a cat switching its tail. In cat and mistress, it was not a gesture to be ignored.

Davey kept his face and manner humble, and said pacifyingly, 'I beg your pardon, mistress, but it was by the master's orders. The master thought it would benefit the boy –'

'Benefit?' she interrupted angrily.

He went on, allowing his voice to crawl. 'Benefit the boy just for a little to run about in the fresh air as the master did himself when young.' She came a step forward into the shadow of the stable. 'You must admit it did the master no harm.'

The crop flicked faster, but she spoke as if she had been pacified.

'If it was the master's orders, I suppose you did right,' she said.

'Thank you, mistress.' Davey turned away deliberately and went to pick up the saddle from the corner. When he turned, he saw she had moved closer again.

'Come here, you – what's your name? Davey,' she said imperiously. He took one step only, in token of obedience, and looked straight at her. She was still staring at him. Now she was out of the sun, he could see her face, and it made him shiver inwardly. She was smiling, but there was nothing of allure in it. It was like a cat's smile, watching a mouse come, step by step, out from its hole into a supposed empty room.

'You have known the master a long time, have you not?'

'All my life.' The movement of the crop called his eye, but he knew he must not look away from her face.

'You must feel grateful to the master for taking you in.'

240

Her voice was edged with sarcasm. He did not answer. 'Grateful to me, too. You know that the disposition of the household servants is the mistress's prerogative. Without my consent, you could not have come here.' He did not answer; his gaze wavered, and as suddenly as a snake strikes, she flicked her crop across his face, not hard, but painfully. Water sprang to his eyes, and she smiled a little, watching him.

'Dumb insolence,' she said. 'I could have you whipped, you know. You think I couldn't? While the master is away, I am absolute here.'

While the master is here, too, his mind added, and she must have seen it in his eyes, for she hit him again, but more lightly, on the other cheek. The tears burst from his eyes, and he felt them on his cheeks. She laughed now, and put out her hand, and lifted a drop from his face on one finger and carried it to her mouth. It was a gesture of such sensuality that despite himself he felt his body twitch in response. She saw that, also in his eyes, and her voice became a purr.

'Did I hurt you? Oh, poor Davey. Cruel, cruel mistress! But I can be kind, too. I can make it up to you, poor Davey.' She stroked his cheek, crimson from her blow, with the tips of her fingers, and they stung him like aquavit on an open wound. 'Would I have you whipped? I wonder. I think perhaps when I saw you stripped, I would relent. It would be shame to spoil such pretty skin with cruel stripes, wouldn't it? When there are much nicer things to be done.'

She was close to him now, and he could smell her sweet breath, and the scent of her skin and clothes. Her face was close to his, and he could see the soft wrinkling of her eyelids under their paint, and the down of fine, colourless hair on her cheek. His body was on fire, and the pain in his groin served to keep his mind on his duty. She looked into his eyes, and her expression changed minutely.

'You don't like me, do you?' she said, and it was nearer to a true thing than anything else she had said.

His breathing was difficult, but he said quickly, 'It isn't my business to like or dislike you. You are the mistress. You are Matt's wife.'

'Forget that, just for a moment,' she breathed. Her eyelids lowered slowly, her face tilted upwards, her lips parted softly and hovered over his. Davey's hands rose without his volition and closed over her arms, and he pulled her towards him; then stopped, holding her immobile with a fraction of an inch between her body and his. The closed eyes opened a slit, and then flew open with alarm.

'Let me go. You're hurting me. Let me go I say!' She wriggled, then tried to wrench herself free, and tears of pain rose in her eyes in their turn. 'You're hurting my arms!' Her voice broke in a whimper. 'I'll have you whipped to death!' she cried, and it was the impotent cry of a child. He eased his grip, set her back from him on to her feet, and released her.

'Better go, madam,' he said evenly. 'There will not be time to change before dinner. You don't want to come into the drawing room in your riding habit, do you?'

She blinked back the tears of pain and rage, and glaring at him hissed, 'You'll be sorry for that, I promise you!'

'No, mistress, I won't, and I hope you won't either,' he said gently. She bit her lip and, turning abruptly, was gone in a rustle of skirt on straw.

Davey was left alone with the steady sound of the horses. He reached out absently and ran a hand over the neck and shoulder of the nearest horse, and it flickered its ears contentedly. 'Oh, Matt,' he said aloud, 'you married a wrong 'un.' The horse sneezed, rubbed its muzzle thoroughly against its knee, and reached for another mouthful of hay.

CHAPTER THIRTEEN

Christmas 1708 was the first Christmas for some years that India had not been large with child, and she determined to enjoy the season to the full.

'Dearest, however hard it seems, I do not want to have another child yet,' she said to Matt. 'Do you think me very wicked? But I don't want to be worn out with it, so that I have no strength. After all, if I am strong and healthy, I will have stronger and better children when I *do* get with child again.'

She did not need to present arguments to Matt. He had long grown accustomed to her governing of their sexual activities, and was not by any means the sort of husband to insist on a pregnancy a year. The servants thought him foolishly indulgent to his wife, and would have been horrified if they knew even the half of it; but how could Matt, who was tender to all creatures, be less than tender to the one he loved best? The missus, on the other hand, was tough enough for both, and liked to quote as an example of her sound good sense the remarks made upon the breeching of Edmund, which happened just before Christmas.

The little boy, just five years old, had paraded before his parents in his new manly clothes, and Matt, smiling through his tears of pride and pleasure, had said, 'Now you are in breeches, you will be able to have a pony of your own, and learn to ride properly.'

The missus, however, had remarked only, 'Now you are in breeches, you will be able to be beaten by Father Cole. You will be a man, after all.'

The master was, of course, said the servants, a very proper feeling gentleman, much given to tears, but might well have foolishly indulged his children had not their tutor had charge of the whippings and birchings. Edmund, on hearing his mother's remark, glanced at his father, and then catching his older brothers' eyes, made a sort of grimace. Beatings did not trouble Jemmy at all, and the castigation seemed only to toughen his already bold spirit, but poor Rob was much downcast by it all, being a quiet, gentle child. It was not possible any more even to avoid beatings by the exercise of virtue, for India, on one of her sudden and brief visits to the schoolroom, had decreed that all the children should be beaten first thing on Monday morning, to give them a foretaste, by way of warning, of what idleness or wickedness would bring them during the week. Matt had intervened only in so far as to tell Father Cole privately that as there was an unwritten rule at St Edward's School that no boy should be beaten twice in the same lesson, his own children in his own house should have at least so much mercy.

Except for Annunciata, who remained in London as usual at that season, the family was all together at Morland Place for the first time in many years. John and Frances came from Emblehope, bringing with them their two-month-old baby Jack, and the news that Frances was pregnant again. Their first two babies had died, one within weeks of birth, the other when he was a year old. They seemed very happy, and marriage had evidently agreed with John, filling out his frame to more manly proportions, while the good air of Northumberland had cured his asthma. His father-in-law Francomb was also with them, grown a little rounder, but as jolly as always, making sly sidelong remarks which seemed to cause the mistress some confusion, and evidently doting on his grandson.

'He'll have a grand place to inherit if he lives to be a man,' Francomb said, holding the baby high against his shoulder and ignoring the attempts of the nursemaid to reclaim her rightful property. 'My son John has some right good ideas about improving the land. I warrant you we'll be growing oats and rye in places where there's been nothing but bog-grass and heather until now.' He grinned amiably at John, who smiled and bore up under the thump on the shoulders that accompanied the compliment. It was evident that the unlikely pair got on well together. They and Matt occupied every spare moment with talking farming, when they weren't talking horses.

Lord and Lady Ballincrea presented a very different picture, being coldly polite to each other, and still childless. Clover had not so much as had a miscarriage in six years of marriage. She listened with evident interest to the talk of marling and crop-rotation, but she spoke very little; Arthur had no interest in the land, and would sooner chatter about clothes to India, and husband and wife rarely spoke directly to each other. They both looked very elegant and well-to-do, but Clover had grown thin and grave, quite unlike the round, rosy, happy creature she had been as a child; while Arthur had put on weight, and looked flabby and disconsolate under his finery.

For the first time in years the family from Aberlady had joined them. Mavis still wore black, for it was the custom in Scotland for widows to stay in mourning until they married again, but it suited her fairness very well, and she looked handsome and prosperous. Her daughter Mary was eight now, a tall girl, handsome in her mother's image, and precociously intelligent. Matt found pleasure in talking to her, and wished more than once that Father St Maur had been there to hear her converse. She spoke with equal facility in English, French or Latin, and far out-stripped Jemmy in her knowledge of mathematics and astronomy.

'What a pity she's not a boy,' Matt said once to Mavis. 'She could have been a great man. Instead of which she will have to marry someone, probably with a poorer mind than her own, and all that education will be lost in childbirth.'

'She is a considerable heiress. She will make a good match,' Mavis said, and then, as if to comfort Matt, she added, 'If she marries nobly, she will have perhaps enough freedom to continue to use her mind. In Scotland there are learned women, even married ones.'

Matt enjoyed being with Mavis again, but most of his enjoyment came from the awareness that her power over him had gone. India had laid the ghost, and he could talk to Mavis without any touch of regret for his lost love.

Sabina and Allan Macallan had changed very little from Matt's memories of them, except that Sabina was thin and pale from her last miscarriage. Since her marriage she had had two miscarriages, and had borne a child that died in its first week of life, but her firstborn son, Hamil, still thrived. He was three years old, and had inherited the Morland colouring from his mother. He looked, indeed, very like her, with the same resolute, bold blue stare and small eager face. Matt remembered she had always talked a great deal, and that had not changed with marriage; but he noticed that even while she chattered, her eyes missed nothing, and there was that about her which suggested to Matt that the flow of talk was a screen behind which she hid a considerable wit.

The season passed happily and in the traditional manner. Matt had made Davey Lord of Misrule, which annoyed India very much, though when pressed by Matt she would not admit any objection except that 'he was not a member of the family – indeed, he was almost a servant'. Matt said firmly that Davey was not a servant but his friend, at which India snorted with derision.

'Friend! A common shepherd's son!' she cried. But one thing on which Matt stood firm against her was his friendship with Davey, and she knew better than to press the matter further. In fact, Davey had settled in very well at Morland Place, and the servants had adapted so far to his equivocal status that when Matt was absent they frequently applied to Davey for decisions and orders – which infuriated India. But Davey was always gravely, punctiliously polite to her, and she had nothing that she could legitimately complain of. If she felt that his humble mien before her was derisive, she could not very well say so.

Davey made an excellent Lord of Misrule, organizing

246

games which entertained and involved everyone and made use of the diverse talents and tastes of the heterogenous party. His centrepiece was a play acted by the children for the adults, in which the principal parts of the King and Queen of Bohemia were taken by Jemmy and Mary Morland, though the entry of small Hamil as a shepherdess, leading Oyster, looking very ashamed of himself wrapped in a white woollen shawl to represent a sheep, produced the greatest sensation.

But throughout the celebrations, India was, and demanded to be, the centre of attention, and Davey, looking on with a cynical smile, saw how she must have everyone paying her homage, how if she were in conversation with John Rathkeale and Arthur came by, she would have to call him over to give his opinion upon some trivial point. It was evident that Arthur, at least, did not object to being beckoned; perhaps, Davey thought, he found India a refreshing change from his sad and quiet wife. The only person who resisted the ploy was John Francomb who, like Davey, watched India from afar with ill-concealed amusement, and if approached by her or called to attend, would slip away, politely but firmly, on some other business.

One result of India's exercises with Arthur was revealed to Davey by Matt. Davey was rubbing down Star after a hunt – it was a job properly belonging to the grooms, but Davey always found it soothing, and knew Matt appreciated the extra care taken of his beloved horse. Matt, who had gone into the house, came back out and sought out Davey in Star's stall.

Davey acknowledged his presence with a nod, and carried on methodically rubbing the damp black coat, and Matt, after lounging in silence against the doorpost for some time, said, 'I grew up with Clover, you know. She was like a sister to me.'

'I know,' Davey said, and Matt looked grateful.

'Yes, of course you do. You were almost one of us. Arthur – Lord Ballincrea – never was, though we were all in the nursery together. The servants treated him differently – he was always little Lord Ballincrea – and then he set himself apart too. He used to bully me. I could never like him.' A pause, and then, diffidently, 'I am afraid that perhaps I let that early dislike prejudice me.' Another pause. 'I cannot like him, even now.'

It was a difficult confession, and Davey said nothing, only nodded calmly, as if they were discussing the prospects for the harvest. Matt went on, as if it were not of great importance.

'He has always got on very well with the mistress, though, so he can't be a bad man, can he? He and the mistress have had many long talks this Christmas.'

'I see they have plenty to say to each other,' Davey said. Matt moved restlessly, and then came nearer, seeking confidence.

'They have no children – Arthur and Clover.' Davey nodded, bending to brush between Star's forelegs, so that his face was hidden. Matt would talk better to the back of his head, he knew. 'India has heard of a new man in London, who has a means to make barren women bear. An operation of cutting with a special instrument and – I don't know what else. She has persuaded Arthur to call in the man to work on Clover.'

Now it was out. Davey straightened up and looked at Matt, and saw the pain and fear and indecision in his eyes. An operation involving cutting involved great suffering for the victim, and a good chance of death. And Matt loved Clover – Matt who was so tender he did not even like to think of his sons being birched for their sins. But what could Matt do? He could not interfere between man and wife.

'Have you spoken to Lord Ballincrea, sir?' Davey asked.

'No. I don't know if I can. Davey, what should I do?'

'Perhaps you might talk to Lady Ballincrea?' he suggested. Matt's anguish deepened.

'But I don't know if she knows yet. If they haven't spoken to her, it will be a shock to her.'

'I think perhaps you might speak to Lord Ballincrea – without the mistress's knowing. She would not like to think you were going against her.'

Matt offered to speak, and stopped. It was difficult for him to accept that Davey knew how India ruled him, even though Davey made no criticism of him for it, not even by so much as raising an eyebrow. He hesitated a moment longer, and then nodded briefly to Davey and left.

Davey never knew whether Matt had done anything or nothing in the matter; but whether or no, it made no difference to the outcome. Arthur was, by the end of Christmas, so set on the idea that he took Clover to London from Morland Place to see the surgeon, and commissioned him to perform the operation at once. It took place in the surgeon's own house on 20 January, and involved the use of a new instrument which, the surgeon said, 'would reduce what used to be an age of torture to but one minute'.

Clover endured the cutting and probing with great courage, permitting no complaint, and only the occasional involuntary groan to escape her, and the surgeon pronounced that she had survived the operation very well and that he had every confidence of success. The following day she was very low, which was said to be from the shock of the execution; but the subsequent morning she woke with a fever, which gradually increased through the day. For two days she tossed in delirium, and in the early hours of 24 January she died.

Arthur was devastated. No one had supposed he had any particular love for his wife, since their marriage had been arranged for financial reasons, but he had grown up with her as much as had Matt, and had been married to her for more than six years. He rode hell-for-leather from London to Morland Place, without even leaving any orders for the disposal of the poor corpse, burst in upon the family with his news, and cried out that it was all India's fault, that she had persuaded him to the thing, and that she had done it out of spite and for revenge against Clover. India turned pale and looked about to faint at the horrible accusation, and when Arthur had stopped ranting for a moment, Matt jumped up and pulled him from the room, and thrust him into Davey's arms.

'Give him aquavit – give him laudanum – anything. He is beside himself. He is out of his wits. I must get back to my poor wife.'

Davey took the sobbing, fainting Arthur upstairs, and ministered to him, and when he started raving again, Davey sent all the servants away out of earshot, for fear of what Arthur might say. Afterwards, he was very glad that he had done so, and when, several hours later, he finally got Arthur quiet and into a fitful sleep with the aid of a quantity of brandy, he looked very thoughtful.

It was at this time, more than any other, that Matt was glad he had found Davey, for Davey proved his worth over and over. As well as the problem of India and Arthur, Matt had his own grief to deal with, and the guilt he felt at not having interfered over the operation – though in truth there had never been anything he could have done. It was Davey who managed Arthur, keeping him away from India and from the rest of the household until he had argued him into a calmer frame of mind; Davey who persuaded Arthur that he would be better off at home in Kendal, and arranged for Clement to escort him there; Davey who travelled to London to make the arrangements for Clover's funeral; Davey who wrote the letters informing the rest of the family of the tragedy.

If, back at Morland Place, Davey was more quiet and thoughtful, less inclined to social intercourse than ever, it was not noticed in the prevailing gloom. Matt hung the house with black and had Father Cole say a Requiem Mass, and the tender sympathy of his wife, who never left him alone for a moment, was his only comfort. Davey watched from the background, resolved to bide his time until the period of wifely devotion was over, and the leopardess revealed her true colours again. Meanwhile he listened more closely to the servants' gossip, and by a discreet question or two managed to guide their meaningless chatter towards the things he wanted to know.

Matt was sitting up late after his supper at the Crown in Wetherby when Davey came in. Matt had arranged to stay the night in Wetherby, not because it was too far from home to travel back, but because he had several pieces of business to conduct on consecutive days at Wetherby, and India had said that there was no use in his tiring himself out riding back and forth, when there was a perfectly comfortable inn to stay in. It was one of the ways in which she displayed her thoughtfulness and concern for his welfare, and he loved her for it. There might, of course, have been many reasons for Davey to ride across and seek him out, but Matt's mind flew immediately to India, for she suspected herself pregnant, and he had been uneasy about leaving her alone, despite her gentle chiding that she ought to be well enough used to it by now.

He jumped up so fast on seeing Davey that he struck his knee painfully against the edge of the trestle, but he did not even notice the pain.

'Davey, what is it? Is something wrong?'

Davey's face was grave. 'Master, I want you to come back to Morland Place with me at once.'

'The mistress is ill!' Matt cried, pushing back the stool and fumbling for his purse. 'I knew I should not have left her.'

'No, master, no one's ill,' Davey said.

'The children –'

'No one's ill.'

'Then what . . . ?'

'I want you to come back with me at once, and alone. Leave your man here, and ride with me.'

'But what's happened?' Matt insisted in considerable anxiety. Davey leaned on the table and looked at him steadily.

'There's something at Morland Place that I think you

ought to see. You ought to know about. No one is ill, I promise you.'

'Then why won't you tell me –'

'Master, please trust me. I can't tell you, because you wouldn't believe it, but you must see for yourself. There is something going on – an injustice, call it – which you must deal with. But it is not a thing I could tell you about. Matt, please trust me.'

The use of his name, the steady voice, the urgent appeal in the eyes, worked on Matt. He thought of injustices, and supposed that a servant was perhaps bullying another, or stealing – but he could not think why Davey could not tell him about something like that. But Davey was his friend. He picked up his hat and said, 'Very well. I'll come.'

Davey took him across the fields, and fast, and it was less than two hours' ride that way. But when they got near Morland Place, he made Matt dismount and tie the horses in a copse, and they proceeded on foot, circling the house and coming to the back door. There Davey cautioned him.

'Step softly, master. No sound. We must not alert them, or they'll be gone before we can catch them.'

Matt pulled back. 'I don't like it. It's trickery. Why can't we face them in the morning with a proper accusation? I don't like this underhand business.'

Davey faced him squarely. 'Master, they have been underhand. They have tricked *you*. The only way to force them to admit it is to find them out in the act. Please. It is necessary.'

And reluctantly Matt allowed him to go on. In silence the men entered the back door: Davey must have oiled the lock and the hinges, for the key turned and the door swung open without a sound. It was dark inside the passage, and when he had relocked the door, Davey groped about and found Matt's hand to lead him. It was damp with apprehension; Davey's was dry and firm. In a moment they had passed through the inner door and into the central courtyard, called Eleanor's Garden. Here, by contrast to the absolute blackness of the passage, there was a glimmer of light from the stars overhead. The house was in darkness, no lights shewing anywhere. Everyone must be asleep, Matt thought. What perfidy was it that needed the cloak of night to cover it?

Along the east side of the garden; past the drying rooms and store-rooms. The last section of the east wing, next to the chapel, was the vestry, which had no entrance from the garden. At the penultimate store-room, Davey stopped, placed his finger to his lips, and crept close to the door. Matt did likewise, and pressing his ear to the door heard at first nothing, then a rustle and a murmur which might have been a voice, or voices, or might have been his imagination. He felt Davey tense himself, and felt the sweat start up along his backbone. Then Davey moved.

The door was flung open; there was a startled gasp, but in the darkness of the store-room, Matt could see nothing. It was used for storing odds and ends of dry goods, and Matt could smell oiled wool and candles and soap and wood, evoking childhood and games of hide-and-seek. The person within could see *him*, however, framed in the doorway, and as Davey began to strike a light, Matt heard a woman's voice, a muffled shriek, 'No! No!' A rustle of more determined movement. Davey's voice, dark with threat, 'Oh no you don't!' and then the spark caught, the small glow blossomed round Davey's hands, and leapt into flower at the candle's wick. He had brought all these things with him, Matt thought with dull shock. He had planned every detail. Shock, because he already knew what he was going to see. Like the victim, he could have cried no, no, had he not been so numb.

The leaping candlelight flung the store-room into existence before him. India shrieked 'Oh! Oh!' more in rage than fear. She was sitting up on a heap of blankets, naked, except for the shift she had snatched against her at some time before the light was introduced. Beside her Father Cole disdained to cover his nakedness. He looked down at his hands, resting on his bare legs, like someone awaiting execution. Matt felt the dull, inevitable pain, like the knife in the vitals which carries the foreknowledge of death without the sensation. India's face looked strangely smeared, as if it were made of some soft substance which could be smudged just as her hair could be ruffled; but even in this moment, Matt could admire her spirit, for she did not weep and wail, or crawl for mercy. Her spirit acknowledged no guilt, only sheer fury at being so surprised. Her first action had been to cover herself, but her second exposed her again, for she dropped the shift to grab for the nearest solid objects that would do for missiles, and still shrieking she began flinging them at Davey.

He ducked this way and that, the candle dipping wildly with the movement, and the missiles thudded solidly against the door and, now and then, against him. She did not look at Matt – he wondered whether she had even registered his presence.

A feeling of nausea was growing in him, and he pulled back from the door, and said to Davey, 'Come away. For God's sake come away.'

Davey obeyed him instantly, following him out and shutting the door, against which a last projectile thumped in departure. The candle flame ducked and went out, and the darkness pressed suddenly close, and Matt felt its safety with gratitude. The nausea was rising in him. He made a choking sound, and then reeled about and vomited into one of the flower-beds. Davey came after him; he felt the strong, warm hands on his upper arms. He tried to push him away, but ineffectually. When the retching was over, he straightened up, and became aware of the quietness.

Abruptly he thrust himself away from Davey and went towards the garden door. Outside there was the close, sweet-smelling darkness of the land, acres of it, enough dark to hide him, to hide his grief and humiliation and shame. He knew it all, all in one brief flash like lightning, that illuminated a whole country in vivid, unforgettable detail. It was not just now, not just Father Cole in the store-room this one night. As he stumbled away, running faster to try to get away from Davey, away from Morland Place, away from himself, the memories came crowding in like people come to gloat over a felon's corpse.

How long? Always? Since the very beginning?

The other priest, the one she had accused of making improper advances to her. He remembered her words, her report of the alleged interview. She had probably told him the exact truth, except that she had put her own words in the priest's mouth, and his into hers. She had petitioned, he had rejected, and in anger she had come to Matt, and Matt had avenged her, dismissed the man who rejected her.

Did the servants all know? Had they been watching, laughing at him?

All the times she had gone away, into the city, to Harrogate – dear God, to Northumberland! He had always been surprised at her sudden affection for Sabine. It wasn't Sabine that attracted her to Emblehope. Little fragments assembled themselves of their own volition in his mind, making a picture that would not be ejected. Jack Francomb. A look, and smile over the shoulder, a gesture of the hand. Riding at the hunt. Dancing with him that Christmas – was that the beginning? He had watched her dance with him, and thought her kind.

Had Sabine guessed?

And before Francomb, who? Between Francomb and the priest, who?

In retrospect he heard the falseness of her voice, the hypocrisy of her declarations of love and care for him. In retrospect her touches were loathsome; the memory of their love-making brought the hot bile to his throat. Now he saw so clearly why she had regulated their marital life. The long abstinences between lovers, the 'uncontrollable' passion that led her to break their fast when she had a new lover.

And that brought him to another thought, a thought so monstrous and painful that he cried aloud, and put his hands up as if he could fend it off. Davey caught up with him, tried to restrain him. Matt turned, hit out at him, cried, 'Leave me alone! Leave me alone! Haven't you done enough?'

'Master – Matt –'

Matt bared his teeth like a cornered, wounded fox.

'Leave me be!'

Davey reached out his hands again, and Matt struck him with a closed fist on the side of the head, hard enough to knock Davey down, though he was bigger and heavier than his master, and stun him. Matt ran away into the concealing darkness before Davey could get up again, ran blindly, as if in panic, heading for the trees of the copse where they had left the horses, and once in the trees flung himself headfirst into the thickets, an arm up to defend his eyes, until the tangle of undergrowth slowed and finally halted him, and he went to ground, exhausted and panting, in a tangle of brush and weed and fern.

The thought he had run from found him again, silently and brutally, as he hunched, panting, amongst the night-fragrant plants.

The children. The children.

How long? Since the very beginning? Since before Jemmy? Jemmy and Rob and Edmund, George, little Thomas, and baby Charles. Were they none of them, none of them, his own? A murderous rage rose up in him, and he saw himself going home, dragging them out from their beds and drowning them pitilessly like unwanted whelps, like the litter of the prize bitch who had gone running off with a mangey, louse-ridden stray. Jemmy, and Rob, and all the others. His children. His sons. The tears came at last, and he lay down on his face, and covered his head with his arms and wept like a child.

When he knew he had lost Matt, Davey turned at once back towards the house. Miraculously, it was still quiet. What would she do, he wondered? She would not raise the house. Secrecy and darkness were a habit with her now. She would be planning, planning, sitting at the centre of her web like a spider. In the bedchamber, thinking out what she would say to Matt. She would not be despairing, not yet. Her reaction had been anger; fear would follow, and apprehension, but she would not believe it was all over with her. She would still believe she could win him back. And why should she not? In nine years of marriage she had manipulated him like a puppet. She would weep, and blame herself; how could she so hurt her beloved husband, who had always been so good to her, whom she loved so much? It was but one, foolish, unimportant lapse. It would never happen again. She was so sorry.

And Matt, gripped by the habit of loving and trusting her, would forgive her and take her back. Davey's face was grim as he let himself back into the house, and trotted silently up the stairs to the great bedchamber. She was there, already in bed, in her nightgown, sitting up waiting for Matt. Her hair was brushed out smooth, her face composed into an expression of humility and regret over a shining, childlike innocence.

'Very touching,' Davey said. Her expression lasted for a fraction of a second before it changed to murderous fury.

'I'll have you whipped!' she hissed. 'I'll have you skinned and burnt alive. I'll poison you!'

Davey wrenched his face into a parody of hers. 'Oh husband, forgive me!' he whined. 'It was a moment of madness! It is you I love!'

'Get out!' India cried. 'Get out of here!'

'Not yet, mistress, not yet. There is a little business we must transact first.' He took a step towards her and fear doused anger like a light.

'I have no business with you,' she said, clutching the bedclothes for protection. 'You had better get out before my husband comes in, or it will be the worse for you.'

'No, mistress. That's all over. You won't impose on him again. Because I know about all the others, too, and I am going to make sure he does.'

'You! He won't believe you!' she said scornfully, but her eyes were watchful.

257

'Oh yes he will. After tonight, he'll believe me. And besides, I have witnesses. You weren't as discreet as you thought. Arthur told me about you and him, and about Jack Francomb. And Clement knows. Lots of the servants know, but they could not tell the master before – he would have thought them mad. But now he has seen for himself –'

'Arthur wouldn't –' she began, but fear began to dawn in her eyes.

'Arthur would – Arthur did. After you killed his wife –'

Now she began to cry. 'That was not my fault. It was nothing to do with me! It was his decision. I didn't want her to die. Why should I?'

Davey waited impassively. At length, her face smeared with tears, she said, 'What do you want? What am I to do?'

'That's better. Now you are being sensible. I will tell you what you will do. You will write it all down, the whole confession, in a letter to your husband.'

'No!'

'Yes! I shall stand here and watch you do it. Everything, you understand?' She did not answer, shaken now by sobs, her tears falling fast like summer rain. 'And then I shall mediate for you.'

'You? Why you?' She was incredulous.

'Because I am best suited to do it. I am his friend.'

'Why should you?' she asked, wiping the tears from her face with her fingers, a gesture so childlike that he was almost touched. Almost.

'I want what is best for him,' Davey said, and it did not even sound like an answer. 'Come, get up. I have paper and ink over here for you. Come and sit here at this table, and write. Make haste. It must be done before he comes back to the house.'

Still sobbing, she scrambled slowly out of bed, and came across to the table, pushing the strands of hair that stuck to her wet face with the back of her wrist, sniffing pitifully. She sat down, and he placed the paper before her and put the pen in her hand.

'Write.' He commanded. She hesitated, and looked up at him, her drowned leaf-green eyes appealing. She was in his power now, and he felt triumphant. She wanted him to command her, her will gone. 'Write,' he said again. 'Dear husband. Dearest Matt –'

She wrote. Slowly, with many pauses and sobs; hand shaking now and then, tears falling on to the page so that the ink ran the words together; prompted, corrected by Davey, she wrote. Docile now, tear-shaken, wet-eyed, wet nosed, obedient, a chastised child, she made her confession. He read it over her shoulder as she wrote it. She had learned to write late in life, and never used the art if she could help it, and it was like the scrawl of a five-year-old child, the spelling eccentric, the script clumsy and unpractised. 'Sign,' he said when she had finished. She signed. He allowed her to stand up, leaving the messy page on the table. She turned to him.

'Can I go back to bed now?' she asked shakily. He looked down with triumph into her face. Where is your beauty now, he thought, where your bold confidence?

'You can sleep now,' he said. 'Sleep as long as you like.'

She did not understand his intent until it was too late. He held her eyes with his own, and he thought that for a moment she expected him to kiss her. Then the fear leapt to her face, but it was already too late. The pressure of his hands prevented her from making any sound but a strangled gulp. She was a big, strong woman, though debilitated by her weeping, and taken unawares; but his hands were a workman's hands, barely softened by a year in gentlemanly service. He held her at arm's length, and her thrashing limbs thudded ineffectually against him.

He held her for a long time after she was still, to make sure, and then, in sudden disgust at what he held, he let her go. He still was not sure whether he had meant to do it from the beginning. He listened for a moment, but the house was quiet still. Matt might come back, a servant might wake, at any minute. He must work quickly.

He opened her clothes-chest and turned over the soft,

scented garments quickly, ignoring the protestation of his senses at this reminder of her living sensual appeal. He found what he wanted – a long scarf of coloured silk, that she had worn as a sash, sometimes around the waist, sometimes over one shoulder. He knotted it round her throat, and then with great difficulty hoisted her up and tied the other end to the hook of the chandelier. When he released her, she hung, turning slowly a quarter turn each way, and her toes just scraped the surface of the floor with a thin, mouselike scuff. A stool, carefully positioned, and overturned. The blotted, tearstained letter lay on the table, the last testimony, pathetic and completely convincing. Under the bed, her dog Oyster cowered in silent terror.

He went quickly away and out of the house again, back towards the coppice, to collect the horses, and begin a search for Matt. Only when he reached the tethered horses did he find that he was wiping his hands again and again down his jacket, as if to clean them of some contamination.

Davey searched all night without finding Matt, and returned at first light to the house, to find it in uproar. Millicent had discovered her mistress, hanging in her bedchamber, when she went to wake her. Clement had cut her down, and sent for the priest, who was nowhere to be found, and the master, who was thought still to be in Wetherby. Matt himself came in shortly after Davey, red-eyed and exhausted, ready to forgive his wife and believe the best of her. Clement told him in broken words what had happened, and led him to the room. Matt stared down at the contused face and the red ring around the throat, and had no more tears to shed. He looked up, his eyes going round the circle of faces with the numb expression of a child who has been so abused as to become almost witless, seeking no relief, only for the direction from which the next blow was to come.

Explanations came bit by bit that day, while Matt sat in a chair where he had been put in the steward's room, neither speaking nor moving, as if bewildered by grief. Davey looked in from time to time, though he had a thousand things to do in the absence of direction from the master. When he went towards sunset he saw that Matt had fallen asleep at last, still sitting in his chair, his head slumped sideways on to the untender support of the chimney wall. Asleep he looked very young, too young to know such pain.

I owed you a life, Davey thought, looking down at him. The debt is paid now. She won't deceive you ever again. The droop of the mouth in sleep was undefended, the dark eyelashes soft and long against the brown cheeks. Davey felt the tears rising in his throat. What would Mat do now? he wondered. When the first shock had passed, what would he begin to feel? He reached out and stroked the cheek very gently with one hand, and in his troubled sleep Matt stirred and gave a trembling sigh. Would it not have been better that he had never known, had gone on happily in his dream of perfection?

I have been no friend to you, Matt, Davey thought, no friend after all. He went away, his shoulders bowed, and before Matt woke again, he had gone from the house, leaving no word of explanation.

CHAPTER FOURTEEN

The war had gone badly for France, and to military defeats had been added the problems of bad harvests and famine, and in April 1711 the death of the Dauphin from smallpox. His son, the Duc de Bourgogne, became the new Dauphin, and his duchess, King James's cousin Marie-Adelaide, Dauphine. Karellie and the King were still together, serving under Berwick that summer, and a certain cautious friendship had been struck up between them. There was a great difference in their ages – Karellie was approaching forty that year, while the King was just twenty-three – but the difference was not so apparent as it might be, for James was unusually grave and mature for his age, while Karellie, as sometimes happened with mercenaries, had remained very young in his ways. They were united by a love and respect for Berwick, and by their sisters back in St Germain.

Both of them received letters from Aliena and Louise-Marie which kept them in touch with things in Paris. The new Dauphine had been very kind to them, and had invited them to a number of parties, and even, on the occasion of a grand hunt, had sent Louise-Marie a horse and a riding habit so that she could take part. King James worried a great deal about his sister, for she was nineteen, beautiful, sweet tempered and intelligent; yet because of her position she had no suitors, no dowry, no pretty clothes, and would probably never be able to marry. There seemed no more likelihood of his being able to reclaim his throne, and though he dutifully fed the slender hope, even writing a personal letter to his half-sister Queen Anne begging her to remember her duty and leave the throne to him, Karellie never felt he really believed much in the prospect. Karellie did what he could to cheer the King, and again that winter broke his promise to Diane that he would spend every Christmas with her. The King, he felt, needed him more, for the war was going so badly that King Louis was already negotiating a peace with England, and a peace treaty would almost certainly insist that Louis repudiate James and expel him from France.

They stopped at Lyons on the way back to Paris, and visited the silk factory there, and each of them bought a length of silk for his sister – King James chose white embroidered with gold for the Princess, and Karellie bought scarlet for his darker sister. Neither of the girls had much in the way of finery, and the silk would at least provide each of them with one new gown.

Christmas at Versailles might have been very gloomy, but for the Dauphine, Marie Adelaide, who determined that they would at least be merry for the season, and she contrived even to make old King Louis a little more cheerful. There were hunts and feasts and balls, and at the centre of every activity was the Dauphine, dark eyes shining, chivvying and provoking the royal family into laughter. Karellie thought she looked very like King James, and when they danced together they might have been brother and sister. The King was always easily affected by those around him, and as Karellie, dancing with Aliena, watched them go up the set, he saw King James throw back his head and laugh in a quite uncharacteristic way.

'That is a good sight,' he murmured. Aliena nodded. 'What has it been like here, since the news?' he asked her. She gave a very French shrug.

'Tears and misery. *Que voulez-vous?* The Queen grows old, the Princess has never seen any kind of life. Without the King, whom they adore, what would be the point of living? Le Grand Roi will not expel *them*, nor stop their pension, but for such as them it is not merely a roof over the head and enough to eat which matters. They try not to be unhappy or ungrateful, but we spend more and more time at Chailly, hiding ourselves, seeking comfort. If the

King goes, the Queen I dare say will soon die, and the Princess will become a nun. Poor little creature.'

Karellie understood her. 'She is so pretty, she ought to be the happiest girl in the world,' he said.

'The beautiful Princess,' Aliena nodded. 'An irony, is it not?'

'And what of you?' Karellie said shyly. 'Not a princess, but all the same –'

Aliena smiled up at him. 'You flatter me, my brother. But I am not to be pitied. The Princess says that her lot is not so hard as her mother's, since she was born in exile, and has therefore never known any better. You could say the same of me. I know no home but St Germain. I am at home, and with my family. What more could I want?'

'A husband, perhaps,' Karellie said. She gave him a strange look.

'Oh no – not that. I do not feel the need of that.' She was watching the King and the Dauphine coming to the end of their walk; now she and Karellie were at the top of the set and must make the parade down the room, and he asked no more questions, though he continued to wonder from time to time what she had meant.

The celebrations went on to the end of January, for the Dauphine, who already had two sons, announced that she was pregnant again, and she delighted in any excuse for making merry. But on 9 February she was stricken with smallpox, and the next day she was dead. It was as though a light had gone out; King Louis was grief-stricken. And then, only a few days later, her husband the Dauphin was taken by the same disease and died a week later, leaving their four-year-old elder son as Dauphin. The Court was plunged into heavy mourning, and even now there was no respite for them, for three weeks later the child also died of the same disease. King Louis had reigned for an almost incomprehensible seventy years, and his sole heir was a two-year-old child, his great-grandson.

There was no possibility of King James leaving Court at such a time, and Karellie felt that if the King stayed, he should stay also. James wrote again to Queen Anne, urging her to name him heir, and this time the Queen replied, saying that if James would change his religion, she would do what she could for him. It was a meagre enough promise, but even so it might have made a deal of difference, for it was known that Anne did not like the Hanoverians, especially her cousin George. James could not, would not, ignore his father's last words to him, which were to honour his religion more than his throne. He wrote firmly that he was satisfied with the truth of his religion, but would never urge anyone else to change, or think the worse of them for differing from him; and that he therefore expected to be allowed the same liberty of conscience that he himself would deny to no one.

March dragged on wearily at St Germain. The Queen and Princess were at Chaillot where their friend Soeur Angelique was ill, and Aliena was with them. Karellie found the palace gloomy, and the King was poor company, restless and moody. He longed for action, and began to consider asking for leave. When he raised the subject tentatively, the King would not hear of it, and said instead that he would ride to Chaillot and beg his mother and sister to return to St Germain.

'It will be better when they are here. It is the lack of female company that makes us dull,' he said.

The Queen and Princess came back; two days later, the King fell ill, and when a rash appeared on his face, the terrible fear descended on them. Karellie waited in an ante-room, pacing up and down. Would this be the end to all their enterprises? he wondered bitterly. He thought of Martin and Kit, dead in battle, of his own long exile, his wasted life. He was forty years old, and had nothing, nothing to shew for it.

It was very late when Aliena slipped quietly in and stood before him.

'It is smallpox,' she said, 'but the doctors say it is a very mild attack, and that the King should come through it. With careful nursing, he should not even be marked.'

265

'Thank God,' Karellie said heartfeltly. Aliena gave a little sigh, and sat down on the nearest chair, putting her hands to her face. 'You are tired,' he said sympathetically. 'Let me call for Mrs Nan to take you to bed.' Aliena shook her head, and a moment later took her hands from her face and looked up at him. She was flushed, and her eyes were unnaturally bright.

'It isn't that, Karellie,' she said steadily. 'One thing that exiled ladies come to know about is disease – we are all expected to be tender nurses. I am not tired, I am sick.'

'No – no it can't be that,' Karellie said. In that moment, he realized how much Aliena had come to mean to him, breaking through with her sweetness the barriers he had erected against her, because of her parentage.

'I'm sorry, my lord,' she said. 'I think I have smallpox.'

It was an anxious time, but after a week had passed, it was plain that both the King and Aliena would recover. Karellie never left his sister, sleeping in an ante-room and sharing the attendance with Nan in a way that amazed and rather embarrassed the servants. He would not permit Aliena to be bled, which made them shake their heads, for bleeding was the first and most efficacious cure for everything. But Karellie insisted that it was bleeding that had killed the Duke of Gloucester, and that the late Dauphine had suffered an instant decline when *she* was bled. He remembered his mother's stories, how Prince Rupert had had the gravest doubts about the efficacy of bleeding, and had refused the treatment himself, and what was good enough for his illustrious grandfather was good enough for his sister.

At all events, Aliena recovered, and a burst of sudden spring weather allowed the convalescents to sit out on one of the terraces. They had their chairs placed side by side, and Karellie noticed how they would sit in silence for a long time, and then exchange a glance which seemed to serve them instead of conversation. They were like an old married couple, he thought. Louise-Marie sat with them and tried to entertain them with cards or conversation, but Karellie saw how little they needed diversion, and occupied her energies himself, to leave them in peace. A few days later Louise-Marie discovered the rash on her own face, but she made light of it.

'My brother and your sister have recovered so well, that I doubt not but it is the same light infection. With God's will, I shall not even have a mark.'

She retired to bed, and the Queen, in great anxiety which she was at pains to conceal, retired with her to nurse her. Aliena and the King were not allowed near, for in their weakened state they might retake the infection, with fatal results. The Princess spent a quiet night, but on the next day the doctors bled her in the foot, and by the evening she was seriously ill. She grew gradually worse over the next few days, not responding to any of the treatments which she bore with great patience. When she had been ill for a week, she asked her mother to send for her confessor.

In the ante-rooms, the King and Karellie and Aliena waited, numb and shocked.

'She has had no life, no life at all,' the King said. At length the priest came out. 'How is she, Father Gaillans?' the King asked.

'She is very weak in her body, sire, but her mind is quite clear. She is resigned to death. She has placed herself in the hands of God.'

'Oh, I pray that God will spare her,' the King said, the tears running over his face. 'I pray God will see we need her more than He.'

'You must pray for resignation, sire,' the priest said gently. 'His will be done.'

Late that night the Queen came out. 'They have given her a sleeping powder,' she said. 'She has prayed that she might live, only to serve God and comfort me. She is so young, so young.'

'You must rest, mother,' the King said, taking her arm.

They leaned together for a moment. 'Let me get them to give you a powder too. Then you will sleep.'

The Princess died in the early hours of the morning, before the Queen woke. She was buried beside her father in the Church of the English Benedictines in Paris, and the length of silk that the King had chosen for her at Lyons, which she had never had time to have made into a gown, was given to the nuns at Chaillot for an altar-cloth for the chapel where she had spent so many peaceful hours.

A few days later the Queen left St Germain for Chaillot, where she hoped to be allowed to live permanently, and the Chevalier St George and the Marechal Comte de Chelmsford left Paris to rejoin the campaign. Aliena remained with the Queen, but Karellie was worried about her, for with the Princess dead she had no official place at Court, which indeed appeared to be on the point of breaking up anyway. She could go to Maurice, of course, but Maurice was retreating more and more deeply into his world of music, and had now taken to travelling round Italy with his father-in-law, producing operas in Rome, Naples, and Florence, coming back to Venice only for short visits. What life could he offer their sister? It seemed to Karellie that the only thing would be for her to go back to England to live with their mother. Whatever Karellie felt about his mother – and it was too complicated for even him to be sure – there was no doubt that she could, if she would, give Aliena the kind of life that Karellie wanted for her. So at their first halt he swallowed his doubts and wrote a letter, telling his mother of the situation and begging her to recall Aliena to England.

On 25 March Annunciata gave a party at Shawes to celebrate her sixty-seventh birthday. Shawes was virtually completed – even the gardens were laid out pretty much as they were meant to be, and she had compromised between the traditional and the Marlborough notions by having planted a mixture of mature trees and saplings. The damming of the stream, which had led to some unfortunate incidents, had at last been adjusted successfully, and the terraced gardens now led down to a small ornamental lake, and the weather being clement, Annunciata had arranged a water-pageant for the diversion of her guests. Vanbrugh declared himself well-satisfied with the house, and claimed that, next to Castle Howard, it was his favourite child. He was still working on Blenheim, though he and the Duchess of Marlborough disliked each other so well that he foresaw a time when he would have to abandon that project to someone else. Thornton, the architect of the new house at Beningborough, had been visiting both Castle Howard and Shawes, and Beningborough would have the best features of both when it was finished. The Bourchiers were amongst the guests at Annunciata's celebration, and try how she might, Annunciata could not conceal every trace of delight that her house was finished first, and was therefore the model and not the copy.

Another guest was Henry Aldrich, whose pet scheme for pulling down the old Peckwater Inn and replacing it with a modern building, had now been under way for some years. Three sides of the new quadrangle were almost completed, and the design was all his own. Annunciata had been to inspect it, and had praised him highly.

'You have been a heavy drain on my purse,' she said, 'but I don't begrudge a penny.' The Dean promised he would have the new quad finished in time to be occupied by the first of her great-grandsons to attend Christ Church, and in return she invited him to her birthday party, and to stay for as long as he liked as a house guest.

Vanbrugh teased her about him, saying, 'You should put the poor man out of his misery and marry him at once. Don't you see to what lengths he is going to gain your attention. If you do not accept him, he will be forced to pull down Wolsey's quadrangle next, or perhaps even the cathedral.'

Annunciata laughed, pleased at the idea. 'Now, Van, I

am too old for love,' she chided him. Vanbrugh looked her up and down judiciously.

'You may be too old to fall in love – that is a matter which only you can decide – but you are certainly not too old to be fallen in love with. I doubt if you ever will be. You put your younger relatives to shame, aye, and most of the rest of York society. If I weren't in too much awe of you to ask, I'd offer you *my* hand.'

It was all pleasant nonsense, but indeed Annunciata was feeling younger, stronger, and more cheerful than for many years before. When her first grandson had been born, she had hated the idea, for it made her aware that she was losing her youth; but now the mathematical sum of her years troubled her not at all, nor the increasing age of her great-grandchildren. Her relationship with Aldrich, her friendship with the inner circle of distinguished architects, her building of Shawes, had all given her a new lease of life. It was more than twenty years since Martin had died at the Boyne, and she had longed to die also.

'We live long in my family,' she would say to Chloris when they talked, as they did more and more frequently, of old times. 'There is so much to be interested in.' Chloris, who was ten years younger than she, seemed older, and Annunciata, full of vigour, would sometimes chide her for wanting to sit in her chair by the fire rather than walk or ride with her mistress. She was bone-thin now, and becoming rather bent, from her habit of stooping her shoulders over her work as her eyesight deteriorated. Her hair was grey, and sometimes Annunciata in absent-mind-edness would call her Birch. Father St Maur was dead now, and Annunciata had a new young priest, a lively man of just one-and-twenty, who had been a pupil of Edmund's at St Omer. His name was Renard, and Annunciata found him very stimulating. They would argue fiercely for hours on end, and sometimes Renard, who was fiery and quick tempered, would stamp away in a rage, only to return a while later and apologize laughingly and give himself a penance. Chloris disapproved of Renard, for she thought that he behaved towards her mistress with a lack of respect. The two of them could also behave in a way that Chloris thought indecently sentimental between priest and mistress, and she said so to Annunciata, but Annunciata would not even be annoyed.

'There is no harm to it,' she would say. 'It is merely pleasant. It makes us both feel happy.'

'If he were not a priest, and you were not so old, you'd be lovers,' Chloris said roughly, and Annunciata laughed.

'But that is the whole point, dear Chloris. It is simply *because* we can't. Don't you see?' Chloris didn't. 'One of the delights of reaching my great age is that I can have love affairs with all the young men without having to do anything about it. Love, as you have so often pointed out to me, is a difficult and dangerous thing and brings terrible troubles upon us. Now I can have the sweets without the troubles. You should be happy.'

She could say so now, though it had been a long time before she could adjust to the idea of never being able to have another child. Architecture, she had come to realize, replaced that aspect of her life. With Shawes she had been able to create something as much her own and as intensely satisfying as any of the ten babies she had borne, and far more enduring. All the same, the letter from Karellie about Aliena moved her in a way she had not thought to be moved again. When she had read it she sat a long time in solitude, thinking of that last and dearest child of hers, trying to imagine her a young woman of twenty-four, wondering whether she would be able to endure the sharp pain of seeing her again. But she had always intended to leave Shawes to Aliena, and it was obvious that her career at St Germain was over. She wrote back to Karellie, and sent at the same time a letter to Aliena, bidding her come home.

'Everything can be arranged,' she wrote. 'I can send servants to fetch you if necessary. Your future will be secure here, and you will be able to marry if you wish, though whether you do or not, you will be mistress of

Shawes after me. The political situation here should not trouble you – we are left alone by those in power, and I have no reason to suppose that will change. Remember you are the Queen's cousin as well as the King's.'

In fact, though Annunciata did not say so in her letter, things were more hopeful in England, for the Whigs had been replaced in power by the Tories, and many of the men in the highest places, like Oxford, Ormonde, Bolingbroke, and Mar, were known to be pro-Jacobite in sympathy. The Queen loathed the idea of being succeeded by George Lewis, and the only bar to James regaining his throne was his religion. Every 10 June James's birthday, brought celebrations and demonstrations, and Scotland had never stopped rumbling since the Union. It was this hope almost as much as everything else that had made Annunciata feel so young and strong over the past year or so.

That things were not going so well in the other branches of the family was known to her, though it affected her very little. Both Sabina and Frances had suffered a string of misfortunes with their children, miscarriages and infant deaths, and though Sabina's firstborn, Hamil, had now reached the age of seven, Frances was left, by the death of her sons John and Arthur in successive years, without an heir. Arthur Ballincrea had not remarried since Clover's death, and seemed to have no intention of disturbing his bachelor round of clubs, coffee houses, London for the Season and the country for the shooting. His work occupied him just sufficiently to prevent him from becoming debauched – three of his houses were at present in the process of being built – but he seemed to prefer the company of other architects and gentlemen to any woman's, and appeared not at all troubled by the idea of leaving no heir.

And then there was the situation at Morland Place. Annunciata had been shocked and horrified at the news of India's suicide, and though she had seen the letter the girl had left, she had always felt that there was a great deal more to the matter than was admitted, even to so privileged a public as herself. There was, for example, the mysterious disappearance of Matt's 'friend', Davey, who had left Morland Place the same night and hadn't been heard of since. That was three years ago, and Matt, like Arthur, had shewed no signs of wanting to marry again, though as he had six healthy sons there was no immediate necessity.

Annunciata had not been to Morland Place since the tragedy, and if she was honest with herself, she had to admit that she had rather avoided the idea. When in Yorkshire she had plenty to occupy her at Shawes, and her polite letter announcing her arrival was generally answered by a polite acknowledgement, leaving her free to carry on with harassing the gardeners, rearranging her furniture, riding out on Phoenix with big Kithra bouncing along at heel, arguing with Father Renard, and visiting acquaintances in the city. The one occasion when she might have expected to see Matt was during race week, and the fact that he was never there she excused to herself for other reasons.

The horse racing which Ralph had begun so many years ago had been so popular that it had become an unofficial annual event, looked forward to by everyone in the district, not only those owning horses, but those who liked gambling, which encompassed many, and those who simply liked an excuse to parade in their best clothes and meet their friends, which included nearly everyone else. In 1709, therefore, when Matt, deep in despairing grief, had declined to hold the races, a committee had formed itself amongst the eminent people of York. They had come to the decision to hold official racing for a week every year, and they had been held in 1709 for the first time on Clifton Ings, the stretch of common land beside the River Ouse, close to the site of Watermill House, which had belonged to Kit Morland's father and had been destroyed during the civil war.

Since then race week had begun to assume a great importance in the social calendar, and every evening during race week there would be balls and parties and assemblies given by the great hostesses of York. Many an eligible daughter had been disposed of favourably as a result of race week assemblies, and last year there had even been an elopement. It could have generated business for the horse-breeding side of the Morland estate, but in the three years no one from Morland Place had even attended, still less entered a horse in a race. Annunciata was not surprised when her invitation to her birthday party was politely refused, and if she noticed that the refusal was only signed by Matt, not written in his hand, she thought nothing of it, knowing how many letters had always gone out from Morland Place in a week.

She was walking about her terrace, enjoying the sunshine one morning at the beginning of May, and throwing a stick for Kithra, who was disposed to be puppyish, when Gifford came out of the house and approached her with more than his usual diffidence.

'My lady, there is someone here asking for an interview with you,' he said, as if that were an unusual thing.

'If it is not important, send them away,' Annunciata said genially. 'It is too early. You know I don't see people until at least eleven.'

Gifford hesitated. 'My lady, it is Clement –'

'Clement the steward? From Morland Place?' Annunciata said, frowning. 'It is not bad news, I hope? No one is ill?'

'He has not come with news, my lady. He asks for a private interview with you, and will not tell me the matter.'

Annunciata shrugged. 'Show him out here, Gifford. I am sure Clement would not trouble me with something trivial. And when you have brought him, make sure we are not disturbed.'

Clement had been Annunciata's steward when she was mistress of Morland Place, and was grey-haired now, though otherwise he seemed unchanged to her. They had gone through the siege together, and knew each other pretty well, and Annunciata, as she studied his face, recognized in herself that she would trust him perhaps more than anyone else she knew. The office of steward at Morland Place had been with his family for generations, and each successive Clement had grown in dignity and responsibility, like a kind of aristocracy. If this Clement had not been born a gentleman, there was nothing about him which would have revealed it to a stranger.

'It is good of you to receive me, my lady,' he said.

She took in the anxiety and weariness in his face, and said abruptly, 'Let us walk in the gardens, and you can tell me what is wrong. We shall not be disturbed or overheard.'

Clement gave her a look of gratitude, and when they were strolling along the formal walks, with Kithra, quiet now, sniffing interestedly under every hedge, he responded to her openness as man to man.

'Things are not well at Morland Place, my lady. I have done my best to mitigate them, but it has gone beyond me now, and I don't know anyone but you who can help. The master was deeply affected by the death of the mistress – that was natural enough. It was a great horror to us all. But in three years he has not come back to himself. He does nothing; he neglects the business; he sits all day in the steward's room with the shades drawn, and sees no one, and eats barely enough to support life. The only time he ventures out is after dark, and then he walks about the grounds in the dark like a ghost.'

'Do you think his reason affected?'

'I don't know, my lady. He hardly speaks to anyone, so it is difficult to judge. Often when I ask him a question, he will not appear to hear, but if I persist he grows angry and tells me to leave him alone and decide for myself. Well, my lady, there is a limit to the things *I* can decide. Without a master, the household is breaking up. Orders are not given that should be given. The servants – the older ones are very loyal, but it is human nature to take advantage of slackness, and some of the younger ones are worse than useless to me.'

'Yes, I can see that,' Annunciata nodded. She, who had

275

run so many large households, could easily picture the growing chaos of a house run without either master or mistress.

'Then there's the children, my lady. They have no tutor, and their father does not interest himself in them at all. The nursery maids do their best, but boys need firmer handling than they can give. Jemmy and Edmund run wild, and it is setting a bad example to the younger ones.'

'What do you want me to do?' she asked frankly when Clement had finished. She stopped and faced him. They were standing beside the little lake, and Kithra began to race up and down foolishly, chasing the ducks and barking.

'Speak to the master, for a beginning, try to reach him. Make him see that he has a responsibility to us all. And if that doesn't work –'

'If it doesn't?'

'Then take over yourself. You have done it before. I know that you have not wanted to interest yourself in Morland Place since – since –'

'Since Martin died,' she finished for him, quietly. Clement met her eyes.

'You are a Morland, my lady, you were mistress of Morland Place, and you are the master's grandmother. We need you, and your place is with us. If it is hard for you, I am sorry, but duty is hard.'

'Harsh words, Clement,' Annunciata said with a little smile. 'You are bold to remind *me* of my duty?'

'My lady, you have known me long enough to know what is in my heart. I would give my life for Morland Place and the family.'

'I know; and knowing that, I should not be surprised that you would give *mine* too.' She sighed, looking across the lake and around at her gardens, where she had been enjoying peace at last. 'Very well, I shall come and speak to Matt, and do what I can. You did right to come to me, Clement. And you are right about my duty. We can't change the blood that runs in our veins, either of us.'

Despite being forewarned, Annunciata was shocked at the change in Morland Place. It looked deserted when she arrived, and though Clement hurried out when he heard her horse in the yard, she noticed that the windows of the house were dirty, and most had their shades drawn, and that there was refuse and dung lying about the yard, as if no one had bothered to sweep it for a day or two, and an unnatural quietness where there should have been bustle and activity.

'The stables are mostly empty, my lady,' Clement told her in a low voice. 'We keep only a few horses here for messages. I had the others turned out, for there was no one to exercise them.'

A young man, whom Annunciata recognized, belatedly, as Clement's grandson, took the reins from her and led Phoenix away, and Clement took her into the house. There was the same air of desertion; everything, while not precisely dirty, looked dingy and neglected, and it was very quiet. There should have been servants trotting back and forth on errands, and the sounds of cleaning and the smells of cooking. The house had a musty smell. While they were crossing the great hall, there was a noise behind them, and a rough-looking boy of about six came running from the passage leading to the kitchen, clutching something in his hands, dashed past them and was heard clattering up the stairs. A maid appeared at the end of the passage, evidently in pursuit, but when she saw Clement and the Countess she slid to a halt, dropped a frightened curtsey, and disappeared whence she had come before anything could be said.

'Who was that boy?' Annunciata asked.

'Master George,' Clement said. 'I think he must have stolen a pie from the kitchen.'

Annunciata glanced at him. She saw that it pained him to admit such things happened in his house, but that he wanted her to know the worst. 'Where is Matt?'

'In the steward's room, my lady. I told him you were coming, but I don't know if he heard me.'

'I'll go in alone, Clement. Stay within call, in case I need you.'

She gave him a gentle shove of encouragement and left him in the staircase hall. Outside the steward's room she paused, wondering whether to knock, and then decided to go straight in. It was gloomy inside, for the shades were half drawn, and there was no fire or candle lit. The room looked shabby and unkempt. There were ashes uncleared in the grate, the sconces were crusted with melted wax and in one holder the stub of a candle leaned out drunkenly, its wick overlong and black, suggesting that it had guttered out for lack of trimming. There were books and papers everywhere, and on the hearth two empty bottles and a plate containing a neglected supper of bread and meat cried mutely for attention. Nearby India's greyhound, Oyster, an old dog now, was lying down, its paws and tail tucked in. It looked up at her with anxious eyes, but did not lift its head. It still wore the diamond collar, and the gems glittered in a way that seemed to emphasize the squalor of the rest of the room. Kithra, seeing Oyster, tried to thrust past her to inspect him, and she shoved the big dog back, and said, low and sharp, 'Sit down. Stay.'

Matt was sitting at the table, his head in his hands, and he looked up when he heard her voice. He was unshaven and unkempt, and for a moment did not seem to recognize her; but to Annunciata, in the gloom, he looked so like Martin that her heart turned over in her, and she was transported on the instant twenty, thirty years back, to the days when Martin had ruled Morland Place and her heart. This, more than any, had always been his room; here, in the days before they were lovers, when he was younger than Matt now was, she had always sought him out, looking for comfort, for cheer, for amusement, and he had sat at the table, in that chair, and looked up at her over the mountain of work with a wry smile knowing that she was about to torment him into neglecting it for her amusement. She had intended to be stern with Matt, but she was seeing Martin, not him, and she could not be other than gentle.

'Matt, I have come to recall you to your duty,' she said. 'You must not grieve in this useless way. We need you. Your children need you.'

He stared at her as if he had not understood her, but in a while he answered, in a voice that sounded harsh with disuse, like a door rarely opened, whose hinges have rusted. 'I have no children,' he said. She walked across the room to him, and saw him flinch back from her. She knew he did not want her to touch him, and deliberately, letting him see her hands as she would approach a frightened horse or dog, she put her hands on his shoulders, and then gently stroked his head.

He shuddered under her touch, and she said, even more quietly, 'I know how you have suffered, and it is right that you should grieve. But all things have their season. It is over now, and you must come out into the daylight and live your life.'

He met her eyes, and the dead look gave way before such an expression of loss that she quailed. What had he to live for? She knew what was in his mind as clearly as if he had spoken the words. What comfort was there?

'Matt, listen to me. I am nearly seventy years old. I have lost, through the course of my life, everything I cared for. Time and again I have made a new start, only to lose again. My husbands, my children, the man I loved, all have gone. I have known grief like yours.'

He was listening to her, his eyes on hers as if he could draw sustenance from them. She went on stroking his head while she spoke.

'I should have come to you before. I left you alone, and that was wrong. My duty was to help, and I neglected it. But I have come now, to help *you* do *your* duty. Come, Matt, come.'

She stepped back and took his hands and drew him to his feet. He was taller than Martin had been, two or three inches taller than her.

'The sun shines as brightly, the air smells as sweet. Life can still give moments of pleasure, though you are filled with pain.' She drew him a step closer. There were tears in his eyes. In the half-light, he looked so like his father that her senses were confused. He came the last step towards her, and she put her arms round him, and he rested his face on her hair, and she felt him trembling.

'I've come back,' she said. 'I won't leave you again.' Her eyes were closed, and tears escaped from under her lids, too, for there was no going back, despite her words. She had come back to Morland Place, but Matt was Master, and Martin had been twenty years in his unmarked grave in Ireland.

BOOK THREE

THE LION AND THE UNICORN

God bless the King, I mean the Faith's Defender;
God bless – no harm in blessing – the Pretender;
But who Pretender is, or who is King,
God bless us all – that's quite another thing!

John Byrom: *To an Officer in the Army*

CHAPTER FIFTEEN

The change for the better did not happen all at once, but from the moment that Annunciata stepped across the threshold of Morland Place, the household breathed a sigh of relief. Even those servants who had willingly taken advantage of the situation to be idle and dissolute found themselves happier for firm orders and certain discipline. Gradually routines were re-established, the house became clean and comfortable, run-down stocks were replenished, and in the atmosphere of purposeful busyness, Matt began to revive.

He did not soon resume his normal occupations, and it was therefore necessary for Annunciata, once she had the house in order, to find subordinates to run the estate and the wool and cloth business. She could not quite bring herself to move into Morland Place permanently, now that she had finished her perfect house, and so she kept most of her personal staff there, and made a point of visiting frequently and sleeping there as often as possible, maintaining the fiction that it was at Shawes that she lived, and that her presence in Morland Place was that of a visitor. But she took with her Chloris, without whom she would not have felt comfortable, and Father Renard, and the latter, in his brisk, efficient way, solved many of her problems.

Once again Mass was said in the chapel at Morland Place. Under India's rule, and by her example, there had developed a slackness about attendance, and many of the servants had claimed to belong to some or other dissenting sect in order to stay a little longer in bed. Annunciata changed that. The decree went forth that every member of the household was to attend Mass twice a day, and any whose religious conscience prevented them could leave at once and find another position. Moreover, everyone must be properly dressed and washed when they entered the chapel, and must behave in an attentive and respectful manner throughout. She had only to dismiss one girl for appearing with her clothing hastily thrown on and her hair unbrushed, and fine one footman for yawning during the service, and her point was sufficiently made. After a few weeks, Matt began to attend also, and Annunciata sighed with relief that the cure had at last begun.

Father Renard, in consultation with Clement, helped Annunciata to divide up the other jobs until such time as Matt took the reins into his own hands again. Clement was perfectly accustomed to doing the accounts, and Annunciata appointed herself treasurer, with Father Renard her secretary, and one of the footmen, who was quick and good with figures, was brought in to assist with all the written work. The bailey was interviewed and found reliable, and was given charge of the farm management, reporting to Clement, with an ultimate reference to Annunciata if necessary.

Several factors had to be found to cope with the businesses, reporting to Father Renard, and it took some time to interview and select the right people. It took even longer to find an agent in London whom Annunciata at all trusted, for in her mind London was full of anti-Jacobites, Whigs and Dissenters; but the most difficult task turned out to be finding someone to take care of the horse-breeding end of things. There were horsemen in plenty in Yorkshire, and indeed the head man at Twelvetrees was well able to manage the day-to-day running, but the overall management was another matter. For the time being she had to take it on herself, which added greatly to her burdens, for there were other matters which the master should have been attending to which could not properly be delegated to hirelings, such as dealing with the personal problems of the tenants. She longed for some adult Morland relatives to share these tasks, and appreciated at first-hand how busy Matt had always been, and his father before him. If

Matt was slow in resuming these tasks, she did not know that she could blame him.

Father Renard took one enormous burden from her shoulders, which was the management of the nursery and schoolroom. The little boys had grown wild and wicked in the years of their neglect, especially Jemmy, by whose example Edmund and George had become quite corrupt. Rob, the second-born, was another matter, and the maids called him the best of children and sang his praises. Annunciata doubted that it was virtue that made him docile, but rather a want of spirit, and a sly ability to make profit of a situation; being the pet of the nurse-maids gave him certain advantages in the matter of sugar-plums and other little gifts that his wild brothers missed.

Father Renard changed all that, instituting a rigid discipline and daily lessons, combined with an adequate amount of running about in the fields, riding, swimming, and playing games. He gave the opinion, startling to Annunciata, that the boys, particularly Jemmy, had been beaten too much, too young.

'But Father, how can you control them without beating them?' Annunciata said. 'Children are not amenable to reason.'

'I do not advocate absence of all chastisement,' Father Renard smiled, 'but you see, when a high-spirited boy like Jemmy is beaten hard from an early age, he grows accustomed to it, and it loses its effect. For the moment I am obliged to beat him with a quite remarkable degree of savagery in order to make any mark on him at all – in the spiritual sense, you understand. That is not good for me, and can only harden his heart if it continues.'

'Then what can you do?'

'I have to gain control of him first, madam. But when I *have* control, then I hope gradually to reduce the beatings until they can take what I believe to be their proper place – punishments for the worst crimes only.'

At first there was little sign that this revolutionary plan was working, for Jemmy continued wild and wicked, and continued to be beaten 'like a mule, madam' as Flora put it; but gradually, as the younger boys came under discipline and found contentment there, Jemmy began to feel left out of things, and to wonder whether learning under 'Father Fox' might not be more interesting than his solitary delinquency. One morning, instead of having to be dragged unwillingly to the schoolroom by two large footmen, Jemmy strolled in of his own accord and was there first, waiting for Father Fox when he arrived. The priest wisely made no comment upon the unexpected pleasure of Jemmy's company, but treated it as a matter of course and thereafter there was little more trouble. By way of recreation, and out of curiosity about her great-grandchildren, Annunciata gave one or two lessons herself, and found the six boys a curiously mixed group. The discovery naturally made her uneasy, for it was evidently Matt's belief that he was father to none of them, and the character of their mother made it likely that at least some were not Morlands at all. But Jemmy, in Annunciata's eyes, was quite definitely Matt's son, having already a great look of Matt about him, and something, she fancied, of herself. She liked Jemmy's spirit, and discovered that his mind was alert and quick of apprehension, and it became one of her pleasures to take him riding and tell him stories of her own past and of the history of the Morlands. He loved to hear about the Civil War, and was immensely proud that Prince Rupert was his great-grandfather, and in that first summer Annunciata took him on horseback out to Marston Moor. His questions soon outstripped her knowledge, and on their return he asked permission to have access to one of the books on the subject. Annunciata gave him Martin's copy of Clarendon's *History of the Rebellion*, and the bond between them was firmly forged.

She found the others less interesting. Rob she thought weak and sly – he was a big-boned, fat, pale boy, with fair hair that tended to reddishness, and she suspected him of torturing small birds and animals, a thing with which she had no patience, though the servants tended to think it unimportant. Edmund and George were small-built, wiry boys, dark in colouring like their mother, and very alike in looks. George was harder and rougher than Edmund, who could be charming when the occasion warranted, and was already a talented thief. Annunciata predicted the gallows for him with no great sorrow. Thomas, who was five and ready to be breeched, a matter Annunciata had attended to quite soon, was idle and inattentive, easily swayed by the last speaker, forgetful of everything that did not please him, and passionately fond of sleep. If he were wanted, a servant would be sure to find him curled up somewhere like a dormouse with his arms over his head. Charles, who was only four, and therefore to Annunciata a baby and indistinguishable from other babies, nevertheless had a certain distinction about him, being already taller than his brothers at the same age, dark as a Frenchman, and of a solemn, thoughtful disposition that made him seem, in his petticoats, older than Thomas in his breeches.

One thing Annunciata found she could not improve, and that was Matt's feelings towards the children. To all intents and purposes, they were orphans. Matt would not acknowledge their existence, grew angry if they were talked of in his presence, and gave orders that they were never to be allowed into a room in which he was sitting, or to be in the part of the garden he was occupying. They were never brought, like other children, to receive his blessing, and in chapel they were sat as far from the Master as possible, and if they made the least noise he flew into a rage.

His temper, Annunciata found, was quite spoilt by the tragedy. He had been a pleasant, light person, she remembered, innocent and childlike in his temper. Now he was sullen, moody and savage; suspicious of everyone, resentful of kindness. He never laughed or played, saw no company, spent his leisure hours alone and in solitary reading, or riding across the moors. Even as he began to come out of his retreat and resume his normal occupations, he did them in silent gravity, shunning all human contact. His horse and the little dog Oyster were his only friends, and the

287

only other exception he made was Annunciata. He treated her, not with friendliness, but with respect, and would listen to her, allowing her to be his go-between with the outside world. But even she must keep a certain distance, and if she ventured into forbidden topics he would first turn his face away, and then leave the room. He had remained a child, she thought, for so long, that his sudden growing-up had spoiled him; but despite that, her affection for him grew, and though she had never been a patient person, she found herself taking great pains with him, and believed that in time she would win him round.

In the summer of 1713 Karellie went to Venice to make a visit to the Palazzo Francescini. The Peace of Utrecht had left him temporarily without employment, and a restlessness drove him from place to place without his knowing quite what he intended to do with himself from now. At the Palazzo, Diane received him with a cool dignity that concealed her genuine pleasure at seeing him, for she was extremely bored. Maurice was away, having gone to Naples where Scarlatti was again Maestro di Capella, in order to collaborate on some works with his father-in-law.

'He is no company even when he is here,' Diane complained to Karellie. 'Since his wife died, he has become more and more disagreeable.'

'Maurice, disagreeable?' Karellie said disbelievingly. 'To you?' Diane tossed her head.

'Disagreeableness is a matter of degree, my lord. When he will not converse, nor play, nor sing, nor even notice that a person is wearing a new gown, *I* call it disagreeable. And on my birthday he arrived late at dinner, and was wearing a suit of clothes that I had seen him wear at least three times before.'

'Oh villainous!' Karellie cried solemnly. Diane's brows drew together in a frown.

'Do you mock me, sir?' she enquired imperiously.

'Madame, I assure you that adoration is the only emotion

288

I am capable of in your presence,' Karellie said. He said it half as a joke, but in fact it was strangely true. The little girl who had commanded him had become a young woman of eighteen, tall, fair, haughtily beautiful, one of the most toasted of all the Venetian beauties, and a singer of note in addition to her physical attractions. She was in great demand for special occasions, and she had frequently been asked to perform at banquets in the company of the celebrated violinist, the red-headed Vivaldi. Vivaldi, also a composer of note, had been so impressed with her that he had recently written a cantata for soprano and continuo especially for her, which she had performed at the feast given by a nobleman on his daughter's taking the veil.

Karellie had grown used to offering her adoration when she was a child; without his noticing, the game had become reality.

'Well, my lord, and what have you brought me this time?' she proceeded, the first principles established. Karellie's gifts had become part of the ritual of his visits, and it had become a point of pride to outdo himself each time.

'Your gift is in my travelling-bag, my lady,' Karellie said. 'I'll send Sam for it.' He made to rise and go to the door to call his servant, but Diane halted him with an upraised hand. 'No need,' she said. 'Giulia will go.' And she nodded to the child, who jumped up eagerly enough and trotted off on her errand. It amused Karellie to see how she had absorbed the two little girls into her 'court', and how willing they were to act the part of her ladies-in-waiting. Giulia was now ten, and handsome in a dark, Italian way, looking very like Maurice; Alessandra was fourteen and unexpectedly plain, her features seeming too big for her small face. With his usual unemphatic kindness, the duke had continued to take care of them, even through Maurice's increasingly frequent and lengthy absences, and the little girls repaid his kindness by acting as suitable attendants to his daughter. Karellie wondered, however, what would happen to them in the future, when Diane should be too grown-up to need them, and they themselves grew too big to be ignored as denizens of the nursery. Maurice did not seem to care much about them, except in the bland, careless way that he cared about anyone who actually forced his attention from his music for a moment. Karellie tried to be kind to them, but they were both very shy and reserved, a natural consequence, he thought, of growing up in Diane's shadow.

'Now tell me all that has been happening,' Diane said indulgently while Giulia was away. 'Where have you been since Christmas?'

'I have spent a lot of the time with the King of England,' Karellie told her. 'You know that the Treaty of Utrecht has forced the King of France to expel King James from France, and in February he had to say goodbye to his mother and cross into Lorraine, where the duke has taken him in, of his kindness. The duke's wife is a kind of cousin of the King's – she is the daughter of Princess Liselotte of the Palatine.'

'Then she must also be a cousin of yours,' Diana said eagerly. She liked to be reminded frequently that Karellie had royal blood in his veins. Karellie bowed in assent.

'It was a very sad leavetaking, for it is not at all likely that they will meet again. The Queen is no longer strong, and sadness has made her old before her time. She lives with the nuns at Chaillot, and without the King –'

But Diane did not want to know about sadness and death. She said, 'What of your sister? She was with the Queen, was she not?'

'I was coming to that. I was very worried that she should be shutting herself away at the convent, when she is so young and beautiful.' He saw Diane frown at the mention of another woman's beauty, and went on quickly, 'I wrote to my mother asking that she be invited back to England, but Aliena would not go. And when the King went to Chaillot to say goodbye, he had a long interview alone with Aliena. When it was over, she came to me to say that she was going with the King to Lorraine. He had told her that he could not endure to be parted from her, and asked if she would share his further exile.'

Diane sighed with pleasure at the romance of it. 'He loves her, then, the King? Will he marry her, do you think; If he does, you will be brother to the Queen of England.'

Karellie shook his head, looking a little puzzled. 'I don't think he could marry her, even if he wanted to. She is a commoner.'

'He could ennoble her. As your King Henry did to Anne Boleyn. Kings have unlimited power.'

'Well, perhaps he could. But I don't think he quite loves her in that way.'

'You mean he loves her like a sister?' Diane said, disappointed.

'I am not sure. He has grown up with her, you see, more even than with his own sister. Yet quite in what way he loves her I do not know. I think perhaps he simply wished to have someone familiar with him.'

He knew he was not explaining it very well, but in truth he hardly understood himself what Aliena had told him. He had asked her much the same questions as Diane was asking him, and she had said, 'James does love me, but not in the way you think. He loves me as he would love a brother.' Karellie did not think he could very well tell Diane that.

'But does she love him?' Diane asked now, eager to salvage some romance from the tale.

'Oh yes,' Karellie said. That much had been obvious. 'Yes,' he said sadly, 'she loves him.'

'Then she is happy to be with him,' Diane said. Karellie nodded. It was a strange situation, and with anyone else other than King James, Karellie would have thought it was a plain case of a King securing the presence of his mistress. It was what any other observer would think, of course, and Aliena's curious mixture of royal blood and obscure origins made it possible for her to hold such an equivocal place in the King's household, where it would be impossible for anyone else. 'So you have been with them in Lorraine,' Diane said. 'What else?'

'I visited my aunt Sofie in Hanover, and then I came here to you.'

'Your aunt Sofie, who hopes to be Queen of England in the true King's place?' Diane questioned him severely, and Karellie stirred uneasily. He did not like her to think he was like those unscrupulous English politicians who kept a correspondence with both sides for insurance against any eventuality. But the fact remained that Aunt Sofie was his relative and very fond of him, and there were many sincere Jacobites whose friendship with her had not been altered by the unfortunate circumstance of her being named alternative heir to the throne.

But he could not argue this point with Diane, who liked her stories clear, simple and romantic, and so he diverted her attention by saying, 'It was in Hanover that I got one of your gifts.'

'One of them? There is more than one thing, then?' Diane said eagerly, quite diverted.

When Giulia came back, followed by a servant carrying the bag, the presents were brought out and inspected. The first was a small golden cage, in which sat a gold bird, studded with jewels; when a clockwork mechanism was wound and the spring released, the bird threw back its head and sang. Diane was enchanted, to Karellie's pride and relief. It had cost him very dear, and had he not lived frugally as a soldier he could never have afforded it, despite his pension from England.

The second present he gave her wrapped in a piece of black velvet. She unwrapped it with a smile of anticipation on her lips, which gradually faded when she saw what it was.

'Why have you given me this?' she asked Karellie.

He looked puzzled, and said, 'It is a miniature of my sister, Aliena. Don't you like it? Do you not think she is beautiful? I thought you would be interested to see her face.'

Diane jumped to her feet, and flung the miniature at him in a rage. 'I am *not* interested! I do not want to see her face – or yours ever again! And you can take this trumpery thing with you – toys for children! I see I have been deceived in you, my lord Earl. I thought you a gentleman worthy of my notice. Leave me now, at once! You are no longer welcome here!'

'But Principessa –'

'I thought you loved me! I thought you cared for me! Instead you come here on my father's generous invitation solely to mock and humiliate me, bringing me paintings of other women you think more beautiful than I, and silly whistling birds, as if I were still a child in pinafores! Well, I see now what you think of me. If I am a child, I had better go back to my nursery. Come, Alessandra, Giulia. We will leave my lord Earl to contemplate his grandness in solitude.'

She whirled around, knocking the bird-cage contemptuously over with her skirts, and went out, and the two little girls, with scared glances at Karellie, went after her.

Her rages never lasted long, and by the evening she was ready to listen to his pleas for forgiveness and his assertions of devotion. But he had had time to think in the meanwhile, and to consider what it was about his gifts that had upset her. The duke was from home, and they dined alone in the presence only of the servants. Diane looked particularly beautiful, in a gown of a subtle grey-blue shade that made her glorious red-gold hair glow like burnished copper. When they had dined, they strolled on the balcony overlooking the lagoon, and watched the moon rising, a faint wisp in the night-pale sky.

'Principessa, I have something serious I want to say to you,' Karellie said. Diane leaned against the pillar at the end of the balcony, arranging herself with a negligent air that made him know she was perfectly aware of how she looked. He stood straight before her like a soldier, and continued.

'I have known you since you were a child, and I have

adored you since the first time I saw you. Now you have grown from a child to a woman, and my feelings for you have grown too. I am a soldier of fortune, but I come from an ancient family of good pedigree. I have royal blood in my veins, I am an earl, though an exiled one. If my humble suit can sway you at all, may I have your permission to ask for your hand in marriage?'

Diane watched him and listened with an expression of gratification, which made her answer the more surprising. 'No, my lord, you may not.'

Karellie was startled out of his self-possession. 'But – I thought – when you were so angry this morning, I thought –' He shook his head. 'I thought you loved me.'

Diane smiled, not a smile of triumph that he would have expected if she were tormenting him, but a smile almost of pity.

'I do love you, and I believe that you love me. Nevertheless, I will not marry you. You were right that I was angry because you preferred your sister's beauty to mine –'

'Not preferred – never that.'

'I forgive you for wounding me. I have loved you, too, since you first came to visit your brother, though I knew that to you I was just a child.'

'But you are not a child now, and I –'

'My lord, it is not that I will not marry *you*. It is that I will not marry. I swore long ago, in your presence, that I would never marry, but would be a great singer. I meant it. I will be the greatest singer in the world. Do you not know that signor Vivaldi has plans to write an opera with the main part especially for me? I cannot allow marriage to interfere with my plans.'

'But –'

'You will not change my mind. Please speak of it no more.' Karellie was silent, and she came towards him and stood close, looking up into his face, for tall as she was, he was taller, amongst the tallest men in Europe. 'You call me the Divine Diane, and that is how I want people to remember me. All the world will one day know me. But I will always love you, my lord, and I pray you will not stop loving me. I need your love.'

'I will not stop loving you,' Karellie said.

Her eyes gave permission, and he bent his head to place the first kiss upon her waiting lips. Afterwards she sighed as if something were accomplished, and then said briskly, 'Let us go in. It grows chilly. I shall play for you until the tea is brought.'

When the Electress Sofia died suddenly in June 1714, it was clear that she had failed by only a narrow margin to succeed Anne to the throne, for the latter had been ailing since the beginning of the year, and could not be expected to survive long. Sofia had been active to the end, and had collapsed unexpectedly while taking one of her energetic walks in the gardens that Annunciata remembered so well. She was eighty-four years old.

How things would go when Anne died was still very uncertain, for her ministry was split, and though most people seemed to dislike the idea of George Lewis coming from Hanover to take the throne, the great dread of Catholicism balanced that in people's minds; besides, it seemed likely that the matter would be decided by which-ever of the principal ministers acted fastest, and plots bred like bats up and down the country. Correspondence with King James increased, and Berwick was also known to be writing to Ormonde and Bolingbroke on the subject of the restoration of his brother.

Annunciata had been in London in the spring of that year, but was back at Morland Place by early summer. The improvement there was marked, and though Matt was still withdrawn and would see no company, he had taken over many of his old tasks, to the easing of Annunciata's lot, and had also began to enjoy at least her company. He liked to walk with her in the Italian garden, with Kithra and

Oyster pattering behind them, and discuss the day's business.

'I can get things clearer in my mind if I have talked them over with you,' he would say. As he came to depend on her more, his formality with her dropped away, and he ceased, when they were alone together, to call her madam or my lady or even grandmother. Annunciata found it pleasant. She was growing very fond of him, and sometimes when they walked about the garden, close but not touching, and conversing desultorily as the mood took them, she could imagine that the years had rolled back, and that she was with her lover. He looked so like Martin, that it was her joy to look at him, and she felt she could never have enough of simply sitting and staring.

They discussed other things as well as the business of the estate. On politics his views were very different from hers, and she came to understand that it was useless to expect a man of his generation, brought up as he had been under the rule of successive usurpers, to feel the same way about the occupation of the throne. She had grown up in a world where everyone felt they knew the King personally; she had gone at the age of fifteen to Court, and had lived in close and familiar contact with King Charles and King James, identifying with their lives and interest; the personalities that were mere names, cyphers to Matt, were flesh and blood people to her.

Besides, he had never been away from Morland Place, and with the exception of his long, blind passion for India, it was the only thing he had ever cared deeply about. His inheritance, his land – that had never let him down. It endured. What was good and right for Morland Place had first sway with him. How could distant kings and princes compete with that? Annunciata felt sadly that there were many all over the country who believed the same. Had their livelihoods been directly threatened, they might have grown passionate about the issues, but as it was they were content for the folk far away in London to worry about the succession while they got on with the shearing and the hay-harvest.

All the same, she enjoyed arguing with him, and once or twice as the summer progressed, she even managed to turn the outermost corner of his mouth in the beginning of a smile at her vehemence.

'If you were a man, what a soldier you'd make,' he said once. 'I'd want you for my general, if I were King.'

By August Queen Anne was evidently sinking fast. Annunciata and Matt were taking their walk one morning when a strange servant came into the garden, evidently looking for them, and Annunciata's heart jumped and her hands became clammy at the expectation that this was the long-awaited messenger. But as the man came nearer, something familiar about him made her look more closely.

'John Wood! It is John Wood!'

'Oh, my lady,' said the man, falling to his knees in front of her, the tears coming to his eyes as he took the hand she offered and put it to his forehead.

'John Wood, what are you doing here?' she asked in amazement, touched by his devotion. He had been long in her service, had served her son Hugo, and gone into exile with her as Maurice's manservant. 'Where is your master?'

'He is here, my lady,' John Wood said, rising to his feet. 'Up at the house. He has come back to England, the little girls too. We arrived in London a week ago, and when we found Chelmsford House shut up, my master did not wait, but set off straight away for Yorkshire. Oh my lady, it is so good to be home. I never thought –' he swallowed. 'I did not think I would see it again.'

'Nor, I, John,' Annunciata said with sympathy. She turned to Matt. 'We must go in at once and greet them. Your uncle Maurice, Matt, and his daughters. Come, come, you must welcome them.'

Matt hesitated, for he had not yet accepted any strangers into his house. Annunciata stamped her foot in frustration, and tugged his hand, but he held back and said, 'You greet them. I will walk a little longer.'

She made a sound of exasperation and, beckoning to John Wood, started for the house. As she left the garden, she looked back and saw that Matt had already gone through the wicket on the far side, evidently bent on putting as much of the estate between himself and the newcomers as possible. He was a long way from being cured, she realized.

She found Maurice little changed, for like many unworldly people he seemed to avoid the crushing realizations that aged the rest of the population. He was forty-two, but his hair was as black as ever, his figure as lithe and youthful, and his dark eyes made his face look younger than his years. He greeted his mother affectionately, but without great display, as if they had been only a week apart, and he had never had any doubt that they would meet again. The little girls stood nervously in the background, clutching their muffs like shields, looking to Annunciata markedly foreign and not at all worthy of being her grandchildren. They spoke no word of English, and when she addressed them in Italian they were too shy to say more than yes and no.

'But what are you doing here?' she asked him. 'And where is Karellie? Is he coming home too? And Aliena? What news, I pray you!'

'England is the obvious next place for me,' Maurice said unconcernedly. 'I have got everything from Italy that there is to be got for the moment. Perhaps you do not realize that great things are happening in London? I have heard from George Haendel – do you remember him? He was Kapelmeister at the Herrenhausen – that the public are very appreciative in London, especially of the opera.'

By which she understood that Maurice meant different things from the great things she thought were going on in London. She stared at him with affectionate exasperation. Here was another man who would shrug over her preoccupation with dynasties.

'I thought I could live at Chelmsford House, if you do not mind it, but when I knew you were in the country, I thought I had better come here first.' He spoke with the unconcern of a man who had travelled up and down Italy for the past seven years.

'And what news of Karellie?' Annunciata asked again, more gently.

'He spends his time between Venice and Lorraine,' Maurice said, 'tugged about by his heart like a compass.'

'His heart? What draws him to Venice?' Annunciata asked quickly. Was it possible her son was at last thinking of marrying and getting an heir?

'Oh he has fallen in love with the daughter of the house where I lived, but she will not have him,' Maurice said with amusement. 'It is typical of Karellie that he can only fall in love where he is quite safe from reciprocation. I'm afraid you have spoiled him for love and marriage, mother – he will never get over his first and strongest passion for you.'

'What nonsense you talk,' Annunciata said crossly. Maurice shook his head.

'I am serious, mother. We are all quite, quite useless for ordinary people. There's Karellie, fallen in love with a goddess-like singer; and me, falling in love with perfect dark-haired, dark-eyed nuns, because they reminded me of you; and Aliena who can only be in love with her King. The only difference is that they don't understand what they are doing, and I do. That is why I have stopped marrying. I have these poor little girls on my conscience already. Now I espouse the Muse – at least a slightly less hopeless love than those of my brother and sister, though equally impossible of consummation.'

'But will they come home,' Annunciata said, cutting through all this. Maurice looked at her with sympathy.

'Not until and unless the King does. That is one thing on which they stand firm. They are less – shall we say adaptable – than you and I, though Karellie at least has learnt to forgive us for it.'

*

Maurice and his daughters were still in Yorkshire when the news came that Queen Anne had died in the early hours of Sunday 1 August. There was tension all over the country as to what would happen next; but the Whigs of the ministry were more prepared and more active than the Tories. The Elector was proclaimed King, immediately in London and within days in the principal cities. Almost with her dying breath Anne had passed the rod of office to Shrewsbury, who took control of the army and the militia, forced Bolingbroke to flee, and sent for the Elector. Whether that was what the Queen had intended it was impossible to say, though it was widely reported that she had called upon her brother's name in her last agonies. Another, sadder story was soon being repeated. Anne had had a thick bundle of papers which for years she had carried about with her, placing them under her pillow at night, and replacing the envelope when it grew worn or soiled. After her death it had been found, sealed with her own seal, and with the instruction on the outside that it should be burnt unread. Her close attendants had obeyed her wish and flung the bundle on the fire, but as the flames had consumed the envelope the bundle had sprung open, and many there were to swear that they had seen King James's handwriting upon the pages.

The Elector arrived in England a month later, and to Annunciata's unconcealed annoyance Maurice immediately left with his household to London to seek his favours.

'It's very well for you, mother,' he said calmly, 'but a musician depends on patronage. As soon as the true King comes back, I shall seek his patronage in place of the Elector's.' Annunciata thought of forbidding him to use her house, but at the last moment repented of it. For one thing, she did not want to alienate her son from her, since she was already so lacking in close relatives; and in the second place she reasoned that the less he was in need, the less he would disgrace her by dancing attendance on the Elector.

She remained in Yorkshire, writing letters and waiting

on events. The Elector was crowned in October, and there were riots in Glasgow and Edinburgh and in some other major cities in England, but there seemed to be no one to organize the rebellious elements into a proper force. Yet the time would come, she knew, and she must be ready. She wrote to Edmund at St Omer, to Karellie, Aliena, the King, Berwick, to Sabina and Allan Macallan in Scotland. People moved and thought slowly, but the time would come. Bolingbroke had fled England and was at St Germain, and he and Berwick were in charge of the correspondence with the leading Jacobites in England and Scotland. The Elector, who arrived with his two ugly mistresses, having left his wife still imprisoned at Ahlden, where she had been shut up alone for twenty years, had already made himself unpopular with many of the principal courtiers, and the old scandal of his treatment of his wife was revived and circulated in many 'secret histories' with much circumstantial detail. Since he had brought an entire German household with him, it seemed likely that frustrated place-seekers would soon join the ranks of whose who favoured the King over the Water, along with those offended by the Elector's obvious reluctance to have come at all.

Something would happen, not yet, for winter was closing in, but next year, next spring. Annunciata would not be downcast. Next year she would be seventy years old – surely an important landmark? – and England would have a King again.

CHAPTER SIXTEEN

When the Venetian ambassador arrived in London in July 1715, it was natural that Maurice Morland should call to pay his respects to that emiment personage, even had the ambassador's party not included his old patron, the Duke di Francescini and his daughter Diane. It did not, however, divert the attention of the Whig spies from the fact that the tall, soldierly blond man who was evidently a friend of the duke's was Charles Morland, Earl of Chelmsford. His presence in London caused a ripple of surprise, for though he had never officially been exiled, he was known to be a firm Jacobite. Yet within hours of his arrival, other rumours had begun to circulate: the earl was tired of exile, especially as his mother and brother had now come back to England, and as the Elector was his cousin, he had come to make peace.

'Diane's servant Caterina makes an excellently innocent gossip,' Karellie explained to Maurice when they were alone together for a moment. 'In fact she is a very sharp and intelligent young woman, and we had not been here an hour before she spotted the Whig spy – a footman with a predilection for lounging idly near closed doors. Fortunately, the man is handsome, or at least fancies himself so, and did not find it strange that the empty-headed lady's maid should find him attractive.'

'And he thinks it most convenient,' Maurice smiled, 'that she should give accidental vent to the very information he is seeking?'

'Caterina says she always knows when he is more than usually interested in an answer of hers, because he looks down at his fingernails as if he really can hardly be bothered to listen.'

'So you are here to make your peace with your cousin,

in the hopes of ending your days pleasantly in England,' Maurice said. 'And in reality?'

'To make contact with Mar,' Karellie said, lowering his voice instinctively. 'The Chevalier St George has charged him with bringing out the Highlands, and I am to help him. There was no possibility of my arriving unnoticed in England, so we thought it convenient to make this reason. Mar is in London too. We will both attend the Royal Levée tomorrow. We don't know how much they know about our plans, though it's certain they know something, so we want to divert their attention by making an appearance of loyalty.'

'And then?' Maurice asked.

'Away to Scotland. Maurice, will you come with us?'

Maurice met his eyes steadily, 'No, Karel, no. I am not like you. I have begun good things here in London, and I cannot leave them yet.'

'Good things? Your music? How can you care about that when here's the throne of England at stake?' Karellie cried with some bitterness. Maurice only looked sad.

'Oh, brother, I wish I could make you see. How can I care about something as unimportant as who sits upon the throne, when there is music at stake?' Karellie looked at him with stormy, uncomprehending eyes. 'Kings and princes all will come to dust one day, but music lives for ever. I love you, Karellie, and I don't blame you for being different from me. Do you not blame me.'

Karellie hesitated only one moment and then flung his arms round his brother in a hard embrace. 'Maurice, when it's known I am gone, they may come after you,' he said, his voice muffled by Maurice's shoulder. Maurice patted Karellie's shoulder and marvelled at the thickness of muscle under the silk coat.

'Don't worry about me, I shall be all right. The Wee German Lairdie that has your King's throne has only one grace in him, and that's the love of music. I have already made myself welcome at Court. I sha'n't be troubled much.'

Karellie straightened up. 'Can you get a letter to our mother, without its being found out?'

'I think so. I'll let her know somehow.'

The Levée was well attended, and Karellie had no difficulty in picking out John, Earl of Mar, despite never having seen him before, for the earl had a hump-back which gave him an odd gait – 'Bobbing John', the common folk called him. He was a small, stocky, fair man, pleasant-faced, but with that slight over-fullness of the lower eyelids that is often seen in those who have been ill a great deal. His eyes met Karellie's in the ante-room, and flicked away again. They must not shew too much interest in each other yet.

The Elector, when he arrived, looked to Karellie little different from the last time he had seen him in Hanover, only older and stouter. Karellie's hands were sweating with nervousness – suppose the Elector shouted for the guards and had him clapped in the Tower? – but when the moment came the little fat man looked up at him with a complete lack of interest, and the dull eyes passed over his face with no apparent recognition.

With Mar it was different, however: the Elector knew who he was, and when Mar went down into his bow, the Elector deliberately turned his back on him and walked away, leaving Mar crouched ridiculously before the empty air. There was a stirring of interest and laughter amongst the courtiers, and Mar looked outraged and aggrieved. But when the royal party had moved on, Mar caught his eye once more with a small nod of satisfaction.

When they returned, later, to the Venetian ambassador's lodgings, Diane took Karellie aside and said, 'Was that the man, the little crooked one?' Karellie hesitated to give her any information that she might later regret having but she snapped her fingers in impatience. 'What, do you think they would put me to the question, my lord? Besides, I know so much already, it were better I knew all, not to give something away out of ignorance.'

'Yes, that was the man. We leave tonight, Principessa, in disguise.'

Diane laughed. 'How can you be disguised, when you tower above ordinary men?'

'I go as one of Mar's servants. Dull clothes, a shabby cloak, and a dark wig.'

'But you walk like a lord, like a soldier. Come, we have a little time, let me teach you how to walk like a servant. And you must hunch up a little, let your knees and shoulders sag so that you don't look so tall. Look, like this.'

Karellie watched, bemused, and allowed her to teach him. 'How can you know such things?' he asked.

'I am an opera singer, my lord, you forget. And as such I am half an actress already. Don't you remember in *Aricia* I had to disguise myself as a servant-girl to get out of the palace?'

He came close and took her hands, and for once she allowed him. 'What will you do when I am gone?' he asked. She held her head high, but looked at him without haughtiness; her eyes were bright, but kind.

'There is a great deal to do and see in London. I shall certainly visit the Court again, and Maurice wil take me to the play and the opera. Who knows, perhaps when it is known I am in London I shall be asked to perform? You may come back and find me the toast of London.'

'I shall only be surprised if I don't,' Karellie said. 'Listen, Diane, I must say something. You know that we go tonight to raise the standard in Scotland for the Chevalier? Every year Mar has a great hunting party at Braemar, to which he invites all the leading Highland lords; this year, when they are assembled, he will make the proclamation and raise the standard. It is a dangerous thing we do, and if battle and death do not claim us, there is still the danger of capture and execution. I may never come back –'

'You will come back,' Diane said defiantly, her eyes bright.

'But if I do not,' he went on firmly, 'I want to have the satisfaction of having told you that I love you. Which I do, Diane, my Principessa.' She looked at him steadily, this tall, handsome man with the great dark eyes, and suddenly saw what a tribute it was to her that he should look so humble before her. 'I am more than twice your age, and perhaps it seems absurd to you, but –'

'It does not seem absurd,' she said gently, and turned her face up to him. It was a very quiet, gentle kiss, not passionate, but the kiss of two adults, not man and child. Afterwards there was nothing more to say, and he went away to prepare himself, leaving Diane thoughtful.

That night Mar slipped out of London and took passage on a collier brig from Gravesend, accompanied by General Hamilton and several servants, including Karellie and his man Sam. At Newcastle they transferred on to a boat owned by one John Spence of Leith, who sailed them to Elie in Fife, and from there they continued on horseback. From that moment, letters began to pass back and forth between the great lords of Scotland, and on the 26th the annual hunt took place at Braemar. After each day's sport there would be feasting and drinking, and Mar would make his stirring speeches about the Cursed Union, the sorrows and miseries of the Kingdom, and the hope of deliverance when the Chevalier was restored to his rightful throne. A month after he had slipped away from London, Mar raised the standard, and the rising had truly begun.

Birnie Castle was cool, a refuge from the heart of August, but Sabina felt as though she was burning up. They had all come as usual from Aberlady to spend the summer there, but this year there was no hunting-party, partly because of the events taking place to the north at Braemar, and partly because Sabina had been great with child and likely to give birth at any moment. This was her eighth pregnancy, and her only surviving child was Hamil, who was now ten years old. Allan Macallan had been doubtful as to the good sense of her journeying to Birnie at such a time, but Sabina had longed for the fresh air and freedom of the moors.

'Besides,' she said, 'the first thing that will happen will be the taking of Edinburgh, and you surely cannot want me to be close to that?'

'But Birnie is close to Stirling, where the army camp is,' Allan had pointed out. 'If you want to be safe, we must travel up to the Glens.'

'We'll be safe enough at Birnie,' Sabina said. 'Our own people will be loyal to us.'

Allan had to give in at length; throughout their lives together, Sabina had always commanded him. Theirs had been a happy marriage, except for the death of all their children but one, for their temperaments were suited: Allan adored Sabina, and loved to serve her, while Sabina liked best of all to be adored, and if there was some part of her heart she could not give him, she never let him know it. They were united in loving Hamil and in worrying over his health, and in relying on Mavis for sensible advice.

Mavis still lived with them, along with her daughter Mary, who was fifteen and growing beautiful. In her black gowns and white caps she looked a little like the portraits of Mary Queen of Scots, and Sabina sometimes teased her about it, saying that she was so vain of her beauty that nothing would satisfy her but that she should be mistaken for a queen. In the last year, however, Mavis had lost a great deal of her beauty, though those around her had grown too accustomed to thinking of her as beautiful to notice it. But her gowns hung loose on her, and the bones of her face seemed more prominent. She complained now and then of feeling the cold, and had taken to wearing a thick black shawl; if this had the secondary effect of hiding the thinness of her neck and shoulders, only Mary noticed it.

Sabina went into labour on the last day of August, the hottest day of the year, and between her groans she said to Mavis, 'You see I was right to come. I should have died of the heat at Aberlady.'

Allan had been out about his estates at Braco, and Mavis sent a messenger after him to say Sabina's time had come, and he came hurrying back, bringing news of Mar's hunt, and the support it had gained.

'Lord Tullibardine has gone over to Mar, taking most of his father's men with him,' Allan said, 'so there is not much thought but that Perth will fall to Mar.'

'That would be a great thing,' Mavis said. 'It must be the only town in the Highlands where an army could assemble, besides being a greater matter of prestige.'

'And it would make a good centre for the Chevalier to base himself – good roads and communications, and centrally placed. But the news is not all positive. The Elector has not been idle. Three regiments have arrived from Ireland, and are moving towards Stirling; Edinburgh and Glasgow have armed; and Admiral Byng has the Jacobite ships blockaded in Le Havre with all the powder and ammunition and guns we've been hoping for.'

'Perhaps they might slip away,' Mavis said. 'Blockades are meant for escaping.'

Allan smiled. 'You are always so cheerful. But now King Louis is dead, there is no doubt that the Regent is less sympathetic to the Chevalier, and the likelihood is that he will not wish to provoke Admiral Byng when he has the entire Channel fleet pointing its guns at Le Havre.'

'We shall see,' Mavis said calmly. 'I must go back to Sabina now. I will tell her about Lord Tullibardine, but not about Le Havre. She asks continuously after you, and she will be glad that I can tell her you are here.'

'I wish I could see her,' Allan said wistfully, but Mavis looked stern.

'Nonsense! You'll see her in good time. And don't worry,' she added more gently, 'everything looks well this time. There is no reason to fear.'

'No reason more than usual, you mean,' Allan said. Mavis shook her head at his pessimism.

'Play a game of chess with Mary, and try not to think

about it. Please do – it will be a service for me. Mary is too sensitive and needs to be occupied.'

Before evening more news came in that Allan would have liked to keep from Mavis, but could not. The Earl of Breadalbane, who was eighty years old, had been arrested. He was a distant cousin of Mavis', but more importantly was the head of her clan and the overlord of her family and all their estates. An order had been passed by Parliament naming sixty-two peers and gentlemen whose loyalty to the Elector was suspected, and demanding their attendance in Edinburgh to be judged. Only two of those named went to Edinburgh, and they were clapped into prison, whereupon most of the rest declared for the Chevalier. Some of the more important, like Lord Breadalbane, had escorts sent to them to bring them to Edinburgh; and the news that, as soon as he had gone, his men all joined General Gordon in declaring for Mar, did not lessen the worry about the old man's safety and health.

That evening just about dusk, Sabina at last was delivered of a son, whose size and strength accounted for the length of her labour. As soon as the cord had been cut, the baby seemed to be looking about him with interest, and his thumb crept to his mouth and was sucked with a vigour that suggested he would have no difficulty in discovering how to take nourishment from his nurse.

Allan was delighted with him, and knelt beside Sabina's bed with great tenderness to thank her for giving him such a fine son.

'What shall we call him?' he asked her. 'Whatever is your pleasure, it shall be.'

Sabina looked at him for a moment with bright, tired eyes, and then turned her head away. 'Oh, call him after yourself. I am too tired to think of names.'

The news passed around the servants and tenants, and the next day they began to come up to the castle to pay their respects. A few days later a deputation came from the town of Braco, bringing a silver cup for the baby, inscribed with his name and date of birth. They had spelled the name

'Allen' and Sabina said, 'So be it, it will be a convenience to be able to distinguish him from you, at least in writing.'

The day after that came the welcome news that General Hay, with the help of Tullibardine's men, had taken Perth for the Chevalier, and that Mar was moving south, gathering men along the way, to join him there. There was good news also about old Lord Breadalbane, who had delayed his conduct to Edinburgh by claiming frailty and ill-health and retiring to bed at every opportunity. Finally he got a doctor to sign an affidavit to say that he was too ill to travel any further, and sent off his escort with it, while he slipped away to join the others in Perth, where he was joyfully reunited with his men.

By the end of September, Mar had reached Perth with his army of Highlanders, and more were expected every day. Meanwhile the Duke of Argyll had been sent from London to command the forces for the Elector, and had been joined by two regiments from the north of England and several bands of trained volunteers from Edinburgh and Glasgow.

Mavis took Allan aside and said to him, 'The time has come for you to take our men and join the others at Perth. With the men from Braco, and those from Birnie, you can take twenty armed and mounted men to General Mar, in addition to money. I have my jewels packed and ready – they are my gift.'

'But I cannot leave you,' Allan cried in surprise.

'You must,' Mavis said calmly. 'The men from my clan in the north have gone, and if I were a man, I would be with them, ready to fight for the true king. But it has pleased God to put me in the body of a weak and foolish woman. I can give nothing but money and prayers, but I can release you for the task by taking care of Sabina and your children. You must go, Allan Macallan: for duty; and if that does not move you, for pride.'

'But what will you do?'

'I shall take Sabina and the children and go back to Aberlady.'

'That will be dangerous.'

'It will be dangerous to stay here. With Mar at Perth and Argyll at Stirling, we are between two armies here.'

'Sabina won't go,' Allan said shaking his head. Mavis smiled.

'Leave me alone for that. I can manage Sabina. We'll travel slowly, and in disguise, so as not to attract attention. The idea of the disguises will reconcile her to the scheme. We'll be safer at Aberlady, for if the worst comes to the worst, we can get a boat from there, to France or Holland. Or escape across the Border. Frances and John would hide us if need be, and it would be a brave man that would follow us into Coquetdale. At all events, we cannot stay here.'

'Yes, I see that. Well, if you are determined, it shall be as you say.'

The next day Allan took his leave of his wife and children, and the day after that Mavis and Sabina, with their servants and the children, slipped quietly away from Birnie, disguised as poor people, with a cart and a farm horse for Sabina and the baby and the luggage, and the rest of them walking. Sabina, dressed in a coarse brown woollen dress, with a length of greasy plaid round her shoulders and over her head, loved it all, and had to be restrained from asking directions of every passer-by for the delight of seeing their reactions. At all events, it took her mind very successfully from the departure of her husband.

Allan Macallan's first task on arriving in Perth was to find billets for his men, and that was none to easy. The town was already crowded with soldiers, and a discreet chaos seemed to reign, though it was evident that attempts were being made to organize foraging parties and various committees to run the day-to-day routine of the gathering army. He soon discovered the Battalion of Drummonds, numbering about two hundred, and led by Lord Strathallan, and decided the best thing would be to report to him, and let Strathallan solve his problems and likewise take charge of the money he had brought for Mar's aid. He found his lordship in a room above the tap-room of the Rose Inn, conversing with a fair-haired man so tall and broad-shouldered that he looked like to burst the tiny room at its seams. The two men were deep in some discussion when Allan knocked at the door and entered. Lord Strathallan glared at him.

'Who are you? What do you want? Wait, I know you now – you're Allan Macallan of Braco! What the devil are you doing here?'

'I've brought twenty men, my lord, fully armed – ' Allan began, but the tall man was staring at him with pleased surprise, and interrupted him.

'Allan Macallan – well well! I claim you as a relative, sir, by marriage at least. If I mistake not you are married to my cousin Sabina.'

The man had large dark eyes like an Italian, and a way of pronouncing his words that was not Scottish nor yet precisely English. His blue silk coat, though hard worn, was of rich material; his wig, flung aside over the back of a chair, was even at a glance a superior one made of real hair which so closely matched the pale colour of his own that it must necessarily have cost him a small fortune.

'Your cousin, sir?' Allan asked hesitantly. The man extended a large, shapely hand.

'Charles Morland, sir, Earl of Chelmsford. Your wife's mother was sister to my father Ralph Morland.'

Allan took the offered hand. 'My lord,' he said, 'I am deeply honoured –'

'So you have brought men,' Strathallan interrupted these pleasantries.

'And money, my lord, and my wife's jewels.'

'Money – that will please Mar,' Karellie said. 'It is no light task to feed an army, as he is discovering.'

'It seems all he can discover,' Strathallan growled. 'He spends all his time talking about money and corn and the

312

price of hay. When are we going to move? Does he mean to sit here in Perth for ever?'

'He has no orders,' Karellie said gently. Strathallan thumped his fist on the table.

'Damn it, that's what a commander in chief is for, to give orders.'

'The Chevalier, my lord, hopes to land in the south-west with Ormonde. The rising here in Scotland is secondary.'

'Then all the more reason for Mar to take matters into his own hands. If the Chevalier and Berwick are not coming here –'

'But my lord, I understood the King was expected here hourly,' Allan said, perplexed. 'The King and Lord Berwick –'

'That's what the men think, and I'll thank you not to tell them otherwise, Macallan. But if what Chelmsford says is right – damn it, the longer we give Argyll to arrange his forces, the worse for us. How long before our men start slipping away, eh?' He was speaking to Karellie again, forgetting Allan's presence as soon as his eyes were off him. Karellie leaned over the table.

'Argyll has the bridge at Stirling, and that puts him between us and the Borderers of Northumberland. Now, if we can get across the Forth at some other point and join up with the Borderers, we'll have the whole of Scotland in our hands.'

Strathallan's eyes brightened at the prospect of some action. 'You have a plan? God damn my eyes, I'd like to hear it. I don't care what it is, so long as it is something to get me off my backside.'

'Not my plan, but Sinclair's – to cross the Firth of Forth by boat.'

'But there are enemy ships in the Firth. Three men-o'-war and God knows how many armed fishing-boats,' Strathallan objected. 'We have no ships at all – what do you suggest, we steal rowing boats?'

'Exactly that. And a diversion at Burnt Island, to draw off the men-of-war while we cross in the dark. We'll need people who know the coast, of course, and the best places to land . . .'

'My lords,' Allan cried excitedly, 'I know the coast from Edinburgh up to North Berwick as well as I know the palms of my hands. I live there – my house is at Aberlady – I have known that coast since I was a child scrambling over rocks.'

Strathallan looked at him with interest.

'Do you, by God? It seems you have brought us something besides men and money. Chelmsford, I think we had better have a meeting with the general as soon as possible.'

'We can go and see him now, and arrange a time. There will have to be others in consultation. Sinclair says Hay knows the Fife coastline, where it will be best to try for boats.'

Strathallan jumped up, ready for action. 'Macallan, you had better come with us, since you have heard so much already. And you can give the money to Mar in person – that will convince him of your bona fides. Where are these men of yours?'

'Outside, sir, in the field at the back of the inn.'

'They can stay there for the time being. I'll give orders to one of my sergeants to find 'em a billet for tonight. With any luck we can be on our way tomorrow.'

Strathallan's hopes were too optimistic, but even so the plan was put into action promptly, and a force of 2,500 left Perth on 9 October, under the command of General Mackintosh of Borlum, known affectionately as Old Borlum, a tall, gaunt man of sixty with piercing grey eyes under ferociously bushy eyebrows, reaching the coast of Fife on Tuesday 11 October.

Sinclair had gone ahead several days earlier to proclaim the Chevalier King in the fishing villages along the Fife coast and to commandeer the necessary boats. On the following day the men laid up quietly and rested, ready for

the first crossing on the Wednesday night. There were to
be two crossings on successive nights, for it had been
estimated that it would not be possible to take over more
than a thousand men in small boats and land them safely
during the hours of darkness. Allan's men had joined with
Lord Strathallan's Drummonds, and Allan was to go in the
first party to advise on the landing. On his recommendation
the boats were to head for three landing places at North
Berwick, Aberlady, and Gullane; the first-comers, including the general himself, could wait safely at Aberlady
House for the crossing to be completed, for the worst thing
to fear was that the force should be split up and scattered.

The crossing was done in fifty or so small boats, and it
was a tricky business, getting the men, some of whom had
never seen a boat before, let alone been on one, aboard in
the pitch darkness, rowing across, landing them, and
rowing the boats back to be in place for the second crossing
on Thursday night. Allan went across in the first boat to
Aberlady in the exalted company of Old Borlum himself;
Karellie was remaining on the Fife side to control the
second night's crossing. As soon as they stepped out on to
the sand, Allan despatched his servant to run up to the
house to prepare them to receive the general and as many
of the expedition as could be accommodated. It was just
less than two weeks since Allan had seen his wife and
children, but already he was overjoyed at the prospect of
holding them in his arms again, even if only for a few short
hours.

The plans for the rising in Northumberland had been in
hand for some time, and the activity of messengers going
from house to house had not escaped the notice of the
Elector's spies. Already warrants had been issued for the
arrest of Lord Derwentwater, for no better reason than he
was a distant cousin of the Chevalier, and Tom Forster,
the MP, because he was deep in debt as well as being a
known Jacobite, and would therefore be expected to be

reckless. Suspicion was also being directed against John Rathkeale, who as the grandson of the Countess of Chelmsford might well be expected to come out for the Chevalier. The gathering was set to take place on 6 October, just outside Bellingham, which was well placed at the junction of several important roads. From there the gathering would move to Rothbury, on the Alnwick road at the foot of the Cheviots, where they expected the east coast people to join them, and from where they could march straight down to Newcastle. The difficulty for Rathkeale and his men was in getting out of their own grounds, for since the warrants had gone out, they were being closely watched, and any move southward would be likely to provoke arrest. A diversionary tactic was needed, and though John hated the idea of involving Frances, her own enthusiasm overcame his objections.

'I have as much right to do what I can for the cause,' she said. 'And Father approves, don't you?'

Francomb grinned amiably. 'She's her mother's daughter,' he said. 'I could never have kept Sabine from it, so you may as well give in now, John.' In his mind was the image of Sabine on horseback charging down on the government agents with terrible yells, just as he had seen her galloping full-cry at the hunt. 'Besides, if you can think of another way to get us out –'

John couldn't, and so it had to be. On the evening before, they lay tenderly entwined in their curtained bed, and though they did not speak, they both thought about the chances that they would never meet again.

'I have been very happy with you,' John said at last. 'I did not give much thought to marriage when I was younger, but when grandmother said I was to marry you, I knew that you were the only person in the world I could ever have wanted to marry. And our son John –'

His voice failed him, and Frances pressed him closer in comfort. Their only surviving child was just two years old, and their joint pride.

'Hush, darling. Don't speak of it. It's the same for poor Lord Derwentwater,' Frances said.

'Worse in a way,' John said. 'He has only been married three years. At least you and I have had ten years together.'

'And his wife is pregnant,' Frances added. 'That must be hard for him.'

'I could wish I was leaving you pregnant, my hinny. Then, if anything happened to me –'

She put her hand over his mouth in the darkness. 'Don't speak of it,' she said. 'I have been happy too, my John. But we'll be happy again. When the King is on his throne, and you come home to me.'

There was no more speech. After some time, when they were drifting together into sleep, he heard her murmur, 'Perhaps you do leave me pregnant.'

He smiled, but was too far gone in sleep to answer.

The next day Frances and two of the women dressed in men's clothing, and with cloaks and hoods for further disguise, they rode out on to Emblehope moor, and set off riding hard in the direction of Otterburn. When they had gone, drawing, it was hoped, the attention of the government spies, the men slipped away in ones and twos to the woods along Rooken Edge, where the horses had been concealed for two days, and there mounted up and rode across Blackburn Common down to Greenhaugh and thence to Bellingham. In the meantime Jack Francomb, mounted on his most hardy horse, undertook the wild and solitary ride over Blackman's Law, down into Redesdale, and by the track up and over Raven's Knowe to Blindburn, to bring out his own men from the old estate. In winter it would have been certain death to attempt the ride, and even in October it was risky enough; but Francomb had been born on the Cheviots, and those bare hills had been his harsh nursemaid. On 13 October, when the Jacobites already gathered at Rothbury had moved on to Warkworth, he rode in at the head of a band of twelve armed and mounted men to join his son-in-law.

*

The second crossing from Fife had not had such good luck as the first. It was not to be expected that the diversionary force at Burnt Island could fool the men-of-war for ever, and the ships came up upon the little boats when they were right out in the middle of the Firth. Karellie had held back to the end of the embarkation, and saw most of what went on, and at first it looked as though there would be no trouble, for the small boats were very scattered, and it was difficult for the big, clumsy ships to do much against them. Karellie saw one boat captured, and forty-or-so men taken into custody, but while that was happening others slipped through and reached the shore, aided by the lights from the ships, which shewed them the direction and made the landing easier.

But then the men-of-war regrouped themselves, and instead of dashing hither and thither after the rowing boats, like great oxen chasing flies, they had the sense to place themselves in a line across the water and bar the way. It was impossible to go forward, and now that the tide had turned and the current was setting away from the coast of Fife, it was impossible to go back. Karellie gave orders to pull for the Fife shore, but the current and tide proved too strong, and after an exhausting few hours of rowing they were able only to land on the Isle of May, in the middle of the widest part of the estuary. It was a tiny, rocky island, wild and windswept, on which a religious foundation had once made its retreat from the world, and they were lucky to have reached it, for beyond was only the wild waste of the North Sea and no landfall before Norway. If they had been swept past it, they would have perished for sure.

The men-of-war could not get close in to the island, because of the rocks and currents, but they stood as close-to as they could, preventing escape. During the night and the following morning, other boats came in, numbering around eleven, and carrying Lord Strathmore amongst others. When it was possible to assemble and count the men, they were able to estimate that around half of the second night's contingent must have got across. There were around two hundred of them on the island. Wearily, Karellie set about making arrangements for the shelter and feeding of his small army.

Allan had found his womenfolk at Aberlady House, and was rapturously reunited with Sabina, who looked none the worse for her journey, and in fact had discovered a new delight, in actually feeding her own baby at her own breast, for the wet-nurse had left them the first night when they passed by her home village, saying that she did not care to risk traipsing about the country when there were so many soldiers about. She was less delighted to see Allan than he was to see her.

'Goodness, what are you doing here?' she asked him sharply. 'Why aren't you off fighting somewhere?'

'We are on the way to fight, my dearest,' he said pacifically. 'Meanwhile, I must ask you to accommodate the general and his staff and some of the men. I cannot tell you too much of the plan, for fear of being overheard, but –'

'Accommodate? I hope you don't mean feed, for we have very little in the house,' Sabina said. Mavis intervened at that point.

'You had better bring them into the hall, Allan,' she said, 'and those who cannot fit into the hall can shelter in the stables and the barn for a while. How long will you be staying?'

'Only for one night.'

'How many men have you actually got out there?' Sabina asked suspiciously.

'There will be about three hundred altogether, and others may come in during the night from –'

'Three hundred!' Sabina cried. 'How in the world do you expect us to feed three hundred men?'

'He doesn't expect it, Sabina,' Mavis said. 'Do make yourself calm, or you will curdle your milk, and the baby will be sick. Allan, you had better go and direct them in here, with as little noise as possible. We don't want to attract the attention of the neighbours, though thank God we are well away from the road here.'

Allan took his departure gratefully, and Mavis turned to Sabina. 'I have never before had to remind you that this house belongs to me, in trust for my daughter, and I hope it is not necessary now. Allan will bring the men in, and we will do what we can for them. I don't understand why you are being so difficult.'

'It's all so ridiculous and undignified,' Sabina grumbled. 'We fly from Birnie at great inconvenience to ourselves, and travel across country in ridiculous disguises,' already she had forgotten her pleasure in them, 'solely so that Allan will feel free to go and join General Mar at Perth, and hardly are we here but he turns up on the doorstep. It is ridiculous. What are they doing here anyway?'

'We cannot know their plans. Perhaps they are going to attack Edinburgh.'

'Well, perhaps they are,' Sabina said, mollified.

'Whatever their plan, it is for us to aid them.'

'Yes, you're right. Sensible Mavis. Come then, let us go and see what we have.' Sabina's moods and poses never lasted long. Now she was being brisk and efficient, the loyal soldier's wife. Mavis sighed and wondered what would be next.

On the afternoon of the thirteenth General Mackintosh moved out the assembled men to Haddington, to make room for the second night's contingent. Allan remained behind to help with the landing and he and his womenfolk watched from the shore with their hearts in their mouths as the great ships bore down on the little boats. They could not remain to watch the whole drama, for soon the men were coming ashore and the women had to go back to the house to succour them, but later when the flood of men had ceased they went back to the rocky promentory to look out. In the beginnings of dawn they could just see, beyond the great ships, the tiny dots of the small boats that had been turned back.

'Lord Chelmsford must be on one of them,' Allan said. 'I pray God they get back safely.'

At least the ships have gone away,' Sabina said. 'It was frightening when they bore down on us towards the shore.'

'They couldn't come in very close. We were safe enough,' Mavis said. 'I suppose you must go away now, Allan?'

'Yes, I must take these men to join General Mackintosh at Haddington,' he said, but his expression was thoughtful. The ships had come close enough to see where the men had been landed, and the news would probably be relayed to the enemy at the garrison in Edinburgh. Aberlady itself might become a target. 'You must leave here as soon as we are gone,' he said abruptly. 'You may be in danger. I think the best thing would be for you to go to Morland Place. You would be safe enough there.'

Sabina opened her mouth to protest, but Mavis put a hand on her arm and silenced her.

'Very well, Allan, we will do as you say,' Mavis said quietly. Allan looked relieved.

'I think now that I have not acted for the best in allowing this house to be used. I may have placed you in danger. But if it is known that the house is empty, I expect they will not trouble with it, and we can come back here safely, when all this is over.'

'You need not worry about us. You may put all your energies into the task before you,' Mavis said firmly.

In the early hours of the Friday morning, 14 October, Allan embraced his wife and Mavis, kissed the children, placed a hand in blessing on little Allen's head, and marched away with the last of the men towards Haddington. The women went back into the house to prepare for their second flight; but, as the day went on, it became plain that Sabina was not well. She tried to hide it at first, but by the afternoon she was flushed with fever and seized by fits of uncontrollable shivering; as dusk drew in she made no protest when Mavis put her to bed, and it was clear that they would not be able to move on until the fever had passed.

CHAPTER SEVENTEEN

Allan Macallan had thought, like everyone else, that as
soon as they were all gathered together, they would march
south to join up with the Borderers, who had been expected
to 'come out' at the same time as they made their crossing.
But as soon as it was light on that Friday, 14 October, Old
Borlum formed them up and gave the order for a brisk
march on Edinburgh.

'What's he up to?' a fellow captain asked of Allan
peevishly. 'We haven't a hope of taking Edinburgh, the
few of us, with no ordinance.'

'I don't know,' Allan said. 'Is it likely that Old Borlum
would act on his own initiative over something as important
as this?'

'Old Borlum would do that in the gates of hell,' the
captain said with a kind of sour respect. 'He's a dour old
creature, and doesn't think much of any flighty young lord
under the age of sixty. But we can't take Edinburgh. Is he
hoping to frighten them to death?'

'Perhaps he thinks they'll surrender. After all, there
must be plenty in Edinburgh who hate the Union and have
no love for the Elector. If they see us coming, maybe
they'll open the gates and march out and join us.'

'Well, one thing is sure, if we did have Edinburgh our
problems would be solved,' the captain said. 'Arms,
money, cannon, everything we needed.'

'And it would cut Argyll off from the south,' Allan said.

In the early afternoon they came in sight of the city, and
halted about a mile from the walls, but there was no sign
of anyone coming out to meet them.

'Perhaps they haven't seen us yet,' Allan said hopefully.
The captain sniffed pessimistically.

'Not them! Look, over there, and there – they're

bringing up shot for the cannon. They don't mean to give in, damn them. They're preparing to defend.'

They stood for about an hour in the thin October sun, and then General Mackintosh gave the order to turn north and march for Leith, Edinburgh's port, and it was evident that whatever help Old Borlum had expected of Edinburgh, it had not materialized. But there was plenty for them to do in Leith. The Town Guard came out, looking nervous and defiant, but in the face of so many men they could do nothing but lay down their arms. Allan was then sent with a handful of men to the Tolbooth jail to release the forty men who had been captured on the second crossing and bring them to join their ranks again. Then they seized the Custom House, where a great many provisions were stored, and also, unfortunately for discipline, a great deal of brandy.

'We'll never keep them to anything once they start opening those bottles,' Allan said in despair. But there was plenty to do to keep the men occupied for the time being. They took over the Old Citadel, a disused fortress built for the defence of Leith city, and set about fortifying it. It was in good shape still, and preparing it was only a matter of blocking up one or two holes and barricading the gates. There were several armed ships lying in the harbour, and they were boarded and their cannon swayed off and set up on the ramparts of the Old Citadel. By ten o'clock that night they were snugly and safely holed up, and the men could begin their long-delayed drinking.

Allan gave up the problem of discipline and got a bottle for himself, found some bread that was hardly stale at all, and some dried beef that had been raided from the ships, and made himself comfortable. The friendly captain, whose name was Black, joined him.

'Well, this is better, all things considered, than I expected,' Black said, taking a pull at the bottle. 'The men will be incapable of moving by morning, but who cares? They can't dig us out of here.'

'Who can't?'

'Why, General Argyll and his men. They marched in to Edinburgh a while back.'

'How many of them? His whole army?'

'No, no, about five hundred, the scout said. Shews he's worried by us. Maybe that's the plan. Anyway, while he's here, he's not in Stirling, and if General Mar has any sense he'll march quick to Stirling and that'll be the end of that.'

Allan thought of Stirling, and the march from Perth that would take the army past his own home at Braco, and the Morland castle at Birnie. And then, by a natural progression, he thought of Sabina and the children. He hoped they had got away by now. Perhaps he was wrong to have left them at all – perhaps his duty was more properly with them than fighting for the Chevalier? But he knew what Sabina would say to that. Sighing, he took another gulp of brandy and handed the bottle to Black.

'Filthy rotgut stuff,' Black said. 'How I wish I had some whisky. However, we must do the best we can. Here's a toast, to the King across the Water – to the Chevalier! And confusion to the Wee German Lairdie!'

He drank the toast with enthusiasm and began to sing:

Sing hey for Sandy Don, hey for Cockolorum.
Sing hey for Bobbing John, and his Highland quorum.
Many a sword and lance swings at Highland hurdie –
How they'll skip and dance o'er the bum o' Geordie!'

And Allan joined in:

Come up among our Highland hills,
Thou wee, wee Germain Lairdie –'

The brandy was warming away his doubts and fears; from different parts of the fortress he could hear other voices raised, some tunefully, others already drunk and blurred.

Argyll had come and gone, had asked them to surrender and when they refused had left without firing a shot. The men cheered, but they wondered what would happen next. There was a general sense of lack of direction, a feeling that they were doing no good to anyone here. Perhaps the general felt that too, for on the night of 15 October he marched them all out and along the sands to Seton, where they took over Seton House, which belonged to Lord Wintoun, who was absent raising the Border Scots for the Chevalier. Several of the men were lost during the night march, presumably too drunk to walk even as far as Seton. The rest were driven to work all through the night and the next day to gather provisions and make Seton House strong, and it went a long way to sweating the drink out of them. Allan had a foul headache himself, but guessed that he felt better than most of his men, who looked near death.

They worked all through Monday, 17 October, and slept soundly that night. On the 18th the first bit of excitement came, when two hundred horse and three hundred foot arrived from Edinburgh, presumably on the departing orders of Argyll, to try to force them out of Seton House. But Seton House was a fortified house of the old style, rather like Morland Place, and like Aberlady House before it had been destroyed and rebuilt, and without cannon they had no hope of taking it. They fired a few shots at the outer walls, stood around for an hour or so, and then retreated.

The men were excited, and cheered derisively at the departing militia. Later that day a despatch arrived from General Mar, and towards evening Captain Black sought out Allan and said, 'Well, that's the end of Old Borlum's initiative. The word from Mar was to join up with the Borderers as soon as possible, and from what I heard it was worded pretty sharply. We march off tomorrow to meet them at Kelso.'

Allan murmured something in reply, but his eyes and his mind were not on the captain; he was looking towards the east, where a strange glow was beginning to shew as the sky darkened.

*

Mavis had put on a brave face in front of Sabina, for Sabina was terrified that she had got smallpox, and it was necessary to reassure her again and again that there were no spots. What the fever was, Mavis did not know, and could not guess, but it was mild and intermittent, and after a great deal of thought she had decided not to call upon a doctor, for she wanted to do as little as possible to call attention to the fact that Aberlady House was still occupied. Only a week ago a house in Haddington had been attacked by a group of neighbours and militia because the owner was known to be a Jacobite supporter, and the son of the house had been killed. Mavis kept the doors locked and the windows shaded, and gave orders to the few servants who remained to keep quiet. She tried always to appear cheerful and confident, but the silence got on her nerves, and the slightest sound made her jump. The children were very good, and Mary kept Hamil amused for hours with card games and stories. The baby was a problem, for he seemed to be getting the fever that was laying his mother low, and was fractious and cried a lot.

By the Tuesday Sabina seemed much better, and Mavis began to hope that they would be able to get away on the next day. It was more than four days since the crossing, and surely if there *was* going to be an attack upon them, it would have happened by now, she reasoned. They must think the house empty, she decided. Many of the large houses along the coast in these parts were used only as summer residences by the great lords.

That afternoon Mavis began to make preparations for leaving the following morning, provided Sabina continued to mend, and as it seemed quiet she sent two of the men out to the village to see if they could buy any food. They were gone two hours, and then returned in a state of great agitation.

'Mistress, mistress, there are soldiers coming,' they cried. 'A great army, out of Edinburgh, marching this way! We must fly at once!'

Mavis quieted them as best she could, and tried to get

326

some sense out of them, though they were so terrified they could hardly speak. Mary and Hamil crept close behind her and listened in silence, their eyes huge. Finally she managed to make out that they had heard that the Jacobites had settled in at Seton House, and that the militia had come out of Edinburgh to try to dislodge them. They had failed, whereupon most of them had gone back to Edinburgh, except for a detachment which was heading for Aberlady.

'Well, we don't know what they are coming in this direction for. They may be going anywhere – to North Berwick for instance. It does not necessarily mean they are coming here.'

But one of the men, his eyes white like a frightened bullock's, began gabbling again that a woman in the village had known who he was, and had told him that the soldiers were coming to burn down Aberlady House.

Mavis thought quickly. The first thing, she decided, was to discover the truth of the assertion. She told the men to stay put, and climbed up to the top of the house and out on to the leads, where she could see for a considerable distance all round. What she saw made her blood chill; the soldiers were coming, all right. No great army, to be sure, but enough of them, perhaps fifty or sixty, she guessed – and what was worse, they were being joined by local people, ordinary citizens who resented the Jacobite activities, or perhaps who simply wanted mischief. As she watched she saw two men run up armed with pitchforks and fall in with the soldiers, skipping about as they tried to match the soldiers' step, and wagging their heads, presumably chattering and laughing to each other.

She went back inside and ran downstairs. Hamil and Mary were alone in the room where she had left them.

'Where are the men?' Mavis asked.

Mary, her face white, but her voice still under control, said, 'They ran away. They said they didn't want to get killed for their pains. Mother, what's going to happen?'

'It will be all right, darling,' Mavis said, trying to sound confident. 'We'll just stay very quiet, and perhaps they'll go away again. Would you go upstairs for me, and see if Sabina is all right? Don't tell her about these people coming. It would only alarm her. And Hamil, run out to the stable, will you, and shut the horses into the stone byre in the yard. They'll be safer there.'

The children ran off on their errands, and Mavis went round the house, looking for the servants, and making sure that the windows and doors were locked. There seemed to be no servants left at all, until she got to the kitchen, and there she found old Kateryn calmly packing up their food into a couple of sacks.

'Where is everyone else?' she asked. Kateryn looked up.

'All gone, mistress, damn their black hearts. There's only me left, and the girl upstairs with Miss Sabina. Who is it that's coming, mistress? I couldn' make out a word they were saying.'

'It's the militia, and a mob from the village,' Mavis said, seeing no reason to lie to this sturdy old woman. 'Someone said they're coming to burn the house down.'

'Did they now? Well that's a poor thing indeed. There was always a deal of bad feeling about this house, mistress, ever since it was pulled down in Lord Cromwell's time, damn his black heart in hell, or wherever he may be. But southerners are a Godless people, and so I've always said. You should have gone home to your own country when your husband died, mistress, and so I've always said.'

Kateryn's soft, slow voice calmed Mavis. She was from the far north herself, and regarded the rest of the world apart from her own glen as an aberration on God's part, and the rest of humanity apart from her own lord and his clan unspeakable barbarians. But while she was speaking, Mavis had been listening subconsciously for something, and now she realized that it was the sound of the horses coming into the yard. Hamil should have been back by now. She told Kateryn to go up to Sabina's room, and went out into the yard. The door to the stone byre was still open, and it was empty. She went on to the stable, and the stable door was also open, and she knew before she looked in that the horses would not be there either. They had been forestalled – someone had stolen them, and with them their chances of escape. But where was Hamil? She was turning away when something caught her eye, some pale gleam in the back of one of the stalls. Heart in mouth, she stepped softly forward to investigate.

Hamil lay face down, his cheek cradled on his bent arm as if he had lain down in the straw for a sleep on a hot afternoon. His nose, still childishly snubby, was pressed against his upper arm, his parted lips shewed a gleam of teeth. But he was not sleeping. The whole of the back of his head had been stoved in by a blow from some heavy object, a rock, perhaps, or an iron pole, and his hair was red and sodden. Mavis felt her gorge rise, and swallowed saliva frantically. She must not be sick now. She knelt in the straw and touched the back of his neck, tried to move his head without touching the mess. The bones of his skull around the wound felt strangely mobile, as a skull should not be. There was no doubt he was dead.

She rose, and stood trembling, looking down at him, unable to think. Her mind was dazed, refused to grapple with the problems that beset her. She gave no thought that his assailant might still be on hand. She wanted to run away, away from the house and the people in it, who should not be her responsibility. And as she stood there, swaying on her feet, she heard the commotion from the front of the house, a confusion of voices and banging noises. Dear God, the mob had arrived! She was startled out of her confusion. Mary was in there. The yard gate was open. She picked up her skirts, whirled around and ran.

She heaved the yard gates closed and ran the poles across, fled into the house and bolted the door behind her. She could hear from the front of the house the tumult of banging, and the horrible howling of the mob, and now and then she could even make out the words: 'Burn the place! Hang the Jacks! String 'em up!'

The house was not defensible – it had not been built to

be defended. They would be in at any moment, and then – she could not think about what would happen. She ran up the stairs towards Sabina's room. Could she get them out? she wondered as she ran, and even then she heard the shattering sound of splintered glass, as they abandoned knocking at the door and broke the windows for access.

Sabina's door was open, Mary stood there, trembling with fear. Mavis shoved her violently back into the room and slammed the door behind her, looking round for something to barricade it with. Downstairs she heard the mob coming into the hall through the windows, their voices rising with excitement. Kateryn and the girl, Bet, were on either side of the bed, where Sabina sat up clutching her baby and looking frantic.

'What's happening?' she cried. 'Who are those people? Where's Hamil?'

There was no time for gentleness. 'Hamil's dead,' Mavis said. 'Those people are a Hanoverian mob, and they've come for us.'

She saw that the fright and shock prevented Sabina from taking in what she had said about Hamil, which was perhaps to the good.

'Can you get out of bed?' Mavis asked tersely. 'Our only hope is to hide. Take the baby and get through into the closet. Here, take these blankets and cover yourself. Try to look like a heap of bedding. Kateryn, help her. Bet, Mary, give me help.'

Kateryn took Sabina's arm to get her out of bed, while Mavis and Mary and Bet grabbed whatever loose furniture there was and dragged it to the door to barricade it. But there were feet on the stairs already, and even as they pushed a chair against the door, it was shoved violently from the other side, the door began to spring, and the chair was pushed back against their legs. Bet screamed shrilly.

Mavis heard a voice outside yelling: 'In here! They're in here!'

The door was shoved again and flew open, and the chair

rammed back against Bet's legs made her fall over. She screamed non-stop, her eyes wide with terror, mindless with it. Three men forced their way in, and others pressed behind them in the corridor. Bet was grabbed, and screaming and immobile was passed like a bundle of clothes over the heads of the mob, and Mavis saw her no more. Mary was behind her, and for a second held firm, and then in terror ran to the window and began struggling with the catch. A man darted after her and grabbed her round the waist, and she clung to the catch of the window with both hands, shrieking, while the man dragged her backwards. Mavis made her last, desperate, futile attempt, seizing the nearest thing to hand, a pewter pitcher, and ran towards the man, raising it over her head to try to bring it crashing down on him. But she had gone no more than a step or two; she heard the sound behind her as the next man in ran forward; and then a silent, violent blow struck her across the back of the neck, like a great painless explosion in her head, and she fell forward into the dark.

Allan Macallan leathered the horse fiercely to make it go faster, galloping towards that glow on the horizon, a terrible fear in his heart. Of course, he reasoned with himself, they had gone days ago; it was probably a fired rick, nothing to do with Aberlady House; if it *was* Aberlady, it was the empty house that was burning. The horse stumbled and almost pitched him from the saddle. He did not know whose horse it was – he had simply grabbed it. Black had called out after him as he rushed away, but idly, thinking him perhaps caught short. He had not had time to adjust the saddlery properly, and he could feel that the girth was not tight enough, and the saddle was slipping. He took his feet out of the stirrups and held on to the horse's long, coarse mane, the better to balance, in case the saddle went over.

The horse was slowing now, wearily, and he yelled at it and kicked and slapped its neck with the reins. It put on a spurt for a moment, then slowed again, determinedly. It was a farm horse, not a gentleman's hunter, and fast galloping was not in its nature. Desperately he tried to push it on, but it would only condescend to trot. He considered jumping off and running, but knew even in his desperation that he was going faster than he would on his own legs.

When he got near, he knew from the direction that it was Aberlady House that was burning; nearer still, and he could see the outline of the house against the glowing sky, and the dark windows like blind eyes. The horse began snorting with alarm and throwing its head about, smelling the fire, and now he did abandon it, flinging himself from the saddle while it still moved and beginning to run as his feet hit the ground, while the horse veered off and fled with a turn of speed it had not shewn before. Stumbling in the dark that was darker by comparison with the flames, Allan went forward. The house had been attacked and looted, he could tell from the debris in the garden, before being fired, and the windows downstairs were smashed and the front door torn off its hinges, perhaps to make the bonfire that began it all.

That was not all that was in the front garden. His stomach sinking in nausea, he saw the dark shapes silhouetted by the flames, and he went forward, almost as if his feet carried him against his will. Two figures hung from the branches of the big oak tree, that was older than the house by far; still and limp, hanging by their necks, women's figures, he could tell by their skirts. He crept closer like a shivering dog. One face, tranquil, unmarked, was Mavis's. The other, contused and almost unrecognizable, was Mary's.

Frantically, he looked round him. Where were his wife and children? He began running back and forth, madly, uselessly, and then spun round and dashed for the house. The hall and stairs were not yet in flames. They must have started the fires in the rooms, where there would be furnishings and wooden floors to help, while the hall was mostly marble, apart from the wooden staircase. He ran upwards into the pall of smoke, and within seconds of reaching the top of the stairs had to drop to his hands and knees, choked and blinded. He knew Sabina's room without being able to see. The door was open, there was furniture broken and scattered about the floor. The bed, he discovered by groping, was empty. He turned to crawl away when some instinct – a sound, heard at the limit of consciousness perhaps – made him go to the closet and open the door. He felt something firm, covered in a blanket, and pulled at it. It cried out and wriggled. He pulled the blanket off, and knew blindly that it was Sabina. He felt about her, found her eyes open and wet, the baby in her arms, and he began to drag her towards the door. She resisted, and he gasped, 'It's me, Allan.'

He heard her draw a breath to speak, but she only began coughing. Now she did not resist him, but shook his hand off and got on to her knees and crawled too. They got to the staircase. Lights seemed to be exploding inside his head, and his sight was so dimmed that he almost fell down the stairs.

Sabina struggled a few steps down, and then said, 'Allan – Kateryn! She was in the closet with me.'

'I must see you safe.'

'I'm all right. You must get her out. Only one – loyal.'

Allan rolled his eyes despairingly. 'Wait in the garden. Keep under cover,' he gasped, and turned back up the stairs on his hands and knees. He found the bedroom again, but it seemed further away than before. Surely it had never been so far? The darkness rolled down over him, his lungs were on fire, his eyes streamed as if they were bleeding. He found the closet, reached forward with fingers that seemed a hundred miles away from him, and numb. He found a bundle – a body. He leaned close, tried to speak. He ran his fingers over the face, with no response. She's dead, he thought, and the thought was a long way off, too. He hooked his fingers into the cloth and tried to pull her with him, but he had no more strength. Abandoning the task, he tried to crawl back towards the door, but it got further and further away, and the red darkness grew heavier and more solid. He collapsed, gasping for breath, and his face felt the floorboards burning hot under his cheek.

John Rathkeale and Jack Francomb and their men did not feel they had achieved very much since joining Tom Forster's army at Rothbury. There had been talk of marching south to take Newcastle so as to have something solid to shew the Scots when they joined up, but news had come of the great hostility amongst the town's officers towards Jacobites, and so that had come to nothing. And then it was time to march north to Kelso.

There they had joined up with Old Borlum and his army from Perth, and the Scots from Kircudbright under Lord Kenmuir, and had made a fine show of men. There had been a wonderful display on the Sunday after they arrived, the 22nd, with a church service, and proclaiming the Chevalier king, and reading speeches, and marching and parading, and bands playing, and the bagpipes of the Scottish regiments, and in the evening plenty of good things to eat and drink provided by the inns and the loyal and grateful populace.

After that things had begun to go wrong. The trouble was that there was no getting anyone to agree on a plan of action. The Border Scots wanted to go back to their own country and capture the main towns of south-western Scotland, and then Glasgow, so that all of Scotland would be in their grasp. The English Borderers wanted to march into Lancashire, which had always been a Catholic stronghold and which, it was believed, would turn out in force for the Chevalier. The English regarded Scotland as a dark and barbarous place, and were strongly averse to penetrating it any deeper. The Scots, on the other hand, regarded themselves as bound only to fight within their own country, and thought the English could sort out their own problems south of the border.

So there followed almost three weeks of indecision, during which they marched first one way and then another, covering hundreds of miles across the Borderlands along tracks over moors and mountains in steadily worsening weather. After the first week it was definitely decided that they would head for Lancashire, and some of the Scots went home in disgust, but most stayed, though pessimistically, rather than be accused of desertion or cowardice. On 5 November they reached Kendal, wet and tired and disheartened, and four days later they came to Preston, after one of their worst day's marching, through teeming rain and thick mud. Preston was a fine town, with good inns, public gardens and squares, even a theatre, and it was decided to stay there a few days to rest and revive the men before pressing on to Manchester where, it was hoped, the long awaited welcome from the people would at last take place. If they could only get to Manchester, great numbers would join them, and they could easily capture the port of Liverpool, which would give them access by sea to France and Ireland.

But on the eleventh news came in from scouts that two enemy armies were approaching under General Wills and the much-feared General Carpenter, and Old Borlum gave orders to prepare to defend Preston. On the morning of Saturday 12 November, the vanguard of Wills' army was spotted coming up the road from Wigan, and the men on the outposts were ordered back behind the barricades. They were only just in time. Even as the last of the men withdrew, General Wills crossed the bridge outside the town and at around two o'clock the first attack came. About two hundred of Wills' cavalry entered Churchgate Street; the Scots snipers, hidden in cellars and attics, fired on them, killing more than half, and they retreated hastily. The battle had at last been joined.

For the next three hours until dark, the Elector's army attacked the barricades on all four sides of the town, and were beaten back. When darkness fell the action was discontinued, though the sniping went on all night, and the intermittent rattle of shots kept everyone wakeful. At first light on Sunday morning there was another attack in Churchgate street, which was beaten off; so far the Jacobites had inflicted heavy casualties, and suffered few losses themselves. Then at around nine General Carpenter arrived, and closed round the town, blocking all escape-routes, and the Jacobites were under siege. By eleven o'clock it was obvious they were in a hopeless position, and surrender began to be talked of.

Forster sent a man under a white flag to parley for terms with Wills, though the Scots were for fighting their way out, to die rather than surrender. When it became obvious that no one else was going to fight with them, the Scots sent an emissary to parley for separate terms for the Scots. The answer to both emissaries was the same – no terms. The Scots demanded time to think about it, and were allowed until seven the next morning, on condition hostages were given. Lord Derwentwater and Colonel Mackintosh gave themselves as hostages, and darkness fell again.

Jack Francomb came to his son-in-law in their lodgings and took him to one side.

'I don't like this business, John. I didn't march all this way to surrender without a fight.'

'But what can we do?' John said despairingly. 'The Scots still want to fight – some of 'em at least – but the rest are so dispirited –'

'They'll hang us, John, every man jack of us – you know that? You'll never see your wife and child again.'

John gave a groan and put his head in his hands, and Jack Francomb leaned closer and whispered in his ear a single word, 'Escape.'

John looked up.

'Just the two of us,' Francomb said. 'I'm pretty sure I can find a way out.'

'But, sir, we've got thirteen men here, two of them wounded. We can't just leave them.'

'We can't take them with us. The wounded men will die

anyway, that's for sure. Thirteen of us trying to escape will be seen. Two of us might make it.'

'We can't leave our own men to die,' John said. Francomb seized the front of his jacket.

'Listen, get it into your head that they're going to die anyway. We all are. You heard what that bastard Wills said – "prisoners at discretion". Do you know what that means? That means we will have no rights at all, not even the right to trial. They'll hang us like dogs – if they don't draw and quarter us. Do you fancy the idea of smelling your own guts as they burn them in front of you?'

'But –'

'Do you want to die knowing they'll report it all to Frances back home? What's the use of dying with the men when you could live? She can't run the farm and bring up the baby alone. For God's sake, John, think!'

Francomb shook him in his agitation, and John thought, despairingly. He thought of the shame of surrender, of what the family would think, of what grandmother would think. He thought of death. He thought of Frances, struggling on alone, grieving for him, trying not to let his son grow up ashamed of his father. Then he thought of arriving home alone, without the men he had set off with. He thought of telling their wives and children that he had left them behind to be hanged. He thought of the way people would look at him ever after, because he had deserted his own people. And he groaned again, because there was no way out.

'Come on, John,' Francomb said. He looked up. His father-in-law was watching him with an expression of calculation. John shook his head.

'No,' he said, 'I can't leave the men. I brought them here – I must stay with them.'

Francomb straightened up, and bared his teeth in what might have been a grin, or a grimace. 'Well, thank God I'm not a gentleman!' he said. 'Have you any message for your widow, when I get back?'

'You're going?'

337

'I'm going – with or without you.'

'Without me.'

Francomb turned away. When he reached the door, John cried out, 'Take care of them, of Frances and the bairn?'

Francomb looked at him with an odd mixture of pity and disgust. 'What in hell did you think I was doing it for?'

Then he was gone. Without him, John felt cold and lonely, and the horror of the death that was to come ate into him. He went along to see the men, who were all crouched together in one room, talking in subdued voices.

'What's going to happen, sir?' they asked him.

'I think tomorrow we will have to surrender,' he said.

'And what then?' they asked. He hesitated, but at the last moment thought, they have the right to decide for themselves too. They shouldn't die in ignorance, like cattle.

'I think they will hang us all,' he said quietly. And then he saw in their faces the resignation that shewed they had known it all along.

'Well,' said one, 'I said goodbye to my Mary before I came, and I didn't think I'd see her again. One death's the same as another I suppose.'

John went away, unable to bear any more. He felt trapped by circumstances over which he had no control. Outside he could hear shots being fired in the distance, as if someone had not yet given up – or were they, he thought with a sudden chill, being fired at his father-in-law making an escape? He started towards the sound, but it stopped immediately and was not resumed, and he could not tell the direction without it.

It was dark, with only a muted light here and there from a window where an officer sat up, perhaps, discussing the situation. Was there no way out? he wondered. His aimless steps were taking him towards the barricades. Perhaps, perhaps. It would be suicide, but what of that? Better for Frances to think of him dying in battle than hanged as a traitor. And as to his immortal soul – he thought perhaps God would understand.

The thing was not to be seen too soon, or he might just be turned back. He crept along, low and quiet, keeping to the shelter of bushes and walls. He was in a little lane called Back Ween, where heavy fighting had taken place earlier on. It smelt of blood, and his nostrils twitched like a horse's. Beyond was one of the fording places of the river, and still further on he could see the flickering of firelight from the enemy's camp, and the great black shadows of people moving back and forth. He stepped out towards the river.

'Halt! Who goes there?' came a voice at once. One of his own side, or the enemy? No Scots accent, but that made no difference. He walked on. 'Halt or I fire,' the voice said, less certainly. He turned towards it, and made a gesture as if lifting his gun to his shoulder. It was enough for the nervous guard. John heard the crack of the explosion and, to his stretched nerves, it seemed like an endless time before the ball smacked into his chest. He was amazed at the force of it, enough to make him stagger backwards. His foot was on something that gave under him, crumbling, and he fell backwards and downwards into cool dampness.

It was one of the drainage ditches that ran into the river, he realized. It smelt of ordure and rotting flesh, and there were other bodies in it. He could hear his executioner rustling about above him, looking for him, afraid he might be going to shoot back.

Dead in a ditch, he thought vaguely. The pain was growing in his chest. There had been no pain at first. And then he thought, shot while trying to escape. That sounded better. He let his head sink back into the mud, and smiled.

CHAPTER EIGHTEEN

For more than a week the tiny island of May supported them. The weather was cold and windy, and food was a problem, though they eked out their supplies with gulls' eggs and seaweed and one or two fish. The few people who lived on the island viewed the arrival of two hundred soldiers with fear, and rightly so, for their stores of food were commandeered for the soldiers, and they foresaw starvation ahead through the winter. Karellie tried to ensure that a little was left for them, but it was difficult to stop the men slipping to the cottages under cover of the dark.

There were other troubles, too – Lord Strathmore's battalion was made up of some Highlanders and some Lowlanders, and the traditional dislike of the one for the other was exacerbated by their imprisonment on this comfortless rock. Strathmore and Karellie did all they could to keep them apart, Strathmore taking the Highlanders to one end and Karellie the Lowlanders to the other, but there were fights every day, disturbances at night, and furious accusations of theft and unfair division of food. Meanwhile the government ships cruised about the island, waiting for the sea to moderate enough for them to get closer in.

On the eighth day the wind veered sharply and increased in strength, and the marooned soldiers saw the government ships, for all their tacking and beating, gradually being forced further and further out into the open sea. Karellie and Strathmore held a hasty consultation. The wind was strong, the sea high, and rowing would be hard in such conditions, but on the other hand there might not be another chance like this for weeks – by which time they would have all starved to death.

'Better we go while the men have strength to row,' Strathmore said, and Karellie agreed. They lost one man in the embarkation, whose hands slipped as he was climbing aboard and who was at once swept away amongst the rocky outcrops. There was an hour of muscle-cracking strain and nerve-racking tension as the men laboured to pull the boats clear of the sharp rocks and pounding waves, but at last they reached open water and were pulling towards the distant outline of Fife. It was an exhausting, nightmarish journey. As soon as they were in open water the boats began to be scattered, according to the weatherliness of the craft and the strength of the men at the oars, and as the cold, wet, grey day drew to its close there were only two other boats in sight of Karellie. Every man was soaked to the skin by the icy green sea; hungry, unshaven, with blistered and bleeding hands, not the least like an army; but as darkness fell they were at last close enough to the Fife shore for the tide and currents to bring them into Crail harbour.

However unwilling the citizens had been to aid the army, they took unstinting pity on the exhausted rowers. Three boats made it into Crail, and every man was comfortably billeted and fed. Other boats had been seen heading for the harbours further south – Pittenweem and Kilrenny – and Karellie sent out messengers to find out the numbers and condition of survivors. One boat had been blown too far and had been seen passing to the north-east of Fife Ness; Karellie sent a messenger up the coast to ask for news of it, but the boat was never heard of again, and it had to be assumed that they had drifted out to sea and drowned.

They lay up in the fishing villages for three days, and then Karellie formed up his men and marched them down to Pittenweem, having sent orders for the other survivors to meet him there. Lord Strathmore arrived with thirty men, and others drifted in during the day, but many had evidently had enough and slipped off home. They spent the night in Pittenweem, and the next morning marched off for Perth with a hundred and thirty men. They arrived in Perth on the evening of 28 October, to discover that General Mar had still done nothing, though his army numbered almost twelve thousand, as against Argyll's reported army in Stirling of three thousand.

The army presented a motley appearance: there were country gentlemen in fine suits trimmed with lace and well-curled wigs; there were Lowland peasants, in simple grey or brown woollen with wooden shoes; there were well-to-do Highlanders in their colourful plaids, with bright feathers in their bonnets and great jewelled clasps on breast and shoulder; there were the wildest Highlanders from the remotest parts who went half-naked, barefooted, and seemed to be dressed mostly in their own hair and beards. The horses, too, were a strange collection, ranging from the fine hunters and blood horses of rich gentlemen, through farm horses, right down to Huntley's 'light horse', who were bare-chested, bare-legged Highlanders mounted bareback on tiny hairy ponies no bigger than dogs and controlled with nothing more than a twist of rope through the mouth. The only bit of finery about these last were their blue bonnets, which could be picked out in any assembly.

Karellie tried to keep his men occupied, and organized training games when they were not on camp- or foraging-duty; for the rest he hung about the other generals trying to ascertain what, if anything, was planned. Mar held himself aloof, and appeared to be waiting for orders. Ormonde was intending to land with the Chevalier in the west of England, and it seemed that Mar must have been waiting for this to happen, for when, in the early days of November, word came that the west-country landing had had to be abandoned, and that the Chevalier was now trying to find a boat to bring him to Scotland, Mar at last called a Council of War.

The plan that was devised was simple, but should be effective: three battalions were to remain behind to hold Perth, while the rest marched towards Stirling. Three thousand would there be detached to deal with Argyll's force, while the rest of the army crossed the Forth and marched on Edinburgh. Once they held Edinburgh they would effectively hold Scotland, and when the Chevalier arrived he could lead them triumphantly into England.

They left Perth on Thursday, 10 November, and by Saturday the twelfth were marching down Strathallan towards Dunblane. It was a clear, frosty day, and Karellie rode along the higher ground above the Allan Water and looked about him at the view of the moor and the low hills on his left, and the higher mountains on his right. They passed the village of Braco, and shortly afterwards Karellie glimpsed away to his right the castle of Birnie, which belonged to his Scottish cousins, but which he knew, from what Allan Macallan had said, was now empty. They reached Kinbuck, with another five miles to go to Dunblane where they were to camp for the night, when a halt was called, and the message was passed back that a boy had arrived from Lady Kippendavie, a local landlord's wife, that Argyll had marched out of Stirling that morning and had just passed through Dunblane, heading in their direction.

It was four in the afternoon and growing dark, and it would have been folly to go on. The horse patrols took up position on the high ground above Kinbuck, and when the main body of foot soldiers arrived at around nine in the evening, they were sheltered for the night in the barns of the tiny hamlet. It was very cramped quarters for so many men, but at least being packed so close together kept them warm. They did better than Argyll's men, whom the scouts reported to be sleeping in battle order on the bare hillside by Kippendavie house.

The men were formed up at six in the morning, on the high ground to the east of the hamlet, and when the sun came up at eight, some of Argyll's horse could be seen on the high ground of Sherrifmuir, little more than a mile away. A skirmishing party was sent out to drive them off, but they disappeared over the brow of the hill before they could be reached. Sherrifmuir was not a flat moor, but a series of low hills, and it was impossible to see anything of the enemy. At about eleven a brief council was held amongst the senior officers, and it was decided that battle should be joined. Mar made a very stirring speech, and everyone but Huntly assented to the motion, but there was little enthusiasm for it. Karellie, looking round the faces, saw distaste in one or two expressions, and he guessed that the sight of those enemy horsemen had made everyone realize that the enemy were not Frenchmen or Turks, but their own kin, Scotsmen, some of them probably even cousins.

For Karellie it was different: he had been a soldier for twenty-five years, a mercenary, and he had fought for many different commanders and never questioned who it was he was to fight against. An enemy was an enemy, simply by virtue of being on the other side; warfare was a science, soldiering an art. He asked himself no embarrassing questions: for him today there was only one reality, his loyalty to his King, and those who set themselves up against the King were the prey of his sword. He formed up his men, and his grave cheerfulness steadied and heartened them, and at half past eleven they began to move forward towards the place where the enemy had last reportedly been located.

Matt had at first hardly noticed the coming and goings of messengers and the frequent arrival and departures of letters, for there was always a great deal of activity about Morland Place, and he was in any case disposed to take notice of nothing outside his immediate concerns, for fear of being hurt. It was six years since India had died, but the wound, though scarred over on the surface, was still tender in its depths.

All the same, the healing process that had begun was continuing in his society with Annunciata, and in the course of being with her, walking and talking and riding with her, enjoying her company and feeling a little lost when she was not there, he was bound in the end to understand that she was being active on behalf of King James or, as she always called him now, the Chevalier. Matt wondered vaguely whether he ought to remonstrate with her, whether such involvement with what was at least technically treason would bring danger on them. He had certain reservations also about Father Renard, who was more Catholic than Matt quite liked, and might be having too much of an influence on the children. But Father Renard was so indispensible to Matt, and Matt was so averse to having to interfere with anything that smacked of personalities and emotions, that he let his doubts remain buried.

But the crack in his perfect defences which had been opened up by his reliance on and regard for Annunciata was slowly being widened. Annunciata was the only person, with the exception of Father Renard, who could do much with Jemmy, who was now a well-grown fourteen, and full of vigour, enthusiasms, and wild spirit. The priest beat the boy into decent behaviour, and bludgeoned him by the sheer weight of personality into absorbing a little learning, and then passed him over to the Countess: she awed him into respect, charmed him into love, and coaxed his mind with stories into greater aspirations than stealing pheasants' eggs and outriding his brothers on the moors. Jemmy was in a fair way to being in love with Annunciata, whom he regarded as a mixture of the Fair Elaine and Queen Boudicea. Since he spent so much of his free time with her, Matt was forced into his eldest son's company, for the alternative was to be forced out of Annunciata's.

It was painful, more painful perhaps than with any of the other children, for Jemmy was his first-born, the first fruit of his great and blind passion for India. Moreover Jemmy looked a great deal like him, with a particularly painful admixture of India's features, and even laying aside his resemblance of his parents, he was a handsome boy, strong, well-grown, and lively, the kind of son any man would want for a firstborn.

Annunciata noticed Matt's painful preoccupation in his son's company, and approached it gently one day when they were walking alone together in the rose-garden. It was impossible to lead Matt to talk about India and the past, but she took his hand and drew it through her arm.

'He *is* yours, you know. You can see it in every feature, every gesture. Whatever you may think about the others, Jemmy is yours.'

Matt turned his head away and stared hard at a cream-white rose as if he had never seen one before.

Annunciata went on, 'He has been placed in your custody by God – they all have. We do not always relish our duty, Matt, but we always recognize it. God will never give you more than He knows you can bear.'

In the summer of 1715, Annunciata persuaded Matt not only to allow Jemmy to ride one of the horses in the races at Wetherby, but to attend the races himself, and when the moment came when Jemmy spurred the black horse Landscape first past the winning-post, Matt was so over-come with excitement and pride that he yelled with the rest of the crowd, and turned to Annunciata with shining eyes and a grin of delight that almost split his face in half. Annunciata laughed back with relief, for she had not been sure how the plan would turn out. Matt soon recollected himself and composed his face into its normal reserve and gravity, but when the grinning and triumphant boy led the big black horse up to his father and great-grandmother to receive his due praise, Matt shook the boy's hand with fervour, and the solemnity of his face slipped a little.

Back at Morland Place Annunciata tackled Matt again on the subject of Jemmy's future.

'There are various alternatives before you,' she said. 'You can send him to University; you can send him abroad; or you can keep him here to be trained in his inheritance. If you do the latter, I suggest that you let him for the time being have more to do over at Twelvetrees. He shews a great instinct for horses, and as a horseman must be born not made, it seemed a pity to waste it.'

Matt would not be drawn into a discussion, and Annunciata let the subject drop for the time being, intending to take it up later. Then, it was ousted from her mind by the beginning of the long-awaited rising, and her conversations with Matt became exclusively concerned with the Chevalier and matters in Scotland. Jemmy, hanging by her side out of what had become habit, absorbed her interests and views almost open-mouthed, and relayed them to his brothers, complaining bitterly that it had all happened when he was but fourteen and too young to go and fight.

At the beginning of November, Annunciata's intelligence was that the Chevalier was crossing France in disguise to take ship to join his men; on the evening of the day that letter came, Matt came to her in great agitation to tell her that Jemmy was missing.

'He has stolen a horse and gone,' Matt cried, his mask of indifference quite off. He had allowed himself to love this boy, and had instantly been punished.

'Gone where?' Annunciata asked.

'To Scotland, to join the rebellion, where else?' Matt cried. 'You filled his head with all this nonsense about the glorious cause and the true King, and he absorbed it all like a sponge, and now he's gone to try to join them, and he'll be killed for sure, if he doesn't perish of the cold on the way in this bitter weather.'

'Matt, Matt, be calm,' Annunciata said. 'Just because the boy is missing, it doesn't mean that he has gone off to Scotland. He has probably just gone for a ride somewhere –'

'He has stolen Landscape,' Matt said, clenching his fists in frustration, 'and taken one of the swords from the long saloon, and packed clothing and food. He got George to steal the things for him and bring them to him at a meeting place between here and Twelvetrees, and he arrived with Landscape and told George not to tell anyone. But one of the men saw them talking, and Father Renard beat George until he told all. *Now* do you see?'

'When was all this? This morning? Then we can still get him back. We'll send men after him. He won't be hard to find – he doesn't know the way, and will have to ask. Besides, a boy so young on a horse so fine will be good and conspicuous. Anyone with any sense will stop him or turn him back. We'll send after him, and have him back by morning, don't worry.'

'It's your fault,' Matt said, turning away from her in bitterness. 'If he comes to harm, it will be your doing. I should never have allowed you to come near him – I should have forbidden him to speak to you.'

'Matt, you are passionate. Even if the worst happened, even if he should be killed, it would be a glorious thing, to die for his King.'

'You think so? It's easy for you to say, when he is not your son. You are free with other people's children, but what would you be saying if he was yours?'

'My eldest son is there now,' Annunciata said quietly. 'My son Rupert died at Sedgemoor. Do you think I love Jemmy less than you? He is the son of my old age.'

Matt stared at her, silenced by the passion in her voice, and she went on, 'We are wasting time. You had better give your orders to your own men. I will send out Gifford and Daniel – they know this country – and I suggest you send Clement and Valentine, each with a party of two or three.'

Matt nodded curtly and walked away. Annunciata gave her orders, and settled down to wait, aware that half of her mind hoped the boy would be found, but that the other half hoped he might get to Scotland and have the chance to draw his sword for the cause.

'But you chose the wrong horse, Jemmy,' she said to herself. 'Next time, take a horse built for stamina, not speed.'

*

The first charge of the battle, of the Jacobite right wing against the government's left, broke the government troops and sent them scattering and fleeing in disarray, some downhill towards the Wharry burn, where they were trapped and cut down, and others towards Dunblane. The Jacobite cavalry galloped, yelling, in pursuit, hacking down any they overtook, delighted with the swift and easy victory. Some of the government men managed to scramble over the Wharry, and others skirted the obvious trap of Dunblane, and these headed as fast as their feet could carry them for Stirling.

'They will not trouble us more,' Karellie said, and began trying to reform his men, to stop their wild gallop, for if they got too spread out they would fall to looting and drinking and be of no further use to the battle. It was an impossible task. Most of them had never fought before, still less taken part in a cavalry charge, and the excitement of it had overpowered them. Karellie, longing for some disciplined troops such as he was used to commanding, cantered after the main body of them, towards Dunblane, where they were scattering down the streets, looking for inns and open houses and easy pickings.

For hours Karellie scoured the countryside all around the town, gathering up stray troopers, exhausted and draggled with the blood of their enemies. He caught a glimpse at a distance of General Mar himself doing the same thing with the men who had gone the other way, towards the Wharry. His own trouble was that as soon as he got a few men together and left them somewhere, they would wander off again. It was a frustrating business, and time consuming.

The Jacobite left wing had had no such easy victory, against the government right wing which was under the command of General Argyll himself. They had lost their cavalry early, through a mistaken manoeuvre, and were therefore alone against the government infantry and its

349

dragoons, who continuously charged them and drove them backwards. The Highlanders rallied every time and renewed the fight, only to be charged again, and after some hours they were driven back right to the Allan Water where, having nowhere else to go, they had to scatter, to save themselves from being driven into the water and drowned.

It was fortunate for them that the government troops held back at that point and did not pursue them further, and were recalled a moment later by Argyll to go back up the hill and face the troops reformed there by General Mar from the original charge. It was a thing that had been seen all over the battlefield amongst the foot-soldiers, the unwillingness to kill each other. Hand to hand, the men had seen and recognized their brotherhood, and quarter was given again and again. A wiry, mouse-haired, grey-bearded man with a bad limp, which he had evidently got from an accident some years ago, to judge by his nimbleness in accomodating it, jumped into the icy Allan Water with the fearlessness of one who had learned early to swim, and got across to the other side, and there he stood in safety, banging his numb arms against his sides, and watching the action on the other side.

What to do, was the question. There was still fighting up the hill, but he was tired, and now that they had been scattered he could see no chance of their winning. The cavalry had disappeared in the first moments of battle and had not been seen since, and without cavalry they had no chance of beating Argyll. He watched the government troops withdraw and go back up the hill, and decided it was over for him. Besides, if he stood in this cold wind for long he would surely perish. He turned and limped briskly in the direction of Kinbuck.

He heard the crying, and at first was inclined to ignore it. The cold and wet had reached a degree of actual pain, and he longed for food and shelter. But there was something about the crying that made it impossible to ignore – it was like a young woman's, or a child's. He hesitated, cursed softly, and went to investigate. It was growing dark, and at first all he saw by the thorn thicket was a large black lump, but when he came closer he saw it was a magnificent black horse lying on its side, with its head in the lap of a young boy. It was the boy who was crying. The horse was looking at him with liquid, trusting eyes, and the boy was stroking its head and weeping, dropping great hot tears on to the black muzzle.

'Hey now, boy, what's the matter?' the man asked gruffly. The boy looked up, his face tear-slobbered, but even so striking enough to make the man draw his breath sharply.

'He's hurt,' the boy cried. 'He put his foot down a hole and fell – we fell all the way down the hillside – and now he can't get up, and I don't know what to do.'

The man knelt down beside the horse and felt it over with skilled, gentle hands. It was tragic, he thought. It was one of the most beautiful horses he had ever seen.

'Did you steal it?' he asked the boy abruptly.

'I borrowed him. His name's Landscape, and we won a race in June at – where I live. He's the best horse in the stable. Will he be all right?' The pride and love had overcome the tears. The man put a hand on the boy's shoulder.

'His back's broken. He'll never get up again.' The boy stared at him with wide, frightened eyes. 'I'm sorry. You know what you've got to do, don't you?'

'I can't!' the boy cried. 'I can't!'

'Then I will,' the man said. He drew his knife, and pushed the boy gently, and he rolled away and fell on his face, burying his head in his arms and sobbing. The man stroked the horse's face and neck softly, talking in an old tongue that he had not used for a long time, and the horse looked into his eyes with puzzled enquiry. He felt no pain; and all his life had been touched lovingly by men. He had no fear of the hands that touched him; and he died with no more than a surprised snort, cut off half-uttered.

After a while, when the sobbing had eased, the man

crawled to the boy and touched his shoulder, and after a moment of resistance, the boy came into his arms and leaned against him, reduced by his grief to the child he had so recently been.

'We'd better get going,' the man said. 'We've got a long way to go.'

'Go? Where to?' the boy asked, sniffing miserably.

'Why, home, where else?'

'To my home?'

'To your home.'

'You know who I am?' Jemmy asked in amazement. The man smiled grimly.

'You were only a child of seven or eight when I last saw you, but you haven't changed much. I'd have known you anywhere.' He stood up and held his hand out. 'Come on,' he said.

The boy scrambled to his feet, glad to have someone to trust in again. He felt very cold, very tired, and very young. 'Will we have to walk all the way?' he asked.

'I dare say,' said the man. They began to walk back towards Dunblane, for Kinbuck was now the wrong direction. The man limped faster than the boy could walk, and had to modify his pace.

'What shall I call you?' the boy asked after a while. The man looked at him curiously.

'Don't you know me?'

'I – don't think so,' Jemmy said cautiously. He did not know any man who had a beard.

'I'm Davey,' said the limping man.

It was growing dark. Karellie had sent back several platoons of men under junior officers, while he himself stayed to gather and rally more, but as darkness came on it was clear that there could be no more fighting. It was obvious that they must have won, having scattered half the enemy in the first charge, and with the strays of their own side being sent back to help the left wing deal with the other half. Tonight they would probably sleep in Dunblane, and march the next day for Edinburgh. He formed up the last few men and started out towards the battlefield, to form up with the others and receive their orders.

He had barely passed the last house of the town when he saw the army ahead marching towards them, looking very battle-weary. He halted to wait for them; the first-comers were not men familiar to him, and he knew too little about the clans to recognize their plaid. A strange officer stared at him, and then wheeled out of line and galloped away towards the rear of his column, and it was only then that Karellie realized his mistake. It was already too late. The men marching towards him were Argyll men, not Mar's. Two officers were galloping back with the first one, to come to a halt one on either side of him. Karellie stared at them in despair.

'You are Charles Earl of Chelmsford?' one of them said. His manner was courteous and his accent impeccably English. Karellie nodded wearily.

'Then, my lord, I must ask you for your sword,' the man said. He sounded apologetic, almost gentle. Behind him Karellie heard one of his own men burst into noisy tears, and he wished he could have that same release. Slowly he drew his sword from its scabbard and held it out, hilt foremost, to the officer. So this was the end of his military career, he thought miserably. Not a glorious death in battle, such as might be sung of, but an ignominious surrender.

'Is the battle over?' he asked.

'Why, yes, my lord,' the young man said.

'And who has won?' he asked. The man hesitated.

'Why, my lord, we have,' he said, but his voice was so far from certain that he might just as well have said, I don't know.

They came to call it the Black Thirteenth, for on that same day, 13 November, came the surrender of Preston, the surrender of Inverness, and the battle of Sherrifmuir. At first both sides claimed Sherrifmuir as their own victory, but as time went on it became plain to the onlookers that Argyll's star was rising and Mar's waning.

At Morland Place there was gloom and despondency, on Annunciata's part because of the defeats, and on Matt's part because Jemmy had not been found, and the more time passed, the more certain he became that the boy was dead.

A week after Sherrifmuir, a covered farm wagon came down the track from the main road to Morland Place, and pulled up on the far side of the moat, and a roughly-dressed man got down from it and came up to the main gate, where he was stopped by a servant. A dispute followed, after which the man was brought, with some reluctance, into the house, and the master informed that a pedlar wished to speak to him most urgently. It leapt to Matt's mind that here at last was news of Jemmy, and almost knocking over the servant in his haste, he ran down the stairs to the hall, where a number of servants had gathered already. Annunciata came from the chapel at the same moment, and the children, hanging over the stairs above, contributed to an impressive audience. The pedlar seemed to relish it.

'Master Morland, is it?' The man had a strange accent which Annunciata recognized as coming from the Border-lands, though to Matt it was merely 'foreign'. 'Well Master, I am a pedlar, and I follow an honest trade in the north, and to say truth, don't often venture this far south. But I have a particular piece of goods to deliver to you, as I was promised it would be made worth my while to bring.'

'What goods,' Matt said tonelessly, his face very pale. The old man looked at him sideways.

'Human goods,' he said. Matt's face trembled.

'Oh thank God, thank God! Bring him in! Why did you not bring him in? Is he hurt?'

'Him? T'aint no him, master. How many goods was you expecting, in the name of fortune?'

Matt stared uncomprehendingly, and the pedlar began to look worried.

'It's a woman, and a bairn, and I was told that they'd be paid for at Morland Place very handsomely. Now if she's diddled me, I shall have something to say!' His anger was rising, and Annunciata stepped in.

'Let us, for heaven's sake, see who this woman is, before any more is said. Bring her in, man, at once.'

'She can't walk, missus, and that's why I left her out there. Have you a couple of strong lads to carry her?'

In the end they all went out to the cart, pedlar, Matt, Annunciata, servants, and the children jostling behind for a better view, their faces alight with the excitement. The pedlar climbed stiffly up on to the wheel-rim, loosed the canvas at the back of the cart, threw it back, and stepped down again, to unlatch the back flap of the cart. Matt still stood dazed, unable to cope with his disappointment, and it was Annunciata who stepped forward cautiously to peer into the cart. It was full of the kind of small trash that pedlars sell, and on a heap of striped blankets lay a woman, dressed in a coarse gown of brown wool, her hair matted and tangled, her face emaciated to the point of death, a very small baby sleeping in the crook of her arm. She looked up with lacklustre eyes at Annunciata's appearance and her lips moved feebly, but no sound issued.

'Holy Mother of God,' Annunciata cried softly. Matt looked in over her shoulder.

'Sabina,' he cried, shocked out of his daze. 'What has he been doing to you?'

It was a day and night before she could speak, and then her story took many hours to tell, for remembering distressed her and talking exhausted her. She told of the attack on Aberlady House and the death of Mavis and Mary and Hamil. After Allan had disappeared into the house, never to return, she had lain where she was in the garden, under a bush, with the baby, for hours, until the fire died down and eventually guttered out. She had been terrified that the mob would return, and it was not until darkness fell again that she had ventured from her hiding place.

She had discovered the central core of the house unharmed, for the fire had raged in the rooms about the hall without spreading to the hall itself. She had been afraid at first to venture upstairs, for fear the stairs would collapse, but in the end she had to find out what had happened to her husband, and had taken the chance. She had found him lying dead on the floor of the bedroom, apparently suffocated by the smoke.

For a long time – she did not know now whether it was hours or days, for her fever had returned, and the shock and horror made everything seem unreal – she had sat on the floor, rocking back and forth, unable to leave her husband's body, unable to think what to do, afraid to venture out of the house again. Eventually, cold and hunger had roused her. She was still in her bed-gown, and had got herself dressed in whatever came to hand, and had then thought about going down to look for food. But when she got to the ground floor, she had heard noises which made her think the mob was coming back, and she had fled out of the house and into the country.

For an unknown length of time she had wandered about, shivering with fever, weak with hunger. She thought she had been heading south all that time, for the only idea in her head now was to get to Morland Place, but she could not be sure. At last she came to a cottage standing all on its own on a piece of heathland, and afraid to knock at the door and ask for help, in case the occupants were Hanoverians, she had taken shelter in one of the outhouses. There she had been found by the goodwife of the house, who had taken her in.

She had stayed there some days, in a raging fever. The goodwife had fed her and the baby, and asked her questions, but she had spoken no word to her, for fear of the consequences. One evening she had woken to find herself alone in the house and the fever temporarily abated. Her own clothes were spoilt from the smoke of the fire, and she had taken a dress of the woman's – the one she had still on her – and had crept away south again. She had walked a long time, eating only what she could find in the way of berries, fruit and, once or twice, things stolen from barns or houses. And then the pedlar had come along. At the limit of her strength, she had risked telling him where she was headed, and had promised him reward if he took her there. She had given him her wedding ring as surety that she was not merely a beggar, and had finally collapsed into unconsciousness.

The doctor was called in, and said that she was suffering from starvation and exhaustion, but nothing more, and with rest and food she would recover. As her body grew stronger, the distress of her mind took over, and she had terrible nightmares about fire and hanging. Awake, her deepest distress was that she could not bury Allan, but had had to leave his poor body lying where it was.

Matt spent a great deal of time with her, sitting by her bed and encouraging her to talk, holding her hand and soothing her when the fits of trembling took her. The baby Allen seemed to have taken no harm from his long journey, and was safe in the nursery where the maids regarded him with astonishment and awe. His survival was the touch of romance they craved in their lives. To Matt it was a terrible thing to see the Sabina he had always known as so strong and determined and full of life reduced to a shivering invalid, jumping at shadows. He swore to himself that he would nurse her back to health. It helped to take his mind from his own desperate worries.

He did not have to worry much longer. A week after Sabina's strange arrival, a man and boy were seen coming along the track on foot, a man with a bad limp, and a boy in tattered clothes, his feet bound in rags. A servant cried out, and others joined in, and in moments Matt was running across the drawbridge to meet them. Jemmy was thinner and browner after his two-week walk, his clothes were ruined, and he smelt like a peasant, but Matt simply folded his arms round him and pressed him close.

'I've been such a fool,' he acknowledged mutely.

'Father –' Jemmy began nervously, wondering how he could begin to explain or apologize. Matt stood back from him to arm's length, and ruffled the matted hair with the palm of his hand.

'Not now, Jemmy. No need. I am just so very glad to have you back, it is all I can manage just now.'

And then he looked at the limping man, and his face paled. His hands dropped from Jemmy's shoulders, and everything seemed to become very still, very silent, as he looked into those brown eyes; eyes in which there was such knowledge of pain that his own seemed to pale into insignificance.

'Davey, is it really you?' he said. His voice was hardly more than a whisper. Davey nodded.

'I brought him back to you, master,' he said. He wanted to say more, to babble with explanations as Jemmy had wanted, but his obstinate lips would not move. He wanted to beg forgiveness, to beg Matt to take this service in payment for that other, unspeakable service that went so wrong, to beg Matt to say this paid for all, so that he could go away and die somewhere in peace. But the longer the silence went on, the more impossible it became to break it; while Matt, staring and staring, could not pick any of the things he was feeling as being the most important one to say. At last Davey's shoulders seemed to slump a little further, and he began to turn away.

'I'll be off, then, master,' he said.

Matt was so dumbfounded he let him take a step or two before he found his tongue, and then he cried, 'No, Davey, don't go!' Davey hesitated, his back still turned, unable to believe what he wanted to believe.

Matt misunderstood the hesitation, and holding his hands out said, 'Please, Davey – please! Don't go. I'm sorry.' Davey turned in amazement.

'*You're* sorry?' he said hoarsely. Matt's face looked suddenly much younger in its innocent anxiety.

'I've lost so much – I can't lose you, too. Not again.'

And Davey was unable to move, even to take the proffered hand, but the expression in his eyes as he looked at Matt was like the Pentecostal tongue of flame.

CHAPTER NINETEEN

Matt went into the stallion-box at Twelvetrees with a diffidence that would better have suited a servant than the Master of Morland Place, and stood for a moment unobserved, watching the man groom the younger of the stud-stallions, Prince Hal. The big red-gold horse was so soothed by the rhythmic brushing that he was dozing, his lower lip hanging loose and his ears flopping, so that for the moment he looked more like a docile old farm-gelding than a Barbary racehorse stud. Davey was hissing through his teeth as he wielded the brush, moving nimbly despite his dragging foot. He had told Matt that he had broken his leg in a fall from a horse when he had been working as a groom on a stud near Newmarket. He had been reticent about his travels since running away from Morland Place, and Matt felt a certain delicacy about bringing up the past. But whatever had happened in between, it had marked Davey – not just by leaving him with a limp. The lines were deep in his face, and his hair and beard were grizzled. Well, Matt thought, he was not the only one. They were both thirty-one years old, but looked older.

Davey became aware of his presence and looked up quickly, and when he saw who it was, he stopped brushing and straightened up, waiting for Matt to speak. There was no hostility in his silence, only uncertainty. It was three weeks since Davey had come back and Matt had asked him to stay, and they were still unused to each other. It was like the shyness of children, but harder to overcome. It would be a long time, Matt thought, before they regained their ease with each other. But the most important thing was that they were together again. Davey had soon seen where he was most needed, and had offered to take over the running of the stud. Matt guessed that he did not want to be at Morland Place too often just at first, and the stud manager had quarters at Twelvetrees; he had agreed willingly.

'How is he?' Matt asked at last. Davey ran a hand down the hard neck of the stallion, who turned his head and blew gently into Davey's ear.

'Coming to his best,' Davey replied briefly. 'He'll do. He only wanted more exercise.'

'He can't replace Landscape,' Matt said mournfully, and Davey nodded. 'There have been more messengers this morning,' he went on. Davey waited. Messengers meant news of the rebellion. 'The Earl of Chelmsford is being taken from Edinburgh to London, to the Tower. They have decided that since he is English he is to stand trial at Westminster with the other English lords – Derwentwater and Nithsdale and the rest. The Countess wants to go to London. She thinks she might persuade the King – the Elector, I mean – to let him off.'

'Let's hope she does,' Davey said briefly. Matt had hoped for more of an answer – it was difficult to converse when one of you spoke so tersely. He fell back on the reason for his call.

'I want you to find a suitable horse for my cousin Sabina. I think it will do her a great deal of good to get out. Exercise and fresh air will help her recover.'

'How is she?'

'Her health is much better, but she grieves terribly.'

'Of course she does, poor lady. It must have been terrible,' Davey said.

'She mourns her husband and her other son,' Matt went on, encouraged.

'Poor lady. But at least she has the baby. Small enough comfort, but better than nothing.'

'But I can't help feeling that it was all such a waste,' Matt said. 'Here's Sabina, terribly shocked and grieved, her family all killed, her home burned down. And my cousin Frances – her husband, killed at Preston, though her father managed to get away, and now Arthur – Lord

Ballincrea – has managed to get most of her men freed, those that survived. And Lord Chelmsford to be tried for treason at Westminster – was it all worth it?'

'*Was?*' Davey said. 'It is still going on. The Chevalier is on his way to Scotland at this very moment. The army is still in Perth –'

'Growing smaller all the time, so we hear. The Highlanders are just drifting away. By the time the Chevalier gets to Scotland, there'll be nothing left. So many dead.'

Davey looked into his eyes. 'Death comes to us all sooner or later,' he said simply. 'One has no choice about that. And what can any man do but fight for his king?'

'That's what the Countess says,' Matt said. 'But I begin to wonder. Well, you will find a suitable horse for Sabina?'

'Yes, of course. When do you want it?'

'If you have something ready, bring it up to the house after dinner, and we'll shew it to her. It may arouse her interest. Oh, and have you seen Jemmy this morning?'

'He was here very early. He generally comes over early on,' Davey said. 'He loves the horses.' Davey sounded defensive, and Matt knew he was worrying that he ought to have discouraged the boy, so he hastened to reassure him.

'I'm glad. Love of horses is a good thing in a man. I think he has grown a little quieter since he came back.'

'He's growing up,' Davey said. 'He's not here now, however. I should think he has gone over to Shawes.'

'Yes, he spends a lot of time there, too,' Matt said. 'I'll see you this afternoon, then?' He met Davey's eyes, and though Davey did not precisely smile, his nod was the next best thing. Matt went away more happily. Things were turning out better than he could have hoped: Davey was back, Jemmy was safe, and looking like growing into a very satisfactory son and heir, Sabina was on the mend, and with Matt's sovereign cure, riding, and the house to oversee, should be well at last. If the Countess could win a pardon for her son, everything would be all right.

*

Annunciata found Chelmsford House in a poor state to receive her. Maurice kept the minimum of servants, and those he had seemed a surly, cheating lot, who skimped their work and took advantage of their master's absence of mind. Though she had sent Maurice an express warning him of her intention to come to London, she was not expected, and one of the servants on being questioned said that Maurice had received the message but had pushed it into his sleeve to read later.

'And there, I daresay, it lies still,' Annunciata said grimly, 'unless he has dropped it somewhere in the street without noticing. Where is he, anyway?'

'He is gone over to Master Haendel's, madam – your ladyship,' the servant said. 'I don't know when he will be coming back. Sometimes he stays there several days.'

'And where are the children?' Annunciata wanted to know.

'Upstairs, my lady.'

'Send them to me. And I shall want a boy to take a message to Master Haendel's. And I want something to eat, and some hot water to wash in.'

'Something to eat, your ladyship?' the servant said doubtfully. 'I don't think there's anything in the house.'

'Then send out for some fresh bread, and cheese, and cold cooked beef. And whatever fruit is best on the stalls. And chocolate – no, forget the chocolate. I'll send my own man for that. Get on with it at once. And send my man Daniel to me.'

When Daniel came, she said to him, 'Go to the Cocoa Tree Chocolate House – you know where that is?'

'Yes, my lady.'

'Bring me back a quart of the best chocolate, and whatever handbills are the most recent. Make haste on your way there and your way back, but in the chocolate house you may dawdle as much as you like. Get talking with the proprietor, or the waiter – whoever is the most eager to chat. Don't say who you are, or who you work for, but find out as much as you can. Do you understand?'

'Yes, my lady,' Daniel said, and Annunciata blessed him silently. It was good to have to deal with her own, well-trained, intelligent servants after battling with Maurice's frowsts.

'Good. Here's eighteenpence. That should be plenty.'

While she waited, Annunciata amused herself in talking to her grandchildren. The girls did not seem to have made much progress with English, and Annunciata had continually to revert to Italian to make herself understood. Alessandra was sixteen now, very dark, with an olive skin and rather plain features, but a pleasant smile and good teeth. Giulia was almost thirteen, and growing very pretty, as dark in her hair and eyes as her half-sister, but with a white skin and delicate features. She was livelier than Alessandra, who worshipped her younger sister and took care of her in a manner half protective and half adoring. They were both very shy with the Countess at first, but when she used their own language they gradually thawed towards her and began to talk more freely. She discovered that they were being taught at a private Catholic school for girls, where the master was a former Jesuit priest. All the lessons were conducted in French, which accounted for their poor English. It may also have accounted for their slowness, for Annunciata could not discover that either of them had learned anything at the school other than embroidery and singing.

The mention of singing brought their minds very naturally to the thing that absorbed and excited them most, which was the presence in London of Diane di Francescini, whose nickname of The Divine Diane was beginning to be used all over London. She had sung at the Opera House before the Duke of Hanover himself, they told Annunciata, and he had received her at Court with great courtesy. Annunciata listened with amusement, partly at their obvious infatuation with the young woman to whom they had acted as willing slaves all their childhood, and partly at the careful way someone, either Maurice or the Jesuit schoolmaster, had taught them to talk respectfully of the Elector without actually calling him King.

'Papa is writing some more songs for Diane,' Alessandra said proudly at the end of a long description of the gown the Divine Diane had worn for the recital before the Elector, 'and she is to sing them at Court for Princess Caroline. Papa says that I may go, though Giulia is still too young.' She looked sorrowfully at her younger sister. 'I wish it could be you, Giulia, really I do. You're so much prettier than I.'

'I shall have my chance later,' Giulia said cheerfully. 'You may have some nice lord fall in love with you at Court, and get a good offer of marriage.'

Annunciata soon tired of their chatter and sent them away. She had a great deal to think about: the following day she would see the Elector to plead for a pardon for Karellie. She had no great hopes of the man's clemency, but she hoped she might be able to stir up his sense of justice.

The Elector, she found, had changed little since she had met him last. She remembered the first time she had seen George Lewis, at Windsor, when as a young man he had come over to inspect Princess Anne as a possible bride. She had not thought much of him then, a short, stocky man, with a pink, plump face, pinkish-blond hair, dull codlike eyes and a loose mouth like a frog's. The plump face was now fat, the eyes more dull and codlike than ever, the jowls making the loose mouth look looser. He wore a chestnut periwig, which made his cheeks look redder, and a brown velvet coat over yellow waistcoat and breeches which Annunciata thought hideous.

They eyed each other cautiously: George Lewis could not have been unaware of why she was there. He looked her up and down as if inspecting her clothes, but gave no indication of what he thought of them. Annunciata's gown was of midnight-blue satin over a ruched and embroidered petticoat of a shade lighter, with silver lace at bodice and sleeves – she had thought a display of solid wealth and respectability would be the best way to impress him and win his support. Her hair was still black enough to wear piled up on the top of her head, dressed with pearls, a loose tail curling down her back – she hated headdresses, though to many her bare head looked not only old-fashioned but vaguely indecent.

'Well, Lady Chelmsford, what is it you want?' George Lewis asked her. His face was devoid of expression, but Annunciata soon learned that it always was, unless he frowned in real anger. She began in English, but he soon interrupted her in German to say that he did not understand her. She did not know whether or not this was true, and it put her at a disadvantage. She began again, but her German was not good, and she had often, stumbling, to search for a circumlocution, or seek an Italian or French word that he might know. He listened impassively, and the only moment when he reacted in any way was when she called him 'cousin' – then he frowned, and she did not know if it was in disapproval of her claiming such a relationship, or in disapproval of her not giving him the title he had taken.

At all events, she came finally to a halt, without knowing how much, if any, of her speech he had understood, or even listened to.

He remained silent for a long time, staring at her, and then said, 'I can do nothing before the trials. He must stand trial with the others,' and turned away from her, not even waiting for her curtsey. Annunciata watched him go in painful uncertainty. Was he implying that he would help, if necessary, *after* the trial?

She left the Palace, pushing away as she climbed into her coach the memories that clamoured like lonely ghosts for her attention, memories of other times at the Courts of Whitehall and St James, when King Charles had ruled and she had been young. She directed the coachman to take her to the Tower, and settled back in the stuffiness of the leather seat, pulling her cloak about her and pushing her hands deep into her muff for the warmth, glad of Kithra's body across her feet. The ghosts tugged importunately at her mind, and she tried hard to ignore them. She had never been able to imagine growing old, and King Charles's Court was still fresh and vivid in her mind: but here she was, an old woman of seventy, feeling the cold this year as never before, on her way to see her son, a son of forty-four, who was very likely going to be beheaded for treason. King Death, she thought, hath asses' ears; but life made fools of them all, just as much as death.

When the grey bulk of the Tower came in sight, Annunciata could not prevent a shudder passing through her. It was the royal residence in the city of London, that was all; a castle keep, a fortified palace; the Kings of England slept here before their coronations, every one, and many had lived her for long periods. But she could not help seeing it as a prison. Here she had been imprisoned, within sight of the place where Anne Boleyn had been beheaded, and where she had expected to lose her own head. The horror of that time, when Titus Oates had ruled London, had never truly left her. And here now Karellie was imprisoned. She gestured to the girl she had brought with her to pick up the basket of food she had prepared, told Kithra to lie down, and stepped out into the dark courtyard.

Karellie's quarters were cramped but comfortable, and he had been allowed to keep his servant Sam with him, and so, had it not been for his expectation of death, he would have been in no bad case. He was delighted to see his mother, embraced her, and for a long time simply stood with his arms around her and his face against her hair, while Annunciata felt with distress the thinness of his body through his clothes, and after a while the heat of his tears on her head. At last he straightened up and released her, making an obvious effort to be cheerful.

'Well, mother, what have you brought me in that basket?' he asked, sitting down on the edge of his cot and leaving the chair for her.

'I did not know how well they would be feeding you,' she said. 'I have brought a few delicacies, but if you are in greater need I can have other things brought in.'

'They feed us well,' Karellie said, 'though plainly. These things will be very welcome. They are all very kind to us here – I think they are all sorry for us. For two pins they would open our prison doors and let us free – only they have their jobs to consider.'

Most of all, he wanted news of the rebellion, and Annunciata told him everything she knew. He listened attentively, moving restlessly now and then, but almost as if he did not know he was doing it. Then he gave her his own news.

'They are going ahead with the trials, without waiting for any further outcome of the rebellion,' he said. 'We are to be impeached some time in January, and tried as soon after that as possible. They want it over and done with, before opinion swings in our favour. There are seven peers apart from me, and we are all to be tried together.'

'Dispatch seems to be the order of the day,' Annunciata said. 'The poor creatures taken at Preston are to be dealt with in January as well – those that are still alive. The conditions of their imprisonment are terrible.'

Karellie nodded at that, but said nothing. A moment later he was up and pacing and she watched him walk up and down the small room, waiting for him to break through his control. At last he turned to her and cried, 'It is being shut up, mother. I can't endure it. The locked door – the small room. You were imprisoned once – how did you bear it?'

'I was very ill. I don't remember much about it. But, Karellie, it is only for a little while. I survived, and so will you.'

'I don't think so,' he said bitterly. 'You, after all, were saved by the King. For us there is no hope. The trials are a matter of form only, the conclusions are foregone. We shall all die on Tower Green, mother.'

'He is your cousin, your own blood kin. He will not kill you,' Annunciata said desperately. Karellie shook his head.

'He does not care for that. And it is not *he* that will kill us, but the Whigs and the Dissenters. They will send us to our death, and he, caring nothing one way or the other, will let the law take its course.' Annunciata said nothing, knowing this was all too likely, and Karellie went on, 'Nevertheless, it is not death I dread so much. A soldier lives with death close beside him. It is this – being – shut – up!'

And Annunciata could say nothing, do nothing, to comfort him.

Annunciata was not allowed to see Karellie again – none of the peers were allowed visitors after the first few days – until the trials began. Derwentwater, Nithsdale, Widdrington, Carnwath, Kenmure, and Nairn were all tried with Karellie in the great hall at Westminster before their peers under Lord Cowper, the Lord High Steward. It was a solemn, and ceremonious occasion, with all the officers of the court in full robes. The serjeant-at-arms read the King's Commission in Latin, the Lord High Steward, with his white rod of office, took his seat, and the Lieutenant of the Tower brought in the accused piers, followed by the masked executioner, his axe turned away from the prisoners. Annunciata, from her discreet seat in the gallery, watched with a renewed shudder, remembering her own procession, with the executioner following behind her too. Karellie looked pale, she thought, but all the prisoners conducted themselves with dignity. They knelt before the Lord High Steward, bowed to their fellow peers, and received bows in return, before they took their places at the bar.

One by one the Articles of Impeachment were read out, and one by one the peers made their answers. Derwentwater, Widdrington and Nithsdale had all prepared speeches, expressing their sorrow for their past actions, and pleading for mercy, and they read them now; Carnwath and Kenmure simply asked for mercy; Nairn spoke anxiously of his being a Protestant and having played little part in the rising.

Karellie said simply, 'I followed my orders, given to me by the man I hold to be my King. What could I do more, or less? And what could any of you have done?'

There was no reaction to any of the speeches from the assembled jury, not so much as a sympathetic sigh. The result of the trial, as Karellie had said, was a foregone conclusion. The Lord High Steward asked the prisoners why judgement should not be passed upon them according to the law, and again each of them was given the opportunity to answer. Carnwath and Kenmure retained their dignity and said nothing; Widdrington claimed his health was poor, Nairn that his family would starve without him. Poor Lord Derwentwater, a young man recently married with two infant children, trembled, and said that the terrors of their lordships' sentence that would deprive him of estates and life and leave his wife and children destitute, robbed him of thought, and that he could only say that he was guilty, but that he had done what he did rashly, and without premeditation. Now it was Karellie's turn.

'Lord Chelmsford, what have you to say?' Lord Cowper asked. Karellie straightened his back.

'My lord, I am a simple soldier, and have no readiness with words. You have accused me of treason, and if I am guilty of treason, I deserve to die. But I have always understood that treason was an act of rebellion against one's lawful king, and of that I am not guilty, for my lawful king is King James III, and I know no other, and him I have served faithfully and with my whole heart, as a soldier is bound to do. Therefore I must say to you that I am not guilty of any treacherous act, and do not deserve to die.'

There was a murmur at that, though whether sympathetic or not Annunciata could not tell.

Lord Cowper said firmly, 'Lord Chelmsford, we are not here to debate the possession of the Crown of England or the legality of the succession. Treason is an act harmful to the common weal of England, and against the head of that weal, which is King George I, who is the best of kings. You have come from a foreign country to levy war against the people of this realm, which is a terrible thing, and worthy of no mercy.'

After that it was impossible for Nithsdale, the last of the prisoners, to say anything, except to plead that he had been very little involved in the rebellion. At last Cowper stood up to pronounce the sentence.

'It is adjudged that you return to the prison of the Tower from whence you came, and from thence you be drawn to a place of execution; when you come there you must be hanged by the neck, but not till you be dead, for you must be cut down alive and your bowels must be taken out and burned before your faces; then your heads must be severed from your bodies and your bodies divided into four quarters, and these must be at the King's disposal. And may God almighty be merciful to your souls.'

The white staff of office was broken in two, and the prisoners left the bar and were escorted out of the hall, followed by the executioner, the blade of his axe turned towards them.

Judgement was passed on 9 February, and the executions were to take place on the twenty-fourth. In the intervening two weeks, Annunciata was not idle. She had heard the sentence with incredulity and horror, and could not believe that Karellie would really die. She paid a visit to him daily, and saw to it that he had a priest with him, for he seemed determined that he would die. Meanwhile she got together with the families of the other condemned peers to make up a petition to go before the House of Lords. Then one evening Lady Nithsdale came to see her.

'I have heard that the King is to go to the Drawing Room tomorrow, and I plan to go with a friend to stop him on his way and plead for my poor husband's life. Now, my lady, surely you will go with me? You must be as anxious about your son as I am about my husband. Moreover, the King is your kinsman, and your presence must help our cause. Will you not come with me?'

'Certainly I will,' Annunciata said, 'though I have no great hopes of this *King* as you call him. But I will try anything that may help, and if you think my kinship with the Elector will weight matters in our favour, I shall come along and cry him cousin.'

'I have had my clerk write out a petition – would you like to read it? If you would like to make one out similar for your son, we can give them to His Majesty before he reaches the Drawing Room. My friend Mrs Morgan tells me there is a long saloon between the King's own apartments and the Drawing Room where we can wait.'

'Yes, I know it,' Annunciata said. 'A long room, with three windows, and seats in the windows. We can sit in the middle window, where he is bound to see us.'

'And I think we should wear black, as if we were in mourning,' Lady Nithsdale said with a glance at Annunciata's finery. 'That will make a better impression on his mind, and may touch his heart.' Annunciata gave her a look of amused scepticism, but agreed the plan.

The following morning they assembled in good time. Annunciata had worn black, as agreed, but had scorned to ape sorrow with plain drab. Her gown was of black satin, drawn back to shew the petticoat of quilted black satin, piped with crimson. The bodice was sewn with jet beads, and in the centre she wore the pearl and amethyst cross her mother had given her, which had once belonged to Anne Boleyn, and round her neck the diamond collar given to her by King Charles II. She thought it wise to remind the Elector that she had been favoured by those who had held the throne, with right on their sides, before him.

George Lewis emerged at last from his apartments, attended by four blue-riband servants, and walked down the saloon towards them. His eyes went from Annunciata to Lady Nithsdale, and then fixed themselves determinedly upon the far door, and Annunciata saw he had resolved to ignore them. She prepared to step firmly into his path and

372

address him, but was forestalled by Lady Nithsdale, who flung herself to her knees before the Elector, clutching at him and babbling a frantic plea for mercy in very bad French.

Annunciata was exasperated, but could only try to make the best of a bad situation. She added her own plea in German, explaining that the kneeling woman was the Countess of Nithsdale, and saying that they both had petitions for him. She held out her petition; Lady Nithsdale, still babbling in French, was trying to push hers into George Lewis's pocket, and the Elector was trying to pretend the whole thing was not happening. He pushed Annunciata's hand away quite roughly, and tried to walk on, sidestepping the kneeling figure of Lady Nithsdale, who grabbed desperately at the tail of his coat and held on so hard that the determined stride of the Elector dragged her forward.

It was a disgraceful scene; the kneeling woman was towed from the middle of the room to the door of the Drawing Room, while the Elector tried to pretend that nothing was amiss. Then the blue ribands grabbed her from behind and forced her hands open, releasing the Elector, who made his escape, whisking into the Drawing Room, whose door was shut hastily behind him. Lady Nithsdale's petition fell from his pocket and was crushed by the closing door.

Annunciata made an attempt to see the Elector alone the next day, thinking she had a better chance without the Countess of Nithsdale, but when the Elector saw her he frowned and said, 'I have nothing to say to you. Rebels must hang. That is the law.'

That same day she learned that the petition that had been placed before the House of Lords had been rejected, and that the Elector had been angry with the peers who had dared to suggest that he pardon rebels. It all looked hopeless. Annunciata sat up all night with Father Renard in prayer and discussion; the following morning she sent Daniel out to a remote part of London to purchase a file.

If there was to be no pardon, she thought, then there must be an escape.

Three days before the date of execution, Annunciata received a visitor. The young woman came masked, and gave her name as Mrs Freeman, the time-honoured pseudonym of the incognito.

'Have you any idea who it is, or what she wants?' Annunciata asked Chloris.

'Her height and her red hair and her voice are all unmistakable, my lady,' Chloris said. 'Mrs Freeman can be none other than the Divine Diane herself, and therefore what she wants is easy enough to guess.'

'Something to do with Karellie,' Annunciata said. 'Is she hysterical?'

'No, my lady, very calm, but excited I should say.'

'Well, she may have an idea, then. Send her in.'

Annunciata had never seen Diane di Francescini, but she had heard about her, both as a singer, and from Karellie, who had said enough for Annunciata to guess a great deal more. She had expected a haughty, shallow, vain charmer, a woman so convinced of her beauty she could afford to reject the love of Annunciata's son Karellie. When the tall young woman took off her mask, Annunciata saw that the beauty and pride had not been inflated in the telling, but that the intelligence and feeling had not been mentioned. There was distress in those great blue eyes, and determination in the set of those lips, which were being prevented by exercise of character from trembling.

Diane, on her part, had not expected the Countess to look so beautiful or so human. An old woman of seventy was, to Diane, a thing past understanding, who must therefore be a creature apart, difficult to communicate with. She found a woman like herself, of pride and self-confidence, and they regarded each other with the frank interest which acknowledged beauty reserves for acknowledged beauty.

'You have come, I take it, on some errand concerned with my son Charles,' Annunciata began. 'Forgive me for not employing all the usual courtesies, but where my son's life is concerned, there is no time to waste. Have you news? or some plan?'

'Thank you for being frank, madam,' Diane said. 'I shall be frank in my turn. I love your son, and want to help him escape from the Tower. He must not die, madam, of that I am determined.'

'Yet you rejected him,' Annunciata said curiously. She wanted to know if she could trust this young woman. Diane drew herself up to her full height.

'I am a singer, madam, the finest singer in Venice, which means the finest in all Italy. I am known as the Divine Diane. For no one can I give up that honour, not even for Karellie, whom I love. I will never love anyone else; but I can love without wishing to surrender. Can you understand that?'

Annunciata could; this was a woman that she could trust.

'You speak of escape,' Annunciata said. 'That is on my mind, too, now there is no hope of reprieve. So far I have only one plan. I shall smuggle a file in to his cell, and a rope, and he shall break out at night.'

'If you will forgive me, madam, I believe I have a better, but it requires your help,' Diane said, her eyes shining with enthusiasm. Annunciata gestured to a chair.

'Please sit down, and tell me about it.'

Annunciata, Diane, Alessandra, and the two serving women, Chloris and Caterina, presented themselves at the Tower to see Karellie on the evening of the twenty-second. Annunciata had been doubtful about involving Alessandra in the plot, but Diane had said she could be relied on, for a lifetime of obeying Diane's orders would make her quick and docile, and would obviate the necessity of explaining the plot to her, which was all to the good. Annunciata was dressed more formally, and more in accordance with her age, than was usual. She was well-covered-up, and wore a thick cloak with a hood, which she said was necessary to keep the cold from her 'old bones'. It was a good thing that she had complained to the guards before about the cold and dampness of the Tower, for the cloak was concealing a great deal. It was a good job also that she was very thin, for she was wearing two sets of everything, and managed not to look unduly bulky.

Alessandra and the two maids chattered to the guards while Annunciata and Diane remained in the cell with Karellie. On Diane's orders, all three came and went from the cell several times so that the guards should not get too fixed an idea of them. Meanwhile Annunciata was having difficulty in persuading Karellie to escape.

'It would be dishonourable to involve Diane in such a thing. It could be dangerous for her,' he objected. Annunciata grew exasperated.

'For God's sake, Karellie, don't you love life? Do you want to die to please the Elector? Do you want to let him execute you for something of which you are innocent? Diane has involved herself, and she will be safe enough – the Venetian ambassador's immunity will protect her, even if anyone should suspect her, which they won't. I say you must not die. Will you break her heart, and mine?'

It took Diane's pleadings as well to persuade him, and then they had to act quickly. Choosing her moment, Diane looked out into the passage and told Caterina to run down to the coach with a message for the coachman; the girl left, and a moment later, on receiving Diane's nod, Alessandra slipped away unseen by the guards, who were talking to Chloris. The guards on the doors below would let her through without question. Meanwhile Annunciata was taking off her outer garments, and Karellie was putting them on, along with a dark wig which Annunciata had brought in the usual basket of food. Diane made up his face, darkening his eyebrows and whitening his skin, and applying rouge to his lips and cheeks, and then draped him in the thick cloak, pulling the hood up over the wig.

Diane looked out again, and called to Chloris. 'Come here at once. Your mistress is unwell.'

'What's the matter, mistress?' one of the guards asked, coming closer. Diane looked coolly at him.

'What is the matter? Surely that is obvious. A mother saying goodbye to her son, who is about to be executed – what do you expect? She is half-fainting with grief. Chloris, come here and take your poor mistress to her carriage. She had better not strain herself with a longer visit. She is an old woman, after all.'

'Yes, madame,' Chloris said, looking suitably anxious. The guard, who was a kindly man, tugged his friend's sleeve and pulled him away, to give the women privacy. A moment later Chloris came out of the cell half-leading, half-supporting the cloaked figure, bent with grief, sobbing into a handkerchief held to the face. The guards stood back sympathetically and allowed them to pass.

Diane said, 'Take her straight home, Chloris, and send the carriage back for me and Alessandra. I will call on you later tonight to see how you are, your ladyship.'

For half an hour more, with the door of the cell closed, Diane carried on a conversation with Karellie of which the guards could only overhear the odd word or two, not enough to distinguish how many voices were speaking. Then she took her leave accompanied by Annunciata dressed in a replica of the clothes Alessandra had been wearing, her face also concealed in the shadow of her hood. Her slenderness was again helpful, for it made her look young enough to be mistaken, her face hidden, for a much younger woman.

The guards stepped back for them, and Annunciata went on down the stairs while Diane hung back to say, 'His lordship is saying his prayers, and is much distressed. I should be grateful if you would leave him undisturbed as long as possible.'

'Of course, mistress. We understand. Poor gentleman, it's a terrible thing, isn't it?' the guards said. They liked Karellie, who had been gentle and courteous to them, and

Diane tripped away down the stairs, feeling rather sorry for the guards, but hoping that they would not be punished too heavily for being hoodwinked.

At Chelmsford House, behind closed shutters, there was a joyful reunion. Karellie and Maurice hugged each other with silent tears, Karellie kissed his mother, and grasped Diane's hand in a gratitude that was almost painful to her. But there was no time to delay.

'They will come here as soon as they discover you are missing,' Annunciata said. 'You must get away – and tonight.'

'But what will happen to you?' Karellie said, looking from his mother to Diane. 'They will know you have plotted the escape.'

'My story is that I knew nothing about it,' Annunciata said. 'The guards saw me leave on Chloris's arm, in deep distress, leaving you to escape afterwards disguised as Alessandra. The plot was between Alessandra and Diane.'

'And what is to happen to them?' Karellie asked, even more distressed. Diane took his hand.

'We shall be safe abroad, where they will not be able to touch us. We are leaving tonight, the three of us – you, me, and Alessandra. My father has hired a boat for us, which is waiting at Dover. He went down yesterday on the pretext of arranging for the reception of the Venetian ambassador's brother, who really is due to arrive in a few days' time.'

'You have worked it all so well,' Karellie said in painful admiration. 'I can never thank you enough. But will not Alessandra mind leaving England and her father?'

'She will be glad to be with me,' Diane promised him. 'Besides, you will visit her in Venice, will you not, Maurice? The soul of music will call you to us again, I am sure.'

'I miss Italy, it's true,' Maurice said. He stroked Alessandra's hair and smiled at her. 'Venice is home to you, isn't it, *cara?* You have never really liked London so much.'

'It's true, Papa,' Alessandra said, 'but –' She looked from him to Giulia and back again.

'We will visit you, very soon. In fact, when the fuss has died down, Giulia can go back to Venice too, and live with you and Diane.'

Annunciata tapped her foot impatiently.

'Come, it is time to go. You must change into your new disguises.'

'More disguises?' Karellie asked in a dismay Annunciata found comic, considering he was fleeing for his life. It was Diane who answered, with half-concealed glee.

'We cannot flee in our own persons, my lord. We are to be Signore and Signora Rinaldi, travelling back to Italy with our maid, Caterina. We came over for the opera, to hear the Divine Diane sing before the King of England – and for the love of God, do not argue with anyone who calls this George Lewis King, until we have got safely out of the country.'

A little while longer, and then there were goodbyes to say. Annunciata had lived through so many of them in past years, that she had no words for Karellie, only a silent embrace that told him everything, all her love and pain. There was little chance that she would ever see him again. Diane she kissed with respect and affection.

'I should have been proud to have you as my daughter-in-law,' she said, 'and I am proud to have known you, all the same. God go with you on your journey, and God bless you for what you have done for Karellie.' And she gave her the pearl and amethyst cross that had belonged to Anne Boleyn. 'I always meant to give this to Karellie's bride when at last he married,' she said. 'I don't suppose he will marry now. In any case, it is you that I shall always think of as his bride. Take, wear it, for me, with my blessing.'

Diane kissed her in return, and a few moments later the three were off on horseback. They had sixty or more miles to go before morning.

CHAPTER TWENTY

It was some time after six in the evening when they left London, and it was full light when they rode into Dover, under the lowering bulk of the great grey castle.

'We must be quick now,' Diane said in a low voice to Karellie. 'Papa said the tide turned at eight, and it must be close to that now. If we miss the tide we will have to stay here all day, and they will surely soon be looking for a tall man travelling with two young women.'

'Where is the boat?' Karellie asked, urging the tired horse along.

'I don't know – we must ask. Papa says she is called the *Songthrush*. But I will do the asking – you sound too much like an Englishman. Both of you, remember that you don't speak any English. Whatever anyone says to you, just stare at them blankly. I will do all the talking.'

They rode down the main street towards the harbour, and Diana stopped the first likely person she saw, and asked in a prettily broken accent the whereabouts of the *Songthrush*. The man directed them to the harbour office, and they rode on. Outside the harbour office they halted, and Diane dismounted and went in, leaving Karellie and Alessandra outside. The officer knew the *Songthrush*.

'She's been hired to take a Venetian party over to Calais – is that you?' he asked. Diane did not understand at first, for he pronounced the French town as 'Callus', and the misunderstanding strengthened the impression she wanted to give.

'That's right – me and my husband and daughter.'

She glanced out to the others, and the officer looked too, and said, 'Why, miss, that young lady is too old to be your daughter.' Diane went cold, and her fingers closed into

380

her palms. The officer went on, grinning broadly, 'You are too young and pretty to have a daughter that age.'

Diane breathed again. She looked at him haughtily, and said, 'But of course, she is my step-daughter. What did you think?'

The officer took her outside and gave her directions to get to the *Songthrush*.

'But what about your horses?' he asked.

'They are to be collected from the Sun and Stars Inn,' Diane said. 'Perhaps you can tell us also where that is?'

'Oh, don't you worry about that, miss,' the officer said. 'There are plenty of boys hanging around the harbour. I'll get one of them to take the horses up. You had better hurry, if you don't want to miss the tide.'

So they unpacked their small bundles from the horses' saddles and left them there and walked rapidly down to the harbour side.

'We have had such luck so far,' Karellie murmured, 'I can hardly believe it.'

'Hush,' Diane warned. 'Where we are.'

The captain of the *Songthrush* was looking out for them, and bundled them aboard without ceremony.

'Go into the cabin, if you please, while we get under way. I'll tell you when you can come on deck,' he said and, grateful to obey, the three of them got under cover, while the sailors cast off and made sail. They felt the ship turn from an inert to a living thing, felt her spring to the tremendous leverage of her big mizzen driver, like a fresh horse leaping under the rider's hands. They felt the difference in the movement of the waves when they cleared the shelter of the harbour bar and came out into the open sea, and then they sighed with relief.

'Unless they send a faster boat after us, we must be safe now,' Diane said. Karellie nodded.

'All the time I kept thinking how suspicious it must all look, three of us, rich enough to hire a boat, yet having no servant and no luggage between us. And borrowed horses, not hirelings. Anyone might have stopped us. When the man at the harbour office talked to you –'

Diane looked thoughtful. 'I wonder if they were all as stupid as it appeared. Papa said he had no trouble getting a boat to take three people to Calais on a certain date. Perhaps they all know what we are, and want to help us escape.'

'But the hue and cry cannot have reached here yet,' Karellie said. Diane shook her head.

'I don't meant that – I mean anyone trying to get across to Calais in suspicious circumstances is likely to be a Jacobite. Perhaps they guess we are Jacobites, and don't mind.'

A moment later the captain stuck his head round the door. 'You can come on deck now if you like, but I warn you the wind's a bit fresh. Very favourable, mind you. It'll be the quickest passage I've done in many a long year.' He smiled at them with a faint air of enquiry and added, 'The wind couldn't have served you better if you were flying for your lives.' Then he withdrew, leaving them bemused.

In England the enquiries went just as Annunciata had expected. A very short time after the fugitives had left, an officer and half a dozen armed guards came knocking on the door of Chelmsford House, looking for the Earl of Chelmsford, and demanding to be let in, to be allowed to search, to have the earl given up to them. Everyone played their parts well, delaying opening the door for as long as possible, and then allowing only the officer in. Maurice was finally fetched, and was suitably furious at having been disturbed when he was writing. He berated the servants in front of the officer for calling him against his express orders, was short with the officer himself, and denied any knowledge of his brother's whereabouts.

'You have not been to see your brother in the Tower at all, sir?' the officer asked suspiciously.

'I have not,' Maurice said shortly. 'I am a servant of

King George – he is my patron – I disapproved of the whole thing.'

'Then you were glad your brother was to be executed?' the officer asked disbelievingly.

'Of course I was not glad. But rebels must be executed. He had done wrong under the law and was to be punished. There was nothing *I* could do about it. If he has escaped I am glad, but I certainly did not help him. And now perhaps you will go away and let me get on with my work.'

He turned away, but the officer called him back.

'I'm sorry, sir, but it isn't as easy as that. I beg your pardon for suggesting it, but you could be lying, and concealing your brother about the house.'

'I assure you I am not,' Maurice said.

'I wonder sir if I could see your mother, the Countess, for a few moments.'

'My mother has retired to bed. She was greatly distressed by this afternoon's visit, and came home in a state of collapse. Her maid put her to bed at once.' He saw the quick suspicion flare up in the captain's eyes, and fed it. 'I cannot in any circumstances allow her to be disturbed.'

They managed to waste another half hour in arguing whether or not the Countess should be disturbed, and when it was decided to call her, there was another long delay while Annunciata was dressed and made ready to receive a visitor. When she finally appeared and was seen to be the Countess, and not, by any stretch of the imagination, the earl in disguise, the captain wanted to search her apartments in case the earl was concealed. Annunciata expressed a righteous indignation.

'I rejoice that my son has escaped from this unjust punishement, but I have had nothing to do with it myself, and I cannot permit you to disturb this house any longer. If you wish to do so, you must return with a greater authority than you have now. Leave me, Captain, at once.'

The captain, in the face of Annunciata's age and authority, had no choice but to withdraw, and the first round of the delaying game was won. Over the next few days other enquiries were made, the Lord Lieutenant of the Tower himself called upon the Countess, and she was invited to St James's Palace to be interviewed by members of the Privy Council, and to describe what had happened on that last visit to the Tower.

'My grief overcame me, I felt myself fainting, and my maid conducted me out to the coach, which brought me home. And that, my lords, is all I know.'

'So you left your son in this room with – whom?'

'With Lady Diane. She and my son were to be married, and she had her own farewells to say.'

'And now Lady Diane is – where?'

'I cannot tell you, my lords. I hardly knew her.'

'Hardly knew the young woman who was to marry your son?'

And so it went on; but to no avail. Annunciata was finally left alone, though whether she had really persuaded them of her innocence she could not tell. For several weeks her house was haunted by strangers – servants out of work seeking a position, pedlars who did not seem much interested in selling their goods, idlers lounging in the street outside – and her servants were put under a great deal of strain by friendly, sharp-eyed men asking them apparently casual questions in the street as they went about their business. She suspected her mail was being intercepted, but it made no difference, for it was almost startlingly innocent of significant correspondence.

The network she had inherited from Clovis functioned smooothly and secretly as it always had, and she was able to send both letters and money ahead of the party to various places along their route. It was a long and unpleasant journey across Europe in the dead of winter, and she knew that they would need all the help they could get.

One consequence of travelling as husband and wife that Karellie had not anticipated was revealed to him on their first night, when they stopped at an inn on the road to

Lille. Presenting themselves as husband, wife and daughter they were given two tiny rooms, and the inn servants conducted Karellie and Diane to one, and Alesandra to the other, in such a way as to make it impossible for them to change over. Karellie faced Diane with distress when they were left along together.

'I had not anticipated this, Principessa. What can we do? Naturally I had supposed that you and Allessandra would share a bed – I had not thought –'

Diane laughed. 'My dear Karellie, it is perhaps the most endearing thing about you, that you had not anticipated this. But of course we will be given a room to share! We are husband and wife in the eyes of the world. We have chosen to be.'

Karellie looked about the tiny room in despair. 'You will have the bed, and I will sit on that chair, and wrap myself in my cloak. And tomorrow –'

'You would not be fit to ride tomorrow if you sat up all night on a hard chair,' Diane said, amused.

'Tomorrow –' he went on firmly, 'we must change our disguises. I must become your foot man or uncle or something of the sort.'

Diane came closer, and despite the chill and damp of the inn room, Karellie began to feel rather warm. 'My lord Earl, can it be that you are afraid of me? You who have faced the cannon's roar, and the yelling of barbarian hoards? You who have charged the enemy's ranks a thousand times, afraid of a simple young girl?' Karellie said nothing, watching her doubtfully. She put her hands against his chest and smiled at him.

'Tonight, my lord, you will sleep in this bed, as will I, and I promise you will come to no harm.'

Behind her teasing smile he could see there was some serious purpose about her and despite himself his body stirred at her nearness.

'We will sleep in the same bed,' he made one last effort, 'but I will stay outside the sheet, while you sleep under it.'

'Sheet? In an inn like this?' Diane said. 'I doubt if there

will be more than a couple of rough blankets.' She began undoing the buttons of his waistcoat, and he started to tremble. She looked up at him, her eyes seeming to slant, catlike. The lids were heavy, her lips were soft and full, she seemed almost slumbrous with desire.

'Diane,' he said. His hands went behind her shoulders, and no longer able to control himself, he pulled her hard against him and kissed her, long and deep, feeling her ready response. She really meant to do it, his mind told him in distant surprise. When at last he released her, panting, she smiled up at him with a confidence that made his blood sing round his body.

'Tonight,' she said, 'and all the nights between here and Venice. It is my holiday from life. I love you Karellie. I shall never love anyone but you; but I cannot marry you, except in this way, in masquerade. Let us enjoy what we have while we have it. Come, husband, come to bed.'

At the beginning of April, Annunciata left London and went back to Shawes, and it was there, a week later, that the message reached her that Karellie and Diane and Alessandra had reached Venice in safety. By that time, the attempt to restore King James to his throne was over. The King himself, arriving too late in late December, had left for France again in February, but there was no home for him anywhere in French territory. With Old King Louis dead, the Duc d'Orleans was Regent for the infant Louis XV, and he had no sympathy for the exiled King's plight. Any country that depended either on France or on George Lewis must refuse to accept James, or even to allow him to pass through, and in the end the only place open to him was the Papal city of Avignon.

Before setting out for Avignon, the King sent five ships to Scotland to rescue as many of his supporters as possible. By then Derwentwater and Kenmuir had been executed, two score simple men had been hanged, and several hundreds transported. Nithsdale and Wintoun had both escaped, and later several others did the same, including Thomas Forster, who had led the Northumberland rising, and General Mackintosh, Old Borlum, who broke out of Newgate jail with thirteen others by the simple expedient of rushing the gates and overpowering the guards.

For a long time it was not known what reprisals would be taken against those known to have, or suspected of having, taken part in the rising, but as time went on it became plain that those who had not actually been captured in battle were to be left alone. For some time Annunciata considered whether it would be necessary or advisable for her to go abroad, but she thought of the prospect with no pleasure. The idea of the exiled Court at Avignon, crammed with penniless Jacobites and living far more precariously even than it had at St Germain, attracted her not at all. She was too old to travel, too old to be without physical comforts. Besides, now that her great passions had died down, she was happy in England, even despite the presence of a Usurper on the throne. She had Shawes, which she knew she would never quite finish adapting and improving; she had Matt and Morland Place to oversee; she had young Jemmy to cheer her old age with his flattering interest in her stories and evident delight in her company.

Annunciata had been at Shawes only two months when a letter came from Maurice to say that his younger daughter Giulia had caught smallpox and died. Despite the heat, Annunciata went up to London at once, for the tone of Maurice's letter was deeply distressed. She found him sunk in despondency from which she could not, for all her efforts, rouse him.

'What have I to shew for my life?' he asked miserably. 'I'm forty-four, a widower, and childless. My life has been wasted.'

In vain did Annunciata point out that he had another daughter – out of sight was out of mind to Maurice in his black mood. In vain also did she point out the music he had written, the operas he had performed: to an artist, only the next work is important, and at that moment he found himself devoid of ideas. At last in exasperation, she said, 'Oh, why don't you go back to Italy? Write some more operas, marry another Italian beauty, have some more Italian brats, then perhaps you'll feel better!'

She meant it more or less in jest, but within a few days the idea had taken root in the fertile soil of Maurice's discontent, and by the end of June he had left London for Naples, where his former father-in-law was still Maestro di Capella of the chapel royal.

Annunciata remained in London a few weeks more, in order to tidy up affairs and to find a tenant for Chelmsford House, which she had decided once again to let. 'I don't think I shall come back to London,' she said to Chloris. 'It is a dead place to me now. London for me was always the Court, Whitehall, St James's, and the people of the Court. It can never be so again, with George Lewis and his dull son to come after him.'

'Do you not think the King will ever regain his throne, my lady?' Chloris asked. Annunciata pulled Kithra's ears thoughtfully.

'No, I don't think so. It has been too long now for England to rise, and Scotland alone is not strong enough to turn the Guelph from the throne. No, Chloris, there will be no more Kings. George Lewis does not rule – he is ruled by the politicians who gave the throne to him, and his son will be ruled also. A nation ruled by politicians, that is what we shall become.'

Chloris thought of her own son, who had died in battle for King James, and of all the Morlands who had fallen. 'Was it all worth it?' she said, unconsciously echoing Matt's words. Annunciata stared out of the window and thought back over her long life in the service of the throne, and wondered what life would be like for Englishmen without a true King to follow.

'Twenty-five years ago,' she said, 'Martin walked out of his house – his safe home – an ordinary gentleman, with no experience of battle, to take his sword and fight and die for his King, giving the service all men must ultimately owe.

No Morland will ever do that again. If there are wars in the future, they will be fought by soldiers; no private gentleman will go out to die for a Hanoverian. There will be no more Kings, Chloris: that world is gone forever, and you and I will be strangers in the new one.'

She turned back to the room, and patted her friend's frail shoulder. 'We'll go back to Yorkshire,' she said, 'and have a little peace.'

There was one more curious little incident before she left London, which was the arrival of a letter with the Royal Seal upon it. It said, simply and without explanation, that the Act of Attainder against Charles Morland, Earl of Chelmsford and Baron Meldon, had been reversed by command of King George I and with the approval of the Houses of Parliament. Annunciata read it through again disbelievingly, and then laughed. So, after all, the cold, codeyed man had not been able entirely to ignore the claims of blood! Perhaps in memory of his mother, or in recognition of Karellie's courage and Annunciata's resourcefulness, or simply because, now that Karellie had escaped, it cost him nothing – but he had done it. Karellie could come back to England if he wanted, and the title could be passed on. It would probably make no difference to anyone, Annunciata thought, but it was something pleasant to reflect on during the journey north.

On a bright July day in 1717, Frances McNeill sat on the window-seat in the great bedchamber at Morland Place, watching two maids dressing Sabina for her wedding. The dress was of pale gold brocade, decorated with small green and white flowers, drawn back over a petticoat of apple green satin, much frilled. The bodice was laced at the the front and clasped with tourmalines, and was pulled in very tightly to shew off Sabina's small waist, and the sleeves, which ended at the elbow, were filled with three layers of lace. High headdresses had gone out of style at last, and the *coiffeur basse* for ladies was the thing. Sabina's black hair was curled all over, the side pieces drawn back into a roll at the back of her head which was decorated with fresh flowers, the back hair curled into heavy ringlets. Round her neck she wore the Queen's Emeralds.

'How do I look?' she asked when the maids had finished. She came across to Frances and spun round on the spot. 'Do the pleats at the back look well? Do you think my train should be longer?'

Frances smiled at that. 'What use to say it should, even if I thought so? There is no time to make a new dress now. Your bridegroom waits below.'

Sabina laughed. 'Very well, you have exposed my design. I do not want your opinion, I want only to be told I look well.'

'Then your frankness shall be honoured. You look – very lovely.'

'Not too old to be a bride?' Sabina asked anxiously.

'You look no more than eighteen,' Frances assured her. The baby Allen, who was not yet two and was at the stage of wanting to push his fingers into everything, upset the box of hairpins with a crash, and Frances darted over to pick him up and set him against her shoulder. Her own son, John, was four years old and it was no longer possible for her to pick him up. He had become the province of a tutor, and she missed the feeling of a baby in her arms.

Sabina watched her, feeling faintly guilty. Frances's best dress, put on for the wedding, was of half-mourning grey, and she wore a cap and coverchief like a matron, though she was a few months younger than Sabina. She had loved her husband dearly, and mourned him so deeply she never spoke of him voluntarily.

'You don't blame me, do you Fanny?' she asked abruptly. 'Allan was a good husband to me, and I believe I made him a good wife. But he's dead now, and nothing can bring him back.'

'No,' Frances said.

'And I have loved Matt ever since I can remember. When I was a child, and he used to come up to Birnie for

390

the summer, I swore I would marry him one day.' She bit her lip. 'You don't think . . .?'

'Of course not,' Frances said quickly. 'God doesn't work in that way. As you say, poor Allan is dead. There is nothing to stop you marrying Matt now. Be happy, darling. I'm very happy for you.'

Sabina hugged her gratefully, and kissed Allen's round pink cheek and said, 'Poor little boy, disinherited before he could ever walk. We will never get the estate back now. Well, at least he will have a father and brothers.'

As soon as she said it, she wished she had not been so thoughtless, for Frances's child had neither. She cocked her head speculatively and said, 'Fan, have you thought of marrying again? I mean, I have been watching the way Arthur looks at you? I'm sure he is interested in you. Has it occurred to you –'

'No,' Frances said, too firmly to allow Sabina to carry on, and then, more gently, she added, 'things don't happen in just that tidy way, Sabina. You can't marry people to people just to get them out of the way. Arthur is a solitary man who enjoys his bachelor life; and I – well, I suppose I am still married, in my heart.'

'I'm sorry,' Sabina said awkwardly. Frances put Allen down and took his hand.

'I think it is time to go down. Are you ready?' she said. Sabina forgot her awkwardness at once, and her face lit up.

'Yes,' she said. 'I'm ready.'

Father Renard conducted the service in the chapel, and Sabina's new stepsons, Thomas and Charles, served the altar. Matt was waiting for her, looking handsome and nervous in his new suit of emerald green satin and a wig of his own hair colour. His nervousness made him look younger than his years. He was attended to the altar by his cousin Arthur and his friend Davey, both very solemn and determined to play their parts correctly. Sabina walked up to take her place beside Matt, and he turned to her with such a smile that she saw and thought of nothing else all through the service.

Afterwards they went to the great hall to receive the long, long line of friends and tenants and villagers who had come to congratulate them, and then they went out into the gardens where, in view of the good weather, the wedding feast was to be held. Sabina was never able to move very far from the one spot, for as soon as one person had finished telling her what a good master Matt was and how happy they were that he was marrying again, another would begin. But over their heads she was able to watch the other guests grouping and regrouping; to observe the Countess, splendid in cornflower-blue silk, with her rough-coated dog always pressed against her legs, arguing some point vehemently with Arthur and a group of eminent architects; to see, with some anxiety, sixteen year old Jemmy being far too charming to the daughter of a wealthy merchant from York; to notice, with pleasure, that Frances was having what seemed to be a very interesting conversation with a well-set-up young man who was one of Matt's friends and who bred horses at a stud near Middleham.

Now and then Matt was able to escape his well-wishers for long enough to address a word or two to his new bride.

'Are you happy?' he asked her, anxiously, more than once.

'Very happy,' she assured him. Since she had come to Morland Place, he had devoted himself to her welfare. When it became obvious to her that he wanted to ask her to marry him, she had had to bring him to the point at last by telling him she had always been in love with him, for his diffidence was such that he might have waited years before broaching the subject.

Now he said, 'It is strange, the way things work themselves out,' and she knew what he meant. Their marrying felt very right to her, a rounding-off of things. It was no wonder that she wanted, tidily, to complete Frances's life in the same way.

When the dancing began, Jemmy went first to ask his great-grandmother to dance, bowing very low, with a courtly flourish, and saying, 'Will you do me the great honour, your ladyship, of standing up with me?'

'Provided you do not expect any great leaps or swift footwork,' Annunciata said, placing her hand in his. He carried it to his lips.

'You are lighter than thistledown on your feet, my lady, as well you know. You should not make such obvious play for compliments.'

'Now, Jemmy,' Annunciata said firmly, 'I have been watching you, and I hope you are not using me as practice for more serious conquests later.'

'My lady,' he said, gazing into her eyes, 'What could be more serious than my attempt upon the citadel of your heart?'

'Your attempt upon the citadel of that young lady's virtue,' Annunciata said, gesturing with her fan towards the languishing beauty Jemmy had been flirting with.

Jemmy looked at her out of the corner of his eye, and said, 'Oh she is all airs and graces, so affected she makes me feel quite uncomfortable. Why cannot young women behave naturally? The giggling and the play with the fan and the averted eyes – how they weary me!'

'Jemmy, you are only sixteen years old – you cannot be world-weary yet,' Annunciata said gravely. 'And now can young women be natural when the world demands otherwise of them? They are told from the cradle upwards, poor creatures, that the sole purpose of their lives is to marry and that to marry they must be as unnatural and affected as possible. What would you have them do?'

'I'll wager my new horse you were never like that,' Jemmy said, pressing her hand. 'Why can't young women be like you? You talk sensibly, about the things one is interested in.'

'I was brought up in a different world,' Annunciata said. Jemmy sighed.

'I know – and how I long for it myself! If only I could

have been born fifty years earlier, when there was a real Court and a real King, and glorious battles, and adventure, and women like you!'

'There were never any women like me,' Annunciata laughed. Jemmy's eyes shone in return.

'I know. But if I had been born fifty years earlier, I could have married you – if you'd have had me.'

Just for a moment, Annunciata's heart turned over in her, and she told herself that it was ridiculous and unseemly for a woman of her age to have that kind of reaction, still less to have it for the words of a child half a century her junior. But he was Martin's grandson, with Martin's blood in his veins, and despite the dilution of the intervening generations, Martin looked out at her from those eyes more clearly even than in Matt.

'If I were fifty years younger, Jemmy, I should not let anyone else have you,' she said, and Jemmy grinned and bowed and led her one more place up the set.

'What do you think of my chances in the race tomorrow?' he asked after a moment and their talk turned to the perennially fascinating subject of horses.

On the following day, as part of the wedding celebrations, Matt had arranged a horse-racing meeting on the flat field that lay beside the boundary between Morland Place and Shawes, and since it was nearer to Shawes than Morland Place, Annunciata had offered Matt the use of her house for refreshments before the racing, and for a ball after it. All the invitations had been accepted: Annunciata noted with amusement that those people who had previously been inclined to 'cut' her because of her religion, her Jacobite sympathies, or her dubious past, were now eager to visit her, and were full of praise and admiration for her new house.

The races were exciting, and much better organized than those Ralph had initiated so long ago. The difference in the horses was very noticeable too – they were all becoming lighter in build, and faster, and there were no longer any farmers pitting their carthorses against the better animals. Jemmy rode his father's best horse, wearing Annunciata's ribbon, just as long ago Martin had ridden Ralph's best horse with her ribbon tied about his arm. Annunciata sat under an awning and watched, feeling happy and strangely tired, as though she had missed a night's sleep. She enjoyed the race, but did not feel inclined to go to the trouble of gambling on Jemmy, nor could she find the energy to stand up and cheer when he came galloping down to the winning post, in the lead. When he had dismounted and left his horse with a groom, he came running to where she sat and knelt at her feet, his flushed face wreathed with smiles, to offer her her ribbon and receive her praise.

When he had gone again, Matt came to say, 'I hope that boy of mine does not trouble you. I'm afraid he may forget himself. If he is insolent, you must tell me.'

'He amuses me, Matt. He does not trouble me.' Kithra sat up and laid his heavy head on her knee and stared into her face in the way dogs have, and she said, 'The older I grow, the more time seems to contract. Sitting here, I can hardly remember what year it is, which race I am watching, whose sons are riding. It gives me a kind of contentment.'

When Matt went away, Chloris came to look over her shoulder and say, 'You are tired, my lady. Perhaps you should go to bed, rather than to the ball.'

'Nonsense,' Annunciata said. 'I am hostess – how can I absent myself?'

'Then will you at least rest before the ball begins? Come now, and I'll undress you, and you can lie on your bed for an hour or two before it is time to dress for dinner.'

'Just to please you, then,' Annunciata said, sighing resignedly. But she was glad of the excuse to rest. She was very tired, and as she stood up she met Chloris's eye and read in them the same question as was in her own mind – was this the beginning of the end?

*

The rest did her good, however, and she dressed for dinner and the ball feeling well and looking forward to the evening. I am a Palatine, she told herself as she went downstairs. We have good eyesight, sound digestions, and strong hearts, and we live to a great age. Compared with my aunt Sofie I am a mere stripling. I have many good dancing years in me yet.

Matt sat on her left, with Sabina beside him, and she gave Sabina an approving nod across his head. She liked Sabina, the more so since Sabina had confided in her about her lifelong love for Matt.

'You are a good Morland,' Annunciata said, 'and you will make a good mistress for the house.' And Matt, Annunciata thought, was becoming quite a satisfactory person now that he had grown up, though it had taken a long time. With both his blind infatuation for India, and his sullen bitterness at her deception behind him, he had become an open-hearted, frank, and conscientious man, the very thing Morland Place needed. He would never, she thought, match his father in any way, but he would keep the Morland family safe. Jemmy, on the other hand – she observed Jemmy cautiously, as he flirted with two young women simultaneously halfway down the table – Jemmy had potential greatness in him, but that same potential could be ruinous to Morland Place if it were not properly channelled. She could control him, but she would not always be here. Suddenly she longed, passionately, for another ten or fifteen years of life, to make sure. What happened to Morland Place and to the family mattered so much to her.

The nap was drawn and the sweets and fruits were brought in, and with a nod to Gifford, Annunciata dismissed all but a handful of servants to get their own dinners. The conversation became more lively, and Annunciata was so absorbed in it that she did not notice the servant come in to speak anxiously to Gifford, nor did she notice Gifford himself until he coughed firmly and discretely in her ear.

'Would you please come out to the hall, my lady? There is something that requires your attention,' he murmured. Annunciata glanced up at him but received no clue from his eyes; still, she knew he could be trusted not to call her for nothing. She excused herself and slipped away after him.

In the great hall she saw a heap of luggage and several strangers, giving all the appearance of a guest arriving for a long stay.

'What is going on?' Annunciata asked in astonishment. Then the nearest stranger turned round – a woman of thirty in a neat travelling habit and a large feathered hat, under which a tired but beautiful face made Annunciata's heart falter and then race on.

'I've come home, mother,' the stranger said. 'I hope that I may stay?'

Annunciata could only nod, for once lost for words. It was Aliena; and she was pregnant.

CHAPTER TWENTY-ONE

The delicate political situation which existed when Holland joined the Triple Alliance in the January of 1717 forced the Regent of France, however unwillingly, to put pressure on the Pope to expel King James from the Papal city of Avignon, which was on French soil. So in February of that year the King set out for Italy, the last possible place for him to find refuge. He sent his household servants with the silver, plate and linen to take ship at Marseilles and sail to Leghorn, while he and the rest of his household, numbering about seventy, went over the Alps.

It was a terrible journey, over the snowbound passes, along rough mountain tracks; a slow journey in the bitter cold. Aliena, in midsummer, shivered at the memory of it as she told her mother about the crying, floundering horses, the comfortless coaches, lurching over bumps so that at the end of an hour you hardly knew where to put yourself to ease the discomfort. After ten hours, Aliena would be weeping; she was not the only one. Every now and then it was necessary to get out of the coach while it was levered by main force out of some rut or drift into which it had lurched, and then, standing sometimes knee-deep in the snow, they would get so cold as to lose all feeling in the fingers and toes. Later the sting of returning circulation was all but unendurable.

Whatever they had suffered, the King had suffered ten times more. He had been ill the autumn before with an extremely painful anal fistula, which had been operated on at the end of October. The operation had not gone as well as had been hoped, and it was a month before he could receive visitors, almost two months before he could go out again. The jolting of the coaches was agony to him, and riding on horseback, except for short periods, out of the question. Added to his physical agony he had the mental anguish to bear – or parting from his mother, whom he was leaving sick and friendless at St Germain, and whom it was unlikely that he would ever see again; and the anguish of being thus sent further and further into exile, ever further from his own country and his rightful inheritance.

There was nothing Aliena could do to comfort him on that journey, other than simply to be there. Her position in the Court had ceased to arouse any comment. She was accounted for, officially, as 'my dear friend, who shared my childhood at St Germain' or 'one who is as dear to me as my late sister, whose intimate she was'. Unofficially, her precise relationship with the King was difficult to describe. Commentators from outside the Court often noted that though the King enjoyed the friendship and admiration of the women in the Court circle, he never seemed to be in danger of losing his heart to any of them. Some said he had taken his father's parting words deeply to heart, and there was some truth in that. Others said that he was, because of his strict upbringing, very young for his age, and sexually naïve, and there was some truth in that too.

'But what would you say you were to him?' Annunciata asked Aliena during one of their many long conversations that summer, that seemed never to begin or end, merely to continue, broken into segments by the necessities of the days and nights. Aliena thought for a long time, and then she shrugged.

'His dear friend,' she said. 'I was his dear friend.'

And it was largely because of her undefined, ambiguous presence in his life that he was able to resist the temptations that surrounded him. In truth, she always believed that he was not ever aware of them *as* temptations: physical intimacy with strange women was something he had set so firmly beyond him at an early age that he was, at twenty-eight, incapable of seeing women in that light.

At the end of February they at last reached Turin, where they were able to rest for a few days at the palace of the

Duke of Savoy, a relative of the Queen's, before travelling south to Modena, the Queen's birthplace. There they stayed at the Palace of the Duke Rinaldo, the King's uncle, and found letters awaiting the King from Queen Mary Beatrice.

'They were such sad letters,' Aliena said. 'An exile's letters, longing for news of home. She wanted to know what were the King's first impressions of Modena, did he like it, did he think it beautiful. And questions about all her relatives, how were they, had he seen them. She begged him to go and see the summer palace, because she had such happy memories of it, forgetting that the weather in March was far too cold and windy. We did not go. James would not leave the palace.'

'She wanted to be a nun, you know,' Annunciata remembered. 'They argued and argued with her to make her marry the Duke of York, as he was then. And how disappointed she must have been when she first saw him. She came to love him later, but he must have seemed to her an old, cold man. She was only fifteen, and very beautiful.'

'Yes,' said Aliena. 'I saw her portrait, in the palace of Modena, taken just before she married. The King has a great look of her, about the eyes.'

It was at Modena that the trouble began. Duke Rinaldo had three daughters, all well-brought-up, pleasant girls.

'They were quite good-looking, though not out of the ordinary, but the King – well, I suppose one must forgive him. He had been under great strain, after that terrible journey, and after being rejected from every country in Europe he had come to the house of his relatives, where the duke received him with such kindness. His heart was already softened. And then, he missed his mother so, and the girls all had a great look of her about them. Especially the eldest – especially Benedetta.'

Within a week the King had written off an ecstatic letter to his mother at Chailly to say that he had proposed marriage to Princess Benedetta, and the Queen wrote back that she could not be more happy.

'They were two children, two unworldly, simple children,' Aliena said, and Annunciata heard a bitterness under the sadness that she could not comment on. 'They wanted each other, and each thought they could use Benedetta as a substitute. It was pitiful.'

In bed with Aliena the first night, he had talked non-stop about the beautiful princess and her imagined virtues, and all the wonderful things that were going to happen when they were married. Aliena had tried to bring him down to earth, to make him see what he was doing, but he was blinded by the perfection of the plan of marrying his cousin, who looked like his mother. As to the intimate side of marriage, he did not give it a thought. Aliena decided that he had not associated physical proximity with the romantic love he was experiencing, and that if she pointed it out to him, he would be shocked and angry. As it was, he told her gently but firmly that he did not think they ought to sleep together now that he was as good as engaged to marry Benedetta, and after that night he did not visit her bed any more.

Aliena found an ally in Duke Rinaldo, who was utterly dismayed at the turn of events. He sought out Aliena, having quickly understood her relationship with the King, and confided in her, hoping that, as his mistress, she could change his mind for him, as mistresses the world over were expected to do.

'It is an impossible match,' he said. 'I have to dispose of my daughters advantageously, and the King, though I respect and love him, has nothing but an empty title to offer. And an empty title, moreover, that would win me nothing but hostility. Modena and England have been friendly for a very long time. We are a small country, we cannot afford to make enemies.'

Aliena understood all this, and asked why the duke did not simply refuse. He looked miserable.

'I hardly like to. The poor young man has had so many

misfortunes – and he is, after all, my sister's son, and King of England, even though he is in exile. And I cannot bear to make him more unhappy. If he really loves her – though I cannot imagine *how* he can, when he hardly knows her –'

'His Majesty has had a very strict upbringing,' Aliena said, 'and his contact with women has always been on a very formal basis.'

'Except with you?' Rinaldo said hesitantly.

'It is very different with me. The King does not understand women. He does not understand *me* as a woman, only as a friend – something between a sister and a brother, though I cannot expect you to understand that.'

'I think I do understand,' Rinaldo said. 'But cannot you influence his mind? Make him see that the thing is impossible?'

'If I were his mistress in the normal sense, I could,' Aliena said. 'As it is, I can only suggest that you separate him from the princess, and hope that time and absence loosen the grip of her charms on his mind. If he is from her, perhaps some other infatuation may replace her.'

So the duke told the King that he would consider the proposal of marriage, and suggested that the Jacobite Court might like to visit the Palazzo Davia at Pesaro. They stayed in Pesaro for a month, and the King was very miserable there, saying that it was a dirty town, and the wine was undrinkable. He waited daily for good news from Modena which never came, complained of the boredom, of the weather, of ill health, and of Pesaro. One good thing to come out of it was that after a few days in the Palazzo Davia he came once again to Aliena's bed.

'I thought that we must not cohabit now you are almost betrothed,' she could not help saying tartly when he first came to her, but she could not refuse him. Loving him had become as much a habit as serving him.

'I am not betrothed yet, and it begins to seem I never shall be,' he replied. 'But I'll go away if you want me to.'

'I don't want you to,' she said.

After a month at Pesaro the King wrote to the Queen

402

asking her to persuade her friend the Cardinal Gualterio to invite the King to stay with him in his palace in Rome, which the cardinal duly did, and at the end of May the dwindling Court arrived in Rome. The King's spirits rose: it was the height of the Season in Rome, when all the plays and operas and festivals were going on, and the main buildings were lit up at night with so many torches it was almost as bright as day. The cardinal had had his palazzo redecorated to receive the King, and had arranged for an audience with the Pope as soon as the King was rested.

'He liked the Pope,' Aliena said sadly. 'He said he found him easy and kindly. He asked the Pope to help bring about the match between himself and Princess Benedetta, and the Pope promised to do all he could.'

The cardinal was tireless in shewing the King round all the sights of Rome, but Aliena was able to introduce him to something just as exciting as the famous churches: the opera. She had not been two days in Rome before she received a visitor, a circumstance which greatly impressed the King. It was, of course, her brother Maurice, who had come with his father-in-law to witness the performance of two new operas, and on hearing of the arrival of the King had come at once to see if Aliena was still with him.

'But now, of course, Signore Scarlatti is his proper father-in-law once again,' Aliena said, 'not just his former father-in-law. Oh, he forgot to mention that to you did he?' she said, seeing her mother's bemused expression. 'Well, he seems to have a predilection for Scarlatti's children. He has married the youngest daughter, Nicoletta – she's twenty-one, barely older than his daughter by his first wife, which Nicoletta seemed to find very strange. Maurice took her to Venice last Festival to introduce her to Alessandra, who is still living with Diane di Francescini, by the way. Nicoletta hardly ever stopped talking about Venice, and her step-daughter who is also her niece.'

'You saw a lot of Maurice while you were in Rome?' Annunciata wanted to know. 'Did he see the King?'

'Oh yes, he came to pay his respects to the King straight

away, but I don't think the King would have taken much notice, except that Maurice happened to be at the Papal palace at the same time as he was, also having an audience with His Holiness. When the King discovered that Maurice has been asked to write a special sung Mass for the Holy Father, he began to take a great interest, and we went to the first performance of Maurice's opera. After that, we all saw a great deal of each other.' She looked suddenly wistful, an unexpectedly young expression for her mature face. 'It was rather pleasant, all of us together,' she said. 'The King seemed really to like Maurice – he treated him almost exactly in the way he treats – treated me.'

It was while they were in Rome, and the King seemed happier than at any time since they left Avignon, and was behaving in such a comfortably intimate way towards Maurice, that Aliena decided she could no longer conceal from the King that she was pregnant. The child had been conceived on that long, bitter journey through the Alps in February. She had suspected that it was on the way when they were at Pesaro, but had not wanted to discuss it with the King when he was so dour and gloomy. Now she was beginning to grow large, and any man other than the King would have suspected long ago. But he was happy now, and must surely, she reasoned, have begun to forget about Princess Benedetta. So one night, when they were in bed together, she told him.

His reaction shocked her, in that he seemed utterly amazed that she was with child, and while it did not cross his mind to suppose that she had bedded with anyone else, it took her a great deal of talking to persuade him that she was not mistaken, and that it was his actions that had caused her condition. When at last he believed her, she waited in vain for pleasure, joy, or even reassurance. The King seemed wholly dismayed, and it was for Aliena to say, 'Well, my lord King, what will you do?'

'What do you want me to do?' the King asked. 'What is there for me to do?'

'You are the father of the child that is growing within

me,' she said, and seeing this did not make any impact on him, she said, 'if it is a boy, it may one day be King of England.'

That shocked him out of his daze. He stared at her. 'You want me to marry you?'

She sat up and gazed down at him, her long hair framing her face and touching his cheek. 'Jamie, why not? I love you – you love me. We are comfortable together.'

'But I am as good as betrothed to Benedetta,' he said. She kept patience.

'You are not as good as betrothed. Rinaldo does not want the match, he is only pretending to consider it because he does not want to hurt your feelings. He does not think it a good match.'

'But I am King of England!'

'Yes, my darling, but only in name. He does not believe you will ever get your kingdom back, and meanwhile he dares not cross the Elector or the Emperor of Austria by allying himself with you. He will never give you Benedetta, believe me.'

He was silent for a moment, and then said, stiffly, 'Even if what you say is true, I could not marry you. I am King of England, after all, even if, as you so harshly put it, it is only in name.'

'But, Jamie, I am as good as Benedetta. I am well-born, well-educated, I have royal blood in my veins. I am, or at least will be, a woman of means. There is a large inheritance for me in England, which will come to me when my mother dies. I am your lover, and I am with child. Do you want our child to be a bastard?' The King only stared at her in distress and embarrassment. She went on, less surely, 'Who knows you better than me? Whom do you know and trust as well as me? If we live the rest of our lives here in Italy, in exile, we can still be happy together as ordinary people.'

'But I am not an ordinary person,' he said – not proudly, but gently, as if explaining something to a child. 'I am the King, and I cannot marry a commoner. How could I make you Queen of England? Aliena, you know how fond I am of you, but after all, you are – well, my mistress. How could I marry you? Everyone knows about our relationship. And if they did not before, they soon will know, when they see you are with child.'

'There are plenty of precedents for kings to get their wives pregnant first. If it were always done, it might save a great deal of unhappiness. What about your uncle King Charles? If he had followed that simple precaution – and suppose you marry a barren princess? What good will her royal blood and stainless reputation do you or England?'

She knew it was no good. He had shut off from her. He sat up and reached for his nightshirt, and in the kindness of his voice came the deadliest of blows.

'Aliena, it is impossible. I owe it to my mother, and my father's blessed memory, to marry in accordance with their wishes. They would not wish me to marry an obscure woman with whom I have already had carnal knowledge. Do not be afraid, I shall not desert you,' he added. 'Our child shall be taken care of. Why, I have had the example before me all my life of my lord of Berwick. It was often said that my father had almost as great a pleasure in him as in me – and so I hope it will be for us.'

He dressed quickly, when he was dressed he kissed her forehead and went away, all without meeting her eyes. She lay a long time, dry-eyed, wishing she could weep, hearing his words over and over again. She did not sleep until dawn, and then only fitfully, for an hour or two. She did not know what to do, or where to turn.

At the beginning of July, the Pope told King James that he had had a palace prepared as a permanent home for the exiles at Urbino, a remote medieval town in the hills overlooking the Adriatic sea, and indicated that the King should go there at once, as his presence in Rome was an embarrassment. The King was not unhappy at the thought of a permanent home, after so much pointless wandering, but to Aliena is spelled the end of hope. The King was being pushed into the background, sent away where he could do no harm and would not be on hand to remind people of his lost kingdom and of what they ought to be doing to help him. No one now believed that he would ever regain his throne, and that was why they were being so kind, and so firm, and sending him to such a remote place. In the time since she had told him that she was pregnant, he had avoided being alone with her, had treated her when they met with a distant kindliness, and she could see that she was being pushed away in just the same way as James himself. The difference was, she knew it, and he didn't.

She packed her own belongings as the Court packed theirs, keeping them separate. Maurice was on the point of returning to Naples, for the Rome Season was almost over, and the heat was growing to unpleasantness, and so she confided in him, and borrowed money from him, and one or two necessities from Nicoletta, who, guessing her predicament, had been kindness itself and begged her to make her home with them. 'There are so many of us all together at Naples, that another one, or two, won't matter,' Nicoletta said. But Aliena thanked her, and refused. She had suddenly been overtaken by a deep longing to go 'home', to England, which she had left as an infant and had never seen since. She had her maid Nan with her, and her laundress, a French girl from Avignon called Marie, and Nicoletta gave her one of her own footmen, for she said a pregnant woman could not travel so far without a manservant; and on the day before the exiled Court left for Urbino, she took ship for Marseilles.

From Marseilles she went by road to Avignon, where she sought help of the Papal Vice-Legate, who arranged her safe passage through France to La Rochelle. From there she took another ship to Cherbourg, where she was able to take passage on a privateer to Folkestone. Everyone was very kind to her on the journey, perhaps because of her condition, perhaps because she was so evidently a lady.

'And what did the King say to you, when you said

goodbye?' Annunciata asked at last, when the rest of the story was told. Aliena looked a little ashamed.

'I did not tell him I was going,' she said. 'I could not bear to. I thought if I did he might beg me to stay, and I would not have been able to refuse him. So I left quietly, and gave a letter to a servant I could trust, to give to him.'

After a silence, Annunciata asked diffidently, 'I wonder, do you not think that if you had gone to Urbino . . .? After all, in an isolated place like that, with no news from Modena, and you beside him, growing larger with child, and more beautiful day by day – he must surely have married you in the end?'

Aliena looked into the distance sadly. 'Yes, perhaps. I think you are right. I thought of it myself, of course, but there was my pride, too. I could not endure him to take me in lieu of anything better. No doubt that is a fault in me, and I shall suffer for it, but it is the way I am. I have the blood of kings in me, and I would not be rejected for an Italian duke's daughter, though her title be princess, and mine no more than mistress.'

Annunciata looked at her with compassion and sympathy. 'I do understand,' she said. In her youth, she had had that kind of pride. 'What had we better tell the servants?' she asked. 'I assume that you will be staying here, at Shawes, for good now that you are home? It will be yours one day, and your child's after you. All my estate is mine to leave, and Karellie and Maurice will not want it. Maurice cares nothing for material wealth, and since Karellie has followed Berwick's example and taken French citizenship, he will not be able to come back to England.'

'But what about his daughter? He may want an estate for her,' Aliena said with a glint of amusement.

'His daughter?' Annunciata asked in astonishment. 'Karellie's daughter? He surely cannot have married, without telling me?'

'No, he is not married. Well, I assume it is his daughter – the child of Diane di Francescini, born last December. A perfectly lovely little girl, so Maurice said – he saw her when he took Nicoletta to Venice. But Maurice thinks all babies perfect, especially girl-babies.'

Annunciata was staring at her, her mind furiously at work. 'During their escape?' she said. 'Possible, I suppose – even likely, since they were travelling as man and wife. But she said she would never marry him.'

'And she has not. She is magnificent, so Maurice says – simply had the baby, refused to discuss it, forced everyone to accept it by simple means of expecting them to. She has not said it is Karellie's child, not even to Maurice, but one must suppose it is, since she has called it Karelia. Well, perhaps I should do the same,' Aliena said with a dark smile. 'I shall tell the world nothing about my child. I shall disdain to explain myself. As your daughter, and your heiress, I can afford to be proud, magnificent, and silent. What the Divine Diane can do, so can Aliena the Obscure. Will you support me in it, mother?'

Annunciata smiled happily. 'You must have heard of the sad affliction known as mother-hunger, that attacks old women when their childbearing days are done? You and I will live in comfort and plenty here at Shawes, and bring up your child, and defy the world. After all –' she hesitated, and Aliena raised an enquiring eyebrow. 'After all,' Annunciata went on, realizing the time for such discretion was long gone, 'I did it before, when you were born, though with less self-confidence.'

'We must just hope that it is a girl,' Aliena replied, with a flash of understanding that told Annunciata more than anything else whose daughter Aliena was.

The baby was born on 11 November, Martinmas, and the birthday of Aliena's father Martin, which coincidence struck Annunciata very forcefully. Aliena was thirty, which was old to be bearing a first child, and the labour went hard with her, and when it was over, she said, 'Thank God I shall never have to bear another.' The child was a girl, a long, dark-skinned baby with a large nose and a matt of black hair.

'Unmistakably a Stuart,' Annunciata cried. 'She will be tall, like her father. What shall you call her?'

'I think I shall call her Marie-Louise, after my poor Princess, God rest her sweet soul.'

'Princess Marie-Louise!' Annunciata said, lifting the baby to her shoulder and carrying her round the room. 'It sounds well. A good name for a royal princess of England.'

Aliena looked at her warningly, but she was too sleepy to protest too much. She said only, 'That is between us, mother. No more of it now, please.'

The first person to arrive when Aliena was allowed to receive visitors was young Jemmy, who arrived bearing gifts and all eagerness to see the baby. He had been much at Shawes during the summer, and was evidently fascinated by Aliena, and what she had to tell, and the long silences where his longing for romance and adventure could fill in great things for what she would not tell.

Now he came to the bed, wreathed in smiles, to give her the respectful and proper kisses and congratulations, and to say, '*Mort-dieu*, I have spent such a terrible time that you would pity me if you had witnessed it. I have plagued the life out of your servants, sending them back and forth for news, and have wearied the ears of all the saints praying for your safe delivery, and worn the soles out of all my shoes pacing up and down in my anxiety, as if the bairn were my own. And now, here you are, looking as blooming and radiant as if it had all never happened. Great-grand-mother, I hope you have not performed any sly trickery with warming-pans and the like?'

'Impudent boy,' Annunciata exclaimed. Jemmy looked stern.

'I warn you, I shall not believe this flower-like young woman can have produced a child until you shew me the evidence. Come now, where is this this floweret, this rosebud?'

Annunciata lifted the baby out of the crib and brought

her across, and Jemmy stared down into the little sleeping face, and then gently took the baby into his own arms. 'I swear I would have known her anywhere,' he said. 'I feel as if I have known her all my life. Why, she is perfect! My brothers were never so perfect as this nor my – that is, the child of a person in the village I know,' he said hastily. 'She is not crumpled and wrinkled as babies so often are, but smooth and silky like a rose petal. And such a lot of hair!' He looked up, laughing.

'It means no more than a gentleman's periwig,' Annunciata said. 'She'll be quite bald in a day or two. But it will grow again. I expect she will be dark –'

'Like her mother,' Jemmy said, with a liquid look in Aliena's direction. It was always difficult to keep anything secret from Jemmy, because he had such a way with servants that he heard all the gossip before anyone else. 'Well,' he said, handing the baby back to Annunciata, 'I think I may say I am very proud of you, cousin Aliena, if I may call you so, to avoid having to work out quite what relation you are to me. And since you have proved everything to my satisfaction, I shall now bring forth the presents. Wait here.'

He darted out, to come back in with a large bag, out of which he took first of all a length of pale primrose silk. 'For the mother, to make a new dress, to celebrate her return to a normal shape,' he said, presenting it with a flourishing bow to Aliena.

She blushed a little, with pleasure and surprise, and said, 'It is beautiful! I cannot think where you could have got it, but the colour . . .'

'Suits you to perfection. Hush! I am a Morland, how should I not know about cloth, even silk? And now, for the baby –' He reached into the bag again, and brought out a beautiful Italian silver cup. 'I mortgaged my soul to get it, so I hope you like it, for I should hate to have to go back on *that* bargain. I shall have it engraved round the inside with the baby's name – which is what by the by?'

'Marie-Louise,' said Annunciata. Jemmy looked at Aliena and raised an eyebrow.

'A name fit for a princess. Well, and why not? To a mother, every child is a prince or princess, is it not? And now,' he went on quickly, 'finally, a present for the grandmother.'

'For me?' Annunciata said in surprise.

'Assuredly. If you love Aliena one tenth as much as I do you must have gone through agonies while she was in labour, so you shall have your reward too. Here – take this.'

He reached for the last time into the bag, supported its contents with the hand inside, and with the other pulled the bag away and let it fall, revealing, held firmly by its middle, a large and sleepy brindled hound-pup. 'To replace, as far as any dog can replace another, your dear old Kithra,' he said – Kithra had died in September, quietly in his sleep, as an old hound should. Annunciata took the pup with a bemused air, and the creature, beginning to wake, started to squirm, and to lick Annunciata's face, paddling its huge, soft paws for a foothold. Jemmy watched her face, well pleased with himself. 'Every child should grow up with a dog,' he added, 'and the little princess will grow up with this one – what shall you call it, my lady Countess?'

'Fand,' Annunciata said decisively. She liked familiar names for dogs. 'I had a Fand when you were young, Aliena – do you remember?'

'Yes,' Aliena said. 'I like that. Marie-Louise shall have the same.'

'Thank you, Jemmy. You are very thoughtful,' Annunciata said. 'Here, now, take the pup again, and hold him for me: the baby has woken.'

Jemmy watched as she went to the crib to pick up the baby again, and said, 'It makes me feel strangely contented, you know, to think of this little one growing up here, with the dog, in this house. I shall come and teach her to ride as soon as she is old enough – if you will let me, cousin? Shall we all ride out together, to Harewood Whin, and Wilstrop Wood and the Ten Thorns?' He sounded so wistful that Aliena laughed.

'Did you think I would shut you out from us? Of course we shall ride together. And especially to those places, whose names have been like a song to me all my life. I hope you know how lucky you are, Jemmy, to have been brought up here? I look to you to shew me every part of your kingdom.'

'With the greatest of pleasure,' Jemmy said, bowing.

In the May of 1718, Queen Mary Beatrice died at St Germain, much missed by all who had known her in the exiled Court. Annunciata sent a letter of condolence to the King at Urbino through her usual channels; she thought that Aliena probably wrote also, and suspected Aliena had written earlier to tell the King about the birth of Marie-Louise, but whether the King had replied, Annunciata did not know, and did not like to ask. Though Aliena seemed to have settled quite happily at Shawes, devoting her life to the upbringing of her daughter, and deriving her pleasure from simple country pursuits, and her amusement from Jemmy's antics, Annunciata could not help suspecting that the hurt she had sustained ran very deep, and there was a great deal that Aliena was reticent about.

The King, so report said, was deeply grieved at the loss of his mother, and now finding himself entirely alone in the world, had set about looking for a wife from amongst the minor princesses of Europe. Annunciata wondered, unsympathetically, whether he ever thought about Aliena and cursed himself for losing one who would have been the greatest comfort to him, the best of wives. She hoped he did, and looked every day for some sign of his repentance.

It came at last in October, just before Marie-Louise's first birthday: a packet sewn into the bottom of a sack of raisins, which, when opened, revealed an envelope sealed with the royal seal. It bore, as was usual, no direction, for fear of incrimination, and Annunciata opened it herself, thinking it more likely that it would be for her. She read it through slowly, twice, and then lay it down and stared at it, hardly knowing whether to smile or weep.

It was a patent, conferring the Earldom of Strathord, to be held in her own right, on Marie-Louise Fitzjames Stuart, the honour to devolve upon the children of her body, male or female; and it was signed by the hand of James III, King of England, Scotland, Ireland and France.

Annunciata looked again, and saw that the date on the patent was the same date as that on which the King had signed the marriage contract with the sixteen-year-old Polish princess, Maria Clementina Sobieski. Was it guilt, she wondered? Or regret? Or simply a rounding-off of things unfinished, an acknowledgement of responsibility? But she looked at the wording again, and knew that it was none of those things. Marie-Louise Fitzjames Stuart – in those names he had given the baby all he had. It was not guilt, it was love.

So baby Marie-Louise was now Countess of Strathord – vain, empty title, gift of an exiled King! Her mother would give her more, land and houses and rents, solid, worthy things. All the same, one day she might be glad to have it. Annunciata picked up the letter and smoothed the heavy paper carefully with her fingers, and went to find Aliena.

DYNASTY 1: THE FOUNDING

Cynthia Harrod-Eagles

Triumphantly heralding the mighty Morland Dynasty – an epic saga of one family's fortune and fate through five hundred years of history. A story as absorbing and richly diverse as the history of the English-speaking people themselves.

THE FOUNDING

Power and prestige are the burning ambitions of Edward Morland, rich sheep farmer and landowner.

He arranges a marriage. A marriage that will be the first giant step in the founding of the Morland Dynasty.

A dynasty that will be forged by his son Robert, more poet than soldier. And Eleanor, ward of the powerful Beaufort family. Proud and aloof, and consumed by her secret love for Richard, Duke of York.

And so with THE FOUNDING, the Morland Dynasty begins – with a story of fierce hatred and war, love and desire, running through the turbulent years of the Wars of the Roses.

Futura Publications
Fiction
0 7088 1728 9

All Futura Books are available at your bookshop or newsagent, or can be ordered from the following address:
Futura Books, Cash Sales Department,
P.O. Box 11, Falmouth, Cornwall.

Please send cheque or postal order (no currency), and allow 45p for postage and packing for the first book plus 20p for the second book and 14p for each additional book ordered up to a maximum charge of £1.63 in U.K

Customers in Eire and B.F.P.O. please allow 45p for the first book, 20p for the second book plus 14p per copy for the next 7 books, thereafter 8p per book.

Overseas customers please allow 75p for postage and packing for the first book and 21p per copy for each additional book.